I love about books. Read it."

Alice Oseman, author of *I Was Born For This*

Other books by Lauren James

The Next Together
The Last Beginning
The Loneliest Girl in the Universe
The Quiet at the End of the World

THE
RECKLESS
AFTERLIFE
OF
HARRIET
STOKER

LAUREN JAMES

WALKER
BOOKS

First published in Great Britain 2020 by Walker Books Ltd
87 Vauxhall Walk, London SE11 5HJ

2 4 6 8 10 9 7 5 3 1

Text © 2020 Lauren James
Cover illustration © 2020 Lisa Horton Design

This book has been typeset in Fairfield, Arial, Ubuntu, Verdana

Printed and bound by CPI Group (UK) Ltd, Croydon CR0 4YY

British Library Cataloguing in Publication Data:
a catalogue record for this book is available from the British Library

ISBN 978-1-4063-9112-1

www.walker.co.uk

MIX
Paper from
responsible sources
FSC® C020471

For my friends, who have never once tried to murder me.

"I didn't mind thinking you were a murderer," said Lady Mary spitefully, "but I *do* mind you being such an ass."

DOROTHY L. SAYERS, *CLOUDS OF WITNESS*

It started with the grandmother.

Or did it? I get the order of things confused sometimes. There were a lot of deaths at one point, but they happened at the end. At the beginning, there was only one death. The girl with the camera.

I had known she would be coming for nearly four hundred years, but I still wasn't ready when she finally arrived.

The first time I saw her was when the Cavaliers and the Roundheads were marching into battle. The girl was doing yoga on the fire escape.

I think it was just after Felix…

But, no. That comes later. Let's go back.

Chapter 1

HARRIET

Twenty minutes before her death, Harriet Stoker stared up at the hazard signs peppering the entrance of Mulcture Hall. The signs were very informative, stating in huge black letters: *DANGER – DERELICT BUILDING! THIS BUILDING HAS BEEN FOUND TO CONTAIN ASBESTOS; UNSTABLE STRUCTURE – UNAUTHORIZED PEOPLE FOUND ON THIS SITE WILL BE PROSECUTED* and *DANGER OF ELECTROCUTION!* Harriet was impressed. Confident of her life choices, she began to climb the chain-link fence.

Harriet thought that even when newly built, Mulcture Hall must have looked like a place where architecture came to die. The colourful graffiti covering the pebbledash walls didn't detract from the overwhelming greyness of the old halls of residence.

She picked her way carefully through nettles to the entrance. It was nearly dusk, so she used her phone to shine a light through a crack between the plywood boards covering a window.

When a face lunged at her from the other side, Harriet

skidded back on her heels. She laughed. It was her own reflection.

She inserted a crowbar into the gap. The board came loose in a cloud of cobwebs and sawdust, and the glass of the window smashed with the first tap of her crowbar. With her hands wrapped in her woollen scarf to protect against the broken shards, Harriet climbed through.

Her stomach was squirming in excitement. She'd been imagining this moment for weeks, wondering what might be inside the building when she was supposed to be paying attention to lectures or helping her gran with housework.

There were endless legends about Mulcture Hall, passing from final-year students to freshers in a decades-old gossip chain. It was rumoured to be a local drug dealer's base of operations, *and* the entrance to a secret underground government facility. It was also apparently haunted by the ghosts of students and workers who had died here back in 1994. Supposedly, the halls hadn't been demolished yet because the Biology Department was running some kind of long-term experiment on fungal growth. Harriet wasn't sure she believed any of the myths.

The building smelt worse than she thought it would – a foul mix of damp and urine. The stairwell was filled with beer cans and ashes left by other trespassers. Wrinkling her nose, she took a picture with her expensive camera, which she'd borrowed from the uni's photography department. Her lecturers would probably think the mess was artistic.

Climbing the concrete steps, she peered up over the

banister at the remains of the roof several storeys above. Then she turned and looked at the first floor. There were doors falling off their hinges along either side of a narrow corridor. The nearest had been propped open, but someone had kicked in the lower half.

She slid through the narrow gap between the door and the frame, trying not to get dirt on her clothes. Harriet always chose her outfits very carefully. Today, she was going incognito, so she was wearing a charcoal-grey shirt tucked into khaki trousers.

A thin mattress was rotting on the floor of the small student bedroom beyond. Rubbish had collected in gaps between floorboards – a mix of bottles and crisp packets and the springs of an armchair. The walls were black with moisture.

Harriet took pictures of the intricate cracks in a greenish mirror; an enamel sink turned orange by the steady drip of the tap; neon graffiti distorted by peeling paint like a long-lost cave painting.

It was even better than she'd imagined. For her last photography project, Harriet had submitted half a dozen pictures of the ducks by the campus lake. Her feedback had said that even the most technically proficient pictures were unsuccessful if there was no emotional resonance. She'd only got sixty per cent for it. While Harriet didn't mind being called emotionless, she did want a good grade. Anyway, that wouldn't be an issue this time – the building was unbelievably atmospheric.

She climbed the next two floors, peeping around open

doors into other wrecked and ransacked bedrooms. The building had the sad, historical gloom of a bombsite, she thought, rolling phrases for her report through her mind.

In a tiny kitchenette on the fourth floor, there was an ashtray on the counter, still full of a squatter's half-burnt curls of Rizla cigarette paper. Next to it lay a yellowing newspaper. She peeled open its mummified pages, catching sight of the words *Diana* and *Blair* before the paper collapsed into fragments.

FELIX

Felix heard the music first, drifting faint and muted from headphones as someone walked past. It took a huge effort for him to summon up the energy to open his eyes. When he managed it, there was nothing left of the intruder but a line of footprints in the dust.

Someone was here. *A human*. They must be playing music on a Walkman.

It had been so long since he'd last seen someone come inside the building. He'd imagined this moment for ever, but now that it was happening, all he felt was – tired. He was *exhausted*.

Felix should probably investigate the stranger. But the stairs alone seemed to be an insurmountable obstacle. Whoever it was would probably find their own way out. There was nothing in Mulcture Hall any more, not for a human.

Felix closed his eyes and drifted back to sleep.

HARRIET

Harriet adjusted the focus of her camera to capture a fern growing out of the top-floor banister, its fronds curling towards the light from beyond the collapsed roof. She caught a glimpse of darting movement in the periphery of her vision and spun around. Glass crunched under her feet, as her heart tripped over itself.

There was nothing but her own shadow, cast across the stairwell in the last remnants of twilight. She needed to calm down. The building was making her skittish. She was alone here. She was safe.

Harriet's phone rang, distracting her from the shadows. She pushed back her headphones to answer.

"How do you get iPlayer up again?" her gran asked, instead of a greeting.

Harriet patiently guided her grandmother through the process of selecting *Autumnwatch* on BBC iPlayer – a nightly occurrence.

She should tell her gran where she was. She had been the one to suggest Harriet come to Mulcture Hall to take photos for her project, after all. They'd walked past it when they'd toured the University of Warwick campus on an open day the year before. But her gran definitely hadn't meant that Harriet should come here alone, at night. She would be worried about her safety.

When she heard the theme music of *Autumnwatch* playing,

she said, "I've gotta go, Gran – I'm finishing my photography coursework. I'll see you later."

But her gran had already hung up. She hated it when Harriet talked through her favourite programme.

Norma had raised her ever since she was ten, after her parents had died. When she'd been accepted into university, Harriet had originally paid for a room in halls on campus, wanting to live away from home for the first time. But a few weeks before classes had started, her grandmother had tripped fetching the post in the morning and broken her ankle.

Harriet had cancelled the rent payment so that she could live at home and look after her. It was only a thirty-minute commute to the university, and the campus library was open all night, so she always had somewhere to go after the bars had closed. She never opened any of the books, but the WiFi connection was very strong, which was all she ever needed anyway. At least there, she didn't need to go to bed at 9 p.m. so that she didn't keep her gran awake.

Harriet usually filmed make-up tutorials in the stacks, recording herself contouring her cheekbones against a background of law books. It was less embarrassing to do it at night, when the only people who saw her were exhausted PhD students running on caffeine. She could handle talking to them. It was the students her own age who made her nervous.

It was starting to rain through the broken roof, in cold, heavy drops that ran straight down the nape of her neck. Shivering, she suddenly missed her overly warm room at home. She could picture her gran sitting under a blanket on the sofa, with the electric fire roaring and the cat stretched out on the hearth.

Twisting to watch the flight path of a plane as it passed overhead, her foot caught on something. Harriet tripped over the edge of the stairwell, with nothing below her but five storeys of open air and the concrete floor of the foyer. She dropped her phone, throwing her hands out to grab on to something.

Her heart thundered. Her camera fell first, unhooking from around her neck and crashing to the ground into a thousand shards. Then Harriet followed.

It happened too fast for her to scream anywhere except inside her own mind. Her head bounced off a jutting steel beam, spraying blood as she twisted over once, twice before she landed with an audible crack of bones on the floor.

A pool of blood dripped from the split in her skull, gathering on the lurid green moss. Everything went black.

There it is. The death that started it all. It's interesting, seeing it from this angle. I've only ever seen it from the past before. It would have been easy to stop it happening. Just a little bit of pressure here and there – a nudge to take her down the stairs instead of walking up them. And nothing would have happened the way it did.

Father was always doing things like that when he was here. And later, when he...

Sorry, sorry, you don't know about that yet, do you? I suppose I should go in chronological order. Everything just makes more sense if you look at it backwards.

For now, let's go back to where Harriet Stoker is lying in her own blood. She's undeniably, irrevocably, dead. Below her, a fern is being slowly crushed. Above her, the shadows are gathering to watch.

FELIX

Felix flung open his eyes, gasping. A golden burst of energy spread through him, shocking him awake. He jumped up, shuddering like he'd just had a shot of caffeine.

What had…?

The intruder. The one with the music. Something must have happened to them. He hadn't felt fresh energy like this in decades. He hadn't expected to ever feel it again.

Felix ran through into Kasper's bedroom. To his relief, he was awake too. Felix couldn't imagine anything worse than being the only one to wake up.

"What year is it?" Kasper asked, opening one eye to squint at Felix. He was shirtless, stretching his arm over his head. The muscles all along his torso lengthened and contracted. There was a shock of blond hair in his armpit.

Felix exhaled. "Last I remember was 2009. You?"

"2011 – a cat died in here. You were sleeping."

Felix was disappointed he'd missed a cat ghost – and then felt promptly sick at the rush of emotion. His feelings kept changing so fast, and he wasn't used to it. He'd spent so long suspended in sleep, feeling nothing. When he was low on energy, he barely even dreamed.

The world was a lot to process again after all that time. Had the fresh air blowing through the window always smelt so rich? Had Kasper always smiled so widely? Felix almost couldn't bear to look at him.

Rima flew in through the open window, glowing with energy too. "Someone new has arrived!" she yelped. "Get dressed, get dressed!"

"What year is it?" Felix asked her. It couldn't have been that long since the cat. He had a brief memory of snow, fluttering in through his window. Winter had been and gone while they slept. Maybe it was already 2012.

"I have absolutely no idea! Have you seen Leah? Where has that girl got to? Let's go! I need to find Cody!" She twirled, jumping into the air and running through the door.

Kasper looked at Felix, raising an eyebrow. "Business as usual with Rima, then."

"I think we could be here for an eternity and she wouldn't change," Felix said. He took a deep breath, trying to control the deep wave of love that rolled over him. He'd missed them all – Kasper and Rima, Leah and Claudia. After so long starved of them, listening to their voices was like drinking rich cream.

While Kasper pulled on his shirt, Felix turned to examine himself in the mirror by the bedroom door. The glass had a crack down the centre. That hadn't been there the last time he had been awake. Then, the vines on the windows had only been tendrils, creeping up the bottom of the glass pane. Now they covered the room in green foliage, flooding over the carpet.

Perhaps it had been longer than he'd thought. They could have been dreaming for decades, sleeping through the days as empty shells of their old selves. It was hard to tell when he still looked the same. He'd always be eighteen, just like the day he'd died.

Felix folded his crinkled collar back into place, then took off his glasses, rubbing them clean with the hem of his plaid shirt. He wasn't entirely sure how they managed to get so many smudges, considering he was incorporeal. It was one of the eternal mysteries of ghosts – and glasses.

Kasper nudged up against Felix's back and rested his chin on Felix's shoulder as he rearranged his hair in the mirror. He licked a thumb and smoothed his eyebrows flat. "Ready, loser?"

Felix folded his hands over his cuffs. It was starting, then. The peace between them never lasted long. "If you're done primping."

He let himself look at Kasper, feeling that deep ache in the centre of his chest. Had he really had these kinds of emotions constantly, before he fell asleep? Surely not. He wouldn't have been able to stand it.

Kasper walked through the door. "Let's go see who brought us back from the brink, then."

HARRIET

When Harriet woke up, the headphones around her neck were still blasting Janelle Monáe. She lay still for a moment, replaying the darkening sky, the sudden loss of balance as she tripped over something unseen, the flash of brightness as she fell, and then nothing.

She could hear voices. She was surrounded by people, talking quickly. Arguing.

She must be in an ambulance on the way to the hospital. The voices were paramedics discussing her injuries. It was likely she was seriously hurt. She might have broken her leg, or worse. She couldn't feel anything, which had to be a bad sign.

She tuned in to their conversation, trying very hard not to panic.

"...can't just leave her lying—"

"You would say that! You always think that—"

"Oh, because what you think is so much more—"

"Would you two just shut the hell up. It's not—"

"Are we actually fighting about this right now? She's not even cold yet!"

There were so many voices she couldn't keep track of them; they were all talking over each other. She opened her eyes. For a moment, everything was blurry. She blinked, and her vision cleared. She was staring at a mouldy breeze-block wall. The voices around her went silent.

"H-heyyy..." someone said.

Harriet flicked her gaze around until she found the speaker – a short girl wearing a hijab and a nervous expression. There were three people huddled around her, none of whom were paramedics – in fact, they looked like students. They must have heard her fall and come to investigate. She relaxed.

Maybe she wasn't badly hurt, after all.

Clearing her throat around a lump of something dusty and thick, she asked, "What happened to me?"

They exchanged nervous glances with one another. A black boy in a neat plaid shirt said, "Are you – are you OK? You had an accident."

Harriet rubbed her eyes. She knew she probably *wasn't* fine. She ought to be in serious pain right now. But she didn't have a single ache or pain. "I was ... falling."

"You remember?" The boy adjusted his tortoiseshell-rimmed glasses. There was a smudge on one of the lenses.

Another boy spoke. This one was white and much more muscular, with a rugby player's shoulders and rakish blond hair. "Why *wouldn't* she remember?"

"Well, I don't remember when I di—" the other boy began, until his friend cleared her throat warningly. He cut himself off. "Di-di-ha. Uh – well, no, not as such..." He trailed off into silence.

While Harriet watched this display, feeling a little perplexed, the rugby player stared at him in disgust. "Chill out, Felix. Jeez."

"You're the one who needs to chill out!" Felix retorted.

Harriet didn't have time for this. She struggled to her feet, feeling just a bit off balance rather than injured. She must have hit her head, because her bun had been knocked to the side, but there wasn't the tender spot of a bruise.

"You fell from the top floor," the girl said to Harriet,

squaring her shoulders and looking determined. She was wearing a pyjama top that said *HERE FOR THE DRAMA!* in pink glitter cursive writing.

"But how did I survive? I would have died." Harriet folded over into a lazy forward bend, testing herself for injuries. She wasn't hurt. At all.

The girl looked embarrassed. "Yeah. Yeah, you would have."

"So … did something catch me?" Harriet stretched her back, running through a few other yoga poses as she tried to decide whether it was possible that she was in so much pain she couldn't feel any of it.

The blond boy grimaced. "You died. You're dead. Sorry, mate."

"I'm…?" She must have misheard him. There was a lot going on – it was to be expected.

"You're dead; we're all dead," he said.

Clearly, they were members of a Role-Playing Society or something. What other kind of students hung out in an old abandoned building during their spare time?

"Right. OK. Well, I'm just going to leave, so you can all get back to … whatever—"

"You can just take a look at your body if you don't believe us," Felix said, gesturing behind Harriet and then quickly rubbing the back of his neck. "It's a bit gory."

Harriet sighed. She supposed she could play along, if it would get rid of them more quickly. She turned around. When she swallowed, the dusty lump was back in her throat.

Lying on the floor in a puddle of congealing blood was her body.

Harriet fought a surreal sense of dissociation. The world rolled around her as she tried to resolve what she was seeing with everything she knew to be true about the universe.

She was here. She was there.

She was dead.

Chapter 2

HARRIET

"Where are you going?" the girl called, as Harriet pushed her way towards the exit. Harriet didn't stop. There might still be time to fix this. Clearly concussion was causing her to hallucinate her own dead body. But if she could just get to a doctor, it would be fine. She was going to be fine.

She tamped down her panic. This would all be treated, and the worst outcome of her whole misadventure would be that she would have to submit her photography coursework a day late. There was nothing for her to worry about. So why did she feel like her life was over?

She forced the feeling away, climbing out of the window. She had lost her phone in the fall, but someone on campus would call an ambulance for her.

"Wait!" the girl shouted, as Harriet breathed in the clean, fresh air. She already felt better now that she was out of that musty wreck.

Three steps away from the property fence, she stopped in her tracks. She ached all over. Swaying on the spot, she tried to push away the pain vibrating through her bones.

The further she moved, the worse she felt. The feeling was an ocean, pulling her in. She was suddenly convinced that it would kill her to take even another step forwards. She wanted to lie down and become part of the world. It would be so peaceful to give up control and just become a mass of atoms, free to move as they pleased.

Harriet closed her eyes, unable to stop the concept from overwhelming her. She could feel her particles sliding free of each other, peeling away and drifting off into the atmosphere.

"HEY! HEY, GIRL!"

The yelling came from somewhere very far away. She ignored it. She just needed to let herself become part of the air and ground and sky.

RIMA

She was leaving! The girl had only just died, and she was already going to make herself disintegrate. Rima hadn't even had a chance to find out her name. It was such a waste too – the new girl seemed so young and pretty. Though her university experience was probably very different to Rima's. She looked like she got invited to all of the best parties. Rima had only ever been invited to a private Usenet server.

"We have to do something! Felix, come on!" Kasper hissed. His eyes were wide with panic, his hand tight on Felix's forearm as the three of them leant out of the window to watch Harriet's progress. Decades-worth of energy was falling away into the wind, precious golden strands disappearing into nothing.

"What do you want *me* to do?" Felix asked, the words turned up high at the end.

"I don't know – something more than gawp at her!"

Rima rolled her eyes. She nudged them out of the way and hoisted herself over the windowsill.

"You can't!" Kasper said.

"I thought you wanted me to do something?" she said and twisted into a form that was easier to control. If she flew, she could get to Harriet without losing as much energy.

HARRIET

A hand grabbed her shoulder, pinching into the muscle and shaking hard. Harriet opened her eyes.

"What?" she asked, swooning slightly, struggling to remember how words and speech and vocal cords worked.

"Stop! Wake up!" a voice said. "You've got to come with me. Now, or you're gone."

A hand tugged her backwards, and the movement made Harriet stumble. As she walked, she remembered that she had limbs, and muscles, and as she focused, they made a human body and she could move again.

At the entrance to the hall, she remembered what being Harriet Stoker felt like and recovered her shape completely. It was only then that she recognized the girl standing beside her, who was looking at Harriet as if she was searching her face for some sign of life.

The blond boy helped her down from the sill as she climbed back inside.

"What *was* that?" Harriet asked. It had felt impossible and horrifying and *incredible*, like Harriet was so much more than just one person. She had felt connected to everything; every atom and particle on the entire planet.

"You were disintegrating," the girl said. "You can't leave. You'll be gone for ever if you do."

"Dis—? *Gone?*" Her brain was fuzzy and tired, but it felt surreal and primitive to have a brain at all, running a consciousness using neurons and muscles. *"Who are you?* What is happening to me?"

"We're ghosts," Felix said. "We're all ghosts. And now, so are you."

Starting from the beginning – or, rather, this beginning at least, which I think is probably the one that will be the most useful – there are signs of it all. You can see it in her behaviour. It's just like his.

When Rima first realized that she was a ghost, she closed off completely. She said later that she wasn't angry or panicked or sad, but guilty, like she'd wasted what little time she'd had. She could have done so much more, if she'd known that those eighteen years were going to be all that she'd get. She didn't cry or shout or try to leave the building. She just sat down and wished and wished that things were different.

It's always fascinating, watching someone when they think they're alone. They sink inside their own heads and perform intricate little rituals that make sense only to them, that they'd never even dream of showing another person.

It says a lot about Harriet that she didn't pause to grieve like Rima. She started looking for a solution to the problem instead. If only she wasn't so good at finding them.

HARRIET

"I'm a ghost. I'm dead. I'm … *dead*." Harriet held up her hand and looked at it, trying to work out how it could possibly be the hand of a ghost. It looked just like anyone else's hand, but somehow it wasn't made of flesh and bone any more. Experimentally, she tried to pick up a lump of brick from the floor. Her hand passed straight through it.

It was impossible. How could she be dead and feel so alive at the same time?

She was only eighteen. She couldn't be stuck here for ever, with no way to return to her old life. She'd had so many plans for her degree and career … her *life*. She'd only just started gaining followers on her YouTube channel. She'd been diligently posting make-up tutorials every other Monday. The hard work had finally started to pay off, and now all that effort had been wasted.

"I barely did anything with my life," Harriet said. "I've never even left the country. Oh God, I only had sex *once*. I wasted so much time in freshers' week!"

The blond boy stepped forward and patted her consolingly on the shoulder. "Don't worry," he said. "We're here for you. I'm Kasper, and this is Rima and Felix."

"What do I even do now?" she said, ignoring him. "Who are you all? Are you the welcoming committee or something? Please say you aren't *angels*."

He shook his head. "We died here, too. A long time ago,

now. You don't have to go through this alone. There's loads of us here."

"Loads. Of ghosts?"

He grinned and pointed upwards with both forefingers to where dozens of figures were standing motionlessly on the floors above, peering over the balcony at her.

"No. Freaking. Way." Harriet squeezed her eyes tightly shut. When she opened them again, the people were still there. They were all staring intently at her. None of them were moving. None of them were speaking.

It was too much. Harriet turned back to her body.

"Is there a way we can close my eyes?" she asked. It hit her all over again how awful it looked, a lifeless corpse lying there in a pool of blood and cracked bone. "I keep making eye contact with myself, and that is *not* something I ever imagined doing."

"There's no way to move your body," Rima said, as another girl appeared. This one was carrying a baby and looked very young and very tired. All the ghosts here seemed to be teenagers, around the same age as she was.

Had this new girl been a student parent when she was alive? In some of the halls there were special rooms with kitchens and en-suite bathrooms for parents.

"Leah!" Rima and Felix said together, looking delighted.

"Where have you been?" Rima asked. "I've missed you *so* much."

"I was sleeping, like the rest of you." Leah let Rima hug her, and then said to Harriet, not unkindly, "Congratulations, new kid. Welcome to the afterlife."

Trying to hide the dart of pain that rippled through her at the words, Harriet made lazy jazz hands at her. "Thanks! I'm hyped that I never have to pay off my student loans now."

Leah shrugged at that.

"I'm Leah. This is Claudia." She peeled a curl of blanket away from her baby's face. The girl's blue eyes slid over to focus on Harriet.

Leah was standing right under a drip of water, which kept falling through her left shoulder in a way that made Harriet feel dizzy. It was like watching an optical illusion. Her body looked completely solid right up until the moment the water droplets touched her and then her shoulder went kind of ... fuzzy. That – combined with her deathly pale skin, cream linen dress and slightly lanky hair – was the most obvious indication that she was dead. The rest of them looked alive, if you didn't pay close attention.

"Do *you* know how to leave the building?" she asked Leah. "They're saying I can't get out, but I have to go home."

Her gran couldn't drive with her broken ankle. She would be trapped at home if Harriet wasn't there to take her around. She wouldn't even be able to go food shopping until Harriet got back. And they were nearly out of milk.

"You might as well quit now. You can't leave the place where you died," Leah said. "Trust me, I've tried. Our souls are connected to the land or building or something."

"But I have to go home. My gran is all on her own. She'll worry about me if I don't turn up."

"Even if you went home, your gran wouldn't be able to see you anyway," Kasper said.

"You can't know that for *sure*," Harriet said. "My gran could be a psychic or something. Are those even real? I hope they are."

She was very aware that she was pretending to be upbeat and calm about this whole thing. If she stopped smiling, she would break down, and that wasn't something she could do in front of strangers. She'd always been taught never to show anyone a sign of weakness, because someone would try to use it against her.

"You can't go home. Forget about it, kid," Leah said, a little more harshly.

Harriet picked at her nails, miffed. "Why do you keep calling me 'kid'? You're, like, seventeen."

"What part of 'ghosts' don't you understand? We've all been here for years. Long before you were even born. You are a kid to me."

"How did you die?"

Leah sighed heavily and looked down at her baby. Apparently, Harriet had just made a severe breach of etiquette.

"Oh, dude, you'll never get how Leah died out of her," Rima replied. "She and Claudia had already been here for ages when we all died. Even I don't know how she got here, and we've been best friends for dozens of years."

"We're not best friends," Leah muttered.

"Sure. Tell that to your half of our *Best Friends Forever* necklace." Rima tapped a pink locket hanging around her own neck.

"I *told you* – I'm not wearing that thing," Leah said, glaring at the jewellery.

Harriet ignored their bickering. Her brain was too full to find room to care about whatever kind of fight was going on there. If it wasn't about her death or her gran, she wasn't interested.

"Anyway, never mind how Leah died," Rima said. "It was probably something like carbon monoxide or gas that did the rest of us in, though. We think."

Harriet blinked. "What, like a gas leak?"

"Yep." She popped the "p", acting remarkably cheerful about it. "Everyone in the building died on the same night in our sleep, so a pipe must have come loose or something. That's our best guess, anyway. We have no way of knowing for sure."

Harriet had heard that some students had died in Mulcture Hall, but she'd thought it was just another one of the uni myths, exaggerated for optimum scandal. Knowing it was true suddenly put a new perspective on the destroyed rooms, rotting mattresses and collapsing furniture. People her age had lived and died right here. And the current students just saw the building as a spooky story.

"I'm sorry, that's awful," Harriet said, though it was hard to feel sorry for someone as lively as this girl.

"I know, right? We'd only just got a modem here too," Rima said, pouting. She was playing with the folds of her hijab, adjusting the material so that it fell more neatly over her shoulders. "Such wasted potential."

"Modem," Harriet repeated in bemusement. "Should I know what that is?"

"What?!" Felix said, and then clamped his mouth shut, looking embarrassed.

"Please don't start talking about computers again," Kasper told him, and draped an arm over Felix's shoulder to slouch lazily against him.

"Does everyone become a ghost when they die? Like, everyone ever?" Harriet asked, changing the subject to something she was more interested in. She tried to be casual, like the answer didn't matter desperately.

Harriet's parents were dead. Were they ghosts, too? Maybe they had been watching from the afterlife for the past eight years, unable to speak to her. They'd died at her gran's house – were they there, right now?

"Most people become ghosts," Rima said. "But some don't stick around for long."

"'Stick around'? Where do they go?"

Rima shrugged. "We don't know what happens to ghosts who disintegrate. It's one of life's unanswered questions. Tell us about you, anyway. What's your name?" She patted Harriet's arm gently.

"Harriet Stoker." She looked down at the hand on her arm.

It would be rude to ask her to remove it. These people all seemed to be very relaxed around each other – they touched each other constantly, lolling around like a litter of puppies. There was something unnerving about it.

Harriet couldn't remember ever touching any of her friends, except for maybe an awkward hug on the last day of term.

"Great! Nice to meet you, Harriet," Rima said, looking genuinely thrilled. "You should stay with me! I'm in Room 2B."

"Thanks," Harriet said, taken aback by the offer. She hadn't even thought about where she was going to stay. Did ghosts sleep? Would she need somewhere to live? There was so much she hadn't considered. "I really just want to get home, though. My gran…" She trailed off.

Rima worried her lip between her teeth. "Well, maybe someone will come looking for you and they can tell your gran what happened. Did anyone know you were coming here?"

Harriet shook her head. "I was trespassing. I didn't tell anyone."

Rima's shoulders slumped. "That's a bummer."

"I was on the phone with Gran before I died, though," Harriet said. Excited now, she realized what that meant. "Could I use it to call someone?"

"We're ghosts," said Leah. "We can't touch stuff."

"It's voice-activated," Harriet said. It might work. It was worth a try.

Rima smiled kindly at her. "Where is it, in your pocket?"

"I think I dropped it on the top floor," Harriet said.

"I'll help you find it!" Kasper said, standing up straight and releasing Felix. He suggested, "The others can stay here and keep an eye on the corp— Er, I mean—"

His eyes went wide with panic. Rima mouthed at him, *"Harriet."*

"Harriet," he corrected. His Adam's apple dipped as he swallowed. "They'll watch your body, *Harriet*. Sorry."

"Great. So glad that someone else is on corpse-watch," Harriet said. She desperately didn't want to think about her body just yet, but the idea of someone keeping watch over it was reassuring. "Er, what's your name again?"

"Kasper Jedynak," the blond boy said, preening slightly. "4B." He scrubbed his hand through his hair, which was surprisingly fluffy.

"Casper? Like the friendly ghost?"

A much-beleaguered look crossed his face. "Bad coincidence. Don't bother with the jokes, I've heard them all before."

"Though he is very friendly!" Rima piped up.

Kasper sighed.

He was kind of cute, actually – in a dim-looking way.

"I'm Felix Anekwe, in 4A." The other boy held out a hand to her.

"You're neighbours?" She tried to remember whether she'd looked inside any of the rooms on the fourth floor when she'd been taking photographs. It was hard to imagine that the wrecked rooms were still homes for these people.

"Unfortunately." Kasper scrubbed a hand roughly over Felix's scalp, who put up a token resistance but didn't wriggle free.

"Boys!" Rima said, in resigned impatience. "Harriet's waiting for you to take her up to the top floor, Kasper."

He released Felix, looking sheepish. "Right. Come on, Harriet," Kasper said with dignity, squaring his (already very square) jaw.

"Don't get lost, Kasper," Felix drawled. "Just keep going upwards, OK?"

"Talk to the hand, Felix."

"Talk to the hand?" Harriet repeated under her breath, bemused.

FELIX

Felix watched Harriet and Kasper walk away. Kasper's hand was casually resting on Harriet's lower back for some reason. He tried to ignore the ghost of Kasper's touch prickling on his own skin.

When Harriet turned, Felix saw for the first time that there was a fist-sized dent in the back of her skull, hidden under her hair. It was the only visible sign of how she had died.

When the two of them had disappeared, the rest of them all started talking at once.

"What was *that*?" Felix asked, as Rima said, "Kasper was *flirting* with her!" and Leah mumbled, "I did not miss this at *all*."

Felix sighed through his nose. "I cannot *believe*—"

"I *know*." Rima shook her head. "A suicide attempt, within the first five minutes! Unbelievable!"

Guiding Harriet through her death was a bit of a shock to the system. Felix had forgotten how much there was to learn about the afterlife when you were newly dead. Everything must seem utterly confusing. Felix had been so busy obsessing over his own issues that he could barely remember what he'd done in the years after his death. Harriet was lucky she had them to help her out.

A fly was buzzing tentatively around the congealing blood near Harriet's right ear. Felix leant closer, thinking: *Go away.* The fly zoomed off to investigate a McDonald's wrapper instead. Felix settled back, satisfied.

"How long do you think the energy will last?" he asked. "Before we, you know … go to sleep again."

Leah, who was the most experienced among them, shrugged. "Could be anywhere from a few months to a year. It depends how much energy escaped and how much she kept for herself. She seems quite strong to me, so probably only a few months."

Felix swallowed. That didn't seem nearly enough time to do all the things he wanted to do. He felt revitalized, born again. No matter how much he prepared, he was never ready to return to that dull, dreamless hibernation.

"Well," he said, lifting up the corners of his mouth in an attempt at a smile. "I suppose we'll have to make the most of it while we can."

Just then, a small fox spirit appeared from the shadows and trotted up to them.

"Cody!" Rima gasped. The fox leapt into her arms, wriggling furiously and twisting upside down to reveal a pure white belly. "I've missed you so much," Rima said, burying her face in her ginger fur. The fox let out a short, squeaky sort of yowl.

"I can't believe she's still here. I thought she'd have disintegrated by now." Felix stretched out his hand, grinning. The fox tapped it with a black-tipped paw.

"She's a tough old thing, aren't you?" Rima kissed Cody's nose.

Before they had all gone into hibernation mode, Rima had been training up the dead fox as a pet. The process had involved a lot of snarling and baring of teeth from both Rima and Cody, but in the end, she'd even got the fox doing tricks.

Cody jumped to the ground, stretching out her front legs, back curving into a bow. She let out another hoarse yowl, then swiftly jumped across the room to chase a mouse into the wall.

Felix stared up the stairs, after Kasper and Harriet. He wondered what they were talking about, and if his hand was still on her back. But most of all, he wondered how he could stop himself from caring.

Chapter 3

KASPER

Kasper led Harriet up the stairs, weaving between the ghosts who were still watching her. They all closed their eyes as she passed, like they were breathing her in. A girl from the second floor – who used to do student radio when she was alive, and sometimes still put on shows for them all – even darted over to touch Harriet's arm.

Kasper couldn't blame them. Harriet was glowing golden bright, even though she'd lost some energy while she was outside. Kasper had been so scared when she'd left Mulcture Hall. He wished desperately that he was as brave as Rima, who had gone after her without any hesitation at all. If only he could have played the role of rescuer to Harriet's damsel in distress.

"What do they want? It's like they think I'm a snack or something," Harriet said, brushing her hair flat nervously. It was woven up in some fancy twist. Her make-up was very fancy too. Had she been planning to go out to a party that night, if she had survived? There were probably loads of boys waiting for her to turn up right at that very moment.

"You're a novelty," he replied. "Besides, your fall was kind of brutal. No one else has *ever* had such a good death, I don't think. Well, I suppose Leah might have, but she's never told us how she died, so that doesn't count."

Having a good death was a gruesome badge of honour. Kasper always wished his own was more exciting.

He summoned up all his courage and added, "Plus … you're well fit. That makes you even more interesting."

Kasper waited with bated breath for her reply, nerves fluttering in his stomach. It had been a long time since he'd said anything like that to a girl.

"Less fit now that I'm a rotting corpse," Harriet muttered, and ran one hand over the back of her head again. There was a dip there, where her skull had caved in. Kasper and the others had been lucky – they had no wounds.

"Oh, I dunno about that," he said breezily. "You've raised the bar for rotting corpses everywhere."

"Thanks, um—" She paused, clearly trying to remember his name.

"Kasper," he said. He didn't mind. She'd gone through a lot, very quickly.

She smiled at him, her eyes lighting up so beautifully that it completely changed her face. "Thanks for coming with me to get my phone."

"No problem. There is something you can do in exchange, though." He let a small smile pull up the side of his mouth in a way that he used to practise in front of the mirror during pre-drinks, back when he was alive and could go to clubs and flirt with all the girls he wanted.

"What do you want?" Her voice was wary.

He bit back a grin. "Well … you don't happen to know how the Sky Blues are doing in the league tables this season, do you?"

Harriet grinned. Something inside him lightened. He had been hoping for this.

HARRIET

As they walked up to the top floor, Harriet made awkward small talk with this boy, Kasper. He had apparently been a rower, not a rugby player; he had been studying Art History; and he'd been seventh in line for a peerage when he had died.

When they reached the fifth floor, it was full of ghosts too. The ones up here seemed different somehow. They weren't watching Harriet curiously, but just sat around, staring blankly into space. Some were slumped against walls or curled up on the ground. They were faint, too – dimly lit compared to the brighter ghosts she'd seen so far, who could almost pass for living people.

"What's wrong with them?" Harriet asked.

"They're still Shells," Kasper said, sounding surprised to see them too.

"Shells?" Harriet moved closer to one, but he didn't react – not even when she touched his arm. There was no sign of life on any of their faces.

"Ghosts with low energy are called Shells. They're like empty husks of ghosts, nearly gone."

"What?"

Kasper shook his head. "Energy doesn't last for ever. When we first die, we're fresh and bright, like you. But after decades, you just sort of use it all up. You stop being able to move around, and eventually your energy runs out completely and you disintegrate. Until today, we were all like this too."

Harriet stared at him. "So what changed?"

He gestured at her. "You arrived. Your death released energy that spread through the building. We absorbed it, and it was enough to wake us up again. We were all Shells until the moment you died. We've been Shells before, but we've always found more energy from somewhere or other before we disintegrated. This time, we came really close to it, I think." A worried look crossed his face.

"Wow." Harriet was a bit miffed. Kasper had taken some of her energy? Surely that should have gone to her. It was Harriet's death, after all. "So why didn't the Shells up here wake up when I died?"

"Hmm. Well, you probably died when you hit the ground floor, right? The energy would have radiated through the building, so the ghosts on the lower floors got the most. By the time it reached this far, it was too weak for the tiny bit of fresh energy to make any difference to the ghosts here. So they stayed like this."

No wonder the ghosts in the building were all watching Harriet. They were waiting for more energy. Well, she wasn't going to give it to them. If losing energy meant turning into a Shell, then she was going to keep as much as she could for herself. When she got out of here, she needed to have enough energy to spend years watching over her gran with the ghosts of her parents.

The night they died was a horrible, panicked blur of fear and misery in Harriet's memory. Her parents had eaten contaminated meat that had given them food poisoning. At first they'd just been sick, but after a few hours neither of them could breathe properly. Harriet had called an ambulance while her gran panicked and dithered, but her mum and dad had both died before the paramedics arrived.

Her whole life had been taken away from her in one moment. They'd been about to move to America for Harriet's mum's new job; they'd sold their house and were only supposed to be staying with her gran until their visas came through. Before the documents ever arrived, they were both gone. Everything Harriet had loved was lost, just like that – her family, her home, her life. Harriet was left with nothing except her grandmother.

The ache in her heart for her parents had never disappeared. Their deaths had been a terrible mistake. But now, more time with them was tantalizingly out of reach. Just.

Harriet and Kasper crossed the hallway, stopping once or twice to let a vacuous shell of a ghost drift past, blown wherever the wind took them. Finally, they reached the place where Harriet had tripped and fallen.

Peering over the edge of the floor, Harriet could see

rust-coloured splatters of blood staining a steel beam that jutted out from the floor below. She must have hit her head on the way down.

Harriet realized she was rubbing at the hole in the back of her head and forced her hand down by her side. The quicker they found her phone and got away from here, the better.

"How big's your pager?" Kasper asked, crouching down and searching the floor for any sign of it.

"Pager? What is this, *Seinfeld*? It's a mobile."

Kasper looked confused, so Harriet said, exasperated, "A *mobile phone*?"

"A car phone? One of those big bricks?" He looked embarrassed. "Sorry. I was never really that bothered about technology when I was alive."

"No, it's like –" she gestured the size of a small rectangle. "It's silver." It blew her mind that he didn't know what an iPhone was. She kept forgetting that although the other ghosts looked like they were eighteen, too, they were a lot older. There was a whole vacuum between their life experiences.

She started searching too. There were bright yellow hazard signs leaning up against the wall, warning that there was a dangerous, unstable edge. Why hadn't she noticed them before? No wonder she'd had an accident, if they were hidden out of sight like that.

Harriet caught sight of a flash of metal hidden behind a fern. "Oh, there it is!"

When she attempted to pick it up, her hand went straight

through the phone. Of course. Disappointed, she said, "Well, I should be able to make a call using voice control."

"How does it work?" Kasper asked. His eyes were bright with excitement. At least someone was happy. "Where are the buttons?"

"You just touch the screen," Harriet said, already dreading having to give a tutorial in twenty-first-century technology.

"How does touching it do anything?" He leant in for a closer look, his hair brushing against hers.

Harriet had no idea how it worked, but she wasn't going to admit to that.

"We don't have time for me to explain. Computer stuff is very complicated. *Unlock*," she said to the phone, before he could ask any more questions.

Something in her chest loosened when the phone registered her voice. She could call her gran before she started worrying. The battery was still on ninety per cent, too.

Kasper gasped. "There's writing on the screen!"

A search result was still open in her browser. She had been looking up information about the building just before she'd entered, but hadn't paid much attention at the time. Now, she paused and read the first link.

22 OF THE WEIRDEST UNEXPLAINED MYSTERIES

17. The 23 students who died overnight in a UK university dorm.

Back in 1994, twenty-three students died during a single night at Mulcture Hall, on the University of Warwick campus outside Coventry. The alarm was raised early one morning when a student from another hall found their friend dead in their bed. Police arrived at the scene and discovered that every student who had been in the building that night had died some time after midnight.

It was initially declared that the deaths were due to a gas leak within the building, and a press release was issued by the university to that effect, including promises to run immediate health-and-safety checks on all of the halls of residence on the campus.

However, the mystery deepened when autopsies found none of the signs usually associated with carbon monoxide poisoning or oxygen starvation due to a gas leak. To this day, the case remains open with the West Midlands Police, who declared the deaths suspicious after a long investigation.

The case has been discussed online ever since, and possible explanations have varied from a simple blood-sampling error at the post-mortem, to wilder theories such as alien abduction. However, it seems unlikely the true explanation will ever be found.

The deceased were mainly first-year students aged eighteen or nineteen, as well as four international post-graduate students in their mid-twenties.

Harriet frowned. That was weird. What could have killed them all, then? Had the police seriously never found anything in all this time?

Before Kasper could read it and get distracted, she said, "Call 'Home'."

When the phone started ringing, Harriet found that for some reason she couldn't breathe. Finally, the line clicked on.

"Hello?"

Harriet exhaled in a gust and said, "Gran. Hey."

She spoke over her. *"Have you been studying in the library all night again? You should come home, it's not good for you."*

"I've had an accident, Gran," she said, a lump in her throat. Her gran always assumed the best of her. As if she'd ever been really studying, all those nights she'd stayed out late. She'd been messing around with mascara and eyeshadow in the empty stacks of the library's Economics section.

"Hello?" her gran repeated. *"Harriet? I can't hear you. I'm going to call you back. I think the line's bad."*

"I'm here, Gran!"

Her gran hung up. Harriet looked at Kasper, who was watching her with a soft, gentle frown. There was a tickling suspicion making itself known in the back of her brain.

The phone rang again.

"Harriet, hello?" Her gran's voice sent ice-cold shards running through Harriet.

"Hey, Gran. I'm here, Gran. I'm so – I love you. I love you so much."

"I think you pocket-dialled me. Come home, will you? I need you to turn the heating on. I can't reach with my ankle." With that, she hung up again.

Harriet really, really wished that she was the kind of person who cried. Her mum and dad felt further away than ever. "She doesn't even know that I'm missing. If I had to die, why couldn't it be where my parents are?"

Kasper didn't reply. She wanted to shake him – and shake all those ghosts downstairs who'd been watching her every move. This was *her life*. Not a TV show.

Furious, she abandoned the phone and marched down the stairs. The Shells let out a collective, mournful sigh as she left. Kasper didn't follow.

There was nowhere Harriet could go without being watched by curious eyes. All the students seemed to be enjoying their reawakening, shouting and calling out to each other. A couple of them were even playing hide-and-seek on the stairs, jumping through the walls and dangling from the floor into the rooms below.

She barged past them. When she reached the third floor, she found a scrawny boy with white-guy dreadlocks resting his ear against the wall and listening carefully.

He bared his teeth at Harriet when she passed. "Back off. Get your own rat! This one's mine."

Startled, she glanced back at him. "I, er, I don't—"

"You're not coming in at the last minute and taking my spirit. Piss off."

Harriet opened her mouth to reply, but she had no idea what he was talking about, and didn't really care to find out.

On the second floor, she closed her eyes and walked

through the door to the fire escape which zigzagged down the side of the building.

Sitting on the narrow metal staircase, she wrapped her arms around her knees. The sun had risen, turning the sky a pale blue. She'd been here all night. In the car park below, the spaces on either side of her car were filling up as people arrived for lectures. If she looked closely, she would probably see someone she recognized, on their way to their early morning Digital Photomedia class.

She hadn't managed to make many friends in her first few weeks of uni. Everyone in her lectures had started joking and messing around right on day one, but she could never find a good entry point into any conversations. Not that they were talking about anything interesting, anyway.

She used to sit on her own before the professor arrived, researching new cameras and lenses online, or planning new videos to film. Photography was what she was there to do, after all. Making friends could wait until later, when she'd achieved everything she wanted to achieve.

Lights glimmered on the horizon. Somewhere in the city, Harriet's grandmother was wobbling across the kitchen in her ankle cast to make tea and porridge, carefully bending down to feed the cat, and probably calling BT to check whether her landline was connecting properly. She would settle down with her knitting, and it would be hours before she realized that Harriet's call wasn't just a phone malfunction.

Disappointment boiled in her stomach, morphing into

something dense and painful until she wasn't sure whether she was sad or angry. This wasn't how things were supposed to go. This wasn't who she was. She was going to graduate with a first-class Photography degree, and then move to New York or Paris and get a job as a photographer for *Vogue*. She was supposed to be happy and successful and beautiful, with a string of glamorous model lovers and a penthouse apartment.

She wasn't meant to die in a crumbling, undignified block of student housing, or abandon her grandmother just when she needed her most. This kind of thing wasn't supposed to happen. Not to people like *her*.

I know, it's painful to watch. She's so desperate to get home.

Everything always comes back to family in the end. To the ones you love, or the ones you hate – the people who are closest to you. To get revenge or get away or get back to them. Blood is blood is blood. This is going to be important later, so pay attention.

Chapter 4

FELIX

To Felix's surprise, Kasper returned to the foyer on his own, shaking his head in disappointment. "It didn't work. Her gran couldn't hear her, and she's gone off somewhere. I think she wanted to be on her own."

Felix exhaled. He hadn't expected it to work, but he'd thought the process of trying might settle Harriet's anxiety a bit. Clearly not.

There was something disappointed in Kasper's expression, like he'd been hoping for more to come from his time with Harriet. Felix wished that Harriet hadn't died, for his own sake as well as hers. He'd grown used to having Kasper's attention to himself, however abrasive that attention might be.

"It was a long shot, I guess," Rima said.

Leah wrinkled her nose. "I suppose we'll just have to ignore the smell until someone finds her body on their own, then."

Claudia let out a burble, wriggling in her swaddling.

Felix sniffed. The corpse hadn't started to smell, not yet, after only one night. But there were other reasons to want it gone – it was safer all around if there was no chance of anyone getting their hands on it.

Kasper dropped down to sprawl on the floor next to Felix, leaning against an old sponge sofa cushion. The university had emptied the building after they'd shut it down, but over the years, squatters had brought bits of cheap furniture in with them – beach chairs and patio furniture, rotting pillows stolen from skips. The squatters didn't stay long, and they nearly always left this stuff behind when they moved on.

"Her phone is so futuristic, guys," Kasper said. "It can go on Usenet without a cable!"

He lounged to drop his head onto Felix's shoulder.

Rima blinked. "The phone works without a modem?"

"Without any cables at all!" Kasper confirmed. "No beeping!"

"It was completely silent?" Felix looked flabbergasted, blowing Kasper's hair out of his mouth. "I don't believe you. I wonder if Harriet would mind if I went and had a look."

Felix had a lot of things he wanted to check online. He'd spent decades agonizing over all the new comic releases he'd missed out on since he died. Who even knew what had happened to Captain America since 1994? There might actually be a film out by now, though he wasn't sure he'd be able to handle seeing Steve Rogers onscreen. His crush was bad enough as it was.

He could go and look it up right now. Though, it was probably rude to use it while Harriet was hiding away somewhere crying. Rima would tell him off with wide, disappointed Disney-princess eyes, and it wasn't worth *the eyes*. He could wait a bit longer. But he'd have to do it before anyone else found out there was a functioning phone up for grabs.

Rima had an ongoing feud with several of the other ghosts in the building, because they didn't have the same standards of moral behaviour as her. She disapproved strongly of inter-spirit theft, resource-hoarding and anti-social hauntings. The others did not.

Because of that, Felix and his friends tended to keep themselves separate from the others. On more than one occasion, he'd had to hold Rima back from a fight with some random student. It was better this way, anyway – Felix got too shy to speak when he was in large groups, and Leah could barely stand the three of them, let alone anyone else. They were very happy as they were. There had been Lisa too once, but she had disintegrated years ago.

"Harriet reminds me of Lisa," Felix said, realizing for the first time why she seemed so familiar.

He regretted it when Kasper flinched at her name, his muscles going tense where they rested against Felix's side.

Before she had disintegrated, Lisa had been just as nonchalantly cool as Harriet seemed to be. Harriet's aloofness came across as effortless and charismatic, but Felix thought she was probably just nervous.

"I hated Lisa," Leah said. "She was too loud."

"You hate everyone," Kasper said.

"I hate *most* people, not everyone," Leah said. "But Lisa was especially irritating. It's no wonder she passed on so quickly; she used up all her energy chatting bubbles."

Cradled in her arms, Claudia blew an idle bubble of her own, spittle forming on her lower lip.

"You know Lisa disintegrated because of the Tricksters," Rima said. "It was hardly her fault."

Rima always jumped to everyone's defence. She was utterly incapable of seeing anything but the good in people. If she wasn't so lovely, it would have been incredibly annoying.

Felix stared down one of the first-floorers, who was drifting closer and closer to Harriet's corpse, trying to act casually. She met Felix's gaze and abruptly turned and left. Felix grinned in satisfaction.

The general population of the halls were scared enough of Felix to stay away from his things, even the overwhelming temptation of a corpse. Felix had seen terrible, zombie-adja-cent activities done to animal bodies in the past. Harriet didn't deserve that. But no one would come anywhere near this one, not now it was clear Felix had claimed it. He'd worked hard to make himself scary by spreading rumours, even if it only worked on people who didn't know him.

"*I* like Harriet, anyway," Kasper said. He scratched at his shoulder, hand tugging down the neck of his shirt to reveal the line of his collarbone.

Felix pushed down a wave of annoyance. "No surprise there."

Kasper always loved pretty girls.

He sneered at Felix. "At least I'm not planning to take advantage of a newbie to use their phone. You know the

Internet isn't a substitute for real human friendship, right?"

Kasper had always been uninterested in the Internet. He had never used it when he was alive, and he refused to accept that it was mainstream now. Even when it was obvious from all the students who walked past the building with mobiles and laptops that technology wasn't just for nerds any more.

Felix scrambled for a retort, flustered. "Well, your, er – your friendships—"

Kasper lifted a brow, waiting patiently. Felix broke eye contact with him, flushing, trying to summon up a comeback from the depths of his banter resources.

Rima stepped in to save him. "Kasper, when Harriet's ghost appeared, you literally yelled, 'Dibs!' because you thought she was hot. I think that's a bit worse than Felix wanting to use her phone."

"Besides," Felix said, finally coming up with a retort, "it's not like you're the essence of cool. Remember that time some girl offered you a cigarette and you lit the wrong end?"

"That was in my first week of uni," Kasper hissed. "How long are you going to keep bringing that up? Or are you planning to post about it on the Internet?"

"Anyway, Kasper," Rima said, "there's nothing wrong with computers. I liked them too. There's that *X-Files* forum I used to go on. I can't wait to see what happened to the other netters."

"You're not a nerd like Felix, though," Kasper said, looking stung. Rima's reprimands tended to have that effect. "He's into lame comics and games and everything."

"At least I can read," Felix retorted. "You were doing a degree in looking at pretty pictures."

Kasper hated when he made fun of his Art History degree. He poked Felix's side, which tickled enough that Felix laughed, against his will.

"I should probably go after her, right?" Rima interrupted, gesturing upstairs. "She's been gone ages."

"Nah, leave her alone for a bit," Kasper said. "We don't wanna overwhelm her."

"But—"

"You can't mother everyone, all the time," Leah told her. "Sit down and stop pouting."

"I wasn't pout—"

"Harriet!" Kasper said, too brightly, looking at something over Felix's shoulder. A huge weight left Felix's back as Kasper sat upright. "You OK?"

Harriet was standing on the stairs, twisting a strand of dark hair between her fingers.

"Hi," she said, and bit her lip. Kasper's gaze was fixed unwaveringly on it, Felix noticed with a bristle of annoyance. There were plenty of other people in the building who had lips. It wasn't like Harriet's were particularly special.

Felix sat up, rearranging his wrinkled clothing. He suddenly felt self-conscious. How long had Harriet been watching them loll around together?

The four of them had some strange habits, after so many years alone together. They were a co-dependent group, with odd rituals and games and in-jokes that had developed over the decades like mutating bacteria cultures. He didn't want Harriet to judge them and decide that they were freaks. Even if it was true.

You should probably know that I had been waiting for Rima, Harriet and the others for nearly four hundred years before they finally died.

They kept appearing in brief, barely comprehensible flashes of the future. The laughing girl with her hair in a wrap, hugging the bespectacled boy who was always staring at the fluffy one. And Harriet, always on the outskirts, watching and waiting.

Everything comes out of order for me. The past and future are all mixed together in a scramble of little moments. But even without context, I could tell that these people were going to be important.

Once I knew what was coming, it was like everything went on hold, waiting for the people in the visions to arrive. Waiting for them to die. When they finally did, all on the same mysterious night, only the girl with the hole in the back of her head was missing.

HARRIET

"What are modern phones like?" Felix asked, leaning forward, elbows on his knees. They had all come up to Kasper's bedroom on the fourth floor so that Harriet didn't have to stare at her own corpse. Clearly, they had all decided she'd had long enough to recover from the trauma of her own death, because they'd started grilling her about various aspects of modern life.

Harriet didn't really mind. She was getting to spill a lot of gossip about Hugh Grant, Bill Clinton, O.J. Simpson and the Kardashians. Rima straight up refused to believe that Princess Diana had died, let alone that Charles had married Camilla.

Harriet shrugged at Felix's question. "Phones are pretty good, I guess. Especially since Instagram updated their filters so you can put bunny ears on your selfies."

They all stared at her, wide-eyed – except Leah, who was dozing in a corner with her baby. She had got bored when they'd started talking about celebrities.

"You guys didn't understand a single word in that sentence, did you?" Harriet asked.

Felix said, "Not one. But the phone works without you touching it? That's amazing."

"You can have a go on it, if you want," she offered. "I don't think I'll be needing it again."

Felix looked thrilled, even as Kasper rolled his eyes.

Harriet had considered using her phone to send a text to the police, letting them know where her body was. But then they would realize that someone had been using her phone anonymously after she had died, and that would only create more problems.

It might lead to an investigation to find her murderer, and her gran would be caught up in the middle of it, unable to mourn Harriet's death for the accident it had really been.

In the end, she'd decided to just wait for the police to find her body on their own. Surely it wouldn't take long? Her car was parked right outside. They'd find it immediately if they started looking for her.

She was half hoping to see police cars through the window now, but the car park was quiet.

Felix cleared his throat. He seemed to be debating whether to say something. "Listen, I can relate to wanting to leave. I have people on the outside too. My twin brother … he was out clubbing on the night of our deaths, and he survived. Oscar's in his forties now."

Harriet had forgotten again how old the ghosts all were. Forty was ancient.

"That must be weird," she said, trying to work out what to say. Rima, who was lying on the floor cuddling a fox spirit, tapped her foot against Felix's back in sympathy. Harriet couldn't offer that to Felix. She barely knew him – and besides, showing affection had never come easily to her.

Felix sighed. "He's had this whole life that I'm not a part of. He's lived longer without me than he did with me."

"I'm sorry," Harriet said. "You must miss him a lot."

"He comes to visit sometimes. To Mulcture Hall, I mean." Felix rubbed his thumb over his lower lip.

A fizz of excitement spread up her spine. "Can he see you?"

"What?" He looked at her, surprised. "No, of course not. He – he just comes and sits in my bedroom. On the anniversary."

"Don't you ever want to talk to him?"

"I do," Felix said. "I tell him everything, even though he can't hear me. He just cries."

Rima shuffled around to hug him, while Kasper patted Felix's shoulder. Harriet's nails bit into her palms. Watching them interact was giving her a lot to think about. She almost wanted to take notes, to try to work out what they meant by everything they said to each other. Her curiosity was mixed with a deep-seated envy.

"He knows you love him," Rima said. "That's all that matters."

Harriet didn't understand how his brother could have visited for all these years and it had never even occurred to Felix to find a way to communicate with him. "But if you tried, if we just searched for a way to talk to him—"

"Harriet, there isn't a way. I know you want to talk to your gran, but it's impossible, just like leaving the building."

Harriet curled her lips around her teeth, restraining herself from shouting at him. They had all just *given up*. They were stagnant. They probably didn't know anything about how being a ghost even worked.

She took a deep breath, calming herself down. She couldn't yell at him. She still needed to get more answers out of them.

"I just want to understand the physics of how it all works," she explained. "Why can my phone recognize my voice, but my gran couldn't? I can't pick things up, but I don't fall through the floor. And I can push my way through doors, but lean against them, too. This ghost logic doesn't make any sense."

"We don't really know how these things work, either," Felix said. "Personally, I've got some theories, but we have no way of proving anything."

"You should talk to Qi, though," Rima added. "She's done all kinds of cool experiments on it."

"Experiments?" Harriet was surprised. What kind of experiments did a *ghost* do?

"Yeah, she was doing a Chemistry PhD when she was alive. She wants to work out what happens to ghosts after they disintegrate by doing tests on animal spirits and stuff."

"Like that fox?" Harriet gestured to the fox spirit that was lying next to Rima.

Rima looked horrified. "No! I meant rats and mice, or insects. Cody is a friend."

"How do you tame a fox, anyway?" Harriet asked Rima, trying to keep the disgust out of her voice. Cody gave her the phantom itch of fleas. She could see its ribs through its patchy fur. It looked like it had rabies.

"Don't even go there," Kasper warned. "If you get her started, she'll never shut up."

Rima said, gruffly offended, *"Hey."* She winked at Harriet. "I'll show you later."

Sighing, Harriet touched the concrete floor to test the limits of her incorporeality. She couldn't move physical objects, but she could make contact when she focused on them. Or was she just imagining what it would feel like?

Her body was operating as if she was still human, because she expected it to. She would probably bleed if her skin was cut too, just because she expected to bleed. She projected her memories of being human on her spirit.

When she lay down, her head popped through the ceiling of the floor below.

A couple, spooning on a mattress, peered up at her.

"Get out of here!" one of them scolded her. He shot what looked like clouds out of his finger, filling the room so she couldn't see them.

"Kids today have no sense of decorum," she heard him say as she pulled herself back through the ceiling.

"The – the –" she spluttered. "The ghost down there made a cloud! From his hand!"

"Nice!" Rima said. "Was it a cumulonimbus? They're his favourite."

Harriet was aghast. "What the hell?! He just grew it from his *hand*."

"It's his power," Felix said.

"Power?" Her voice was fraying at the edges.

Felix pushed up his sleeves, looking for all the world like

a professor settling in to give a lecture. "All ghosts have a power of some sort or another. It's something that happens when you've been around for a while."

"Felix can hypnotize people!" Rima added.

He grimaced. "It's a bit more complicated than that, but sure."

This was impossible. They must be playing a prank on her. Harriet pulled an unconvinced face. "Oh my *God*."

"You've got a power, too. We'll have to wait and see what it is when it manifests," Felix said. "Everyone's is different. I have a theory that this is why humans have loads of different myths about ghosts. Each culture invented their own stories about ghosts – *poltergeists, bhoots, strigoi, dybbuk, baku, Antevorta* – there are hundreds of legends, all giving them different powers. Because every ghost does something different."

He was *serious*, she realized. They weren't messing with her.

"Why didn't you tell me this before?" This might be the answer to her problems. Was there a power that would let her talk to her gran, in a way that her gran would be able to hear? Or, even better – Harriet sat bolt upright – was there a power that would let her leave the building and go home?

"What sort of powers are there?" Harriet asked.

"Anything you can imagine," Rima said, grinning. "There's a girl who can transform clothes into different outfits! She made me this T-shirt. She owed me a favour."

Harriet stared at the glittery T-shirt. It didn't look magical. It looked totally real and solid. These powers must be really strong, if they could do things like that. What if her own power was something useful? It was impossible to clamp down on her hope.

"How long do they take to appear? I need to find out what my power is. Can we do that? Now?"

"It's early days," Kasper reassured her, while lazily watching a delicate brown mouse steal the filling from an old armchair for its nest. "Mine took so long to appear that I thought I didn't even have a power for ages."

"Can you even imagine," Rima said, laughing, and did a little mock shiver. "No powers!"

"Powers aren't all that, Harriet," Kasper said. "You'll be fine."

Harriet *really* wanted a power. She wanted one right now. "But how do they work? Where does the magic – thing – power come from?" She hadn't felt the slightest urge to cast magic spells yet.

"Well, when you tried to leave the hall and started disintegrating, it was because your energy was weakening with distance, right?" Rima said. "Energy is what keeps us all here as ghosts. It's what our powers run on."

Harriet's head felt like it was going to explode. "What happens if you use it all up?"

"Then your time's up," Rima said. "You disintegrate."

She remembered the feeling of her atoms dissolving when she'd left Mulcture Hall and shivered. "OK. This is a lot to take in. Are there any other hugely important things about the afterlife that you haven't told me yet?"

"Nah, mate. You're good to go," Kasper said.

"Though I do have one question for you," Felix added. "It's something I've been dying to know. How much do Freddos cost now?"

The rest of them don't understand Harriet quite yet. But you don't need to be able to see the future to predict what she's going to do.

Let's go back to 1994. You haven't been there yet, and it's about time I looked back at it from this angle. It's funny how you can see different things, each time you look. Like turning over an object to see it from different sides.

So. Here's Felix on the first day he met Rima and Kasper. He's nervous. He's unpacking his things in his room when his brother, Oscar, brings him a bin bag full of clothes that had been taken to the wrong room by accident. He's brought a girl with him, someone who has a room near by. This is Rima. Felix has no idea that she'll become one of his best friends.

It's strange to me, that when everyone else meets people for the first time, everything about them is completely new. Nobody has any idea of what is to come. How do you all know which stranger to remember? Which conversation to pursue?

When Oscar introduces Felix, Rima grins at him, a little shy herself. Oscar suggests that they all go and grab lunch — he wants to help Felix make friends, so that he doesn't spend all his time alone. But he also likes Rima. She never even noticed. I don't think she knows about his crush, even now.

As they're walking down the stairs, talking about what A-levels they studied, whether they applied to

Oxbridge and where their second choice of uni was, Felix bumps into a boy by accident. They both stumble, and an alarm clock falls out of a box he's carrying. It smashes on the ground.

The boy is Kasper, obviously. He sneers at Felix, annoyed. Embarrassed, Felix forgets to apologize and flees down the stairs. Kasper yells something sarcastic after him, looking at the broken clock in dismay. It was brand new – a gift from his dad for starting uni. He wanted to make sure that Kasper didn't sleep in and miss his lectures (he'd nearly missed one of his exams last summer).

Later, Kasper and Felix will both be mortified when they realize that they are neighbours and must share a bathroom for the next year. But that's still to come. For now, Oscar tells Rima he'd better go after Felix and make sure he's OK. That they'll do lunch another day.

Rima nods her understanding, then kneels to help Kasper pick up the pieces of smashed glass. They go their separate ways without even introducing themselves. (That would take another three weeks.)

But do you see yet? How hard it is to stop yourself from caring, even when you know you shouldn't? How much family matters?

Oscar knew. Felix knew. Harriet doesn't know yet. But she will.

Chapter 5

HARRIET

Harriet's power was locked up somewhere inside her where she couldn't reach it. She tried to create clouds out of her fingers, imagining rain and thunder, but nothing happened. She needed to talk to this Qi person right now.

While the others were cooing over Rima's fox, she turned to Kasper, and pleaded, "Will you take me? To see – er, Chi?"

"Qi, yeah," Kasper confirmed. He squirmed and looked at Rima. "I don't know, though. Qi is kind of busy."

Harriet remembered the way his eyes had been filled with longing when he looked at her earlier. Her gran had taught her when she was very young that if you wanted something from someone, you had to work out what they needed. If you could find a way to offer it to them, then you'd have them eating out of the palm of your hand.

Kasper wanted love. Or the excitement of first lust, at least. That was the simplest thing in the world to give to him. She'd watched a lot of people flirting, especially in freshers' week. There were girls who drew constant attention simply by tilting their head in a certain way, or rearranging their hair over their shoulders. She drew on those memories.

"*Please*, Kasper," she said, pitching her voice low and intimate, so quiet that the others didn't hear her speak. She lifted one side of her mouth to make her cheek dimple. "Can't you make an exception, as a favour to me?"

Out of sight, she took his hand and rubbed his thumb with hers.

Kasper looked down at their entwined fingers. There was a moment when she thought he might be about to say no again, but then he mumbled, "I guess we can go and talk to Qi. It can't hurt."

He stood up, pulling her to her feet. "Catch you guys later," he said to Felix and Rima, who stared at them in bafflement.

Harriet bit down on her victorious smile. That flirting thing had been a lot easier than she'd expected. Making friends was far tougher, but this, she was good at.

"How are you dealing with everything?" Kasper asked as they walked to Room 4E, where the mysterious Qi apparently lived. "It's a lot."

"It is, at that," she said dourly. "I don't know. I guess … I just thought it'd be different, you know? I didn't believe in the afterlife when I was alive. I assumed once you died, then that was it, fade to black. But I always thought, if there was something after death…"

Harriet picked at her fingernails, trying to work out what she wanted to say. "I thought it would be so incredibly amazing that I wouldn't care about my old life any more. I wouldn't want to return to real life, because it would be even better afterwards. Being stuck here, I feel kind of cheated. The afterlife should be less … dusty, I think."

She fell silent, aware that she had been talking for far too long. Kasper had stopped in his tracks and was staring at her, wide-eyed. He had long, pale eyelashes.

"Wow. I prefer your version."

She let out a low laugh. "Me too."

His hand crept onto her lower back again. "Listen, I think you should be prepared for this to fail. Qi will try her best to help you, but it would be easier if you accepted that it's not going to work."

She let out a noise of exasperation. "Never," she said firmly. She was going to find a way to go home, with or without a power.

With infinite care, he took her hand in his again. He did it in a way that made her suddenly regret ever initiating contact.

"OK, then," he said. "Let's hope Qi knows what she's doing."

Just then, Rima ran up behind them. "Wait, I'll come with you! I haven't seen Qi in ages." She eyed their entwined hands, then added, "Unless I'm interrupting something?"

"You're good," Harriet said, relieved, just as he replied, "Kinda."

Harriet turned to Kasper, who opened his mouth to speak but no words came out. When Rima choked on a laugh, he let go of her hand and strode on.

Rima caught her by the elbow, holding Harriet back. "You know he's flirting with you, right? Kind of blatantly."

Harriet couldn't help the smile that twisted her lip. As if she could have missed that. "Oh, I know."

Rima hesitated, then said, "You should know that Kasper might act cocky, but he's actually a lot more vulnerable than he seems. Be gentle, OK?"

Harriet must have slightly overshot the mark on the seduction front, if she was already getting the "best friend" talk. "Is this the part where you tell me that if I hurt him, you'll kill me? Because I think you've missed the boat there."

Rima laughed. "Sorry! I just wanted to let you know. I wasn't trying to warn you off, or anything. I think that you could be good for him, because he and Felix have this really odd... Well, I think this whole place makes everything a bit toxic. We're all cooped up together all the time, and it can get a bit much. So new blood is always a good thing. Go for it, is what I'm saying."

Harriet was drowning in other people's problems. She was trying to get home, not catch up on decades' worth of missed gossip.

"Thank you for the intel," she said at last. "Now watch and learn, baby." She flipped her hair over one shoulder and walked after Kasper. He looked hunched over and embarrassed, and was busy pretending they didn't exist.

Rima called out, slightly out of breath, "I think you might be the coolest person I've ever met!"

When they reached Room 4E, the back of Kasper's neck was still pink. "Dr Pang?" he called.

A soft voice replied, "Come in, Mr Jedynak."

Inside, a Chinese woman in her mid-twenties was sitting on the broken remains of a bed. She was wearing a dressing gown and slippers, and there was a glow around her. It was as if all the dim light in the room was pulled towards her.

"This is her, then," Qi said, holding out a hand to Harriet. "The source of all the –" she breathed in deeply "– fresh energy."

When Harriet took Qi's hand, Harriet could have sworn that her own skin seemed to dim a little. She blinked down at it. Had she imagined the sensation of pins and needles that spread through her fingers?

She quickly pulled away, clearing her throat. "It's great to meet you. Kasper said you might be able to help us work out what my power is?"

Qi leant forwards, inspecting Harriet carefully. "It's very early for a power to manifest, if you've only been dead for a few hours. But I'll try my best."

She touched one hand to Harriet's forehead. Holding still, Harriet ignored the definite itch spreading across her scalp. She felt drained suddenly. Was Qi taking her energy, somehow?

"Interesting," Qi said, and licked the tips of her fingers with a thoughtful expression. "Rima, can you get me a rat?"

Rima started. "Hang on a sec!" She ran from the room.

There was a minute of silence, in which Kasper arranged himself in an artistic slouch against the windowsill and Qi stared unblinkingly at Harriet.

She shifted awkwardly under her gaze. She tried to focus

on the reason she was here – to find a way to get home. Any amount of discomfort was worth that.

Then there was a noise at the door. Harriet turned, expecting it to be Rima, but instead an enormous tawny owl flew into the room, carefully holding a rat between its teeth. It dropped the rat at Harriet's feet and put a claw on the rodent, looking up at Qi expectantly.

At first, Harriet thought the rat was stunned but unharmed. Then she realized it was a ghost.

"Harriet, be ready to absorb the energy," Qi instructed, and then gestured at the owl to continue.

"Right, but what does that mean?" Harriet asked, as the rat's spirit shuddered, seeming to collapse in on itself. A brightness – or something – peeled away from it into the air.

"Quickly!" Qi said. "Before it dissipates! Take its energy."

Repulsed, Harriet jolted away from the rat. But as the cloud of energy drifted towards her, she found herself reacting on instinct. She pulled the energy towards herself. To her surprise, the rat blurred at the edges, shuddered in and out of focus once or twice, and then disappeared completely.

Harriet swayed as a rush of giddy strength spread through her, like she'd done four shots of vodka in a row. It was a delicious rush that made her feel invincible.

"How do you feel?" Qi asked, cradling Harriet's head between her hands and gazing into her eyes. Harriet resisted the urge to push her away. She could see the veins pulsing in her eyeballs.

"Powerful." Harriet let out a stunned, delighted laugh.

This was so much more fun than anything she'd done when she was alive. "I feel incredible!"

"But she's not doing anything," Kasper said, from somewhere distant and unimportant.

"Interesting," Qi said again. "I think we need another."

"Yes!" Harriet gasped. "Please, another!" Nothing mattered but getting more energy, as soon as possible, so that she could feel like this for ever.

The owl leapt upwards, its feathers disturbing the air as it flew out of the room, dust twisting into clouds. Harriet leant into the wind. She felt abruptly convinced that she could fly too if she had more energy.

When the owl reappeared with another rat, Harriet couldn't wait a second. She fell on the ghost, sucking down its energy until it was nothing but a wisp of dust. The feeling buzzed down her veins, and she let out an indecent, lengthy moan. Collapsing onto all fours, she rested her head on the ground and relished the rush of pure joy.

"I need more," she told Qi. "Make the owl get more."

Qi frowned at her, then looked at the bird. She shook her head. "No more."

"No! I have to! Please!" She had to experience that feeling again.

"It's no good," Qi said. "There's nothing there."

Harriet ground her teeth together. She wanted to scream at Qi, to force her to do it anyway. Who was she, to show Harriet this thrilling high and then tear it from her grasp?

She wrestled with her anger, trying to push it down.

The owl leapt into the air. It twisted on the spot, breaking up into a cloud of dust.

Adrenaline gushed through Harriet. She braced herself, ready to suck up the bird's energy too. Before she could pounce, Qi tugged her back with a sharp yank at her wrist.

"Oh no, you don't, missy," she growled. There was a line of glowing light wrapped around Harriet's arm like rope. Qi was holding the end of it, pulling Harriet away from the owl.

Harriet shuddered, trying to escape the rope, but it grew thicker and thicker until she was unable to move at all.

"Stop this!" Qi shouted, as Harriet fought her grip. "You're stronger than this! Calm down!"

Harriet snarled at her, eyes fixed on the owl. But the lightning rope was too powerful for her. Eventually, she ran out of strength and fell still, gasping for breath.

"Look at me, Harriet." Qi moved closer and held Harriet's eye for a long moment, searching for something in her face. She must have found it, because she released Harriet, and the rope of light disappeared into Qi's palm. Her outline throbbed strongly as she reabsorbed the lightning.

Harriet fell back, exhausted. "What was that?" she gasped. "How did you do that?"

Qi didn't answer.

"Harriet, that was mental," Kasper yelled, elated. "You're wild!"

They both ignored him. Qi was still watching Harriet with

dangerously rapt attention, assessing her, as though looking right inside her.

Finally, finally, Qi looked away. The breath left Harriet's chest in a rush. For a second, she'd been certain that Qi had seen something terrible inside her, something Harriet had always feared was there, lurking. Her gran looked at her in the same way sometimes, especially when Harriet was angry. Like she was waiting for her to do something.

It was only then that she remembered to look for the owl. It had disappeared, and in its place stood Rima.

"What?" she asked, shivering now that the energy had died away. "Wait – *what?*"

Rima shook out her clothes. A few feathers drifted into the air.

Rima?

Rima was an *owl?*

"Hey." She brushed a trace of rat blood from the corner of her mouth. "I probably should have mentioned sooner that I can shapeshift."

In the corner, Kasper chuckled.

"You can what?" Harriet asked. "That's your power?"

Rima smiled briefly at her but then looked at Qi. "So? What's your conclusion, Dr Pang? Any idea what Harriet's power might be?"

Harriet jolted. Maybe she was a shapeshifter, too? She couldn't immediately think of how that would help her get home, but she could probably work with it.

"Well, firstly, I've never seen anyone respond so strongly to energy," Qi said, looking worried. "Especially not just a couple of *rats*."

"She's fresh," Kasper pointed out. "She's brimming over with her own energy as it is."

Qi nodded, but she didn't look convinced. "On top of her own energy, yes, I suppose it could have been a little overwhelming for her system."

"I don't understand what happened," Harriet admitted.

"Sometimes people need a little push to help them manifest their power," Qi explained. "The best way to do that is to inject more energy into your system. A rat's energy is usually enough to kick-start the process."

"I had to absorb one, too, when I first died," Rima said. "I couldn't quite work out how to shapeshift before then. It was like – I knew what was supposed to happen. Under my skin, like a skill I hadn't unlocked yet. When I ate a rat, it became instinct. I turned into a rat myself without even realizing it."

"But ... nothing happened to me," Harriet said, thinking this through. "I was supposed to – to grow leaves or clouds, or turn into an animal, or something? And I didn't?"

"It's ... unusual, to say the least," Qi mused. "Most ghosts' powers normally respond to energy, but you ... I've never seen anything like it. And I've kick-started several dozen ghosts."

Harriet was struggling to understand what this all meant. There was a sinking, horrified feeling in the pit of her stomach. What if she didn't have a power? Surely there had to be a mistake.

She *must* have a power. She had to get home!

"No!" she burst out, louder than she meant to. "This can't be right! We need to try again!"

"Definitely not," Qi said firmly. "After your reaction to the energy, this is not up for discussion. Your power will manifest in its own time, I'm sure. It's early days. You need to be patient."

"No! You have to try again!" Harriet insisted. "I need to know!"

She looked desperately from Qi to Rima to Kasper. None of them spoke. A muscle jumped in Kasper's jaw.

Qi shook her head again. "I'm sorry, Harriet. I don't want to risk attempting another absorption, not today. Perhaps you can come back in a month or two?"

The thought of waiting a month – or *two* – made her snarl, "Listen! I need to – I need to go home to my family today. You were *supposed to help me*!"

Qi's mouth tightened. "How I wish I could have a cigarette right now," she muttered. "Save me from self-righteous teenagers."

"We should go," Rima said, in a careful voice. "Qi, I'll keep an eye on her."

"You don't need to keep an eye on me," Harriet said, more nastily than she'd intended. "I'm not a child!"

No one spoke. Their silence said that she was acting like one. Harriet huffed out of the room. She hated that they were right.

I think Qi realized why a rat wouldn't be enough to make Harriet's power manifest. Sometimes there's just something wrong inside a person that stops them from being who they are meant to be. A mental block or purposeful denial.

Those kinds of problems can't be fixed with energy – they need years of therapy and psychoanalysis. But Qi has always been more interested in the science than the story. She doesn't care about motives if she can analyse the molecules instead.

I think she already knows what's going to happen here to Harriet. She's just hoping that there'll be lots to study when the chaos begins. It's a shame that it will be too late by then.

RIMA

Harriet walked quickly down the hallway on trembling legs, leaving Rima and Kasper to trail behind her.

Rima shot him a baffled look once Harriet was out of hearing range. "What was *that*?"

Kasper shrugged. "I've never seen anything like it. She went mental!"

"And it was only a rat. That's not exactly loads of energy." Rima thought Harriet's death must have spooked her badly. Firstly, she'd run out of the building, and now this, lashing out at Qi and ordering them all about like servants. She hadn't even asked them what their powers were yet, even though she was obsessed with finding her own.

Harriet clearly wasn't all there mentally. She must be recalibrating to her new life still.

Rima said, "We should take things slow from now on. She obviously needs some peace and quiet. Let's not pressure her about anything." She shot Kasper a knowing glance. "Tone back the flirting for a few days."

He looked belligerent, but agreed. "I can be chill."

Rima doubted that immensely. Kasper was the most dramatic person she'd ever met – except herself, probably. Sometimes their arguments about *The X-Files* got so loud that Leah would banish them to opposite ends of Mulcture Hall.

Rima had never had a group of friends when she was alive. She'd gone to an all-girls school and spent most of her time with the only other non-white girl there. When she'd started uni, she had decided that things were going to be different. She was going to be bubbly and chatty and make friends with everyone. But making that happen had been harder than she'd hoped. She'd spend an hour talking to someone over lunch in the dining hall, only to never see them again around the huge campus.

By the time she'd died, she was still the lonely girl who read while she ate dinner, and spent her evenings watching *The X-Files* in her room or going on the net in the empty computing lab.

Everything had changed when she became a ghost. Leah, Felix and Kasper had been the group of friends she'd been waiting for her whole life. She wasn't lonely any more. She had found people who really knew her, well enough to tease her and laugh at her jokes before she'd even finished them.

Rima hoped that they could be the same for Harriet, too. The girl needed friends just as much as Rima had.

HARRIET

Harriet dropped onto the top step of the fourth-floor stairs, resting her head in her hands. She couldn't even begin to process everything that had happened. She shuddered, mortified at the memory of dropping to her hands and knees, sucking up a dirty rodent while Rima and Kasper stood watching.

The last traces of energy were still fizzing in her chest, but the feeling was numbed slightly by shame at the way she had behaved. The possibility of getting more energy had sent her out of her mind. She'd thought she had more self-control than that, but the angry thing she had always buried deep inside herself had nearly burst free.

"It's OK," Rima said, approaching Harriet as gently as if she were calming a spooked horse. "It happens to the best of us."

She sat down next to her, wrapping an arm around her shoulders. Harriet automatically tensed, then carefully, painfully, made herself relax into the touch.

Harriet choked back a laugh. "Really? *That* happens to all of us?"

Kasper dropped to a crouch in front of her. "Trust me," he said, in a more serious voice than she'd heard from him before, "we all lose control sometimes."

It had been a long time since anyone had treated her so gently. Not since her parents had died, really.

"You don't want to see Kasper when he's angry," Rima whispered in her ear. "He's like the Hulk."

Kasper let out a gasp, nudging Rima's shoulder in affable outrage. "I didn't come here to be disrespected."

"You're disrespected everywhere you go," Rima replied. She stuck her tongue out at him, hamming it up for Harriet's benefit.

Harriet's friendships had been nothing like this – no in-jokes and silly comedy routines. In sixth form, she'd once spilt her drink down her shirt during lunch. Georgia, the girl she always sat with, had looked away in embarrassment on her behalf. Harriet couldn't imagine Rima being embarrassed about anything Felix did. She'd be more likely to make a joke out of it. Kasper would probably pour coffee all over himself too in solidarity.

Was that what friendship was supposed to be like, when you found people who really understood you? Or were these people odd because they'd spent over two decades trapped alone together? Maybe they were all crazy, and she was the strange one, for being jealous of them.

Kasper folded his arms. "How *dare* you?! I am the backbone of this group. I deserve respect."

Rima literally snorted with laughter. "*Backbone*. You're a fumbling baboon."

"RUDE? So, so rude!"

Harriet couldn't help it; her lips curved into a smile.

"I thought *you* were the backbone, actually," she said to Rima. "You seem to run the show."

"Yeah, I do," she said, preening. "Leah says I'm the mum friend. I think she meant it to be an insult, but, you know, I own it."

"You *are* the mum friend," Harriet said, with dawning realization.

"Kasper can be the dad friend," Rima added.

"Er—" Kasper stuttered, flustered. "I, Rima – I'm flattered, but I don't think of you…"

Rima's cheeks turned pink. Harriet thought she was really pretty when she was flushed and laughing. "I didn't mean like that! I meant you try really hard to look after everyone, but you're kind of bad at the emotional stuff."

He shifted, looking bemused, like he wasn't sure whether to be offended. "Are you saying that I'm clumsy?"

"You have no idea how to handle social situations, is what I'm saying."

Kasper huffed a sigh. "OK, that's it. I'm out." He turned and walked away.

"Dad, wait! I'm sorry. Don't ground me!" Rima called after him, laughter in her voice.

Kasper waved a hand at them over his shoulder, not looking back. He stopped to say hello to a ghost that Harriet didn't recognize – a boy in a rugby shirt and boxers who was carrying a hedgehog spirit under his arm.

Kasper and the boy chatted for a bit, but they weren't joking around like he'd done with Rima. His behaviour seemed a lot less relaxed. Clearly, this boy was just a neighbour, rather than part of the inner circle.

It surprised Harriet that they seemed to have invited her to join their little group, when there were so many other ghosts around the building. What could they see in Harriet?

Rima turned back to Harriet, and her amused grin disappeared. "Seriously, though, are you OK?"

"Yeah. Yeah, I'm OK. Thanks, Rima." Harriet bit her lip. She should use this opportunity while they were bonding to try and get Rima to help her. If she had managed to get rat spirits for Qi, there was no reason why she couldn't get them for Harriet on her own. Then Harriet would be able to find her power without Qi's help.

She remembered her gran's advice again – to get people on your side, find out what they want and give it to them. What did Rima want? She seemed to value friendship more than anything. It was clear that she loved Leah, Felix and Kasper, and showed her affection by teasing and bickering with them. She wanted people to joke around with her and have fun. Maybe Harriet could give her that, too?

She wasn't sure she was brave enough – the idea of inviting ridicule made her feel too exposed.

But she could show affection in other ways. She could compliment Rima.

"You know, you're not just the mum friend," Harriet said. "I think you're really funny."

Rima plumped up with pride, her eyes going bright. *"The funny one.* I like the sound of that. Thank you, Harriet."

Harriet smiled back, then pictured her gran frowning at her, and her smile disappeared. She was losing focus – this was about getting Rima to help her.

Harriet tilted her head, pretending something had occurred to her. "How did you kill that rat, by the way? I thought we couldn't touch anything. Is your animal form corporeal?"

Rima shook her head. "I don't need to touch the rat's body. You can kind of – grab the spirit and tug it free of the body.

Any ghost can do it, but most humans aren't fast enough to catch them; rats are kind of speedy. I can only do it in owl form. Kimaya on the first floor has these, like, tentacle pincers, so she's way better at it, but—"

"So the rat dies?" Harriet interrupted. "And you absorb its energy, or give it to someone else to absorb?"

"Yeah. Some of the energy from the death gets released into the atmosphere, like when you died. But most of it stays in the spirit, which makes it easy to trade with. It's a small amount – not enough to do anything useful, like bring a Shell out of stasis. It's just a little pick-me-up. I tend to swap the spirits with other people most of the time, rather than absorbing the energy myself. I get a little hyperactive if I have too much extra energy."

Harriet squinted at the ceiling, considering this, while Rima went off on a tangent about someone who had never paid up after a trade.

Did it only work with rats, or could you kill a larger animal that way? Surely the bigger the animal, the more energy it would release? If she'd felt that good after consuming the energy from a rat, how might a squirrel or a fox make her feel? Something so huge would surely be enough to help manifest her power.

Rima had stopped talking, so Harriet belatedly made an impressed expression. "That's really cool!"

"Honestly, I mainly use my power to talk to animals, not hunt them. That's how I got Cody to be friends with me – by turning into a fox. I started training her in that form, but it still took absolutely ages. She kept getting distracted by random things like dust and bumblebees. It took a few years before she would even sit down on command."

"Wow." That made sense of everyone's obsession with the fox. But it was taking them off-topic. Harriet gently steered the conversation back in the direction she wanted it to go. "You're so talented. I'd love to see you in action. Do you think that you could get me another animal spirit? Something bigger than a rat would be amazing. It would be a massive favour. Please?"

Rima's smile dropped. "I'm sorry, Harriet. I don't think it's a good idea. Qi was right – your reaction to the energy was too strong. If things went wrong, I wouldn't be able to control you like she did. I mean, you nearly tried to consume me too." She laughed, then added, clearly worried that Harriet would take that the wrong way, "Not that you actually would have done it, if you'd known the owl was me, of course! It was an involuntary reaction. You're just too fresh."

Harriet smiled stiffly. So much for the power of friendship. Even when she was nice to her, Rima wouldn't help her out. "No problem. I totally understand."

She'd have to find someone else.

Rima squeezed her shoulder. "I really am sorry. Shall we go and find the others? Kasper and Felix are about due for their daily argument, and we want to get front-row seats. It might cheer you up?"

"Actually," Harriet said, standing up, "I've got something to do. I'll catch up with you guys later, OK?"

She hurried off, trying not to feel guilty about Rima's hurt look. She had to use her time wisely, and there was no point making friends with people who couldn't help her get home.

It was like her gran always said: *Take what you need and move on when you're not getting it.* People were valuable until they weren't – and Rima and the others had stopped being worth the investment.

Chapter 6

HARRIET

On the stairs between the second and third floors, Harriet stopped next to the scrawny dreadlock guy she had seen before. She realized now what he'd been doing – hunting rats for energy.

"Er, excuse me?" she said.

He held up one hand, listening to something inside the wall. After thirty painful seconds of silence, he stepped away and turned to her, grinning toothily. "It's gone. You must have disturbed it. Hi, newbie."

"Hi. I was wondering if you could get me a rat?"

"You're quick off the mark, aren't you?"

Harriet exhaled through her nose. "Sure. I mean, I guess. I've been here for almost a day, so..."

"Hey, I'm not judging. Have you got something to trade? What's your power?" He tugged up his trousers, which immediately slipped down again. Their clothes all seemed to come along with them when they died, which Harriet thought was interesting. It was as if people's clothing was an extension of their spirit. Or maybe it was just that people always imagined themselves in clothes, so their physical form mirrored how they saw themselves?

Harriet frowned. "My power hasn't manifested yet. That's why I want a spirit. To see if I can make it happen. What do you want for one?"

The guy let out a laugh. "Not anything you can offer, princess."

Harriet swallowed a sigh. Time to turn on the charm again. She twisted a curl of hair around her finger, tilting her head sweetly at him. "Please?"

He snorted. "Goodbye."

"But—" She stopped. Her instinct was telling her to back down.

"Thanks for all your help. I really appreciate it," she said instead, as sweetly as possible.

"Whatever," he muttered, and stuck his head into the plasterboard.

Harriet brushed back her hair, straightened her shoulders, and walked away. There was no point asking anyone else for a rat if they'd laugh in her face like this guy. To stand a chance of making a trade, she had to work out what the ghosts valued. Then find a way to get some of it.

Every innocent conversation seemed to reveal some new discovery about ghost life. She needed to talk to someone who knew everything there was to know about being a ghost, who had theories about powers and mythology. She had to talk to Felix.

I know it won't help you much yet, but can I show you something?

When I was born, my mother had to hide me from my father. I was a girl, which was a disappointment. I was also nearly dead – born too soon and barely moving. She kept me alive, until I was strong enough that he wouldn't have an excuse to kill me. I remember a moment from my childhood when he stared at me with unconcealed bemusement, like he couldn't even imagine what was supposed to make him love me. The whole concept of fatherhood was completely foreign to him.

My mother adored me, and I think that just confused him even more. He couldn't understand why.

That's the way that Harriet looks at the others, when they are laughing and joking together. Like there is something that she's missing. I wish there was a way to help her find it.

It's hard to see what's really going on if you love someone. They can mistreat you as much as they like, and you ignore it because you don't want to acknowledge the truth. If you did, then you'd have to deal with it. And that can mean the end of everything.

FELIX

Felix was on a tour of the building, saying hello to all the people he hadn't spoken to in decades, since the last time they were all awake. He was trying to find a guy who always exchanged comic-book theories with him, singing to himself as he walked, when he bumped into Harriet in the entrance hall.

"Have you got a moment to talk, Felix?" she asked.

"Sure," he said, surprised.

They sat down together near the dusty, graffiti-covered reception desk on the ground floor. Harriet fell quiet.

She seemed distracted. He didn't want to push her to speak, in case she needed time to compose herself before talking about her death.

Silence always made him slightly worried, though. It was just so *loud*. It set him off thinking of reasons why the silence could be awkward, until he wasn't able to tell if it actually was an awkward silence or a comfortable one. By the time the other person spoke, he was usually sweating with anxiety.

He worried a lot about whether people hated him. Felix had been the self-conscious sort, when he was alive. He'd never taken any risks or stepped out of his comfort zone, just in case he was judged.

So, of course, he hadn't made many friends in halls until after his death, which said a lot about how shy he had been when he was alive. It had taken literally an eternity for him to open up enough to make real close friends, rather than casual acquaintances. Even then, he'd only managed it with Rima, Kasper and Leah.

When he was little, he'd always been worried and quiet. His brother was the brave and outgoing one. He pretended that Oscar was here now, rolling his eyes at Felix's nervousness. What would he say to Harriet? What would he think of her? He'd have known exactly what to do right now. A yearning for his brother opened up inside Felix again.

"Can you show me your power?" Harriet asked.

Felix was relieved that she clearly didn't need coaching through a death-related therapy session. This was a topic of conversation that he could handle. He'd been wondering how long it would take Harriet to ask what their powers were.

Instead of replying, he looked at Cody and thought: *Roll over.* The fox immediately rolled onto her back and started licking in between the pads of her back foot.

Harriet didn't look impressed. "Rima can do that, too."

"Yeah, but she uses commands," he explained. "I hypnotized her." His power was less hypnotism and more insistent suggestion, but hypnotism sounded more impressive.

"That's so extra," Harriet said.

Felix preened. He always had to resist the urge to brag when he told people about his power. *He* had an excellent one. Not like poor Kasper.

There was a new gleam in her eyes. "What other kind of things can you do?"

"Well, I can make people see things that aren't there. Look."

He focused on Cody, imagining a pink butterfly fluttering around her head. She opened her eyes sleepily, then snapped her jaws at it. The butterfly flew out of reach, making Cody leap after it, wiggling her bum.

"Brilliant!" Harriet said, watching the butterfly dissolve into dust. "Though if you can hypnotize her, why did Rima bother training Cody? You could just force her to do whatever you like. You could have an army of foxes!"

Felix shook his head, frowning. "I would never do that. She has to *want* to do stuff for Rima, otherwise it's not fair."

Harriet blinked, looking very much like she was struggling to process this. "Right. Well, could you make Kasper pick his nose?" She grinned.

Perhaps she hadn't understood him. "No," he explained patiently. "I don't use it on other ghosts. I'd get sent down to the basement."

He didn't use his power fully much at all. Sometimes he worried that if there was ever an emergency, it would be useless, like a muscle he hadn't exercised. But the threat of it was usually enough to keep people scared of him.

She frowned. "People don't ask you to use your power for them? Is that not the kind of thing you trade for stuff?"

When had she learnt about trading? She'd only been here for a day. "No," he said slowly. "I don't trade my power."

Harriet raised her eyebrows. "Why? If there's something you want, surely it would be easy to use it to get stuff?"

"I can't go around making everyone do things against their

will." A tinge of horror made its way into his voice, without his permission.

Harriet's expression froze for a second, but she recovered quickly. "No, obviously. I was hypothesizing." She let out a short, fake laugh. "But what do you trade instead? Like, what would you say most people are after?"

Why was she asking about trading so much? What had happened with Qi? Harriet clearly hadn't found her power, based solely on her miserable expression. Was that why she was digging for information? Felix picked at his fingernail, thinking about how to answer her.

In the end, he forced a smile. "Oh, I'm a simple sort. I don't really need much. I've never really traded anything. Some people trade stuff for rats—"

She cut him off. "The spirit energy, yeah, I know. But what else do people want around here?"

There was such an intensity in her eyes it almost scared him.

"The same things as everyone, I suppose," he said, pretending to misunderstand her. "I mean, what kind of things do you want?"

Her face went stiff. "I want to go home." She bit her lip. "My parents are dead, too. I think they might be ghosts at my gran's house. Maybe even my grandad – he had some sort of medication overdose after dental surgery when I was a kid. He died in bed at home. I want to see them all again. I want to talk to my mum."

Felix softened. He could understand that. He missed Oscar every second of every day.

"It's hard being stuck here. Everyone has someone they want to see again, whether they're alive or living as a ghost somewhere else. But there's no power that lets us leave the place where we died. If that's what you're looking for, you won't find it. I'm sorry, Harriet."

Harriet looked away from him. The muscles in her neck were tight with tension. She swallowed.

"Right," she said. Her voice was cold, brittle. "I guess you would know. You're the expert."

He tried to unravel the thoughts behind her expression. It was almost like she blamed Felix and the others. Did she think they were keeping her here on purpose? They didn't make the rules, just tried to live by them. He found that hard enough, most of the time.

It had been impossible to control his power when he'd first died. Unlike Rima, whose power hadn't manifested for almost a month, Felix had been able to hypnotize people the moment he died. Distraught, panicked, and terrified – whenever he had felt a strong emotion – he'd accidentally inflected his words with hypnotism.

It had caused quite a bit of trouble. Especially around Kasper.

Kasper and Felix had hated each other before their deaths – they had been famous for never managing to sit at the same table during lunch without arguing over something or other. Their hallmates used to place bets on them.

That was nothing compared to their arguments after they died, though. Once, Felix had accidentally hypnotized Kasper into shutting up in the middle of an argument, and only realized after he hadn't spoken in a week.

Once they became friends with Rima, she managed to stop them fighting. She helped Felix realize that most of Kasper's bluster was designed to cover up his fears and worries. He was more delicate than he wanted people to believe.

Harriet was staring into space with a frustrated expression that made Felix's skin prickle. He wondered whether he should apologize to Harriet for not being able to help her leave. Everything about her was disquieting.

To his relief, Rima jumped from the first floor into the foyer before he had to cast around for something to say.

"You should have killed me when you had the chance!" Rima yelled at Kasper, hitting the floor in a barrel roll. She was almost giggling too hard to get her words out properly.

Kasper dived over the banister after her. They were clearly in the middle of some intricate play-fight involving a hero and villain face-off.

"You could have just taken the stai—" Felix started to say, exasperated, and then gave up. They were shouting too much to hear him anyway. Besides, Rima had spent years perfecting the art of the dramatic entrance. She took pride in it.

"You aren't as funny as you think you are!" Kasper yelled at Rima, stalking her across the room. "Once I overheard you memorizing puns in the bathroom!"

Leah had followed them downstairs more sedately, with Claudia balanced on one hip. She interjected, "He's right. You said that even your *mum* never used to laugh at your jokes, Rima."

"*All* of my jokes," Rima corrected. "I said *all* of my jokes. And I told you that in confidence, Leah! If you keep this up, I'm gonna stop being best friends with you."

"When?" Leah asked, longingly.

Rima gasped, insulted, her hand flying to the *Best Friends Forever* locket around her neck. It was in the shape of half a heart. She'd traded another ghost for the two necklaces years ago on the black market and given the other half of the heart to Leah. Felix had never seen Leah wear it, but he'd also never seen her get rid of it. He suspected that it was hidden inside one of the pockets in her shift dress.

On more than one occasion, Felix had entertained private imaginings about giving Kasper a locket, too – or better yet, being given one by Kasper himself. The daydream was buried very deeply in his brain though, where it was going to stay until the moment he disintegrated. There were some things the world didn't need to know.

Kasper was still stalking Rima across the entrance hall. She twisted into a bat and flew up to a ceiling light. She bared sharp, vampiric teeth at Kasper, hissing.

"You set the image of paranormal creatures back by thirty years when you do that," Felix observed. "Stop being such a stereotype. You're a ghost, not a vampire."

Rima turned back into a human, dangling from the light. "Don't be such a buzzkill, Felix! You don't have to be a vampire to turn into a bat, just like you don't need to be a werewolf to howl at the moon!"

Kasper yanked his shirt over his head and started flicking it at the light fixture. "Get down here Hamid, this is cheating!"

Two girls were coming down the stairs, but they stopped when they saw the play-fight going on. A flush crept up Felix's neck. He knew the other ghosts thought he and his friends were slightly ridiculous. The girls usually spent all their time looking out of the windows at passing humans, so they could spread the news of the latest fashion trends around Mulcture Hall. They'd never mess around like Rima and Kasper were doing.

"What are you fighting about, anyway?" Felix asked, seizing the chance to talk while nobody was yelling. Having a conversation with them was like herding cats – they tended to scatter.

"Well, Harriet and I came up with this theory earlier that I'm the funny one of the group," Rima explained to him, making a little grateful curtsey in Harriet's direction. "I was telling Leah about it, and Kasper said he reckons he's the *charming* one, which is bull! The only thing he could charm is a damp dishcloth."

"Well, we all know it's not Leah," Kasper said. He was rubbing at the back of his head, fluffing up his hair in such a cute way that Felix felt furious about it.

"How dare you?" Leah said, serenely. "I have charisma. If

I really tried, I'd have you all blushing, stuttering and buying me flowers within the hour."

"Oh, sure!" Kasper spluttered. "You decide, Felix. Who's the hottest, me or her? You're the clever one, after all."

Felix felt like he'd been punched in the chest. Kasper thought he was the clever one? "I, er ... well—"

"Sure, she's cute in an anaemic, gothic sort of way. But how can anyone beat me?" Kasper fluttered his eyelashes.

"If anyone is the charming one, it's Harriet," Felix said.

Kasper nodded in an "I'll allow it" gesture. "I suppose Harriet is a more worthy opponent for the title."

Harriet, who looked a bit overwhelmed by them all, raised her eyebrows. "I'm *clearly* the famous one who leaves half-way through Season Three. It's only a matter of time before Hollywood discovers me. I'm 'pre-famous'."

Felix laughed. Harriet was funny, when she let herself relax enough to joke around.

Harriet looked both surprised and gratified. She smiled down at her lap.

"There's more dust in this building than common sense," Leah muttered as she sat down next to Felix, yawning. "Can you take Claudia for a while?"

Felix swung the baby over his hip in one well-practised movement. He'd been babysitting Claudia – and, before that, his older sister's daughter – for years. The baby dropped her head onto his shoulder, letting out a small noise of content-ment. She always smelt the same. Warm and milky, with a hint of honey. He kissed the end of her button nose. She giggled.

"Hey, Leah?" Harriet asked. "What's your power?" Her voice was casual, but Felix could see the intensity in her eyes. Her obsession with powers was back again. Did she ever think about anything else?

Felix pretended not to be listening, leaning forward like he was scrutinizing Kasper, who still hadn't put his shirt back on.

"I can see through time. Sometimes," Leah told her. Felix was surprised. It had taken nearly a decade for Leah to tell them that much. In fact, Felix was sure that she'd told Rima she didn't have a power. Rima had believed that for the first few years of their friendship.

Harriet's eyes widened. "Wait, really? You can see the future?"

"And the past."

"That's amazing! Do you think you could find out what my power is? Knowing what to aim for might help me to manifest it more quickly!" Harriet was speaking faster and faster in excitement. When they'd all been messing around, she'd just stared down at her lap – even when she was joining in with the jokes. But now she was genuinely joyful. She was a mystery.

"Can you look into the future for me?" she asked Leah.

Felix scowled at the ground. What right did she have to ask Leah for a favour? They'd only spoken once.

Leah sighed. "I don't look into the future. Not any more. It takes too much energy. I can't sustain it these days. I used to be able to change things in the future sometimes whenever I used my power. Now I can't even look."

This was news to Felix. He'd thought she'd only had visions, not the ability to manipulate things through time.

"Wait, so you can actually *change* the future?" Harriet asked, eyes wide. "Could you get my gran to – I don't know – come here with the police or something?"

"It doesn't really work like that, even if I did have the energy. I could never control it that carefully. And these days I can barely see five minutes from now. Sorry, kid."

There was a tension-filled silence. Eventually, Harriet nodded. "No problem." It was clear from her voice that this was indeed a problem.

Felix's heart-rate accelerated. These new social dynamics weren't doing great things for his anxiety.

In answer, Leah turned away from them all, and lay down. Clearly this conversation was over.

"I don't think Leah likes me," Harriet whispered to him. Felix wished he could pretend to be asleep too.

He shook his head, letting Claudia tug at his hair. He didn't want to get involved in another tense conversation with Harriet. Once was enough for one day.

"No, she does. She's just like that with everyone. It's not you. She's got – well, we think she's got – postnatal depression," he said, his voice dropping to a whisper.

Harriet's eyebrows rose. "Really?"

"Yeah. We think she had it when she died and got stuck like

that. She sleeps a lot, even when she's got plenty of energy."

Harriet blinked, aghast. "Wow." She shook her head. "I suppose I got off lucky. She's going to be really tired and depressed … for ever? For the whole of eternity?"

He winced. When she put it like that, it sounded a lot more horrifying than he'd realized. "Not for eternity. We're all going to disintegrate one day, anyway."

"What happens to ghosts when we disintegrate? Do you know?"

"Nobody knows. I've always wondered."

"When I went outside the building, it felt as if I was breaking into atoms," Harriet said. "Like it was a final end and I was losing all consciousness. Becoming part of the universe."

Felix took this in. He'd not really considered it before. Clearly there was something that contained human consciousness, that left the body and became ghosts when they died. For lack of a better word, a soul – a personality, made up of the energy they all craved. But what happened after the ghosts disintegrated? Where did those souls go?

"I don't really believe in a god," he said. "But I do wish there was more than disintegration. That sounds so … final. Surely there's some sort of cycle? Our energy has to go somewhere, right?"

Before Harriet could reply, there was a cry as Rima ended the fight with Kasper by turning into a bear and throwing herself at his chest. He plummeted to the floor, shrieking as she licked his face with a slobbery bear tongue.

"TRUCE!" he screamed. "You're hilarious, I swear! And I'm – I'm the cool one!"

Rima settled back on her haunches, turning back into a human. "You can have 'cool'. 'Cool' is less obnoxious than 'charming'. Your ego can handle it."

Kasper hopped to his feet, brushing off his shoulders and strutting like a peacock.

Felix was about to ask whether Rima was absolutely *sure* Kasper's ego could handle it, when Kasper winked at Harriet and said, "Hey, Stoker, it's Halloween tomorrow, and we're having a party in Rima's room. Do you want to come with me? It's usually pretty fun. If you like pretending to be drunk and celebrating our spirit lives."

Felix's whole body seized up in a wince. Devastation was too strong a word. Devastation was something he had no right to feel, not about Kasper. But it hurt. He couldn't tell whether it was disappointment or embarrassment – that Kasper was doing this in front of him; that Rima and Leah were here to see his reaction; that Felix couldn't stop himself from caring.

Harriet shrugged. "Sure. It's not like I have any plans."

Felix glared at the ground, swallowing a thousand comments before they had a chance to be verbalized. He told himself that he wasn't jealous, just concerned about Harriet's attitude. And he was. But still, still, still…

She was dangling something precious from her fingers, when it should be cradled against her chest, nurtured between warm palms. She had Kasper, *his Kasper*, and Felix suspected it was only because she was bored. That aloof distance had never left her gaze.

Next to Felix, Leah let out a long, hoarse snore that almost sounded real.

"I'm going to go and check my phone for new messages," Harriet said. Kasper murmured something about helping and followed her out of the room.

"Just in time," Leah said, when Harriet was gone. She sat up, stretching. "I was getting pins and needles."

"Do you not like Harriet?" Rima asked Leah, surprised.

"Not particularly."

Rima sighed. "I don't think she means to be so abrupt; she's just shy. It doesn't seem like she's had many friends before."

Felix frowned, shifting Claudia slightly. "There's something really odd about her, you know. She's so obsessed with the idea of powers and leaving the building. She's got it into her head that her power will help her do that."

"Felix, she *just* died," Rima said. "She wants something positive to focus on. It was so exciting to find out what our powers did, remember? Plus, she had an odd reaction to energy when Qi did the rat test. She's probably still recovering from that."

Felix frowned. The rat test was the most basic form of energy distribution – if Harriet hadn't been able to handle that, then she must be volatile, to say the least. How could Rima not see that? She was always far too trusting. She had told him once that before they died, she'd lent someone her coursework so they could double-check an answer, and they had handed it in as their own. She had failed the module. The way she had told Felix this story had made it clear that this was a big, dark, shameful secret for her. Of course, Felix would never have lent anyone his coursework in the first place.

"Harriet's just struggling to adapt," Leah agreed, cupping a hand over her mouth to hide a yawn.

"No, it's something more than that," he said. "I mentioned my power to her, and she didn't even seem to understand why going around *hypnotizing people* wasn't allowed."

"Are you sure you're not overreacting because you're … you know?" Rima chewed on her lip, looking uncomfortable.

"I'm what?"

Rima looked away. "Because you're jealous, Felix."

Felix blinked twice, very quickly, going hot all over. "What?" he said and winced when his words came out strangled. "I'm not jealous! What reason do I have to be jealous?"

Leah sighed. "Drop the act. We've all known about your crush for decades. Your entire identity is based around your feelings for another man."

"I don't like Captain America that much!" he attempted to joke.

Rima and Leah both pulled unimpressed faces at him, so he stopped even trying. It would probably be rude to disintegrate in the middle of this conversation as an avoidance tactic. "Does everyone know? Does *he*?"

Rima touched his arm. "Oh, no! I don't think so. Kasper's

kind of oblivious. And your crush mainly manifests itself as …
how should I put this…?"

"Unresolved sexual tension?" Leah suggested.

"Immature squabbling," Rima said instead.

"Right," Felix said, feeling dizzy. "Good to know."

"Anyway, it's completely understandable that you'd feel anxious about a new girl coming and taking all his attention."

"Taking all his attention? I'm not an idiot," he hissed. "Kasper's straight. I know he'll never be interested in me, so what would I have to gain from accusing Harriet like this unless it were *true*? I'm going to keep an eye on her, whatever you say."

Chapter 7

HARRIET

Kasper followed Harriet up the stairs to the first floor, telling her the plan for their Halloween party date in great detail. He even asked her favourite kind of flower – apparently he had a friend whose power let them grow bouquets, or something.

Harriet answered his questions, trying to work out how to shake him off. She'd only agreed to the date because she thought it would be a good idea to keep him on her side. He might turn out to be useful. But the way he'd lit up when she'd said yes had made her regret it immediately.

Harriet had found herself joining in when they were all messing around. She'd even made a joke that they'd all laughed at, which had been a surprise. She wasn't used to being funny. During primary school, her class had voted for their star class-mate of the week, whose picture was put up on a display board. It was a popularity contest, mostly. Everyone in the class got picked at some point, either on their birthday or because they'd made up a fun game in the playground. Everyone except Harriet.

Making Rima and the others laugh was like finally getting

chosen as star classmate. But she had to stop wasting time and distracting herself like that. Having friends wasn't going to help her.

When Kasper tripped on a step, mid-sentence, and started stumbling forward, Harriet felt something stretch inside her chest. She reached forward and grabbed his arm before he could lose balance. If a ghost fell, it was possible they might just keep falling down through every floor of the building.

"Thanks," he said, righting himself.

The bubbling feeling inside her chest disappeared. Harriet frowned, trying to work out what it had been.

"Shall we meet in my room?" Kasper asked. "Then we can hang out before the party starts."

"Sure," she said, rubbing her sternum distractedly. "Is it OK if I have some alone time until then?"

"Oh!" Kasper said. "Yeah, no worries. You must still be processing everything." He gestured vaguely at her ghostly form.

"Mmm."

"See you soon." He backed off down the hall, grinning at her in a lazy, pleased-with-himself manner.

She gave him a little wave, then sighed with relief. She'd have to do her best to avoid him until the next day. When she was alive, she hadn't been invited to many parties after freshers' week had ended. A Halloween party could be fun, she supposed, though it was slightly annoying that she couldn't change any of her clothes. She was stuck in the boring khaki outfit she'd died in.

At least she could change her hairstyle, to make it more suitable for a party. Her make-up was fine too – she'd been wearing her most popular YouTube make-up tutorial look when she'd died, 'Boss Babe Hustle Eyes'n'Lips'. It wasn't a bad look to have for all eternity.

Finally alone, she went to check her phone on the fifth floor. Her gran had left a series of increasingly frustrated voicemails.

"Harriet, darling, where are you? You know how I worry about you. Call me."

"Harriet, where are you? It's very unfair of you to leave me in the dark like this. I'm not well. Please call me back immediately."

"Harriet, if you don't come home this evening, I'm afraid we're going to have a serious discussion about your curfew. This is unacceptable."

Harriet leant back on her heels, wondering what to do now. The messages had left her squirming with guilt and determination. How had she already wasted so much time?

She had been wracking her brains to think of things that she could trade for another animal spirit. Now it occurred to her, as she stared down at her phone, that all the ghosts seemed to be fascinated by the technology. Felix had practically begged for a chance to test it out. Maybe she could trade time on the Internet for more animal spirits. It was worth a shot.

Harriet explored each floor, searching for the rat-hunting guy she'd spoken to on the stairs earlier. She found him in the third-floor kitchen, with his head stuck inside the fridge.

"I have something to trade now," she said to his rear end.

He jumped, the back of his low-slung jeans slipping down even further. "What if I let you use my phone for a bit?"

"Oh yeah, princess?" he said, extracting himself from the refrigerator. He considered her through narrow eyes for a moment. "What's the point of that? Who would I call?"

"It goes online. A lot has changed since you died. You can look up whatever kind of stuff you want now."

"On a phone?" He sounded sceptical. "I can look up anything? Like, X-rated stuff?"

"Uh." She paused. It wasn't like she was ever going to use the phone again – the battery would be dead soon. There was no reason not to let him infect it with viruses. The tips of her fingers were tingling at the memory of the rat energy rush. She needed another, whatever it took. "Sure."

He looked at her more carefully, then. "What did you say your name was?"

She hadn't. "It's Harriet Stoker."

He grinned. "All right, Stoker. Lead the way. I'm Greg."

She took Greg back up to the fifth floor. A few ghosts were chatting on the stairs, and they looked between Harriet and Greg in surprise.

"Sup," he said to them.

To Harriet's surprise, the girls pressed up against the stairs to avoid him, not acknowledging his greeting.

Upstairs, there was a Shell floating over Harriet's phone. She flapped her hands at it, pushing the boy away. Greg inspected the phone in wonder. "How does it work?"

"It's voice-activated. I'll unlock it, then you can just tell it what you want to see. Only … wait until I've gone, please." Harriet hid a grimace. She didn't even want to imagine what Greg wanted to search for.

"All right," he said, and held out a hand. "You've got a deal."

Harriet went to shake it, and then pulled back. He'd agreed suspiciously quickly. "What are you giving me for it? I'll let you use it for fifteen minutes for one rat spirit."

He frowned down at his outstretched hand, then back at her. "I don't have any rats at the moment, but I'll give you a mouse for it."

"Three mice."

"It's worth a mouse and a half at the most." He waggled his hand. "Come on, Harriet."

"Two mice," she said.

He sucked his teeth. "All right. Two mice. Shake on it?"

She paused, eyeing him. What did she really know about Greg? Those girls on the stairs hadn't even wanted to make eye contact with him. He could be trying to swindle her somehow. "I want the mice before you use the phone."

"Sure. Whatever you want." He pushed his hand towards her again. She finally took it.

When her skin touched his, all her doubts left her mind. He was on her side – of course he was. She couldn't remember why she'd ever doubted him.

"A mouse and a half, then," he said, grip tight around her palm.

"Sure," she said faintly.

He released her hand. Harriet swayed slightly, blinking.

Greg grinned at her, a lazy smile tugging up the side of his mouth. "Perfect," he said, and pulled a mouse spirit out of his shirt pocket. He breathed in deeply, his tongue curling around the tail, then passed the other half over to Harriet. She closed her eyes and inhaled, letting the energy roll over her. It was amazing how quickly it worked to make her feel more alive.

It wasn't anywhere near enough to manifest her power, but the buzz was still worth the trade. While Greg spent his fifteen minutes using her phone, Harriet found herself gazing deep inside a cobweb threaded across the ceiling.

"Phew!" Greg stretched his arms up behind his head. "I haven't had such a good time in ages."

Harriet was surprised – the fifteen minutes had gone by in a dreamy energy high, as she tried to spot the spider among the petrified insect cocoons. It was like the energy had done something to her brain, sending her thoughts slow and stretchy like toffee.

Harriet smiled affectionately at him. He was a funny one. Good old Greg. Why had she ever thought he was strange? He felt like a long-lost brother now, familiar and comforting. She found herself telling him the truth: "I was trying to manifest my power with the mouse, but it didn't work."

"Oh, yeah?" said Greg, eyebrow raised. "I might know some people who can help with that. You'd need to have something to

trade, though. They run a black market where people swap …
particular favours and information."

That sounded perfect. Anyone Greg recommended would be able to help her, she was sure of it. Harriet beamed at him.

"Can you take me to see them?"

"Stoker, it would be my pleasure."

Oh dear. I was hoping it would be a while before you had to meet the Tricksters. They're tangled up in everything – past, present and future – so you're going to have to face them eventually. It might as well be now.

You see, ghosts have lived here for a long time. Not just since the halls of residence was built in the seventies, but long before that, in a series of cottages and barns and huts and camps throughout history. In all that time, people have died, like they do.

Gather enough people together, whether they're dead or alive, and they'll make some ground rules, put laws in place and develop some kind of society. There are lawmakers and lawbreakers here, just like anywhere else. Sometimes the lawbreakers are the more interesting ones.

Look at Greg – his power makes anyone trust him, utterly, after skin-to-skin contact. That's allowed him to get away with a lot.

It's a power that makes him valuable to people like the Tricksters. He's an enforcer; an inside man. Harriet hasn't been here long enough to know who she should avoid and who she should trust.

If she'd asked Rima before talking to Greg, she would have been warned to never, ever, shake Greg's hand. But it's too late for that now. She's already made a big mistake – one that it's going to be hard to recover from. But her next mistake will be even worse.

HARRIET

Greg led her down to the basement floor, through a doorway marked "Recreation Room". As he stepped through the wooden door, the entrance lit up in bright white light, and then dropped back into darkness. Harriet was worried it would burn her, but she trusted Greg, so she stepped through. The glowing light was painless.

The floor of the basement room was covered in a black, gunky damp from flooding, and it was full of junk – broken tables and chairs, old suitcases and crates. Ghosts were crammed into every centimetre of space.

"What was that light thing on the door?" she asked Greg.

"It's the lock," he said, scanning the room. "People get sent to the basement for breaking the rules. That girl there, in the orange nightgown, used to go around starting fires a couple of years ago. The boy with the Mohican stalked one of the third-floorers before the millennium. Once you're sent here, you don't get out again. Qi Pang's lightning fries any of them who try to cross the doorway."

He gestured back towards the bright light that had flashed when they'd entered. Harriet shivered, remembering the feeling of Qi's lightning wrapped around her arm. She could imagine what would happen if one of the imprisoned ghosts tried to pass through it.

Greg walked over to where a group of ghosts were crowded around a pool table. One of the balls on it was skittering around, rolling over to hit a second one and sending it flying. The crowd let out a roaring cheer, and one of the ghosts patted a short, grinning girl on the arm.

From the other side of the table, a boy stared at another ball. It tilted to the side, then back. The guy frowned, staring unblinkingly at it until it started rolling.

The ball missed the pocket, and the crowd let out a long groan as the girl did a little happy dance.

They must be using telekinesis. Harriet was impressed. Was there no end to the potential powers ghosts could have?

"Are they the ones who run the black market?" Harriet asked Greg.

He shook his head. Suddenly mute, he pointed to two men she hadn't noticed, standing alone on the far side of the room. They weren't paying any attention to the pool game, but just watched everyone, completely motionless. The sight of them ignited some long-lost instinct inside Harriet's spine that told her to run.

"Those are the Tricksters," Greg said. "It's their market."

They looked like old-fashioned movie stars; all smoothed-back hair and artistic stubble. Their hair was completely white – a shockingly bright white. But there was something unnatural about their disproportionate handsomeness. It felt artificial, like a neon poisonous frog.

The urge to flee gripped the back of Harriet's neck, seizing up her muscles. They couldn't notice her, her hindbrain was telling her body. She had to hide.

"The *Tricksters*?" Harriet said, her voice a little shaky. One of them turned his head, his eyes landing on hers. "Are you sure this is safe?"

"I promise." Greg pressed one hand to her elbow.

She breathed out. If he thought this was safe, then she was going to be all right. "What's that feeling, then? It tickles."

"Tricksters collect energy from fear," Greg said, under his breath. "That feeling is their power feeling you out, that's all. It's harmless."

"I'm not sure about this…" Harriet looked back at the doorway. "I think I should go."

"You don't want to waste your time with that lot upstairs." His hand touched her forearm. "If you want to get things done, the basement is the place to be."

"Maybe I should go and talk to Rima first…"

Greg squeezed her shoulder reassuringly, his fingers touching her neck. Harriet went dizzy, her thoughts going cloudy. When she could focus again, Harriet couldn't remember what she'd been so worried about.

"Let's just go and say hey," Greg suggested. "They'll be able to help, I promise. You trust me, don't you?"

He was right. These were exactly the kind of people she had wanted to find – the real people in charge. It was good that she was afraid – a sign that she was pushing herself as far as she could go. Her gran would never run away from anything. She was stronger than that, and so was Harriet.

She let Greg lead her over to the Tricksters, where he made

a tinny cough to get their attention, hovering in front of them.

Eventually, the taller Trickster deigned to look at him. "Yes?"

"Hi, Rufus. Vini."

The second Trickster didn't look at them but inclined his head slightly.

All of Greg's confidence seemed to have dried up now. "This is, er, Harriet Stoker. She's new, she fell—"

"We know," Rufus said, sounding bored.

"Right. You're very well informed."

"Get to the point."

"I want to discuss a trade." Harriet tried to pitch her voice at the assertive tone her gran used when she was trying to gain control of an argument. Something about these men reminded her of her gran. "I need information. In exchange, I'll give you time using a mobile phone. It has some music on there, and a few episodes of a TV show called *Loch & Ness*. It also lets you access the Internet."

"The Internet is, er—" Greg started explaining.

"We know," Rufus said again, cutting him off.

"... *for porn*," Greg trailed off, under his breath.

"What kind of information do you need?" Vini asked.

Harriet wondered what question she could ask that would give her the maximum amount of information. If this was her only chance to make a deal, she had to get the most out of it. "I want to find a way of choosing my power when it manifests."

For the first time, Rufus moved, turning his head to

exchange a glance with Vini. He had been absolutely, inhumanly still until now.

"We want the phone," Vini said. "Not just time using it. Permanently."

Harriet pretended to consider this. She had come prepared to barter. The phone would run out of battery soon, so she didn't want to give it away completely if she didn't have to. "I'd rather lend it to you by the hour. Just to make sure I'm getting the information I need."

His eyes glinted. "Give us the phone afterwards, if you think we've helped you. We know how to do this."

"How do I know I can trust you?"

Rufus cleared his throat pointedly at Greg, whose hand squeezed the back of Harriet's neck.

"They're on your side, I promise," he whispered in her ear.

Harriet grinned dopily at Greg. "Fine, it's yours," she told Rufus.

As she shook their hands, Harriet noticed Rufus had a neat rectangular tattoo on his forearm. It looked suspiciously like a spreadsheet. Was it a record of black-market trades?

Their ice-cold skin made pins and needles spread through her hand. They were sucking out her energy, like Qi had done. As quickly as she could, while still looking polite, she pulled her hand away.

Vini put a hand on Greg's shoulder. "You should go outside now."

Looking more than a little relieved, he backed away. "I'll,

er, be outside," he said to Harriet. "Catch up with you later."

Harriet closed her eyes, taking a moment to settle herself and focus on whatever was about to happen. She couldn't let herself panic again, not if they fed on fear. She'd come this far; she had to keep going. These Tricksters were nothing compared to how disappointed her gran would be if she didn't get home soon.

"So," she said, and then cursed herself for breaking the silence first. It betrayed her nerves, and they would leap on any sign of fear. Whatever agreement might be in place, they would break it in a second if they saw an advantage. "Tell me."

"You don't eat fear like us," Rufus said. "But—"

"Doesn't she?" Vini interrupted. "Are you sure?" He leant forward and took Harriet by the chin, staring deep into her eyes. She held herself very still.

"No," Vini said a full six minutes later. "You're right. She's something else."

They were very close. Suddenly, she was aware that they were licking their lips. She imagined herself as prey, being hunted, and then, just as quickly, pushed the thought away.

Instead, she tried to imagine herself as a predator, strong and equal to them and not at all afraid. It was too late. They were both breathing in her fear, fingers grasping her wrists and wide teeth catching at the edges of their smiles. Pins and needles frayed away her skin where they touched her.

"Stop it!" she said, her voice tight and high. She pulled her arms away. "That was *not* part of the deal."

"Apologies," Rufus said, stepping back. "Vini," he added sharply.

His brother moved away from Harriet, still watching her hungrily.

"The only way to choose your power is to take one from another ghost," Rufus said, pitching his voice low.

Harriet swallowed a lump in her throat. "How do I do that?"

"You'll need to take their energy. All of it, if you want the power to be yours permanently." His gaze was boring into her.

"All of it," Harriet repeated, feeling faint. *"All of it?"*

"Every last atom," Vini confirmed. "Or it won't be permanent."

Were they saying what she thought they were? "How do you know? Have you tried?"

In unison, they shook their heads. Vini's right earlobe was torn, the skin dangling from the lobe like an earring. She carefully avoided staring at it.

"Then how do you know it will work?"

After a long pause where she thought that neither of them was going to bother answering, Rufus said, "Because it's been done before."

This time, Harriet was the one to step closer to them. Her fear had gone. "By who?"

"You've met Leah and Claudia by now, I presume?"

Harriet was so shocked that she actually gaped at them. *"Leah?"*

"Not Leah." Vini smirked. "The baby. Claudia."

Our powers aren't random. They represent part of us – something we value, whether that's our culture, personality, strengths or beliefs. My power comes from my desperation to have control. Rima wants to be friends with everyone and everything – including every animal she meets. Felix doesn't know how to talk to people, so his power lets him make sure he's never put in a social situation he can't fix.

And Harriet? I guess we'll have to see what her power is, when it manifests. But I have my theories.

Most of the time, the powers you think will be the most valuable are not very useful at all, and boring ones turn out to be surprising. Rima's power, for example, is very desirable. Ghosts can be tattooed using porcupine quills and black squid taken from a shapeshifter's animal forms. People are constantly asking Rima to trade supplies on the black market. But nothing can convince her to trade with Rufus and Vini.

There's a long history of ghosts on this site, with more powers than you can imagine. There were five of us, in the beginning – one of the beginnings, anyway. A family, bonded through blood and bone and fealty. Nothing like Rima and Felix and Kasper, who found and chose each other. That kind of family is easy and gentle, but it's weak, too. A bond that's grown from friendship can be broken. Blood is more powerful. Blood bites back. Blood defends itself.

Blood or bond? Harriet hasn't decided yet. She doesn't even know that she's going to have to make a choice.

She hadn't even noticed the baby until the tricksters mentioned her. Now she thinks the baby is important. But she has no idea.

Chapter 8

FELIX

"Mars bars, for sure," Felix said, tilting his head up to take in the early morning sunlight. He was sunbathing on the moss-covered metal fire escape with the girls. It was one of the only occasions when Leah seemed anything other than ambivalent about life.

"McCoy's crisps, too! I would give anything to be able to eat food again," Rima said, as she wrestled Cody. The fox nipped at her arm and jumped on her chest. "Oh, well *done*."

Felix reached out to rub Cody's head. She licked his palm with a very pink tongue, as Rima twisted into another wrestling move. "That's a half nelson," she told the fox. "You know, I would have made the best professional wrestler."

"You would get out of breath opening a jam jar," Leah told Rima decisively.

"My haters never rest, apparently," Rima told Cody, huffing.

"I think you'd be a good wrestler. You have a very high pain tolerance," Harriet said, admiringly watching Cody gnaw on Rima's thumb.

Harriet's gaze followed the movement when Claudia

reached out from where she was curled into Leah's side to touch the silky material of Rima's hijab with minuscule, soft fingertips.

"You know, that's not usually something that people look for in friends," Felix pointed out.

Harriet shrugged, unperturbed. She was staring at Claudia now. Not looking, but *watching*. Earlier, Leah had passed her baby over to Harriet to hold. She had stood stock-still, staring down at Claudia with stiff arms and a forced smile until Rima had taken pity on her and tucked Claudia under her arm instead.

"I was studying Dentistry really," Rima told Harriet, apparently under the assumption that she would otherwise genuinely believe that Rima had been doing a degree in Wrestling when she was alive. "But only because my parents wanted me to. I rushed through all my coursework so I could watch TV. What did you want to do when you were older?"

Harriet looked up at the sky, wistfully. "I was going to work for *Vogue* one day. I've got a channel online where I post videos of make-up tutorials. Contouring and stuff, you know? I had some collabs lined up with other YouTubers – bigger ones, so I could get some more subs. I thought it'd be the kind of thing *Vogue* would be interested in."

"You should start a ghost *Vogue*," Rima said, looking amused by the idea.

"Kasper would love modelling for it," Felix said. Kasper had modelled for a Rowing Society charity calendar when he was alive, which for some inexplicable reason had involved all the Soc members posing nude with baby animals. Felix had once walked into their shared bathroom, only to find Kasper and five of his friends waxing each other's bums, while covered in tanning lotion. He'd backed out again immediately, then pre-ordered five copies of the calendar.

Tragically, the issue hadn't been delivered before he died. There was a parcel for Felix tucked into one of the postal pigeonholes down in reception. For decades, Felix had been wondering whether the package was the calendar, or if it was a package from his mum.

When he was homesick during the first term of university, she used to send him envelopes full of things she'd ripped out of magazines and newspapers. Oscar had thought it was silly, but Felix had found it comforting. It showed she was thinking about him. Oscar had never got homesick, anyway. He was too busy having fun and skipping lectures.

Felix missed his brother so much. He always got nostalgic in the autumn, near the anniversary of their deaths, and Oscar's escape. Soon he'd come for his annual visit.

It hurt in a good way, seeing how much he had changed. Becoming a man, a husband, a father – even a divorcee. Doing things that Felix would never have the chance to do. The hardest part of dying had been adjusting to surviving without Oscar.

"Do you have a *Vogue*?" Harriet asked Felix.

"I wanted to be a computer programmer," Felix said, immediately. He was the only person in Mulcture Hall who had been studying Computer Science. Kasper, who had been reading Art History, had only been scheduled for a third of the number of lectures as Felix, which had been a constant source of irritation.

"What about you, Leah?" Rima asked her. "You must have wanted to be *something* when you were little. Even Kasper wanted to be a teacher."

Rima was constantly prying into Leah's life even though she was very, very clear about how much she disliked it. Rima even kept a list of facts, which she'd told Felix once. It included:

1. Leah had been alive at one point in time.
2. Leah had died at another, later point in time.
3. Leah had once had a mother and a father.
4. Claudia also had a mother and a father.
    a. Leah was Claudia's mother.
    b. Claudia was between zero and seven months old.
5. Leah had hated coriander.
6. She had been allergic to dogs.
7. Leah's power let her look into the future.

Felix had been reluctantly impressed by the thoroughness of the documentation.

Leah flopped over onto her stomach, pulling up the hem of her dress to sun her thighs. To Felix's surprise, she started talking. "My – my family ... we weren't raised to have careers. Not girls, anyway."

"And you got pregnant when you were, what, seventeen?" Harriet said. "I guess that makes it hard to plan ahead."

Rima touched one finger to Claudia's cheek. "It was worth it, though, for little Claudia," she said eventually.

Harriet's gaze kept returning to the baby. "How have you avoided disintegrating, in all this time? Did you get more energy from somewhere?"

Leah stared at her stonily. "We're not *that* old."

Harriet blanched. She finally looked away. "Right. Sorry."

"Harriet and I were discussing this earlier," Felix said, trying to break the tension like a bubble. "About what happens to us after we disintegrate, I mean."

Rima grinned. "Did you mention my reincarnation theory?"

Felix rolled his eyes. "Of course I didn't. It's ridiculous."

"No, it's not! It makes a lot of sense!" Rima turned to Harriet. "I've got it all worked out. We came from living human bodies, right? It makes sense that when we disintegrate, that energy goes to another human body and the cycle starts again. It can't just disappear into the air. Right?!"

"I think maybe that sounds a bit far-fetched…" Harriet said slowly. "It's too magical."

Rima fluffed up in indignation. "We're literally ghosts! How much more magical can you get?"

"Yeah, but at least ghosts make sense. We're still the same people we were when we were alive. But what you're talking about – being reborn? – we'd forget who we were. What's the point of us being born again if we don't remember our old lives? We might as well start from scratch each time. It doesn't make any difference in the long run."

"If reincarnation was real, wouldn't we all remember our previous lives?" Leah pointed out, shaking her head. "We live and we die, end of story."

"I don't know—" Felix said, and then abruptly made himself stop talking. It was silly. "Never mind."

Rima nudged him. "What were you going to say?"

"Well, it's just that I had a cousin who used to talk about his past life when he was a toddler. He used to describe these vivid memories of places he had never seen. We assumed he was describing stuff from the TV. But what if he wasn't? What if it was real?"

Rima glowed. "See! I'm totally right. I knew it. You're all suckers."

"Ugh," Leah opened her eyes to say, and then, exhausted, closed them again. "Let's change the subject. Why don't you play a game or something."

"Ooh!" Rima said. "Felix – Kiss, Marry, Kill. *Kasper, Ruf—*"

"Kasper," Felix interrupted.

Rima slowly closed her mouth. "I haven't even said the other options yet."

"No need."

The corner of Leah's mouth twitched.

Rima said, "You'd … kiss, marry *and* kill Kasper?"

Persevering, Felix said, "I stand by what I said. Unless Captain America is one of the other options."

Harriet made an *"Ohhh…"* noise, like she'd figured something out.

135

The back of Felix's neck went hot. He had been out for ages, but it still felt weird when he came out to someone new. It was such intensely personal information to just announce to the world. He tugged Claudia into his lap, tickling her until her cheeks dimpled and she started waving her hands and making tiny, adorable giggles.

"You're LGBT?" Harriet asked him. "I'm pan."

Felix raised his eyebrows. "I call it being gay. What do all those new letters stand for?"

Harriet explained the most recent terminology to them, including something called demisexuality. Felix still didn't know what to make of her – he didn't really understand her at all – but there was something warm in his chest at the thought that she wasn't straight. He was no longer the only one who was different. She was like him. However strange she was – that, at least, made him grateful she was here.

Kasper jogged up to the window and climbed out onto the fire escape.

He must have been running laps up and down the corridors, because he was shirtless. There was a scattering of small freckles across the tops of his shoulders, his collarbones and curling down the back of his neck. Remnants of a past life spent in the sun. The marks were so beautiful that Felix felt the pit of his stomach turning to liquid.

"You all right?" Kasper asked them, panting, as he stretched out his hamstrings. Glowing pink, he wiped sweat off his brow with one forearm.

"We were just talking about bisexuality," Rima told him. "You know, being attracted to both men and women?" She watched Kasper carefully.

Felix was amused. She clearly wanted Felix to deal with his thing for Kasper, but did she think this would help? Was she expecting Kasper to say, *"Yes, Rima, you know, I am in fact bisexual myself. I also have a crush on Felix. I am going to kiss him!"*

Felix bit his lip, flushing. Actually, that wouldn't be so bad. *"You're my universe, dude,"* Kasper could say, maybe. Not that Felix had thought about it much.

It had always been weird to him that you could think about someone as much as you wanted and they would have no idea. How could Kasper not see it on his face at every moment?

Kasper shrugged, too busy looking at Harriet to pay attention. "I've, er, heard of it. I guess."

When Harriet met his gaze, his body language went … softer.

Felix rolled his eyes at Rima, feeling exasperated.

Harriet completed the image that Kasper wanted to present to the world: a sporty lads' lad with an attractive girlfriend. This whole infatuation was just based on appearance – his own, as much as Harriet's. Kasper was terrified to step outside the norm in any way.

"I'm looking forward to our date tonight," Kasper told Harriet. He rubbed at the hair on the back of his head, fluffing it up with his fingers. "Can I use your phone before the party starts? I want to make you a mixtape."

"Oh. Er, my phone's battery died. Such a shame," Harriet said in a voice so flat that it was almost a monotone. "A mixtape would have been lovely."

"Oh." Kasper deflated. "Did the Shells break it?"

"The Shells?" Harriet frowned, then sat bolt upright. "Oh. *Oh*. I have to go."

Seconds later, she was gone. Kasper collapsed onto the fire escape in a sulking heap. Felix tried not to watch him mope. He hated this.

Let's go back to the day that Rima, Kasper and Felix met, when Felix knocked Kasper's alarm clock to the ground on moving-in day. Afterwards, Oscar had to persuade Felix not to delay uni and take a gap year to recover from his shame.

When Felix got back to his room, the door to the bathroom was half open. Someone had moved into the adjoining bedroom.

I was watching, of course. It would have been impossible to drag myself away. I'd been waiting for centuries. Nothing could have made me take my eyes off every move they made, trying to understand what was so special about these people.

Kasper stuck his head around the door and said hello, making a joke about how organized the bedroom already was, compared to Kasper's own. His friendly grin disappeared when Felix turned around.

They both recognized each other at the same time. Kasper said, "Oh," and Felix visibly blanched.

"Listen," Felix said, rubbing his palms on his thighs,

"I'm so sorry about bumping into you earlier. I can pay for anything that broke."

"Forget about it. What are you studying, then?"

"Computer Science. You?"

"Art History," Kasper said.

"Um…" Felix wrinkled his nose. "What kind of job are you going to get with that?"

"What do you mean?"

"Sounds like something you only do if you've not got to worry about money."

Kasper glared at him. "So you're a snob, are you? I bet you think it's only for dumb rich kids."

Felix folded his arms. "Well…"

"You're calling me stupid, too? You know what, you can pay for the clock after all," Kasper bit out, his eyes hard. "It was thirty quid."

Felix grimaced. There was only a ten-pound gift voucher for WHSmith in his wallet. "Actually … I just put all my money on my uni account for meals."

Kasper snorted. "I should have known it was an empty offer. Thanks for nothing."

Three nights later, Felix lay in bed listening to the sound of Kasper and a girl through the thin wall. When Kasper ran into Felix the next morning, Felix couldn't help but snap out a sarcastic comment about keeping the noise down next time. Kasper responded, *"Just because you aren't getting laid, doesn't mean the rest of us need to hide it."*

Felix had stopped talking to him completely after that. He hadn't told anyone that he was gay yet. He'd got a pin badge at the university freshers' fair that had PROUD *to be at* Warwick *written in black curlicue letters over a pink triangle. He took it out every few nights. A few times, I saw him pin it onto his coat, leave it there overnight and then take it off and put it back in his drawer just before he left the room for his morning lectures.*

He was still waiting for the right person to tell when he'd died.

HARRIET

Striding up the stairs, Harriet left the group sunbathing on the fire escape. After the Tricksters had told her that she could steal a power from another ghost, they had sent her up to the fifth floor with a telekinetic ghost, who apparently owed the Tricksters a favour. The ghost had made her phone levitate, walking down to the basement with it.

Harriet had only the smallest tinge of regret about losing the phone. It was a useful thing to have, but the information she had obtained in exchange was better. Though she couldn't quite remember how she'd come to make the deal with Rufus and Vini. It was all a strange blur in her memory. At least Greg had been there to support her.

Rufus had asked Harriet, with a smirk that she had refused to let scare her, whether there wasn't anything which might make her consider staying in the basement with them. He had mentioned an intriguingly vague selection of "services" that she was "welcome to make use of", if she stayed. She hadn't asked for further information, shaking her head so vigorously her hair fell out of its bun.

Ever since then, she had been wondering whether she could take a power from another ghost. It sounded easy and painless, but taking energy from another person was so personal. It was invasive. She had to get home though. She'd been telling herself for days that she'd do anything it took to get back to her family – and now she was backing out because it was suddenly getting too real? Her gran would disown her if she could see how pathetic Harriet was becoming.

"Don't let anything stop you, once your goal is in sight," she had once told Harriet. "Other people will stomp you into the ground if they get the chance. You have to make sure you beat them to it."

She had still been wrestling with her dilemma when she'd found Felix and the girls. She was aching with curiosity about what had led to Claudia stealing someone's energy, but hadn't found a way to ask about it.

She had surprised herself by actually enjoying the conversation. She hadn't meant to reveal so much about herself to them. There had even been a moment when something had shifted in her chest, a strange bubbling sensation that she'd thought might be affection. Unnerved, she'd pushed it away. She couldn't let herself grow closer to them. She might have to steal a power from one of them.

Felix's power would be useful, but he seemed to distrust her already. He wouldn't even let her get close enough to give it a shot.

Rima's shapeshifting would be a handy power to have. But Rima had all these connections with people like Qi that might be useful, if Harriet kept her on side. Plus, she could get animal spirits for her if Harriet asked nicely.

Meanwhile, Leah had said her power was too weak to work any more, and Kasper hadn't even told her what his power was yet. He just kept staring at her with those big doe eyes, like he was inventing a love story in his head.

She was going to have to let him down gently, if Felix had a thing for Kasper. She should have been paying better attention – she hadn't even noticed that he liked him, but it made total sense now she knew.

She could kick herself. Knowledge like that was invaluable for negotiations. She'd been focused on getting Rima and Kasper to help her by offering them the things they wanted most – friendship and romance. But in doing that, she'd forgotten to think about what Felix wanted most in all the world.

Well, if Felix wanted Kasper, then he was welcome to him. She would have to turn Kasper down after their date. Felix's hypnotism made him more useful than Kasper, in the long run.

None of their powers were worth stealing. That left Claudia. The baby was apparently the only ghost here who'd taken someone's power. All that wasted potential was just waiting for someone to come along who would appreciate it.

While she was considering the awful possibility of taking Claudia's energy, Kasper had mentioned the Shells. She'd completely forgotten about them. There was her answer, right in front of her. She had a ready-made power supply waiting on the fifth floor.

The Shells couldn't even use their powers any more. It wasn't like it would hurt them, if she took some of their energy away. They might not even notice it. The Tricksters had said she would need to take all their energy, if she wanted to steal a power. But the Shells were so old and weak it would probably be easy.

It would be fine, she was sure of it.

On the fifth floor, wind gusted through broken windows, sending dust into spirals. Harriet herded the Shells into a crowd. There were eight in total. She had no way of knowing what powers they had, so she'd just have to choose one at random and hope for the best. Any power was better than nothing at all.

Before she could chicken out, she grabbed a girl with curly hair, sucking down her energy, open-mouthed. It was like a dam had been released. The energy rolled in a wave through her body, and it kept coming and coming and coming.

She shuddered, tilting her head back. The golden haze of potent energy thrummed in her blood. How would she know whether she'd taken the power yet?

The girl convulsed, and a high-pitched, pained whine burst from her throat. Harriet held on tight, desperately trying to chew down more energy.

She had only meant to take her power, but now her mind was blissfully blank. Even as it poured into her in an endless gust, it wasn't enough to sate her. The Shell's chest collapsed in on itself, a wormhole of swirling atoms that disintegrated under Harriet's touch. A grating noise of pain was still coming from the girl's mouth.

Harriet tore at her neck to get more energy. It pulsed under her skin, starting to burn now, like the shocking heat of a hot bath when you first step into the water. Her nerves were on fire, but she kept going. She couldn't stop.

Around them, the other Shells wailed in a chorus of mournful commiseration. Harriet shook their fingers off her shoulders. The Shell was almost gone, and she couldn't stop until she'd gathered every last drop.

Too quickly, it was over. The Shell disintegrated, her atoms spreading through the air. Harriet's arms were empty. The girl with the curly hair, a long-forgotten student of Mulcture Hall, was nothing more than a memory and a boost in Harriet's cells.

She threw the other Shells across the room, with a strength she'd never imagined possible. Her skin was bursting, like it would split under the swollen richness of the energy.

Harriet stumbled across the wrecked room to the window, gasping down cold, fresh air. The buzzing feeling inside her had changed from thrilling to frightening. She fell to the ground, wishing she'd asked Rufus and Vini how to control the energy before it fried her flesh.

Curled in a shivering ball on the floor, Harriet braced herself against the painful burn. She was going to disintegrate. She couldn't possibly survive this. What had she done?

This is what the Tricksters do. They lend you enough rope to hang yourself, and then charge interest on it. Harriet thinks she's forging her own path, but these moments have been planned for a long time. Nothing can be done to stop this now.

My father used to say that you have to find what people fear the most and focus your attention there, even if there are easier, weaker links. He said that it's worth spending the time trying to break people open in a way that will last. Then you only have to do it once. He planned everything he did meticulously, and then made it look like it was all a spur-of-the-moment decision. People would carry on underestimating him, that way.

Harriet isn't at that level yet. She's trying, but she lacks experience.

The Tricksters clearly had their reasons for telling Harriet how to take a power. I'm not even sure they gained anything from this chaos, except for the visceral satisfaction that comes from knowing you're responsible for another person's destruction.

I've known Rufus for a long time, and he's always been this way – just like his brother. If other people are unhappy, then he's satisfied. By the end of all this, he's going to have made Harriet truly miserable.

Chapter 9

HARRIET

When Harriet opened her eyes, days or hours or minutes later, the sky was dark. Her entire body ached, like her flesh had been attacked with a meat tenderizer.

She tried to move her arms, but a searing, scalding pain ran down her muscles. She wanted to sleep for three months. This must be what being electrocuted felt like. Being electrocuted whilst running a full marathon. Dehydrated. Post-surgery. Her mouth tasted of chemicals. She fell back into a deep sleep.

When she woke up a second time, the pain had gone. This time, she felt ... *fantastic*. Better than fantastic – invulnerable. The thrilling feeling had come back once more. Harriet let out a giddy, overjoyed laugh; shouting it into the night sky.

She had done it! She had absorbed a Shell's energy!

She had done it.

The Shell had disintegrated, which was disappointing. She'd expected to be able to pull the Shell's power free, leaving the girl to drift aimlessly around the fifth floor like before. Instead, the Shell had dissolved into nothing.

But … they were brain-dead anyway, weren't they? It was euthanization, really. If she gained a new power from it, then it had to be a worthwhile sacrifice. Anything to get home.

The Shell had tasted so *good*, too. Better than anything she'd eaten when she was alive. Nicer, even, than that first rat spirit. Harriet had always struggled with food. Her gran had never been a good cook – leaving meat slightly raw and drowning food in bizarre sauces and gravies that she'd invented. She'd just said Harriet had a sensitive stomach and certain things made her feel woozy, but Harriet had never managed to pin down what exactly she was allergic to. The Shell's energy had been a revelation.

Closing her eyes, she tested her control to see if she had gained a power. Nothing was different, but then, her body was still exhausted. Meanwhile, her mind was racing.

In the distance, the university tower's clock struck eleven. Somehow, she had found her way onto the remains of the concrete-clad rooftop, alone under the stars. It was peaceful, with only the sound of the wind blowing through the rotting rafters.

She was supposed to be meeting Kasper for their date at the Halloween party soon. A party suddenly seemed like the best idea ever. She needed to do something with this high of victory and energy and adrenaline. She had never felt this good.

KASPER

Kasper felt light enough to float up to the ceiling. He was actually going out with Harriet on a legit *date*. Squinting into his cracked bathroom mirror, he readjusted his fringe so that it stuck up, then nudged it so it fell over his eye. He wished he could still use hair gel. It was so much harder to sculpt without it.

Ineffectually, he tried to pat the creases out of his shirt and peered out of the window to see if it had stopped raining. The Halloween party had to go perfectly. He'd been preparing all day. Rima had helped him to memorize the patterns of the constellations, and he was ready to point them out to Harriet.

He'd also managed to make a trade with one of the ghosts who lived on the floor below him. In exchange for a future favour, the third-floorer had grown some of Harriet's favourite flowers to decorate the room. Basically, it was gonna be freaking flawless. It would be *right* in a way that things had never been with any of the other girls in the building.

There was a space inside him that craved and ached for someone who was his. Someone who turned to him first; who loved him most. He had been consumed with a low-level loneliness for so long now that he had forgotten how anything else felt. Sometimes his stomach fizzled just talking to *Felix*, which had to be a sign that he needed to start dating again.

Maybe Harriet needed someone as much as he did. He had only known her for a few days, but she was special.

They had arranged to meet in his room. When the clock tower struck eleven, a deep fear rose from where he'd buried it. What if she stood him up?

To his relief, she stuck her head through the door a few minutes later. She had dressed up, too. She was bright with energy – in fact, she was almost glowing with it. She'd somehow transformed her grey shirt into a more elegant formal look; tying her scarf around her waist like a belt and adding some sort of twist to the side of her shirt.

"Your, er—" he waved at her hair, which she'd managed to manipulate into a plaited twist. "Looks nice."

"Thanks," Harriet said. "It's a fishtail plait; they're hard to do without hairspray."

"Oh?" he asked, holding out his arm. She took it, talking him through the hairstyle step by step while they walked to Rima's party. Kasper nodded along, as if he was listening instead of coasting along on pure relief that he hadn't had to come up with a conversation topic just yet. Girls were so much harder to talk to than Felix.

A group of lads were pre-gaming the party on the stairs to the second floor. They were playing volleyball with someone's shoe.

"Harriet's staying at Hotel Back Yourself, I see?" Jonny from Rowing Soc cat-called.

Kasper ignored their wolf-whistles, hurrying Harriet past. This was why Kasper spent so much time with Felix and the girls. The other ghosts here were a lot meaner.

Hotel Back Yourself was something the Rowing Society boys had done when they went travelling. They didn't book hotels, instead trusting that they'd find someone to take them home. Backing themselves.

Jonny meant that Harriet was only dating Kasper so that she'd have somewhere to sleep in Mulcture Hall. But that wasn't what Harriet was doing. She was going on a date with him because she *liked* him, obviously! Wasn't she?

He led Harriet over to the window in Rima's room, grinning. "I've got something to show you."

Kasper launched into a running jump through the window, grabbing on to the edge of the floor of the balcony above. He swung out over the side of the building, twisting his hands one over the other, spinning to face Harriet.

She looked confused, but he gave her a moment to stare at him dangling from the floor above. He was fully aware of how large his biceps looked when he flexed them to hold up his own body weight. Sometimes he caught Felix – who was lean instead of muscular – staring at his shoulders in jealousy.

When he couldn't hide his smirk any longer, Kasper tugged down the cascade of honeysuckle which the third-floorer had grown for him on the balcony above. It tumbled over the edge, hanging in a perfumed curtain of tangled leaves and flowers. The sunset spread through the ghostly pink blossoms, making them glow almost golden.

Kasper dropped back down to the floor, ridiculously pleased with himself. He'd got the idea from Felix, who (very occasionally) had conversations with Rima about what their dream weddings would look like. Felix had described an altar covered in flowers, and the idea had stuck in Kasper's mind. He hadn't been sure it would work, though. If it had failed, it would have been as embarrassing as the time he'd forgotten the word "elbow" in front of Felix, who was basically a walking dictionary. He'd called them "arm knees". *Arm knees.* It had taken Felix six years to stop bringing that up.

He should stop thinking about Felix. This was supposed to be about Harriet.

"Very fancy," she said, admiring the flowers. "I bet you do this for all the girls."

Kasper's smile dropped. He had been trying to make her feel special, not one in a long line of girls.

"You've got me all wrong," he said. "I'm not like that."

He plucked one of the flowers and tucked it behind her ear, twisting a curl of hair around his finger. He let the backs of his fingers touch the skin of her neck.

"Hey," she said suddenly. "Do you know anything about these ghosts who live in the basement? The Tricksters?"

He grimaced. Where had Harriet heard about them? She'd only been here a few days. "You should stay away from them. They're no good."

"Why?"

Kasper's brain and mouth didn't seem to want to cooperate. The truth was, the Tricksters terrified him. "They're always trying to collect new powers to add to their trade. They'll do anything to get the ones they want." Kasper shivered. A girl called Lisa had got into debt and disintegrated a few years ago. She'd got fainter and fainter as the Tricksters called in interest on the debt.

She'd begged Kasper to help her, but there had been nothing he could do. Whenever he'd gone down to the basement to ask them to release her, Rufus had just silently picked at his teeth with a slither of bone. Then one day, Lisa was gone completely.

"Wow," Harriet said, taking this in. "How did the Tricksters get control of the whole building like this? Practically everyone is scared of them. Who are they, really?"

This was not the romantic date he had imagined. "I don't know. I heard Rufus was a priest when he was alive." Kasper shivered. "And not a good one."

Rumours about the Tricksters spread through the building like wildfire. He'd heard that Vini had a weird and incredibly specific predilection for squirrel spirits – no one ever wanted to say why.

He'd also heard that Rufus made the ghosts in the basement gather every full moon to listen to his operatic concert performances in the pale moonlight that reached through the vents. He doubted if that one was true, but it was possible.

"But what do they *want*?" Harriet asked.

"They want control," he said dully. "They want everyone here to do what they say without question, immediately. They keep sending their goons after me, to try and force me to use my power for them. They hate the fact that I won't do it."

Greg came to find him sometimes, trying to bring him down to the basement to see the Tricksters. Greg could make you do what he wanted, if he set his mind towards persuading you. His power was potent. You couldn't even use threats to frighten him off, because apparently the Tricksters had eaten all of Greg's worry years before.

He'd heard that the Tricksters fed on emotions until they were gone completely. It was how they convinced people to work for them. Greg had no conscience now. He wasn't scared of anything people said to him any more, and he got threatened *a lot*. He would do everything the Tricksters asked of him, in exchange for rewards. Even if it meant condemning someone to disintegration.

Harriet leant forward. It was the first time that the full focus of her attention had been on Kasper. "Why are they so determined to have you? What *is* your power?"

There was a glint in her eyes. Kasper was flattered. She really wanted to get to know him, inside and out. This was it; he could feel it. She was finally connecting with him; looking at him like he was someone. *Her* someone.

He took her hand. Her warm skin was even softer than it looked. His thumb glided over the grey slick of her nail varnish.

Carefully, he kissed her. Harriet froze, and then her lips yielded. While Kasper's brain was buzzing with the rush of it all, she took control of the kiss.

With one hand in his hair, she tilted his head further to the side, guiding him into a deeper kiss. When her tongue pushed its way into his mouth, Harriet became everything. Nothing mattered but the softness of her hair; the forceful, determined way she held him in place to kiss him.

Was this how Felix would kiss, or would it be different with a boy? Not that he would ever know, of course.

All too soon, Harriet pulled away, her hand tightening on the back of his neck.

"Now … tell me about your power," she murmured, tickling the hairs on his forearm with her fingertips, "*babe*."

Before he could reply, Rima burst into the room, followed by Felix and Leah.

"It's party time!" Rima hollered. She must have made a trade with someone, because she was wearing a skeleton costume over her pyjamas. She was the kind of person who got *really* into parties. She didn't just celebrate her birthday on the day itself. The whole month beforehand revolved around planning the festivities. Between birthdays, death days and Halloween, they practically had a reason to celebrate on every day of the year.

"Let's rattle our booooones!" Rima yelled.

Kasper was suddenly filled with immense relief at the sight of his friends. The reaction surprised him, because he'd been enjoying kissing Harriet. It was hard to talk to her, though. Especially when she asked about his power.

FELIX

They were drunk. That was inherently obvious, even to Felix, who was almost certainly the most drunk of them all. In autumn, the air was filled with scattered energy from disintegrating insect ghosts and fallen leaves. It was possible to take it in, if you made a very determined effort.

"Unhand me, cur!" Leah said to Rima, as they duelled along the edge of the balcony wall.

Rima jabbed her in the side, making her wobble. "You aren't ever going to fit into modern society if you keep talking like that."

"Do I look like I have ever, in life or death, wanted to be part of society?" Leah hooked her ankle around Rima's calf, dislodging her.

"Foul villain, daddy-o!" Rima shouted. "Lily-livered airhead!"

"I think you're mixing time periods," Felix said, a laugh rumbling in his chest.

Rima tumbled off the wall and dive-bombed into the bedroom. The crowd parted in self-preservation. She had invited all their friends in the building, including some of Kasper's rowing mates and the fashion girls from the fourth floor. Even Qi was dancing in the corner with Marilena, a girl from the second floor who had once accidentally burst into flames when she'd lost control of her power.

"Wait! I've – I've got..." Rima towered above Felix and Leah, laughing too hard to finish talking. "Haha, wait, wait,

I've got – I've – hang on, gimme a sec, hah, I…"

"Absolute scenes here tonight, guys," Kasper said, when it was clear she wasn't going to stop laughing any time soon. He had the deep creases around his eyes that Felix knew meant he was trying hard not to laugh. "Simmer down, will you, Hamid?"

Kasper was curled up on the windowsill, almost sober even though he'd been drunk as often as possible when he was alive. Below him, Harriet was leaning against the wall. She seemed happy to just watch the party, though her quietness could have something to do with Kasper's dangling arm. His fingertips kept grazing her collarbone.

Something had changed about her, but Felix couldn't work out what it was.

"I've got an absolutely brilliant idea," Rima finally said. "Let's play Don't Get Me Started."

"Noooooo," Leah moaned, just as Kasper crowed, "Yes! Leah *has* to go first! Last time was classic!" He told Harriet, "The idea is to give someone a topic, like global warming or Ant and Dec, and see how long they can rant about it. Leah absolutely smashed it last time – she managed to complain about 'the calendar' for seven hours!"

"October really should be the eighth month," Leah said sullenly.

Lisa had loved this game, before she disintegrated. She was always the best at it, when Kasper brought her along to play.

"What's the topic?" Felix asked. He always invigilated when they played party games – it was his universally accepted position. Otherwise they'd get nowhere. "How about 'the Tooth Fairy'?"

This was so obviously the right choice that Leah, a glint of simmering rage already visible in her eyes, began talking immediately. She passed Claudia to Kasper, who juggled the baby with expertise gained from decades of babysitting.

"Don't get me started on this bloody Tooth Fairy nonsense. I hate it!" Leah began. "You want to know why? Firstly, it's immoral to lie to children. I know it's a cliché, but socially speaking..."

Felix found himself zoning out the longer she spoke. By the time Leah had finished, his buzz had died down.

"Way to harsh my mellow," Rima muttered. "You've officially ruined that game, Leah. That was the worst two hours of my life."

"It was only forty minutes, technically," Felix pointed out. "Unless you're taking into account the time-dilating effects of boredom."

Kasper started laughing at Felix, despite himself. He tipped his head back, revealing the underside of his jaw. "You get so articulate when you're drunk. *Vodka increases my productivity by thirteen per cent, I'll have you know*," he said in Felix's voice, adjusting invisible glasses.

"Hey," Felix said, and then, a beat later, "Yeah, all right. I get slightly more effusive when I'm drunk."

"Effusive!" Kasper repeated, delighted.

* * *

Sometime later, Felix realized that Harriet and Kasper were missing. He wandered into the next room and found them wrapped in each other's arms.

A long groan tugged its way from Kasper's throat. If Felix had to choose a word to describe their kissing style, it would be … *frantic. Desperate. Hungry.*

Felix's heart was pounding: a dull throb of pain racing in his chest. He took three deep breaths and twisted away, unable to watch.

Harriet closed her eyes, ignoring him. He wanted to tell her that Kasper was his, that she couldn't touch him – but he had no right to. He couldn't justify how much he hated the flow of her hands over Kasper's skin, tracing the lines of the muscles running over his ribs – and Felix was watching him again. He needed to look away. Right now.

Harriet was so much better than him. Felix couldn't compete. It wasn't like he was even trying.

Rima bumped into his back and gasped, tugging him back out of the room. Felix wasn't watching, he wasn't, he wasn't, he wasn't…

He wasn't picturing what they were going to do in there. He wasn't.

Felix wasn't drunk enough for this.

Felix was crying.

"Oh," Rima said, distraught on his behalf. "Oh no!"

She wrapped her arms around him, pulling him down to her level.

Felix sobbed into her shoulder, and when Rima tugged Leah closer, he pulled her into the hug, too, dropping a kiss onto Claudia's baby-warm head.

"I hate this so much," he said, snotty and embarrassed. He rubbed tears from his eyelashes, and his hands came away wet.

"I know," Rima said, pained. "I know."

HARRIET

Harriet tugged down Kasper's trousers, toppling backwards with him onto the mattress. She was suddenly starving with the need for touch and attention.

The energy from the Shell was doing something strange inside her. It wasn't like being drunk any more. It was like overdosing. Harriet had to pay absolute attention to keeping the energy under control, or it would start oozing out of her pores in a golden glow.

Her brain was running on double-time, struggling to keep up with the flow of information coming from her nerves. It made her jumpy and desperate, but the feel of Kasper's fingers on her skin gave her something human to focus on.

Kasper was moaning quiet exhales of noise into the pit of her neck. She dug her nails into his back, guiding him inside her. This was exactly what she needed to stop the energy taking over completely. It was lying dormant beneath her skin like an unexploded bomb. She still hadn't worked out whether she'd gained a power from the Shell at all.

"*Harriet,*" Kasper moaned, gasping into her mouth.

She rolled him over, cupping one hand over his mouth as she climbed on top of him.

"Just – quiet," she hissed.

He lay silent, staring up at her. Throwing her head back, Harriet tried to pretend that he wasn't there.

When he groaned long and low below her, she bit down on the urge to tell him that she wasn't *done*, and twisted her hips.

Shuddering, she finally came. She didn't know whether she was imagining the calming of her molecules, the reduction of the buzz of her energy. When she opened her eyes again, Kasper was gaping up at her with wide, amazed eyes. She didn't want him to look at her. She didn't want him to see this. This was for her, not for him.

His expression changed, then. He looked confused – and scared? Why would he be scared?

She glanced down. Her body, from head to toe, had turned clear. Wherever Kasper's limbs rested against hers, there was only air.

She was see-through. She was *invisible*! The Shell's power must have manifested!

Harriet had a moment of joy, and then pure fury swept over her – because this wasn't right. This wasn't the power she'd wanted. Invisibility wouldn't help her to get back to her family.

"Harriet?" Kasper asked, hands gently touching her sides, testing to see if she was really there.

"I'm here," she gasped.

"Your power!" He belatedly realized what was happening, and tried to kiss her. He missed, smashing his lips into her invisible cheekbone. "Wow, Harriet! Congratulations!"

"Thanks."

He let out a chuckle. "I feel like I'm getting to know the real you, at last," he said blissfully.

Harriet nodded, unnecessarily hiding a wince. She wasn't even sure who the real *her* was, it was so far buried beneath fabrications and stolen personality traits.

She felt numb. This wasn't what she wanted. What use was invisibility? She was going to have to try again, with another Shell. Immediately.

The energy in her veins insisted that she keep trying. She had to grow stronger. Right now, everything was spinning out of control.

Chapter 10

RIMA

The first thing Rima did when she woke was slide out from underneath a snoring Leah, who had fallen asleep with her head on Rima's stomach. Then she went to find Harriet. While she searched for her, Rima carefully ran over exactly what she wanted to say – for the third time. She'd been planning this conversation ever since Felix had started crying in her arms.

Rima hated telling people off. She really, truly hated it. But the look on Felix's face when Harriet had kissed Kasper had destroyed Rima. He'd grimaced as if his heart had crumbled into ash. Harriet had *known* how Felix felt, and she'd done it anyway.

Harriet wasn't in Kasper's room, or in the corridor. She wasn't in the foyer, where her corpse was starting to smell. Rima was walking back up to the fourth floor, wondering if she'd somehow missed Harriet dozing somewhere, when she ran into her on the stairs.

"Harriet!"

Harriet looked up, startled. Her face cleared when she saw Rima. "Oh. Hey."

Rima was about to launch straight into gently berating her, but Harriet was barely recognizable.

"Your hair has gone white! What…?"

"It has?" Harriet touched her head.

"It looks like—" Rima cut herself off. "You look like the Tricksters," she said dully.

She'd thought the Tricksters had white hair because they were ancient ghosts, losing their colour as they slowly drifted further away from their humanity. But Harriet had only been dead for a few days. Why was her hair so unnaturally white?

"Huh." Harriet brushed it back over her shoulders. "Weird. Maybe I'm their long-lost sister!" she joked.

Rima tilted her head. "I did hear a rumour that they used to have a brother, actually. He was apparently the worst of them all." Leah had said that he used to poison people, but Rima didn't know whether she had just been teasing her for believing idle gossip.

"Oh?" Harriet said, but she clearly wasn't interested. She was inspecting a strand of her snow-white hair.

"Are you OK?" Rima asked, concerned. Harriet was glowing almost golden with excess energy, pupils blown wide with the buzz. "You're all – blurry. Energy is pouring off you."

Harriet looked down at herself, brushing her hands over her thighs like she was trying to wipe the energy away. "I found a dead rat in the hallway. No one had got to the spirit yet. No big deal."

"No, it's something else…" Rima squinted at her. Her arm

kept slipping in and out of vision. "Harriet! You found your power!"

A look of surprise crossed Harriet's face. When she saw that Rima was pointing at her arm, the excitement changed into something like disappointment. "Oh. Yeah."

Rima wanted to dance. It had been heartbreaking to watch Harriet's panicked attempts to work out her power. "I'm so glad!"

She grabbed Harriet's arm, amazed that it was totally firm and yet completely invisible. "Can you do your whole body? Can you make other people invisible too? Do you still have a shadow? Do—"

Harriet was looking past Rima, like she had somewhere important to be and couldn't wait any longer. Rima cut herself off. Was Harriet only listening to her to be polite? "Are you...? Do you need to...?"

Harriet's eyes flicked back to hers. "No, sorry. I'm listening."

"Right. Anyway..." Rima swallowed. It was probably time. "I wanted to talk to you about something important." She cleared her throat. Her mind had gone completely blank as a wave of heat washed over her. "About last night. It wasn't fair to kiss Kasper in front of Felix like that."

Harriet's forehead furrowed. "What do you mean?"

"You knew that he liked him," she said, annoyed at how small her voice came out. She rubbed her fingers over the ends of her sleeves, pulling them down over her knuckles. "Felix was really upset when you two went off together. He *cried*, Harriet."

Instead of apologizing, Harriet rolled her eyes. "It's not like I'm stealing Kasper away from him. Hasn't he ever heard of a one-night stand?"

"One-night...?" Rima repeated, slightly squeakily. "You mean you don't even like Kasper? And you *did it in front of Felix*? Harriet, that's not how you treat your friends! That's—"

"Oh, bugger off, Rima. I literally could not care less about this petty playground gossip stuff. I've got more important things to worry about than some weirdo's hurt feelings."

Rima flinched as if she'd been slapped, ice spreading through her stomach. She'd thought that Harriet liked them. But all this time she thought they were *weirdos*?

"Right." Rima looked down at the concrete steps. Her vision was blurry, and she blinked rapidly. She couldn't cry, not in front of Harriet. "I should, er..."

She was turning away, wiping her eyes, when she registered the sirens. There was an insistent electronic horn outside, getting louder and louder.

Behind her, Harriet gasped. "They've found me." The scorn had disappeared from her voice, replaced with pure, unfiltered excitement. "They've come for me!"

Rima let out an exclamation of surprise, but Harriet was already running, crashing her way down three flights of stairs to the foyer.

Rima swallowed down her hurt. There would be time for Harriet to apologize later. For now, her corpse was more important than a little fight, especially one that was probably a misunderstanding anyway. She had to wake up the others.

Pushing her way through the bedroom door, Rima ran over to shake Kasper awake. He was sprawled over a rotten bare mattress in his boxer shorts.

He rubbed sleep out of his eyes. "Rima? What's…?"

"The police have come for Harriet's body! Get up, get up, get up!"

"Where is she?" His voice was thick.

"I found her upstairs. She's gone down to the foyer already. Her hair is white now, did you know? FELIX! GET UP!"

Felix was curled up on the floor in Rima's bedroom, his head resting on a pile of Chinese takeaway menus. Without opening his eyes, he groaned mulishly and pressed his face into the concrete.

"The police are here! Can't you hear the sirens?"

Felix stretched, limbs splayed out like a starfish, and let out a lengthy, extravagant yawn. "I thought it was your terrible singing."

"We need to go," Kasper said, pulling on his shirt. "Harriet needs me."

Felix's expression dropped into pure despair. "Right. Harriet."

Rima looped her arm through Felix's, as they followed Kasper downstairs. They left Leah asleep on the fire escape. This was nothing she hadn't seen dozens of times before.

"We have to talk later about Kasper," she whispered in his ear.

"Do we?" Felix replied, sounding like he wanted to stab something.

Rima squeezed his arm. Unfortunately, they probably did. Before this love triangle business got even messier.

Harriet's hair went white for the same reason she's starting to lose control. Her body can't handle so much energy. It's sending her nerves into overdrive. Every molecule of her body is vibrating at a frequency that's much too high, trying to keep all that energy under control. The lightning-bright flow sent her hair white with the shock of the electric force.

Even worse, it's affecting her brain too. All those subconscious thoughts that we work so hard to keep hidden? Harriet won't have the capacity to control them any more. They're roaming free. Her darkest desires – the ones she's ashamed even cross her mind – are coming to the forefront now. The energy is eating up her fear and guilt and empathy and spitting out anger and reckless determination in their place. She's come a long way since her death.

Rufus and Vini were quick enough to tell Harriet to steal powers, but they'd never do it themselves. They know that they'd go mad if they did. Instead, they stick with just the one power, and let their subordinates take the risks of gathering more.

I think it's time to look back at the moment Harriet died, now that the snippets of the future I've seen over the centuries have begun to reveal themselves. I can start planning and testing theories for how we'll get from Point A to Point B.

When I first saw her in the future, I tried to find the moment of her death. But it's like trying to find a needle in a haystack. Dipping in at random periods is no way to find answers. I usually saw snapshots of Kasper snoring in his bedroom, or Rima stroking Cody's fur, or Felix wiping his glasses. Quiet, peaceful moments. No big conversations that revealed exactly the information I needed to know. No dramatic showdowns.

But now I know when and where Harriet's death happened, I can find it again. I can go back to the past and see those important seconds before Harriet cracked her skull open on the steel beam.

Let's replay it. Harriet is walking up the stairs to the top floor of Mulcture Hall. She's taking photographs and listening to pop music. She's getting a call from her grandmother.

It's about to happen. You've seen it before, so you know the score. This time, shall we look at it from another side? You might see something different.

Harriet walks towards the edge of the stairwell. She

doesn't notice the barriers, pushed up against the walls – or the dust-free places where the bright yellow warning signs used to stand. But we do, don't we?

Someone moved them. Those barriers were there to stop people from going too close to the broken edge of the floor, where it had collapsed. Now they're stacked up against a wall, out of sight.

There's something else I didn't see before. Right at the edge, before floor becomes air becomes a deadly fall, there's a wire. Strung at ankle height, in the perfect place to make someone trip over the edge.

There she goes now, past the barriers and warning signs, talking to her gran about Autumnwatch. *And her shoe catches, as we knew it would, on the hair-thin tripwire.*

And then she's nothing but blood and shards of bone and a very angry, very confused ghost.

Someone made this happen. Harriet Stoker's death wasn't an accident.

It was murder.

Chapter 11

HARRIET

Harriet crashed into the foyer, taking the stairs three at a time, just as the police officers in bulletproof vests piled out of their cars. She stood by her corpse, waiting with clenched fists. Her hands were slipping in and out of visibility, but she couldn't focus enough to control it.

She pressed a hand to her forehead. Her temples burned. Her brain was melting. Everything ached. Had she made a mistake, going back up to the Shells?

After Kasper had fallen asleep the night before, she'd slipped away to the fifth floor to claim the powers of another Shell. The excess energy made her ignore everything except getting another fix.

She felt guilty, but her hunger outweighed everything else. It no longer mattered if the Shell disintegrated. That concern felt blurry and far away. She couldn't even remember why she'd been so worried about it. Getting powers was more important.

When she reached the top floor, the Shells had all skittered in a panic. She had chased them from room to room, finally pinning them in the corner of the building, up against an outer wall where they couldn't escape.

Choosing a boy at random, she had tugged him forwards, ignoring the petrified shrieks that burst from his mouth. This one struggled more than the last, and it had taken all her strength to hold it long enough to suck it clean of energy. It screamed the whole time.

It didn't last long enough, but her body had still cried out for more energy. Mindless, she had lunged at another Shell. They were all wailing now.

The second Shell disintegrated in her grasp, which was frustrating – and quite clever, for a Shell. To her horror, the others all followed suit, collapsing into the ashy remnants of their molecules before she had a chance to take them in.

Harriet had been furious, screaming up at the early morning pink of the sky, and feeling her rage unravel. She'd tried to push it back inside, like she usually did when she felt this way, but the fresh energy had made that impossible. She'd screamed until the feeling subsided.

Her skin had started glowing with a fluorescent, hyper-bright colour. Energy oozed from her pores, harsh and electric. It ached in the roots of her teeth, a bone-deep throbbing richness. It would keep her going for a while, even without any more Shells.

The energy was still thrumming through her veins, but the buzz had calmed down enough that Harriet was aware of what she was doing again. It was like she was watching her actions from a great distance. Even as Harriet had shouted at Rima, she had known that she shouldn't be doing it – that it wasn't fair or rational. But though Rima had looked hurt and sad, hunching her shoulders inwards and avoiding Harriet's gaze, she couldn't stop herself.

The energy was twisting everything in Harriet's head.

In one night, she'd messed up all her progress – sleeping with Kasper, upsetting Felix, shouting at Rima. It was going to be hard to convince them that she would be a good friend now.

Plus, Rima might still be helpful. Harriet had put a lot of work into staying on her good side.

The entrance hall was crowded with so many ghosts that Harriet couldn't even see her corpse. Qi and Greg were there, along with most of the other ghosts she'd met during the last few days. Presumably, they were waiting to see if Harriet had a catastrophic emotional breakdown when the police moved her body.

The police officers shone torches around the foyer, illuminating spiderwebs, broken glass; and then stiff, yellowing skin; the black congealed blood surrounding Harriet's head.

An officer let out a gasp, her hand rising involuntarily to her throat. "Jesus *Christ.*"

Harriet couldn't control her breathing – she gulped air down uselessly, faster and faster. She could feel the eyes of all the ghosts on her, waiting for a reaction. She wasn't going to give them one.

Don't show weakness. Don't give them anything they can use against you. Her gran's words comforted her. She stood straighter.

There was a long moment of silence – among both the living and the dead – and then it was all action. Radios began crackling with static, and the room filled with more police. When Harriet still didn't start wailing, several of the ghosts drifted away, disinterested.

Kasper appeared at her side. He silently tugged her towards him, fingers sliding up her wrists to smooth warm lines down her veins.

"This is good, right?" he said, trying to read her expression.

Harriet was too tired and numb to care what her face was telling him.

She couldn't even bring herself to reply. She was so sick of the feelings that her death had forced on her. In the last few days, she had needed to acknowledge more of her own emotions than she had since her parents had died.

After a few minutes, the radio dispatcher said, *"Can someone tell the grandmother?"*

Harriet's heart stuttered. Her gran was going to be told she was dead, that her only surviving family member had died. She was the last one left, having lost her husband, her son and his wife, and now her granddaughter.

Harriet wanted to cry. No, she wanted to hit something.

The forensics team were taking samples from the bloody concrete around her corpse, filling evidence bags with tiny fragments of her skull. Harriet's hand rubbed at the hole in the back of her head, hidden under her hair. If she pressed hard enough, she could feel the sharp edges of bone. She shivered, pulling her fingers away even though it didn't hurt at all.

Qi came over and said, "My condolences, Miss Stoker. I do hope you'll feel more settled, now that this inconvenience is out of the way. You'll be able to move on."

Harriet tried to accept this kindly. Her body was more than an inconvenience to her, even if that's all it was to Qi. But she wasn't going to snap at Qi like she had at Rima.

"I hope so," she said.

"You're looking very bright today. The new hair is pretty. You must be getting on well?"

Heat rushed through her in an odd mixture of guilt and dread. Was it that obvious that she'd absorbed so much energy? Harriet couldn't meet Qi's eye in case she worked out what she'd done to the Shells. To explain why she was glowing so much, she said, "I've been very well, thank you. Everyone has been generous. I've been given lots of rodents."

Qi said, bemused, "How unusual. I've clearly underestimated the kindness of the Mulcture Hall residents. This was a gesture of goodwill, was it?"

"Something like that," Harriet replied. She could barely manage to make the words audible. After everything, Qi still scared her. The memory of her lightning bonds skittered over Harriet's forearms. She wrapped her arms around her torso.

"What else have you been doing?" Qi asked. "Apart from charming everyone into giving you spirits, of course."

Harriet swallowed. Why was she asking these questions? Did she want something from her? "Nothing much. Getting to

177

know everyone, you know! Idle chit-chat. Nothing too exciting."

"I hear you've explored the lower floors, too. Someone saw you going down to the basement earlier."

Harriet blanched. "The basement? Huh. No, I don't think that was me."

Qi eyed her. "Hmm. Let me know if you need any advice. I'll be keeping an eye on you, in case you … get into any trouble." She stared hard at Harriet for the length of three heartbeats – long enough for Harriet to start planning her escape route if Qi attacked.

Qi smiled and clapped her hands together. "Well! I hope the police finish up quickly. I can never get to sleep when there are humans in the building. Everyone gets far too overexcited."

Harriet relaxed a little. Maybe she'd imagined Qi's suspicion? She couldn't find the words to say goodbye, so she just dipped her head.

"Bye, Qi!" Kasper said, apparently oblivious to the undertones of their conversation.

"Have a good one, Kasper. Now, I'll be off. I'm in the middle of the most interesting experiment with a woodlouse spirit."

Harriet hoped that the woodlouse disintegrated on her. "Have fun!" she said brightly.

Qi didn't die on the same night as the other students. They all died together in a sudden, inexplicable accident which baffled the police.

But Qi wasn't part of that. She died ten years earlier in her sleep from an early-onset heart failure. In 1994, she was here to greet everyone. Qi was the one to explain how to be a ghost to Felix, Rima and Kasper. She put up with their tears and denials and anger, until she got too absorbed in her research.

She was even there the first time Felix came out. Rima had told him how much she'd liked his cute brother Oscar, who had survived the mysterious incident. She'd then smiled shyly at Felix as if she liked him too.

He'd blurted it out immediately – "I'm gay, sorry!" Then, "Oh. That's the first time I've ever said that."

Qi had been the one to say into the surprised silence, "Congratulations!" Then she'd glared at the others until they'd rushed to agree.

For all this time, she's been studying the physics of ghost powers, hypnotism, shapeshifting and possession. She's learnt a lot, but despite all her time and effort, it won't be enough to make a difference.

HARRIET

"We should go," Kasper said in Harriet's ear, after they'd stood watching the police work for three hours. "You don't have to watch it all."

He'd taken hold of her hand again. He was clearly enjoying playing the role of supportive boyfriend in front of the other ghosts.

"No." She said it through clenched teeth. It wasn't enough to watch the police meticulously file and process every aspect of her death. When they lifted her corpse onto a stretcher and carried it through the front door, Harriet sprang into action. Time was running out. This was the perfect opportunity to try to leave Mulcture Hall again.

She would dissolve outside of a building, but what if she could follow her own body? Maybe that was different. She could tag along with her body in the ambulance, and from there, she might be able to get home.

There was a police car parked only a few metres from the entrance. If she could make it that far without disintegrating, the car might take her to her gran's house, when they went to tell her the bad news.

Surely, with all her new energy and powers, she was strong enough to get that far? It was a crazy idea, but right now she was desperate enough to try anything.

She walked towards the main entrance, tugging her hand free of Kasper's grip. As she passed, she waved her hand in a police officer's face, but he didn't even blink.

Beyond the line of police cars, students from the nearby buildings had gathered to see the crime scene. She caught sight of a girl from her lectures. Harriet had tried to chat with her before class once, but it had been awkward and strained, and the girl hadn't sat near her again, after that.

Now, Harriet focused on her, concentrating on moving towards the police cars, and keeping her atoms firmly in place.

"Harriet?" Kasper shouted in panic. "Harriet?!"

The girl had curly hair, dyed pink at the tips.

Harriet took a step. She was not disintegrating. Not this time. Her new power was seconds away from kicking in, she knew it. She was going to leave this awful place.

The girl's glasses were horn-rimmed, round and glossy, and Harriet was completely, totally corporeal. Her atoms were behaving like normal atoms and staying inside her body.

Harriet took a step. Harriet took a step. Harriet took a step.

The car was close, but out of reach. If she could keep going, then she would be free.

The girl was still there, talking to a police officer guarding the entrance. Harriet knew she was there, but suddenly she couldn't see her. Her eye twitched, involuntarily.

The noise of the crowd and the car engines had disappeared, replaced by a high-pitched, aching thrum in her eardrums.

Harriet stopped. She stared down at where her feet would be, if only she could see them, willing herself to take another step.

But she didn't have feet, and there was nowhere to step to,

and nothing existed, and Harriet couldn't even remember what she was, was, was, was, was, was, was, was…

KASPER

What was she *doing*? Harriet had been dealing so well with the police. She'd held his hand as she watched the whole thing without even crying. But then she'd pulled away from him and left the building.

Kasper had to go after her. She was disintegrating. Harriet was disintegrating, and he had no choice. He was petrified.

He took a step forwards then stopped, foot hovering outside the building. He couldn't do this. He wasn't like Rima, who had gone charging outside after Harriet without a second thought last time. His heart was thundering in his ears, and all he wanted to do was run and hide, but he could see Harriet's atoms peeling away faster and faster as she walked.

She was only ten metres away. He should run after her. His muscles refused to move. He was going to throw up.

Kasper hated himself. Harriet needed him, and he was a coward. Just like he had been with Lisa. Kasper had been too caught up in fear to stand up to the Tricksters when she'd begged Kasper to help her. Even when it was clear that the constant demands on her power were causing her to disintegrate. Even when Rufus had offered him a way to save his friend, by asking Kasper to let them use his power.

He couldn't do that again. Not to Harriet. He wasn't going to let her disappear right in front of him after one night together.

Kasper shook himself. He could do this. He could.

He swallowed a lump of pure fear that had stuck in his throat and broke into a sprint. Somewhere behind him, Greg let out a delighted holler of disbelief.

Kasper made it to Harriet, sweeping her up in his arms. But when he turned, the air felt gelatine-thick around him. Her limbs were heavy and loose, her expression vacant.

He managed to walk a metre back towards the building, powered by pure determination, before he started to forget what he was supposed to be doing. His speed slowed, and he pushed back against it.

It was too late. Harriet was a cloud in his arms, shivering back and forth in the breeze. This was a suicide mission. They were both going to disintegrate.

Kasper pressed his lips to the remains of Harriet's cheek. He couldn't tell which atoms were his and which were hers. He had failed. He hadn't been brave or quick or strong enough to save her. Gorgeous, confident, clever Harriet, who had trusted him. He had never deserved her.

When the force of an impact shivered through him, he was unprepared. Something had passed through him. *Someone.* That was all it took for his subconscious to come alive.

It awakened some base instinct inside him – the power he'd pushed down for decades seized control for the first time.

Human. Soul. Take it.

Kasper turned his head, the ragged edges of his mouth forming a gaping, hungry chasm. Whenever he was near a living human, all he could think about was possessing them. He got the urge to join their souls inside the bodies and take them for himself. His power repulsed him. He never let himself think about it.

Sometimes, he found himself daydreaming about this moment, completely overcome with the desperate need to know what it felt like. Whenever a human entered Mulcture Hall, his power whispered at him, persuading him to try it, just the once. He'd come close before, but he'd always held back the monster inside. Even when it hurt, he'd always stopped it. Being in the entrance hall with the police had been just bearable – he could push the hunger down, ignore the saliva that collected in his mouth whenever they passed close by.

But nothing could stop him now. The human had touched him, and all his control was gone.

Dropping Harriet, he latched on to the police officer who had walked through him. He passed inside the body, which jolted at the force of his determined entry. It was easy and natural, now that he wasn't fighting against himself.

A feeling of panic and revulsion passed through the neurons to Kasper as the body's soul fought him. He pressed it deep down into the subconscious to make room for himself.

Stretching out, he took a second to acclimatize, and then connected. His soul clicked into place in the brain. Immediately, vision jolted through him. Light became shapes became eyes, and then a mouth and face and a body. *He had a living body.*

Kasper let himself spread out, feeling along the nerves to find the fingers and toes, firing electric instructions down the pathways to wriggle his new limbs. Deep inside the body's brain, a voice screamed. Kasper ignored it.

He stared around at the world with real vision for the first time in decades, breathed air with lungs that were fresh and new. The old soul's terror changed into Kasper's delight, and the body smiled.

Abruptly, Kasper remembered who he was, and what he'd done, and what had happened to Harriet. He twisted, stumbling as he found his new centre of gravity. He searched the air for any last remaining traces of Harriet. There. A twisting spiral of grey.

He pulled the cloud of molecules inside the body with him, keeping what was left of Harriet safe.

Kasper walked towards the building in slow and stumbling steps. He could feel Harriet was struggling for freedom, so he squeezed her reassuringly, pleased that there was enough of her left to panic. The small voice in the depths of the brain was still screaming.

Inside the foyer, he released Harriet. For a moment, he thought it was too late for her, but then the cloud twisted in mid-air and re-formed as Harriet. She gasped for breath, heaved like she was about to vomit, and then stood upright.

"Kasper?" she asked, looking wide-eyed at the body.

He opened the body's mouth, trying to remember how to vibrate vocal cords and speak.

"Me," he forced out, and then, "Yes – it's – me."

"You've possessed her," she said, eyes widening in what was either shock or delight. "Is that your power?"

Kasper twisted the body's muscles in a slow smile. He couldn't understand why he'd resisted the urge to possess all these years. It felt so good. It felt inevitable.

He lifted a hand to touch Harriet's cheek, but Felix dived for Kasper, pushing his way inside the body and colliding solidly with him.

Kasper pulled Felix close, pleased that he'd joined him. It would be so much better if he had someone here with him. That would drown out the sound of screaming.

"Let go of the body, Kasper. Now," Felix said, his voice layered with the full force of his hypnotism.

Against his will, Kasper found himself releasing his hold on the brain. He slipped free of the body, as the soul he'd pushed aside expanded back into the space he'd taken from it. Kasper fell to the ground with Felix sprawled out on top of him.

It took Kasper a second to process what had happened. Then he burst into action, furiously writhing underneath Felix. He had to get back inside the body and retake control before it disappeared for ever. It was his, and Felix had no right to force him out. It had felt so good, being inside something so warm and alive and full of energy. He needed that back, right now.

Felix hissed, *"What the hell are you doing?"* and held on more tightly to Kasper.

"It's mine!" he yelled, struggling to escape. "Let me go! I need it!"

Panic exploded in his mind like fireworks. He couldn't live without a body, not now he knew what it felt like. It was so cold and vulnerable and dull out here without a solid form. His instincts had been right all along. He was meant to have a body. It was his right.

Felix fought him, pinning Kasper to the ground with a surprising amount of strength.

"Someone *help me!*" Felix yelled, voice thin and frantic. He clamped his hands around Kasper's shoulders, knees locked to the ground, but his arms were trembling. He couldn't hold Kasper down for long. And the body was still there, frozen in shock while its current soul tried to process what had just happened.

He still had time to claim it. For him and Felix. It could be theirs, to share. Kasper heaved upwards with all his might, and in one smooth movement rolled Felix over to the side. He broke free of his grip and staggered to his feet.

Then a hand touched the back of his neck. Gentle, soft fingers stroked the skin, and then sharp fingernails dug in.

Suddenly, he was filled with a staggering, overwhelming terror, so complete that it stopped him in his tracks. Everything went monstrous and threatening. He was so so scared. Whatever it was, it *hurt*. Kasper's vision went blurry. He fell forwards as everything abruptly faded to black.

In the late twelfth century, there was a ghost here
who could possess people, like Kasper. This was before
Mulcture Hall was built, of course. When there was
nothing here but farmland, ancient ruins and one little
wattle-and-daub barn.

It was quiet, for a century or two. The only time we got
new company was when a tramp took shelter alongside the
cattle and died in his sleep. Though for one golden summer,
the farmer's son brought the butcher's daughter here every
night at dusk. That kept us all entertained for a while.

We fed off the spirits of calves and lambs from the
slaughterhouse next door — and sometimes, when everyone
got bored, we'd hunt the youngest ghosts and feast until we
were bright with energy for a few more decades.

One day, a pedlar took shelter in the barn during a spot
of light drizzle. He hit his head on the door frame, dying
quickly. He adapted to being a ghost even faster.

The pedlar's power worked like Kasper's, but he wasn't
afraid to use it. The farmer was convinced the barn was
haunted, because any time he came near, he would lose

control of his limbs and dance the jig. It made us all laugh – and stopped us from hunting the pedlar down, for a little while. That didn't last, but the pedlar had a good run of it.

After a dozen possessions, the farmer started to change. He became jumpy and confused, holding tight to his dog's collar for comfort whenever he fetched something from the barn. He would often stop and stare into space, lost inside his own brain, like he had forgotten how to think for himself after having someone else take the reins so often.

Still, it was a lot of fun. Kasper is missing out – I don't know what he's so worried about. But then, I'm still getting the hang of morals and ethics and all those modern concepts. My father raised me according to his own rules, which valued power, secrets and control above ethical concerns. You haven't met him yet. You've only seen traces of him, heard echoes all over the hall.

You will meet him soon enough.

Chapter 12

FELIX

Felix's breath left his chest in a *whump* when Kasper collapsed on top of him, unconscious. Harriet was staring down at them both in complete shock.

"What just happened?" Felix asked, wheezing. It had been so quick that his brain was threatening to short out. Kasper had rescued Harriet, and then lost control and accidentally possessed a police officer. Felix had used hypnotism to force him to release the woman and then Harriet had touched his skin, and – what? What *had* Harriet done to him?

"I don't know," she said, and looked from Kasper to her hand, still raised from where she'd gripped his neck. "I think I knocked him out."

"What?"

Behind them, Felix heard a paramedic say to the police officer, "Are you all right, Petra?"

"Just had a dizzy spell for a second there," Petra said, sounding stunned.

Felix winced. Kasper – who was completely unconscious and breathing damply into Felix's collarbone – was going to be horrified when he woke up and realized what he'd done. His biggest nightmare had come true. He'd accidentally possessed someone. Kasper wouldn't be able to live with the guilt. For his sake, Felix hoped that he stayed asleep for as long as possible.

"Sorry, what did you do?"

Harriet was still staring at her hand, blindsided. "I think it's my power." Slowly, like a cobra preparing to strike, she smiled. The expression, combined with the unnaturally white hair, sent shivers down Felix's spine. "I think I can control emotions. I can see them all inside you – like harp strings waiting to be plucked."

Felix was chilled to the core. Harriet was dangerous. And stronger than they'd ever imagined.

"I don't understand," Rima said. "*Invisibility* is your power. Isn't it?"

Harriet shrugged.

Harriet had *two* powers? He'd never heard of such a thing.

At that moment, Kasper gave a little groan.

"Come on," Rima said. "Let's get Kasper upstairs. We can make him more comfortable there."

Felix helped her carry him up to the bedrooms. Their bystanders stared after them in disappointment, clearly wishing they could carry on watching the drama. It was probably the most exciting thing they'd seen in years.

They propped Kasper up in the corner of Rima's room. He groaned again.

"Where's Leah?" Felix asked. He hadn't seen her down in the foyer.

"I'm here. Unfortunately," Leah said, coming in from where she'd been sleeping on the fire escape with Claudia. When she saw Kasper, and noticed Harriet's bone-white hair, she raised her eyebrows. "What did I *miss*?"

As Rima brought her up to date, Felix stood at the window watching the police cars pull away. Kasper was starting to come around. He leant forwards, his head falling heavily between his knees. There was sweat on the back of his neck. Felix could hardly stand to look at him, knowing that he was hurting but unable to offer any comfort.

Right after Lisa had disintegrated, Kasper had retreated to his room in grief and guilt, convinced it was his fault because she'd asked him to help her stop the Tricksters. Felix had sat with him in the dark and the light and dark again. He'd wrapped his arms around Kasper, who hadn't said a word through all the long days. Finally, in a voice rusty with disuse, he'd told Felix, "If you hum any more Christmas songs, I'm going to scream. It's *August*, you monster."

Afterwards, Kasper had acted like his long grieving period hadn't happened. Felix had never been able to work out what to say to bring back the peaceful, trusting companionship that Kasper had allowed for such a brief time. Eventually, he'd given up trying. It was easier to return to the old bickering dynamic their relationship had always had.

"How do we know you did anything to Kasper at all?" Rima

asked Harriet. "Maybe the possession was just too much for him and he passed out on his own. Two powers is impossible, it's—"

"No. I did it." Harriet's expression was vacant, like she wasn't seeing them at all. "I thought he had gone crazy and was going to hurt that human. When I tried to pull him away, something clicked in my head, like a sense I hadn't known I had. I realized that if I touched him, I could push a feeling of fear over him and immobilize him."

No. Felix felt sick. It couldn't be true. She couldn't possibly have two powers.

"Prove it," Leah said, voice tense. "Show us your powers."

Harriet held out one hand to Rima, palm upwards. "Can I?"

Rima looked from the hand to Felix, tilting her head questioningly. He nodded once. He had to know for sure whether Harriet could do this. Surely she wouldn't risk doing anything to hurt Rima, not while the four of them were here to stop her? Well, three of them. Judging by Kasper's still vacant expression, he wouldn't be much use in a fight.

Rima swallowed tightly and took Harriet's hand. Her brow furrowed as she focused on where they touched. Almost immediately, tears welled in the corners of Rima's eyes. She wrenched her hand away.

"Stop!" she gasped, as tears flooded her cheeks. "Oh, make it stop, plea—"

Rima clutched at her stomach, bent double, then shivered and transformed into a silvery grey wolf. It tipped its head back and howled, the sound as painfully mournful as anything Felix had ever heard.

Kasper watched from the corner, looking queasy and confused. Harriet looked astonished, mouth half open.

"Harriet!" Felix yelled, horrified. "Stop it!"

Jolted into action, Harriet touched the tip of the wolf's ear. It stopped mid-howl, throat billowing.

The wolf tilted its head to one side, curious and confused. Then it twisted around and began happily licking its rear end as if nothing had happened.

This is actually the first time I saw Rima. This moment, a flash of the future – Rima twisting into a wolf, while Harriet watches. I saw it during the Jacobite risings. Just like this.

For me, Harriet was there from the very start. I assumed she would arrive along with Rima and the others. That's why it was such a surprise that Harriet came later. There was always an empty space waiting for her. Her shadow was standing among us, and only I could see it.

Then, one night, I was sleeping in the corner of Rima's room while she watched VHS tapes of The X-Files. *A bright flash woke me up, but before I realized what was happening, it was already over. There was no time to react. Something had happened, and Rima was dead.*

I still don't know what caused it.

FELIX

"Well. That worked." Felix licked his suddenly dry lips. It had worked. *It had worked.*

"Can you turn back, Rima?" Leah asked, stroking one hand down the wolf's back. The wolf twisted back into Rima, who sat on her haunches and *glared* at Harriet.

"You couldn't have picked joy instead of sorrow? That was the most depressing thing I've ever felt in my entire life!"

Harriet shrugged. "You're a very cheerful person. I had to make you do something out of character."

"It was still shitty. And how have you got *two powers*?"

Felix swallowed. "Did you accidentally take some energy from the police officer while Kasper was inside?"

Kasper made a pained, cut-off noise, and buried his head in his hands.

"Er, no. I don't think I took anything from her. Can you even take powers from living people? Is that a thing?" Harriet asked.

"I have no idea. But how *else* could you have two powers?"

"Right," Harriet said. "About that…"

Felix jerked his head up. She knew why this was happening. "Harriet?"

She folded her arms, already on the defensive. "I wanted a power. I couldn't wait. So … I sped up the process a bit."

"What did you do, Harriet?" Leah asked. She hadn't seemed bothered by Harriet's drama until Rima had been hurt. Now she was watching Harriet with a wary, preparatory expression.

Felix was pleased that someone else finally saw what he did in Harriet – danger.

Leah continued, "Your hair is white, which means you must have got a whole lot of energy from somewhere. What have you been playing at?"

Eyes on the ceiling, Harriet said, "I went to see the Tricksters."

Rima swore, short and fast. "What did they do? Did they hurt you?"

"Not as such. They explained to me how I could take, um, leftover powers."

Felix frowned. He'd never heard of any powers being *leftover*. "What does that mean?"

"You know, where they aren't being used. Going to waste. Like … with the Shells."

Rima gasped. "They made you steal a power from a Shell? Oh, Harriet, you poor thing. You should never have gone near the Tricksters. They can't be trusted."

Kasper looked wide awake now. Rufus and Vini had been trying to persuade Kasper to possess humans for them for years, ever since they'd found out what his unused power did. They would probably be delighted when they heard that he'd finally used his power. If they'd got to Harriet, too, who knows what terrible things she could have learnt?

"How did you do it?" Felix asked. There was something about the set of her shoulders that made him think she was hiding something.

Harriet froze. She looked between them and swallowed hard. "I... It wasn't that bad, I promise." She was pleading with them now. Whatever she'd done, she clearly really wanted them to forgive her for it.

Immediately, Felix understood. If it was possible to take someone's power, then there was only one way that could be done. "You took their energy, didn't you?"

Harriet looked trapped. "No!" She paused. "OK. Yes. I did."

Taking another ghost's energy was forbidden. It was the absolute most important rule – the unthinkable thing that would get you sent straight down to the basement. Even the thought of doing it made Felix want to throw up. It was cannibalism, pure and simple.

"How much? A little bit of energy, a taste? Or – or all of it?"

She didn't want to answer. Her denial was clear from her expression.

"Did they disintegrate?" he pressed. "Harriet?"

Every muscle in her neck was tensed when she nodded.

"No," Rima said, the word cracking down the middle.

"How many?" Leah's voice was hard as stone.

Felix's mouth was dry. Too dry to speak. Felix had been a Shell just days ago. It was only luck that meant he'd absorbed some of Harriet's stray energy when she died. He could easily have been up on the fifth floor instead, still a Shell even now. He could have been the person Harriet had killed.

Harriet couldn't meet their gazes. "Two. A girl and a boy. The others disintegrated on their own."

Rima had turned pale. She looked like she was about to faint. Kasper had gone green, wrapping his hands around his knees as he hugged himself.

This was worse than anything Felix had imagined Harriet was capable of. She had done this more than once. She hadn't just tried it and found it repulsive and sickening. She'd gone back for more.

Now all of the fifth-floorers were gone? *For ever?* Felix cursed himself for not doing something to help bring them back from being Shells. He'd been too distracted to think about them and now they were gone for ever.

Felix thought vaguely that they would have to send Harriet to the basement now, but he didn't know how to make that happen. Usually, when someone was sent to the basement, there was shouting and violence and anger. They were marched downstairs by Qi, who would imprison them inside with lightning. But Harriet was still looking at them like she'd made a terrible mistake. Like this was all a trick that the Tricksters had played on her. Was she a victim here?

"You destroyed them," Rima said. She was clearly struggling to believe it.

"You told me that the Shells are close to disintegrating," Harriet said. "It was inevitable. I hurried it along a bit, that's all." She was staring out of the window, watching a pigeon fluff its feathers on the sill. "It's euthanasia, more than anything."

"It's murder," Kasper said.

Harriet went very still.

"They only needed a bit of energy and they'd be just like the rest of us." He had his head in his hands. "I told you that, when we went to find your phone. You can't pretend you didn't know."

Harriet's face twisted in a conflict of emotions. "It's irrelevant now, anyway. I put them out of their misery."

Felix was suddenly furious. Harriet was a liar. Nothing she was saying was true. She had never thought about anyone but herself, not once since she'd arrived.

"You made them disintegrate!" he shouted at Harriet. "That's far worse than being a *Shell*. You can't pretend that you did it for their sake, when all you've ever cared about is yourself!"

Harriet lunged at him, teeth bared and pure hatred in her eyes. Kasper was at Felix's side in an instant, as Felix skittered back on his heels. He pushed Felix behind him as Leah leapt forward to block Harriet's path.

Felix had a sudden vision of Harriet sending them all into comas. All she would need to do was touch them and she could knock them out, or take all their energy like she had with the Shells. He had to stop this before it got that far.

"Everyone, calm down. This isn't productive," he tried to say, but the air was so full of voices it was impossible to distinguish any words. Rima was yelling, and Harriet was hissing out threats, and Leah was muttering something ancient and lethal while Claudia wailed in her arms, and Kasper— Felix focused his attention on him; carefully attuned to his timbre after decades of practice.

"Harriet," Kasper was pleading, "just stop. This isn't like you. There's something wrong. Someone's—"

Felix brought his fingers to his mouth and let out a single piercing whistle. Immediately, there was silence. Rima sobbed.

Before Felix could speak, Kasper said, "Harriet, why didn't you come to me if you needed help? Why did you go to the Tricksters instead? I thought we were—" He reached for her hands but she slipped her fingers out of his grasp.

"You thought what?" she said, calmer suddenly than she'd been throughout the whole conversation. "That we were going to be *together for ever*? This isn't a love story, Kasper. You were a bit of fun. A means to an end."

Kasper's face crumpled. He took one step back, eyes begging her to take it back, to say it was all a mistake. He pressed the base of his palms against his eyes, hard enough that Felix saw his skin turning white. He inhaled, quick and devastated, and then dragged his hands down his face. When he opened his eyes again, they were glistening but resigned. "Right. Sorry. My mistake."

"What happens now?" Rima asked, when nobody spoke. Harriet and Kasper were staring at each other. It was like picking at a scab – Felix couldn't look away from them, even when it hurt.

Leah had her lips pressed to the side of Claudia's cheek, rocking her back and forth reassuringly. She was glaring at Harriet with murderous intent.

"Look, there are obviously a lot of problems here that we need to address," Harriet said.

"Problems that *you* created!" Felix yelled.

"Not just me!"

"YOU ALONE!" he repeated. "YOU."

Before anyone could respond, someone walked through the door. Adrenaline made Felix jump in self-defence. To his surprise, it was Greg. He spent most of his time hunting rats while he waited for orders from the Tricksters.

"What do you want, Gregory?"

Greg smirked at him, wandering into the room. Felix took a step back, keeping carefully out of touching distance. You could never be too careful with Greg. He was a slimy person, always searching for the most profitable deals.

Harriet clearly didn't know to avoid him, because she let him touch her wrist. "Harriet. It's Rufus and Vini. They want to see you. They have something you need to hear."

Chapter 13

HARRIET

As they walked down to the basement, Harriet listened to Greg's chatter in a dreamy kind of calm. All of the fight had gone out of her as soon as he'd touched her. She was relieved to be leaving Rima and the others behind. She needed time to collect her thoughts before she carried on talking to them. Otherwise, she was likely to do something rash.

It was getting harder and harder to control her words, or focus on anything but the energy inside her. It was a miracle she could hold a conversation at all, when inside she was screaming.

She wished she'd left before Rima and the others had started asking her questions. She'd messed up. However much she had wanted to stay quiet, these horrible things kept tumbling out of her mouth, one after the other, until she was shouting at them. Their faces had grown more and more horrified the longer she'd talked and she hadn't been able to find the right thing to say to fix it. They thought she was a monster. Harriet had ruined everything.

They wouldn't help her any more. That was why she was so

upset. It wasn't because Rima would stop inviting her to sunbathe on the fire escape or celebrate Halloween with them. Harriet wiped a tear away from her cheek. Who cared if they hated her, anyway? They were *nothing*.

Besides, she'd got this new second power from the Shell. If she could control their feelings, she could force them to like her – or love her, even. They would be her friends whether they liked it or not.

Greg stopped outside the basement. "I'll, er, catch up with you later," he muttered. "Things to do, you know."

"Yeah," Harriet said, wondering what Rufus and Vini wanted to tell her. Did they have some new information for her? Maybe they'd found more Shells she could use, now she'd run through the supply on the fifth floor.

"See ya." Greg bolted down the corridor. What was up with him?

Harriet stepped through the door, which lit up in that bright white light again. She was immediately pinned to the wall by Vini.

"What do you think you're doing?" he spat in Harriet's face, arm pressed up against her windpipe, so tightly he must be able to feel bone.

Harriet spluttered. What had she done? His lips were drawn back in a snarl, seconds away from ripping her cheek open with his teeth.

Behind him, the ghosts of the basement had stopped their game of pool to watch. Rufus strolled up to Harriet and hooked his finger under her right eyelid, pinching the flesh between his forefinger and thumb.

Her vision blew out, fear sending her blind with panic.

"Let go of her, Vini." He spoke like mist.

Vini's arm dropped from her throat. She held her head totally still, very aware of the fingers steadily holding her eyelid in place. The flat of his nail was touching her eyeball.

"What did I do?" she gasped. "I don't know what this is about!"

Rufus dug his fingernails into her eyelid, squeezing until the skin tore and his fingers met. Harriet screamed. Nothing had ever been so painful. Blood began dripping into her eye.

"Do you think we're fools? Do you think we haven't dealt with snakes like you before, time and time again?"

"I didn't mean to—" She ran over everything they'd talked about, trying desperately to work out what had happened. "I really don't know what—"

She gasped. Suddenly she did know.

"Oh," she gasped. "The phone."

It must have run out of battery. They had realized that the deal she'd made with them for information was worthless.

"The *phone*," Rufus confirmed, furiously calm, and dragged his hand backwards. He tore a hole along the length of her eye, pulling the lashes away from the lid.

The pain kept coming in waves, worse and worse, and a scream forced its way from her throat. "St-*ahhhh-hhhhhhhhhhhhhhhhhhhh!*"

Vini had his hand on her elbow, steadily leaching her fear away from her. The familiar pins and needles turned into a white-hot fire, and then disappeared into numbness. Was this what the Shells had felt, when she'd sucked them dry – a slow, burning loss of sensation?

Finally, Harriet managed to control herself enough to speak. "Stop! Wait! I can fix this!"

Rufus paused. Carefully, he slid his fingers free of the hole in her eyelid. He held the torn piece of skin on the end of his finger, inspecting it carefully, then folded it into his palm.

He surveyed her. Harriet met his gaze through the destroyed remnants of her eyelid.

"How are you going to do that?"

When she blinked, pain came screaming back into her eye. "What do you want? I'll get you anything you want to replace the phone!"

His eyebrow twitched. "What makes you think you have anything to offer us?"

"I have powers now. I can use them to trade. They're strong ones."

His gaze fixed on Harriet's newly white hair. He leaned in to sniff delicately at her temple.

"Three?" he asked, surprised. "Oh, you've become a perfectly creeping horror, just like you always wanted. Well done, you busy girl."

Vini grinned, revealing sharp eye teeth. "Leave some for the rest of us."

They could tell how many Shells she'd consumed just by smelling her? "Two and a half, actually."

"A half?"

"One of them disintegrated before I could get its power."

"Ah. A waste of a good murder."

Harriet ignored this. She hadn't *killed* the Shells. They hadn't been alive at all. They were practically brain-dead, whatever the others thought.

"I can turn invisible and manipulate emotions," she said. "Surely those are worth keeping me around for?"

"If you don't trick us again. Would you care to explain why you never told us the phone would shut off when we made a deal?" Vini smiled through rigid lips.

"I was distracted. I forgot. It was an honest mistake."

Harriet wished she'd never come to the basement. She was no match for the Tricksters, she saw that now. She was an amateur.

Rufus was waiting for more.

"I'm telling the truth." She tried to smile, but it hurt too much to move her face. "Only an idiot would try to trick you. Even I can see that."

"You *forgot*," he repeated. "You came down to the basement to make a deal with the most dangerous beings in this building, and you were so preoccupied you *forgot* that your phone's battery would run out. Well. How nice it must be, in that little brain of yours."

Harriet blanched. "I'm sorry. Really. Please. Let me make it up to you."

Rufus turned to Vini. They conferred silently.

Harriet waited, listening carefully. She caught the words "Leah" and "not strong enough". The basement air tasted rotten on her tongue. Her eyelid twinged.

Finally, Rufus spoke to her. "Do you know Qi Pang?"

Harriet curled her lip. "We've met."

He nodded, a minuscule movement. "Fetch her."

Vini was still leaching fear from her arm, and Rufus pushed his hand away, like he would a dog begging at the dinner table.

The Harriet of a week ago would have asked "Is that it?" but she knew better. If they wanted Qi, then it wasn't for a cup of tea and a chat. She wasn't going to escape unscathed. They were asking her to give up Qi in Harriet's place.

She didn't bother asking what Qi had done. It didn't matter. She couldn't negotiate. Either she gave Qi to them, or they destroyed her. The Tricksters might be trapped in the basement, but they had strong people on the outside, like Greg. If they wanted Harriet gone, there would be nowhere she could hide.

Harriet looked inside herself, questioning whether this was something that she could do. If the Tricksters were planning to hurt Qi, then she would be complicit in that.

But then, why shouldn't she do it? What was she holding back for? Qi was already suspicious of her, so it wasn't like she was losing an alliance. Plus, the thought of helping Rufus strangely fed the hunger of the unstable energy brewing inside her.

For years, Harriet had been ignoring the urge to bite and tear, to pounce, pushing that desire down into the darkest corners of her brain, limited to imagination only. But the fresh energy was giving her darkest desires the space to grow.

She had devoted so much of her effort to hiding that part of herself away, and for what? She'd burned her bridges with Rima and the others. They had decided that she wasn't good or kind or *one of them*.

Harriet couldn't stand the way they had looked at her – appalled and disgusted, like she was a monster. If it was all over with them, what was the point of even trying to be normal any more?

She might as well indulge herself, in the only way that she could. Harriet would give them something to really be afraid of.

There was no one left who would care if she burnt herself to the ground and reinvented Harriet Stoker anew.

"Give me ten minutes," she said, relief flushing her with pure adrenaline. "I'll bring Qi to you."

Rufus folded his arms, a small smile playing at his lips. "Good girl. And don't bother running off. We'll get Greg to track you down again if you don't come back. He can be … hard to refuse, as I'm sure you've found."

Harriet met his gaze, holding her bleeding eyelid open with a huge effort. "I understand you perfectly."

Rufus is working so hard, in every moment of every conversation. He wants to be just like his older brother. He needs his approval, even when he's long gone.

He's always been that way. I've checked. I've watched them play together as children. Pretending to be centurions and savages, with blue paint and wooden shields, back when Vini was a baby. Rufus let his brother order him around, hunt him down and beat him up. Rufus idolized him.

He was a sweet boy, until he realized how much more fun it was to be cruel. He learnt from his brother, just like Harriet is learning now.

Circles. It's always circles.

HARRIET

As she walked up to Qi's room, Harriet formed a vague plan for sneaking up on her while she was invisible. She would push an emotion into her then, but she hadn't decided which one yet.

Now that she'd made her decision to go through with this, she was resolutely refusing to question or second-guess herself. She knew she'd never manage to do it, if she thought too hard.

Harriet held her breath until she became invisible, and stepped through Qi's door. Something immediately punched her in the chest. She staggered backwards, electrocution ringing through her jaw and down her limbs. The doorway was glowing with a pure white light, like the barrier on the basement door did when she stepped through it. But this one hadn't let her through.

Rubbing at her jaw, she touched the light with one finger. A stabbing pain ricocheted into her palm. She pulled back, hissing. The light was sparking around the doorway, growing brighter and brighter. Her hair started to sizzle, filling the air with the acrid scent of burning.

"Who's there?" Qi called from inside.

Harriet took a moment to let the pain recede, and then said, in a chirpy voice, "It's Harriet! I think your door is broken! Can you let me in?"

She gave a little false laugh, high-pitched and girly.

"Harriet. I see." Qi's voice was inscrutable.

"I have an urgent message for you from Rima," Harriet

added, when the light started to glow even brighter. "You'd better let me in!"

"You know what, Harriet? I don't think I will. You're up to no good again."

Harriet sunk back against the opposite wall, furious and terrified. This wasn't going to work. Qi had been suspicious of her from the beginning. There was no way that she was going to believe her now.

She'd failed.

"Really?!" she said, laughing through a snarl. "You're making a mistake, you really do need to let me in! Rima needs your help!"

"Goodbye, Harriet," she said, quiet and firm.

Harriet pictured herself punching Qi. She replayed the image in her mind, turning it over and over like a boiled sweet on her tongue, embellishing it, adding spitballs and bite marks and clawed fingernails separating skin from flesh.

She tore her apart in her mind. And then she set the image free.

She smiled.

"No worries if you're busy!" she said, cheerfully, hiding her teeth and claws and nails. "Sorry to bother you!"

She hadn't even come close. She was going to have to go back to the basement empty-handed. The Tricksters would send someone after her if she didn't return to pay off her debt. Someone worse than Greg, with his mysterious aura that made her do whatever he said. It was starting to occur to Harriet that she always seemed to make bad decisions when he was around. It had been Greg who'd made her walk into the basement just now, totally unprepared for what was waiting for her. He'd done something to make her less alert.

She could see how someone could use up all their energy trying to pay back the Tricksters. Once they had you, there was no way out.

Well, if she couldn't give Qi to them, then someone else would have to do. It would be a distraction, so they didn't quench their bloodthirst on Harriet. Choosing a first-floor door at random, she turned invisible and walked inside. A boy was dozing on a rotting mattress. It was Kasper's rowing mate who'd accused Harriet of staying at Hotel Back Yourself. Jonny.

She touched the base of his neck, deciding to send him some lust, with a bit of loneliness. That should do the trick.

A shudder ran through Jonny when she pushed the emotions inside him. He groaned. Making herself visible again, she shook him awake. "Hey, pal."

His eyes dropped to her chest. "Er..." His pupils were already blown wide, and there was a bulge in the front of his trousers. "Hi," he replied in a hoarse voice.

She draped one hand across his chest, and purred, "Hi. Are you busy? Would you like to come –" she paused, watching him swallow – "for a walk?"

"Anywhere," he said on an exhale, and stood up. She took his hand, smiling over her shoulder at him.

She hovered outside the basement door, while he stared at

her arse. Could she really do this? There was no coming back from this, or way of denying it – she was sacrificing a stranger, wholly and undeniably. But wasn't she fighting for her own survival here?

She stepped through the lightning barrier, hoping desperately that it would let her out again. Jonny followed her in, leaning against her back and breathing in the smell of her neck. Rufus and Vini were waiting for her.

"I couldn't get Qi," she admitted, all her muscles braced for attack. "But I brought you someone else."

Rufus curled his lip. Jonny moaned and licked her neck in a haze of lust. She nudged his head away.

She couldn't tell if Rufus was furious or just disappointed.

There was a pause, and then Rufus laughed. "Of course you couldn't catch Qi. She's far stronger than a little thing like you."

They'd been setting her up to fail?

He flapped his hand at her. "Don't look so traumatized. You tried your best. You can live for another day. And look at this independent thinking, bringing us a snack instead. Quite a self-motivated worker we've got here."

Vini tugged Jonny away from Harriet. "You might want to wait outside," he told her.

As soon as his skin stopped touching hers, Jonny finally paid attention to their surroundings. "What…?"

Harriet stepped out of the room just as the Tricksters descended on him. She stood outside and listened to the screams. There was something immensely satisfying about causing pain, emotional or physical. It made her feel *alive* again, drowning out the energy buzzing inside her. She wasn't pretending to be normal, not any more. She was something ... better. Something stronger.

She gave the Tricksters five minutes, until the boy went silent. Then she went back inside.

Rufus had a sated curve to his mouth. Vini was snoring blissfully, curled up in a puppy pile with some other ghosts. Both Tricksters were glowing a little bit brighter.

"That hit the spot." Rufus raised his arms above his head and bent backwards, long and luxurious. He flicked his eyes at Harriet. "We're even. Now get out of here. If it turns out there's anything else which you've ... *forgotten*, we'll find you."

"I can go?" Harriet was surprised. She'd been expecting them to say that one random boy didn't equal Qi. From what she'd heard, she'd thought they'd ask for another two or three ghosts. But Rufus seemed satisfied already. It was like he hadn't been interested in getting her to pay off her debt at all. Had he been testing her? To see if she'd actually go through with it?

And she'd done exactly what he wanted, like an obedient little lamb.

"You can leave. Unless you'd like to make another deal altogether...? There's still a lot I could teach you." His voice was like tar, slick and rich and thick enough to trap her.

"No, that won't be necessary." Her eye was still crying out in pain.

"No hard feelings, hey?" He ran a hand through his silvery

white hair, the colour that perfectly matched her own. "It's just business."

Harriet's mouth tightened. "I'm not sure I have any feelings at all. Thank you for all your help. Goodbye."

Before Rufus could reconsider their temporary peace, she walked out. Greg was hovering nervously in the hallway, holding a wriggling mouse spirit like a joint. The sight of it made Harriet's mouth water. The more energy she consumed, the hungrier she seemed to get.

When he saw her, his worried face brightened into a beam. "You survived!"

"You could have warned me what they were like. I was totally unprepared." Harriet fixed her hair, which had been roughed up during Vini's stranglehold. Her eye was unsalvageable, but there was no reason the rest of her shouldn't look good. "What do they even want a phone for, anyway? Why do they care that it ran out of battery?"

Greg shrugged. "I heard that they were looking up a woman on the Internet. Cynthia down in the basement said it must be someone they knew when they were alive, but I swear they've been dead for hundreds of years. Everyone they know must be long gone by now, right?"

"Whatever," Harriet said, dully.

Greg squinted at her. "You know you've got blood in your eye?"

"Yes, Greg, I know that there's blood in my eye."

Did ghosts heal? How long did it take? She'd have to ask

someone, after she'd worked out what to do next.

"Huh. It doesn't suit you," he said.

"Would you piss off, Greg? I'm taking this." She tugged the mouse spirit out of his loose, surprised fist. "Thanks for nothing."

"No need to take it out on me. I was just following orders." Greg turned to leave, dreadlocks flicking over his shoulder.

She was too eager to be ashamed, and slumped against the wall to absorb the mouse. It was only a small boost to her energy. Once again, nothing happened when she tried to force her power to manifest.

No matter how useful her invisibility and emotional manipulation were, she still hadn't found a power that let her leave the building. There weren't any Shells left, either, so she'd have to be creative.

Harriet remembered how Kasper had possessed that police officer. He'd pulled her inside the body when she'd been on the verge of disintegrating. It had protected her.

Was there a way that she could get him to do that again? They could walk right out of the building, safe and snug inside the living body, all the way to her parents.

She could manipulate his emotions to convince Kasper that he wanted to possess a human, to show his love for her.

It was the perfect plan – or it would be. If all of the humans hadn't already left Mulcture Hall. The police had finished dealing with her corpse and packed up. There was no one left for her to hitch a lift inside.

Greg was halfway down the corridor by the time Harriet realized that he could help her. "Wait," she called after him. "Don't go."

Greg turned and raised one eyebrow at her. "You're sending me mixed signals here, princess."

"Can you find me a human? An alive one?"

He smirked. "What will you trade for it? You don't have that lovely phone any more."

Harriet huffed and touched his elbow. He leant into her, grin widening. He didn't know she had a power yet, so he didn't suspect a thing. By the time she had twisted his emotions, it was too late for him to stop her using his own power.

She pushed admiration and love into him, with a hint of desperation. That should do the trick. He was clearly taken by surprise, because a misty look entered his eyes.

"Are you *sure* you don't want to help me? If you could find me a human, I'd be *ever* so grateful."

Greg swallowed. "I'll be right back, princess."

*Harriet is following in her family's footsteps. She always has.
I'm guilty of it, too. We can hardly hold that against her.*

*When the Tricksters trapped Lisa in a debt, she wasn't
as ruthless as Harriet. They asked her to bring them
a sacrifice too, but she refused and gave up her own life
instead.*

*I reached through to the past to try to help Lisa,
afterwards. I thought I could nudge things in a different
direction. But there's only so much I can do.*

*It started because Lisa wanted a pet owl. Rima isn't
the only one with a pet – Felix had a badger at one point.
Or maybe he's going to have one? I forget.*

*For years, Lisa had tried to find a dying animal and
tame its spirit, but she'd never had any luck. Eventually,
she went to the basement. She didn't realize what the
Tricksters were really like, or how dangerous their black
market could be.*

*She struck a deal with them to get an owl spirit that
a ghost had been training up, in exchange for using her
power on the black market ten times. Her power let her*

change her physical appearance – she could make her hair red or blonde or pink, add freckles or dimples or beauty marks. She could do it to other people, too, but it took a lot more focus. She had to maintain the changes constantly, or they'd revert back to their original form.

Greg came to find Lisa the week after she got her owl, which she named Jujanna. Rufus wanted her to use her first favour to change his eye colour to green. Lisa did it happily enough. It only used a tiny part of her energy to make sure the green didn't disappear. (The new colour did suit him, actually. It was a great contrast to his white hair.)

A week later, Vini asked her to straighten his teeth. Lisa agreed, a little more reluctantly. A week after that, she removed a bump from Vini's nose from the time he'd been punched over an unpaid bar bill when he was alive.

Lisa was starting to feel a little weaker now. The constant drain on her energy was catching up with her. Then Rufus asked her to add silvery highlights to his white hair.

Lisa started fading. If she kept this up, she would become a Shell long before the tenth favour. She asked if she could pay off her debt in another way.

Rufus lit up. This must have been what he was waiting for. "You know that boy Kasper Jedynak, don't you? I'd be happy to accept his power instead of yours. In fact, one favour from him would be enough to wipe out the rest of your debt."

Lisa was confused. "Do you know what his power is? I'm not sure it would do much for you. He can ... possess humans."

"I think that will work perfectly. Why don't you ask him to come and see me? Otherwise, I have another favour I'll be needing from you tomorrow morning."

"I can't give up any more energy." Lisa turned pale.

"Kasper can come along any time – my schedule is completely free," Rufus replied.

Lisa left, disturbed.

I've watched her story a few times over, and I think that Rufus planned this from the beginning. The bargain was designed to put Lisa in debt, beyond what she could afford. Then all he had to do was wait to pounce.

But Kasper refused, very firmly, to use his power. He told Rufus that he was willing to help pay off Lisa's debt – but not by doing that.

He wasn't terrified of them, not yet. That would come later, once he'd seen what they could do. For now, he was just annoyed.

Rufus said that it was Kasper's power or nothing. The next morning, Lisa had to paint his nails red, sharpening the ends into points. She was so weak that she couldn't even make it out of the basement.

Hours later, Vini woke her up and asked her to remove a scar from his wrist. It was just a small white mark, but Lisa fainted. Her light glowed and dimmed as she breathed in and out. She was nearly a Shell.

After this all happened, I went back to that moment. I can nudge the past and the future, just slightly, if I need to. It's like reaching through a window inside my mind. I can push against the membrane between time, calling out to people.

I tried to push some of my spare energy into Lisa — enough that she would be able to wake up and crawl outside the lightning barrier. I couldn't spare more than that. Her faded form did glow a little when she absorbed my energy, but she didn't wake up.

When Kasper realized they'd taken her again, he raced down to the basement.

Edging around the walls, his eyes fixed on Rufus, he pleaded, "Please, she's going to disintegrate. You have to release her."

Rufus admired his sharp red nails and said, "You know what we want. If you're too scared to give it to us, then Lisa will have to pay the price for your cowardice."

"I can't!" Kasper hissed. "I would never do that to a living person."

"It won't kill them, you know. If that's what you're worried about. Humans do survive being possessed."

"It might not kill them, but it's — it's rape. I can't be that person."

"And yet you'll let Lisa disintegrate? How is that not as bad?"

Kasper was breathing hard. "She's already dead. It's different."

"Well, then. If you've made your choice, I suggest you say goodbye. She doesn't have long left. But Mr Jedynak, one day you're going to have to face what you are, however much it scares you. Because the parts of yourself that frighten you? They're not going anywhere."

Lisa disintegrated six hours later. The Tricksters didn't get what they wanted, but they didn't exactly lose, either. They play the long game. Kasper's still caught in their web.

Chapter 14

KASPER

Kasper couldn't sleep, pacing the empty hallways of the fifth floor. Now that the Shells were gone, he could wander alone, crippled with complete and overwhelming guilt.

He'd possessed someone. What had come over him? He hadn't ever wanted to stop. If it hadn't been for Felix, he'd still be inside that poor, innocent woman. Like some sort of—

He was a monster. He really was. He'd tried to be good. He'd thought for a while that he was, but clearly his true nature had just been biding its time until there was an opportunity to strike.

He was disgusting. He could still feel it, the hunger underneath his consciousness. The demon inside him was just waiting for another human to come close enough that it could take control. He wanted to tear off his skin to get rid of it.

He wasn't safe to be around, not any more. He should join the other criminals in the basement, so that Rima and Leah and – and *Felix* – weren't ever forced to look at him again. He had to disappear for ever, before they came to kick him out of the group anyway. They'd be better off without him.

After Harriet had gone with Greg, Kasper had left the room without speaking. He couldn't bear to hear the others break off all ties with him. Since then, he'd been doing loops of the corridors, up and down and spiralling around the fifth floor, the thumps of his feet resonating through the floors.

He couldn't seem to sit still. Whenever Kasper stopped moving, he started thinking, and so he ran.

He turned at the top of the stairs to do another lap. There was a tiny noise behind him. Felix was standing there, looking sleep-crumpled and shattered.

They've sent him, Kasper's brain whispered. *He's here to kick you out of the group.*

"Hello." They both ignored how his words came out pained.

Felix rubbed at the shorn hair on the back of his scalp. "Do you, er, want to talk?"

Kasper's breath left him in a rush. Felix was here to talk. They weren't getting rid of him then, not yet.

They sat down together against the breeze-block wall, staring at the window opposite. Ivy had crept in through the cracks in the pane, spreading across the plaster in thick, creeping fingers. Light fell into the room through the leaves, casting a green glimmer over the mouldering wood of the windowsill.

Usually, Kasper would pull Felix under his arm, into a headlock or a man-hug. He wanted to, more than ever. But he was suddenly afraid that Felix would jerk away in repulsion. He carefully moved his arm so they weren't touching, in case he made Felix flinch back.

Kasper didn't understand why they didn't hate him. They should – his behaviour was unforgivable. Yet here was Felix, right by his side, where he had always been, for as long as Kasper could remember.

To his surprise, Felix lifted his arm meaningfully. Kasper blinked. Felix had never – not once – offered Kasper a hug before. He grumbled enough when Kasper hugged him.

Kasper shuffled closer, pressing himself against his side. Felix's heavy arm dropped across his shoulder, the pressed cotton of his shirt smooth against Kasper's neck.

Kasper let out a long exhale, relaxing in increments. He had so much he wanted to say, but he held his tongue. Felix had supported him before, after Lisa disintegrated. He'd forgotten how awful and guilty he'd felt then, trembling with fear every time there was the slightest noise, in case it was Greg, coming again to demand that Kasper use his power for the Tricksters. Felix had helped him through it all.

"I'm sorry about Harriet, Kasper."

Kasper stared hard at the floor. There was something in his eye. "I should have known that Harriet would never want to be with a monster like me. Not for real."

He was aiming for self-deprecating, but the words came out too honest.

Felix twisted, touching Kasper's chin until he met his gaze. There was a tense fury in his expression. "*Kasper*. You are not a monster. Not even a little bit. If anyone is, it's Harriet."

Kasper closed his eyes for a second. When he opened them

again, he felt stronger than before. Braver. Felix had seen Kasper at his very worst: frothing at the mouth with the desperate desire to cause pain. Yet he didn't blame him for what had happened. He didn't think that Kasper was worthless, spineless, horrifying.

Felix's gaze was flickering back and forth across Kasper's face. "You aren't going to do it again. I know you aren't."

Kasper's chest swelled. He leant his forehead against Felix's shoulder, hiding his face. He wasn't sure what his expression was doing, but he didn't want Felix to see it. "I don't know how you can be so sure. I'm not."

"Because I know you. You're good, Kasper." Felix's eyes were dark when he lifted his head.

Felix still trusted him. Kasper felt winded by the knowledge. He looked at the way the dim light hit the curve of Felix's nose and wondered if he'd ever really seen him before at all.

Felix would never have been weak enough to possess someone. He was much braver than Kasper, in so many ways. Kasper's weaknesses were Felix's strengths, like they were two halves of one whole.

Felix was always there, just when he needed him. But Kasper never gave him anything in return.

"I think Harriet made a mistake," he said eventually. "I don't think she knew what she was doing."

Felix looked away, his jaw set tight. "If she's not to blame, either, then who is? I don't trust her, Kasper. Not even a little bit."

"She's acting a bit bonkers," Kasper admitted. "But I need to give her a chance to explain what happened. It sounds like the Tricksters manipulated her into destroying the Shells. I know what they're like. I can't cast judgement if there's still a chance she's telling the truth."

Felix sighed. "I don't know how she could possibly have an explanation that will redeem everything she's done. Please brace yourself, OK? Even though you – you know, like her—"

"I don't like her," Kasper said in a rush. "I used to, but – I made a mistake. Clearly she's not the person I thought she was. I want to be with someone who actually cares about me. Not someone who pretends to."

Felix was staring at him, eyes wide, expression beaten raw. Kasper was suddenly very aware of how long and black his eyelashes were.

He swallowed, feeling hot and shy. He could trust Felix not to use this against him, but it still felt strange to spill his heart to him. It was different from their usual playful banter. It was … intimate.

Maybe it was time to pull back. He tried very hard to never think about this. *Felix.* Whatever they were both doing, beyond spending time in each other's company.

"I want to give Harriet the chance to make things right," Kasper said at last, forcing himself to focus. "And if it turns out she's…" He trailed off. He couldn't say it.

Felix finished for him. "We'll deal with that if it comes to it."

Kasper sighed, rubbing his face against Felix's shirt. He wanted to stay here for ever.

228

Kasper was almost asleep when Rima found them.

"Boys!" she yelled. "There's a kitten in Felix's room! Come look!"

Kasper grinned. Whenever a cat died in the hall, every ghost wanted to stroke it, because they could actually touch the spirits, unlike living cats – or Cody, who only ever let Rima cuddle her.

He pulled Felix to his feet so that they could follow her downstairs. A cat day was better than Christmas. It was just what they all needed.

HARRIET

Harriet had to find Kasper. There was a thrumming under her skin whispering, *Hurry, hurry, HURRY,* which refused to be ignored. She needed to get him down to the main entrance, so that when Greg found a human for Kasper to possess, they'd be ready and waiting.

As she searched Mulcture Hall, she couldn't stop rubbing at her eye. It stung, throbbing in time with her breaths. When she finally spotted Kasper in Felix's room, they were all passing around the spirit of some small animal, taking turns inhaling it. No, they weren't inhaling it. They were *cuddling* it.

There was no way she'd be able to get Kasper to come with her if the others were around to defend him. They wouldn't even let her touch his skin, now they knew what she could do.

She was going to have to wait until she could get him alone. He'd give up his energy easily, then.

In the meantime, it couldn't hurt to hear what they were saying about her. She turned herself invisible and slid inside the room to listen.

Chapter 15

FELIX

"What are we going to do about Harriet?" Rima asked.

Felix stopped cooing over the tiny black kitten that was cradled in Kasper's lap. There was a long silence.

"I don't think she meant to do anything bad," Kasper said eventually. He sounded raw. He also sounded unconvinced.

"I disagree," Felix said. "There's been something off about her from the very beginning. I tried to tell you all. We shouldn't trust her."

The kitten batted at his fingers. It was newly dead, still full of enough energy to want to play. It wrapped its mouth around Felix's thumb, gnawing on him with sharp teeth.

Rima sighed. "I don't think she did anything wrong. She's new. I think she just misunderstood what the Shells are."

Felix had a sudden moment of doubt. Kasper and Rima were both such staunch defenders of Harriet. Were they seeing something in her that he'd missed?

But, no. She'd *killed* the Shells. Kasper was being guided by his libido, and it was a historical fact that Rima was too trusting of everyone she'd ever met. Felix was right.

"She wasn't thinking about them!" Felix said. "She was only thinking about herself. *How can you not see that?* She made Kasper possess a police officer!"

"She had nothing to do with that," Kasper said defensively. "That was all me."

Rima immediately leant over the kitten to hug Kasper. "It wasn't your fault, either. You can't help what your power is."

"You managed to avoid possessing anyone for decades," Leah added. "I think the fact that you only succumbed now says more about your strength of will than anything."

Kasper looked embarrassed, and relieved. "Thanks guys. I, er. Just, thanks."

"We love you, Kasper." Rima kissed his cheek. When no one else spoke, she prompted, *"Right, guys?"*

Leah leant over to ruffle his hair. "You're a decent sort."

Felix clapped Kasper on the back, biting back the urge to declare how he felt about him.

"We're a family. We're going to get through this." When Rima finally stopped hugging Kasper, the kitten had made its way from his lap to the inside of her cardigan.

Kasper ran a hand through his hair. "Can we talk about something else now, please?" He'd turned slightly pink, to Felix's delight.

"I think we should make her give up the energy she took from those Shells," Rima said. "Even if it was a mistake, we can't let her keep it. It sets a precedent."

Leah made a noise of disagreement. "When did we decide

that it *was* a mistake? People have been banished to the basement for less before."

"But she's new," Rima said. "She didn't understand the rules. We can't punish her for that."

Felix rolled his eyes. Rima was being completely ridiculous. Before he could reply, someone outside said, "Hello?"

Felix turned to look at the door, thinking in a second of pure panic that it was Harriet. But Qi stepped through the door.

"I thought you'd probably want to hear the news," she said, folding her arms. "Greg's gone. He disintegrated."

Felix was baffled. When Greg had come to fetch Harriet for the Tricksters, he'd been glowing with energy, like normal. He spent most of his time hunting rats and topping up his energy with them. Plus, he got a lot of favours from the Tricksters in exchange for working for them.

What had happened, since he'd led Harriet down to the basement?

"He walked out of the main entrance," Qi said. "Several people tried to stop him, but evidently he didn't listen."

"Why would he do that?" Kasper asked, confused.

Greg hadn't seemed the type to commit "suicide", like some ghosts. He had been very calm and content as a ghost, as far as Felix had been able to tell.

"He claimed he was going to fetch something for his girlfriend."

"What?" Felix said. Greg had never had a girlfriend. Felix had kind of thought he was gay.

Qi cleared her throat. "His girlfriend, Harriet Stoker."

That was even more interesting. What was Harriet up to now?

"Harriet and Greg weren't dating," Rima said, but she sounded unsure.

"Greg was quite insistent about it, I believe."

Kasper was pacing back and forth like he was trying to get rid of his shadow.

"It must have been a new thing, then." Rima met Felix's eye.

What could Greg possibly have been trying to get for Harriet that meant he had to leave the building? Harriet wouldn't use her power to manipulate him into disintegrating – would she? That seemed beyond cruel, even for her. Why *Greg*?

"I would like to add that I don't trust that girl," Qi said. "If she continues on her current path, it won't be long before she is banished to the basement. If you need me, I will be waiting for word."

After Qi left, Rima said, "Do you think that Harriet's got something to do with *that*, too?"

"Of course she does," Felix said, groaning. How much evidence would it take? "The last time we saw her, she was with Greg. Now he turns up dead? Before Harriet arrived, the biggest drama of this millennium was someone stealing my glasses. But since she arrived, awful things have been happening *constantly*. This has Harriet written all over it."

"But how?" Rima asked, baffled.

"She must have used her emotion control to make Greg go

outside. It's the perfect murder. No evidence," Felix said darkly.

"For someone who looks so innocent, you really are morbid," Rima said, both horrified and fascinated.

The kitten crawled into his lap, rolling flat on its back and purring deeply. Cody stared fixedly at it, shifting impatiently. Felix hoped that she wasn't going to pounce.

"He's right," Leah said. "That's what I'd do, too. If someone knew something I didn't want to get out, I mean."

"I don't think Harriet's capable of this," Rima said. "What reason does she even have to go after Greg? It's one thing to fight with us, but she's not a serial killer."

There was a moment of silence. Kasper was now doing restless pull-ups on the door lintel. The lines of muscles stood out on the curves of his shoulders. He looked like he wanted to run, as far and as fast as possible.

Cody let out a rumbling noise in her chest, inching across the floor paw by paw towards the kitten.

"No!" Rima said to the fox, and then added, soft and disappointed, "We *talked* about this."

Cody sat back on her haunches, licking her lips.

"It doesn't matter what her motive is," Felix said. "First the Shells, and now this? It's time, like Qi said. We need to have a vote on whether to banish her before she starts manipulating our emotions, too."

"We *can't* send her down there with Rufus and Vini," Rima insisted. "What if she's innocent? The Tricksters made Harriet go after the Shells in the first place."

Harriet and the Tricksters deserved each other, Felix thought.

"I agree with Felix," Leah said. "I think we should vote on it."

"Let's vote," Kasper said, to Felix's surprise. "It can't hurt. Just to see."

Felix's fingers wriggled on the kitten, pleased. Kasper was on his side. He didn't trust Harriet, either.

"Are you really going to decide on my fate without me?" a voice said from behind them. Harriet was leaning against the windowsill, arms folded.

Felix broke out in a cold sweat. When had she come in?

"Harriet!" Rima had gone scarlet with mortification. "Hello!"

Harriet curled her lip, unimpressed. There was something misshapen about her face. The eyelashes on her right eye were dangling in a twisted, unnatural position, and leaking blood in a steady trickle down her cheek.

Taking advantage of the sudden silence, Cody pounced on the kitten spirit. It let out a feeble *meow* and collapsed into a cloud of energy, disintegrating for ever.

"What happened to your eye?" Leah asked.

Harriet's hand darted to her face. "I ran into a door," she said, not even trying to make the lie sound believable. "Will it heal?"

Rima shook her head. She was trying very hard not to gape at Harriet. "No." Her voice came out shrill. "We don't heal, if we're injured."

Harriet hummed. She didn't sound particularly disappointed.

Rima cleared her throat. "Actually, you can't bruise yourself on a door. You'd walk straight through it. Only another ghost can hurt a ghost."

Harriet shrugged. "I had a little disagreement with the Tricksters. Rufus has a strange intimidation style. He apparently decided that keeping hold of my eyelid would be a good souvenir."

Felix blanched. She should probably try and get that skin back, at some point. There was a lot that could be done with part of a ghost's body, especially by someone like Rufus. What had she been fighting with them about? Had Greg been involved? Is that why he'd left the building?

There was an excruciating silence. Rima looked desperately at Felix for support. He shrugged helplessly. He couldn't help – he created awkward silences just by breathing.

Kasper was twisting his hands back and forth, back and forth, bending his interlinked fingers at impossible, violent angles. Carefully, Felix pressed his shoulder against his.

"So," Harriet said, sounding unaffected. She looked out of the window. She was facing away from them. "What happens next, in these votes of yours? Does the defendant have a chance to speak before or *after* they are banished for eternity?"

"We wouldn't have..." Rima said, horrified.

Harriet blew out a breath through her nose. "Don't worry, Rima, I understand. You have to do what's best for the hall. If I'm a danger, you need to get rid of me." She paused, and ran one carefully manicured finger along her bottom lip. Rima was frozen, watching her unblinkingly. "It's interesting, you see, because I wasn't aware that you four were in charge of making decisions for the entire building."

"We aren't," Felix said, when it seemed like no one else was going to. "If we think that you should be punished, then we'll call a general meeting. The whole building will vote."

"Very democratic." Harriet's expression turned disinterested, but there was something that contradicted her sudden boredom. "Surely what I did doesn't deserve that, though? I made a mistake. I won't do it again."

"What happened to you?" Rima's lip trembled. "The Tricksters did something to you, didn't they? That's why your hair has turned white! This isn't really you."

Harriet's fingers pressed lightly against the white strands like she'd forgotten about it. "The Tricksters did nothing to me except actually answer my questions."

Rima swallowed. "But – I thought you were like us. We got on, didn't we? We had fun."

There was a vulnerable expression on Harriet's face for a moment, and then it disappeared and hardened into something new. "Let's break this down into digestible chunks. Just because we have the same *sense of humour* doesn't mean we have the same morals. It doesn't mean I'm anything like you. I didn't…" She faltered for a moment, almost imperceptibly. "I was using you, obviously."

Rima turned away, choking off a sob.

"You're making a mistake here, kid," Leah said. "You're going to regret this."

"What's new there?" Harriet spat back. "I regret everything that's happened since I came to Mulcture Hall."

"What did you do to Greg, Harriet?" Felix asked. "The Shells might have been a mistake, if you got misled by the Tricksters. But what happened to Greg?"

Harriet rolled her eyes. "Should he be allowed to discuss this?" she said to Rima, gesturing at Felix derisively. "We all know he hates me because he's obsessed with—"

Felix made a noise of panic, but before he could cut her off, Kasper got there first.

"*Harriet!*" he shouted, furious.

Felix jerked his head around, shocked. Rima shouted at people out of love. Leah, to make them leave her alone. Kasper, though. Kasper only told people off when he was very, very angry. And it took a lot to rile Kasper.

"Just stop, OK! Stop it." He let out a furious gust of breath. "You can't talk your way out of this. You made a mistake. You have to deal with the consequences."

Harriet tilted her head to one side. She touched his elbow. "Kasper, *babe,* don't be like that."

He jerked his arm away. "I think you should leave. Please. Until we've all had a chance to calm down."

She looked surprised. "But…" She touched his elbow again, frowning hard like she was concentrating.

Kasper shrugged her off. "What are you – are you trying to make me…? Never mind. It's not going to work. Yeah, I liked you. No, that's not going to change anything. Not now, not ever."

Harriet squared her jaw. Her fists were clenched, braced like she was about to start shouting. Then she visibly backed down. She nodded her head, twice in quick succession.

After she left the room, it took a long time for anyone to speak to fill the vacuum she left behind.

HARRIET

It hadn't worked. It had worked on Greg. *Greg* had scurried off to do everything Harriet wanted with a little push of love and desperation. He'd been so desperate to please her that he'd literally walked out of the building, after he realized there were no humans inside. He'd let himself disintegrate for her.

When she'd used the same power on Kasper, he'd shrugged it off. He'd acted like the love she'd made him feel for her was nothing. He had felt the emotion she'd pushed into him – he'd even commented on it – but it hadn't changed his actions. He must be so used to ignoring his emotions that it didn't affect him.

How was she going to convince him to help her leave this place now? Her plan had failed completely.

Seething, Harriet marched up the stairs, pushing her way past a crowd of idling ghosts. She'd thought this power was useful, but if people could ignore what she made them feel, then what was the point? She'd have been better off with Felix's power of hypnotism. At least then people couldn't use their *common sense* to ignore the compulsion.

Once again, she'd been left with a useless power. And lost Greg, who might have been stupid, but knew more about the ins and outs of Mulcture Hall than she did. He had been valuable, in his own way.

At least she'd acted sensibly when talking to the others this time. That was the only positive outcome from the last few hours. Harriet had been absolutely furious, listening to them discuss sending her to the basement. It had taken all her self-control not to reveal herself and immediately start shouting.

But instead of yelling, she had purposefully kept her cool, trying to copy the quiet control Rufus always had. That was the way her gran spoke to people too – keeping her distance and intimidating them with long pauses. She would sometimes knit whole rows between sentences, eyeing Harriet over the top of the wool in disappointment.

Harriet had embarrassed herself during the argument after Kasper's possession. She'd attacked Rima and Felix like a toddler having a tantrum. The energy overdose had burnt the surface off the inside of all her nerves, taking her common sense with it.

She was going to have to wait for a human to appear on their own. Surely someone would come soon – maybe a caretaker, unable to resist nosing around the crime scene. When they did, she would get Kasper and try this again. This time, she wouldn't fail.

RIMA

Rima felt cheated. Harriet really had been using them from the very beginning. Surely deep down, below the panic and desperation that her death had created, Harriet must be a good person. Or was Rima just delusional, like the others said?

Harriet's energy glowed brightly inside her, so strong that it must be hard for her to keep it under control. What if her erratic behaviour was because that extra energy was influencing her? Rima's mind kept returning to the vicious way Harriet had spoken to Qi, hours after her death, because she'd been given one little rat. If only there was a way they could bleed some of the energy out of her. Then she might calm down.

Rima was at a loss for what they should do next. There were too many missing pieces to the puzzle. Had Harriet knowingly killed the Shells? Was she connected to Greg's disintegration? Why had she been fighting with Rufus?

She was acting so randomly that it would be hard to stop her. They needed more information. It was time to ask Leah for help, even if the thought alone made Rima hate herself.

"Look, I didn't want to do this," Rima said. "But, Leah, I think we need to know what happens next. Don't you?"

Leah dropped her head, hair falling in front of her face so that Rima couldn't see her expression. Rima rubbed her nose once, twice, three times, trying to hide her desperation. Leah's power let her see the past and future, but using it drained her.

It was a big risk. But they had to stop Harriet, before she could hurt anyone else.

"Please, Leah? We can't do anything unless we know what Harriet is planning to do." Felix and Kasper were quiet, leaving this to Rima.

Leah ran her finger down the side of Claudia's cheek as she thought about using her power. The baby watched her, blinking leisurely. She opened her lips and made a small, soft burble.

Finally, when Rima was about to take back the request out of sheer awkwardness, Leah nodded. "OK. I'll look for you, Rima. But you should know that I'm very low on energy. And Claudia may – overreact."

Rima swallowed. Leah looked … scared. It was a new expression on her face.

Rima suddenly regretted asking at all. "What does that mean?"

"The last time I used my power, I didn't wake up immediately afterwards. My energy was too low. Claudia thought I was going to disintegrate, and she panicked." Leah looked up at the ceiling. "She took energy from someone nearby and pushed it all into me."

"What?" Kasper looked horrified.

Rima looked aghast at Claudia. Could a baby do something like that? Surely Leah was mistaken. It wasn't possible. She was only a few months old.

Leah explained, "When I woke up, the person had

disintegrated. It was … unfortunate. I've explained to Claudia many times that she shouldn't do that again. When it's my time to disintegrate, she can't stop it. She seems to have accepted that now, but you should keep your distance. Just in case."

"Maybe we shouldn't do this," Rima said, trying to keep her horror off her face. Leah made it sound like Claudia was … developed. Perceptive. Communicative. That couldn't possibly be right.

"I have to try," Leah said. "If Harriet is putting the whole building in danger … I can't let her hurt any of you."

Rima looked between her and Claudia, still unsure. Finally, she turned to Felix. "What do you think?"

He was staring at Claudia, too, and doing a much worse job of hiding his horror than Rima had.

"Felix?"

He jerked his gaze away from the baby, turning to her. "Sorry?" he asked hoarsely.

"Do you really, genuinely think that Harriet is a murderer? Do you believe that enough to put Leah and Claudia at risk?"

Felix swallowed. He wrapped his arms around his chest, pressing his chin into the crook of his elbow. "I – I don't—" A pained look crossed his face. "Yes. I'm sorry, Leah, I'm really sorry, but – yes. I really do think that she's dangerous. And I think we're going to need all the information we can get."

Kasper nodded his head, too, slowly at first, then more quickly. "She's going after the weakest people here. We can't allow that, not while we've got the strength to stop her."

A feeling of pure terror washed over Rima. How could things have escalated this quickly?

"OK." Leah carefully laid Claudia down in her lap and adjusted the material around her face. She leant down to press a kiss to her forehead, and whispered, "Please be good. You know it's time."

The baby wriggled in her blanket, letting out a feeble cry.

Rima looked away, uncomfortable.

Leah said, "It will only take a second. Please don't touch us. At any point."

"Good luck." Rima slid back on the floor until she found Felix, blindly squeezing his hand.

Leah took a deep breath and tipped her head forwards. She was completely still at first. Then her fingertips started trembling. The shudders spread up her limbs and across her body. In her lap, Claudia started wailing, an endless, terrible noise that pierced Rima's eardrums.

Kasper wrapped his arm around Rima's shoulder. She was crying, and pressed her cheek into his bicep, unable to watch but unable to look away.

Leah's light was dimming. She hadn't been very bright before, but now her colour began fading rapidly. After only a few minutes she was so dull that she was almost black and white. She was staring at something inside her mind, something the others couldn't see.

Leah swung her head back around, eyes wide. Looking right at Felix, she said, petrified, *"We have to stop her!"*

Then her eyes rolled back in her head and she tipped over to one side, unconscious.

Claudia let out an agonized screech, legs kicking in her unresponsive mother's lap. None of them touched her.

Leah had become a Shell.

You know, ghosts have myths. They're passed down from generation to generation – ancient, millennia-old ghosts passing on stories they heard when they were newly dead, from other ancient ghosts on the brink of disintegration.

The stories stretch back all the way to Neolithic times, before stories were told in words. Back then, language was crude and essential, nothing more than a way to help humans work together to hunt and eat and sleep.

Those stories don't make much sense now. They don't follow the forms of tales we know. They are short and to the point: the man saw a deer on the eastern slopes and cornered the deer in a small cluster of trees. It tasted good. The hide was strong.

Those early humans weren't interested in entertainment. It hadn't been invented yet. There were no happy endings or romances, or heroes. The stories nearly always ended in death. A hunt, a defeat, a victory, a bad case of food poisoning.

But those stories – if you can call them stories – all have one thing in common, as far as I can see. They might not have plot, or characters, or beautiful writing. But there is always one thing: a lesson. A moral. A new piece of information, worthy of remembering and passing on.

I haven't decided what the moral of my story is yet. The lesson that needs sharing. What here is worth remembering a millennium from now, if we survive that long? Worth passing on to the generations of ghosts that come after us?

I think the message might be that it's never over. Even when you think someone is gone for ever, they can return. Whether you're desperate to speak to them one last time, or terrified to see their face. Life always finds a way.

Chapter 16

FELIX

Felix and Kasper sat together in the laundry room. Leah was in Felix's bedroom, but he couldn't sit there and stare at her like Rima could. Instead, they were sprawled in here, opposite a line of the few remaining washing machines that hadn't been scavenged.

Kasper was lying with his head in Felix's lap, eyes closed. They didn't speak about the important things – that the whole ecosystem of Mulcture Hall had been destroyed since Harriet's arrival; that none of them had any idea what they were supposed to do about it; that Leah still hadn't woken up and Claudia wouldn't stop crying, curled up alone next to her mother because they were all too scared to go near her. Most of all, they didn't speak about the way Leah had looked at Felix after she'd seen the future. She'd looked right at him, like – like he was...

Felix was going to disintegrate. Leah had seen it happen and looked at him afterwards with horror. They all knew it. It was only a matter of time.

"I'd give anything to hear Leah play Don't Get Me Started right now," Felix said.

Kasper coughed a laugh, looking up at Felix from the corner of his eye. "Maybe we should talk really loudly about the Tooth Fairy next to her," he suggested, toying with Felix's sleeve, folding the fabric into concertinas and then smoothing it flat. His thumb pressed against the smooth skin of Felix's wrist. Felix shivered.

Felix's smile disappeared, laughter dying in his throat. "I always knew she was older than the rest of us," Felix said. "But I never thought that meant she might leave us one day."

"I can't imagine a Mulcture Hall without her," Kasper agreed. "It feels like she's always been here."

"Do you know how old she is?"

Kasper closed his eyes and said, "No, do *you*?"

Felix shook his head. "I've always been too scared to ask. Rima asked her once, and I thought she was literally going to bite her head off."

Kasper smiled. His thumb was still rubbing against Felix's wrist, dipping down to press into his palm. "That does sound like Leah."

They'd tried to feed rats to Leah, to wake her again. But there just wasn't enough energy there to recover from being a Shell. They just had to wait and see if she woke up on her own.

There was a bird's nest inside one of the rusting tumble driers, layers of intricate sticks and moss padding the steel barrel. Felix would have to come back in the spring and see the chicks, if they weren't all Shells by then.

Oscar had loved birds. Even as a kid, he'd been obsessed with owls and eagles and herons. Felix had always teased him about being a twitcher, which Oscar had hated. He'd thought he was too cool for that sort of thing.

Felix had been right, of course. Sometimes, on his visits, Oscar would stand at the window and pull out a pair of binoculars. Based on the things he said when he was here, it seemed Oscar was divorced now, and constantly embarrassed his grown-up children with bad jokes. Felix supposed there weren't many things nowadays that his brother was too cool for.

"Whatever Leah saw, I'm absolutely certain it wasn't what you think," Kasper said, apropos of nothing. "Even if she saw you, that doesn't mean that it was something … bad."

Kasper's roaming touch trailed down Felix's fingers, bending and straightening the joints, comparing the length to his own.

"I hope not." Felix sighed through his nose. Why hadn't he done something about Harriet earlier? He shouldn't have left her to wander the building, leaving chaos and destruction in her wake.

Kasper sat upright, suddenly. "Felix, I never said thank you."

Felix blinked. "What for?"

"After Lisa disintegrated, you were there for me. And again, when Harriet – you know – dumped me. You were there for me again. I realized that I never said thank you afterwards."

Felix was shocked. Kasper was voluntarily talking about

feelings. Usually he seemed terrified of even admitting he had any emotions at all.

"I…" Felix stuttered, but Kasper clearly wanted to get the words out in one go.

"It meant a lot. That's all I wanted to say. And – and I appreciate it."

Felix's eyes dropped to the ground. He smiled. "Any time, Kasper." Then he looked up, distraught. "And I don't mean that in a 'I hope you get your heart broken again' kind of way. God."

Kasper laughed. The sound was relieved, filled with a rush of affection. He hauled Felix into a hug, squeezing him hard. Felix's nose hit his cheekbone, too hard and painfully real. He twisted his face to the side.

"Thanks, buddy. You're a really good mate." Kasper rubbed his hand up and down Felix's back in familiar, gentle strokes. There was something awful in the words when combined with those intimate movements, so tender and personal.

Felix went still. Kasper was saying one thing, and doing another. It wasn't fair on him, not one bit. He couldn't call Felix his friend, and then touch him like they were more than that. This was something more than friendship, at least for Felix.

"No," Felix said, quick and rough. "No, sorry. I can't do this."

"What?" Kasper said, confused.

Felix clenched his fists so tightly that the muscles in his hands popped. A whiff of dust, mixed with the humid scent of a brewing thunderstorm, hit his nostrils. "I can't live like this any more. It's not enough."

Kasper was floored. "What? I don't, I mean – *what?*"

"I thought it would be enough, to just be here for you when you needed it. But you have to – you have to know. It's not like you don't – it's not – I can't keep doing this. I can't always be here when you need me, and then pretend I don't care when you're fine, because it hurts too much, OK? It hurts."

Felix's eyes were wet. He wiped at them roughly with the back of his hand. "I've spent decades trying to get rid of this thing, this torch I've been carrying around for you, and all that keeps it burning is pure pigheadedness, but I can't any more. OK? I can't. For my own sake. I'm sorry. You're going to have to find someone else's shoulder to cry on."

"Felix," Kasper said, sounding like the words were torn from his throat. He looked petrified now, rabbit-heart pounding in his neck. Felix had seen that expression on his face before, whenever Felix made too many jokes about being gay.

Kasper was afraid to even hear the words. Why was Kasper so *scared* all the time?

Before Kasper could say anything else, Rima appeared in the doorway. There were dark, hollow bags under her eyes.

"He's here! Felix, Oscar is here!" she yelled, with pure panic in her voice.

Felix stopped thinking about Kasper immediately.

"Oscar," he said, fear running through him. Oscar was here while Harriet was on the loose. This couldn't be happening.

HARRIET

There was a reason Harriet had liked make-up so much when she was alive. It was a way to control how people saw her. She could make sure that everyone's first impression of her was positive: someone who was careful about her appearance; sociable and fashionable. They would never see the real person, hiding behind the mask.

Because Harriet had always known, deep down, that she was a mess. She was inarticulate, embarrassing. She could be mean. If people got to see the real her, they would hate her immediately. It was better that they only saw the filtered, artificial Harriet that she'd made up.

She wished desperately that her old disguise still worked. Because she was exposed now, completely and utterly. Everyone here saw her for who she truly was, regardless of her perfect eyeliner.

Harriet hid on the roof, giving her energy levels a chance to equalize and calming the torrent of emotion inside her. The sky went dark, and then a pair of headlights lit up the road below. A lone figure parked and walked over to Mulcture Hall. A human was coming into the building.

Harriet let out a yelp of delight – she could use this! Her plan of possession could still work! Then she saw their face.

The man looked familiar. A bit older, but his features were almost identical to Felix's. Didn't Felix say he had a twin? He'd said that his brother always visited on the anniversary of his death. Oscar, his name was.

This was perfect. She knew exactly where Oscar was going to go – and she was willing to bet that where Felix was, Kasper would follow. With both Kasper and Oscar in the same room, the rest would be easy. Kasper had leapt inside that police officer without any hesitation. If she got him close enough to Oscar, then all she had to do was make sure that she was there to piggy-back the possession.

Harriet ran down to Felix's room. She would be nice, and give Oscar a bit of time to mourn before she made Kasper possess him.

To her surprise, Leah was sleeping on the floor. She looked faint and muted, like the Shells had been. Claudia was curled up at her mother's side with one tiny fist wrapped in the fabric of her dress, whining softly.

"… Leah?"

The girl didn't stir, but there was a tormented expression on her face. When Claudia caught sight of Harriet, she stopped crying. She rolled over onto her back, regarding her with a surprisingly intelligent expression. Then she reached out towards Harriet with chubby arms, looking at her almost greedily. Harriet crouched down to wrap her hands around the baby's torso, but someone ran into the room before she could touch her. Surprised, Harriet jumped backwards. It was Felix.

"What the *hell* are you doing?" Felix shouted, as Claudia started screeching.

"What do you mean?" Harriet asked. "I was trying to stop her crying."

"Not the baby! Is he here yet?" He looked around, wild-eyed and chest heaving. "What are you going to do to Oscar?"

She sighed. She'd been hoping that Felix would never have to know about this. It wasn't like it would *hurt* Oscar to be possessed. Once they reached her gran's house, he'd be free to leave, confused but unharmed.

"Go away. This is none of your business."

"What … what are you planning? I know you attacked Greg. I'm not letting you take my brother too!"

Rima and Kasper appeared behind him in an act of perfect coordination, looking equally furious. How did they all fit together so well? Why had they not made space for her?

"I didn't do anything to Greg – he made his own choices. I didn't realize you were close." She kept her voice disinterested, as if she didn't care that they were looking at her like she was a monster.

"Why is everything a *game* to you?" Rima sounded winded, like she'd been punched in the chest.

"I want you to leave this room before Oscar gets here," Felix commanded with remarkable single-mindedness, walking towards her.

Harriet held her ground. If he came close enough for her to touch, then she would make him feel fear worse than he'd ever even dreamed possible.

"Absolutely not." Harriet tilted her chin upwards determinedly.

"You can't stop me. I'm not going to hurt him."

"You can't touch him," he said, fear sending his voice paper-thin.

"I'm not going to do anything life-threatening. Honestly. Please calm down." She wished Oscar would walk a bit faster. He was taking so long to arrive. Had the police boarded up the entrance and windows again, after they'd cleared away her corpse?

"Felix, use your power," Kasper said.

Felix stretched his hand out towards her. It was a growing tickle at the back of her mind; the compulsion to *go to sleep*. She shook her head, forcing the feeling away. It snapped.

Felix's brow furrowed. *You don't want to do this,* he whispered into her mind. *You want to sleep for a long time. You're so tired.*

It was harder to resist now, as he moved closer. She yawned, and then shook it off again, snapping the connection once more. It hit her like a physical blow that he could stop her from doing this. She should have hidden, invisible, until Oscar arrived. Felix was more dangerous than she'd planned for.

"Felix," she said, voice oozing charm, "Felix, relax! I'm not going to do anything bad. I promise."

Felix's gaze flickered, but he carried on moving towards her. A muscle stood out on his neck. *You want to go into the basement. You want to leave Oscar alone. You want to see the Tricksters.*

Grinding her teeth, she focused on the ache deep in her

gums and fixed her feet to the ground. If he came nearer, she could use her power and make him scream in agony. Though if he came close enough for her to touch him, he'd have her completely under his control. They were at a stand-off.

Felix's plaid-clad shoulders were tight with tension as he pushed the message into her. Again, she snapped the control, feeling the command ricochet back at him. He winced.

"You don't need to do this," she told him, as he recovered. She could feel herself weakening. She wouldn't be able to hold off his next attempt. "It's immoral to hypnotize people without their consent. You told me so yourself."

Felix frowned. "It's not immoral to do it to protect people."

She scowled. Fine. If he wanted to be like that. "Then again, Kasper could ask you to *murder someone* for him and you'd leap at the chance, drooling for more."

At that, Felix lunged at her. Harriet ducked, spinning across the room as the tail-end of his words hit her.

... to the basement.

When Kasper tried to grab her, she pressed a burst of pain into his fingertips. He let go reflexively, like he'd been burnt. She pushed past Rima, who moved to stop her, too late.

Running into the corridor, her main thought was to get away, but then she heard footsteps. Real, human footsteps, shaking the rotting wooden floorboards as they moved down the corridor. Oscar.

Behind her, Felix yelled, *"No!"*

A man in a well-tailored suit was walking down the hall. He

kept his head ducked, focusing on not tripping over the endless debris filling the building.

For one crystal-clear moment, nobody moved. Harriet stopped thinking about Felix and started preparing. It wouldn't take much. She just had to get Kasper close enough to touch him and he'd latch onto Oscar like a mosquito. With a bit of confusion sent Kasper's way, Harriet would follow him inside the body. She could make him go to her gran's house immediately.

She ran. She could feel the air move behind her as Felix followed. He was slow, too slow. She was going to beat him. She grabbed Kasper's wrist, tugging him along with her across the room with all of the strength her new energy had given her. He let out a yelp, tripping over his own feet as he tried to jerk his hand free of her grip.

Oscar had the same dark cropped curls of hair as Felix. There were lines on his face in the places that creased when Felix smiled.

Flames shot up between her and Oscar, and Harriet jumped back, startled. Where had the roaring fire come from? She couldn't feel any heat on her skin. Tentatively, she touched it. It was cold. Felix had sent the vision to her with his power, making her hallucinate a fire blocking her way.

She strode through it, ignoring the flames. At once, they disappeared. Felix let out a groan behind her. Harriet grabbed Kasper by the waist, using his stumble to throw him towards Oscar.

"No!" he cried, and reared back, clawing at her cheek as he tried to escape.

Let go.

Harriet released Kasper automatically. When she fell, Felix's grip on the back of her neck was the only thing that stopped her from hitting the floor. Cody was hanging from Harriet's leg, teeth sunk deeply into her calf. Rima leapt on her, tiger claws digging into her skin, sliding down her back in deep gouges. Harriet pushed pain into Rima until she yowled, jaws stretching wide in agony and claws digging in harder.

Softer emotions like lust and love were easy to push away, because people did that all the time anyway. Everyone had a crush they tried to ignore. But pain? That was harder to dismiss.

Harriet stumbled across the floor with Felix and Rima, struggling to break free. They knocked into Kasper, who flew forwards and passed through Oscar. The human stopped walking, a dizzy look crossing his face.

Kasper stopped in his tracks. He snarled and jolted forwards, reaching into Oscar's skull. His instincts had taken over.

"Kasper, no!" Felix yelled, letting go of Harriet to stretch his hand out towards Kasper. His command came again: *You want to go to the basement,* and then, distorted, a version he must have meant for Kasper: *You want to let go of my brother.*

Harriet laughed. Felix couldn't control them both. This was going to work.

She flung Rima across the room, ignoring Felix's orders telling her to leave. It was weaker now that Felix's attention was divided. He couldn't hypnotize them both at once. It was her or Kasper.

Felix commanded, *Leave Oscar alone,* pulling back Kasper, who fell limp into his arms. His mouth was a hungry, gaping void, but his eyes were pained.

Harriet threw herself at them, knocking the pair into Oscar's body. Her skin was slippery with blood from Rima's tiger claws, deep gouges running down her back and chest.

Go down to the basement. The command was weak, desperate now. Harriet didn't even try to wave it off.

The three ghosts wrestled inside Oscar, who made a cut-off, instinctive jerk of alarm. Harriet could feel Kasper trying to latch on to Oscar's soul. Every time he got close, Felix tugged him away until he lost his grip on the human's brain.

Harriet hooked her fingers around Oscar's soul, guiding it to Kasper. The three of them stretched and pulled at the human's body, fighting for control of the delicate layers of energy that held it together.

When Felix jerked Kasper outside the body, something came loose. Oscar grunted – a chest-deep, involuntary noise of shock. His soul split open as it was torn away from his body. There was a sudden explosion of golden energy.

Harriet couldn't help herself. She gulped down Oscar's spirit. It swelled inside her, burning along her veins faster than she could control. There was more than she'd anticipated – far more than the weak remnants of life she'd absorbed from the Shells.

She tried to pull away, but the torrent was too strong. The

energy came faster and faster, and she couldn't make it stop. Then she didn't want it to stop, and relaxed in ecstasy, letting it gush into her in an endless stream of delicious life.

Oscar screamed.

Kasper screamed.

Felix wailed.

Harriet moaned. She could feel the tender skin on the pads of her fingers splitting open from the pressure of absorbing so much energy.

Finally, the flow of energy slowed to a trickle. Oscar collapsed to the ground, completely limp. A white fire burned inside Harriet, so strong that she didn't know if it was killing her, or the only thing keeping her alive. She'd thought that she had overdosed on energy before, but this was something new. Her brain was rewriting itself, blowing out the nerves and replacing them anew. She wasn't just Harriet any more – she was a god.

Harriet looked down and smiled.

FELIX

Felix knew the second that Oscar died, because Kasper went limp in Felix's arms, gasping for breath as the urge to possess left him.

"Is he…?" Felix asked.

Harriet looked like she was *laughing*. He wanted to rip her heart right out of her chest.

"Yes," Kasper said. "He's dead. I'm so – I'm so sorry."

Belatedly, Felix released him. Tears dripped from his jaw. He rubbed them away absently.

He'd always braced himself for his brother's death. The year that Oscar didn't turn up, when Felix would know that he'd lost his brother for good. He'd never expected to watch the life sucked from Oscar's body. He'd had the power to stop it happening, but he was too weak.

He sobbed, closing his eyes against it all. He couldn't process what had happened. He didn't want this to be real. He didn't want to have to deal with this. He couldn't.

His twin was old, but not old enough. Felix had wanted to see what that hair looked like when it was grey, what that face looked like covered in wrinkles.

He dropped to his knees, wishing desperately that he could touch him, and feel the last traces of warmth leach from his skin.

Kasper laid a hand on his shoulder. And then gasped.

Oscar's ghost was hovering above the corpse, looking around in confusion. He saw Felix and broke into an enormous smile.

Oscar stepped forward. "Felix," he said, arms outstretched to hug him.

Felix jolted forward into the embrace. They touched for the first time in over twenty-five years. Then Oscar trembled and disintegrated into nothing.

Felix's heart broke in two.

Chapter 17

RIMA

Two days after Oscar Anekwe's death, Leah sat bolt upright and shouted, "She's going to kill Oscar!"

She was glowing with the energy released throughout the room when Oscar died. The death had released too much energy for Harriet to take it all, and Leah had absorbed the rest.

Even though it had brought her back from the edge of disintegration, Leah hadn't woken up. Rima had been terrified. She'd worried that they'd just pushed Leah too far, and something inside her had broken, even when she wasn't a Shell any more.

"Oh, Leah," Rima said, beyond exhausted. "You're too late. Far too late."

As Claudia cooed up at her mother, Leah closed her eyes, pained. "Where is Felix?"

Rima winced. "We don't know. He disappeared after Oscar disintegrated."

The day before, more police had come to check the building. Presumably Oscar's family had reported him missing. They'd taken away the corpse, commenting on how much of a safety risk the abandoned building was becoming.

Rima couldn't believe that Oscar was gone. There was something so tragic about him actually dying here, but not getting to become a ghost or see his brother. Especially after he'd loyally come back year after year to grieve for Felix.

Oscar had been so nice to her, when they were alive. He'd once found Rima struggling with some calculations for an assignment about painkiller dosages. He had been studying maths, so he'd explained it to her, drawing out diagrams and making sure she understood it all. It took hours. Afterwards, they ordered pizza and watched *The X-Files* together.

A few days before Rima's death, she had taught him how to boil an egg in the kitchenette on the second floor after she'd found him trying to boil one in the kettle. They chatted as the eggs bobbled around in an actual saucepan, and then carried on talking over soft-boiled eggs and crumpet soldiers.

Harriet had no idea what she'd destroyed.

"How are you feeling?" Rima asked.

"I'll be all right." Leah rested her head on Rima's shoulder and absorbed three rat spirits Rima had caught for her. She glowed a little brighter as she inhaled each one. "I've been a Shell before. If Claudia didn't hurt anyone, then it was all worth it."

Rima had been trying hard not to think about the baby. Claudia had gone to sleep for the first time since Leah had passed out, curled up serenely against her chest.

"Where's Harriet?" Leah asked.

Rima stared out at the sunset, glowing pink and yellow behind the campus buildings. No one had seen Harriet since the fight, but there were rumours. Rumours were all Rima had to go on, now that Felix was missing, and Kasper was overwhelmed with guilt for attacking Oscar.

"She's on the fifth floor. We think. Oscar's energy was a lot to absorb. She's probably still recovering from it."

Leah nodded. "OK. So … how are we going to get rid of her?"

"I have an idea. But we should probably find Felix first."

Leah was a bit shaky standing up, but seemed mostly unaffected by her extended sleep.

"Leah, how old are you?" Rima asked, as they began searching the building for Felix and Kasper. She had never seen anyone pass out after using their power like that – not even the oldest ghosts. She clearly couldn't handle accessing her power at all any more.

Leah tucked Claudia onto her hip and sighed. "My full name is Aeliana Flavius."

Rima repeated *"Aeliana"* under her breath reverently. Leah so rarely spoke about herself that the knowledge was something to treasure.

"It's Roman," she added.

Rima blinked. "Roman?"

"It's Roman, because I'm Roman."

Rima's jaw dropped. "Roman. Roman? Like, from Rome?"

"Roman, as in I'm nearly two thousand years old. Around

that, anyway. I'm not exactly sure when I was born. I try not to think about it. I didn't exactly have a pleasant time, when I was alive."

Absurdly, the first thing that came to Rima's mind was: "But you speak English. Not Latin."

Leah smiled. "You pick these things up. *Facillimum est.*"

"How are you even *here*?" Rima's words came out hoarse. "This building was built in the seventies!"

"My home is buried under the foundations. Venonae, it was called."

"A ruin is enough to keep you here?"

"For now."

Rima shook her head. Leah – her *best friend* – was two thousand years old. Even *Claudia* had lived for millennia. They had been here during the Roman invasion of Britain. The collapse of the Roman Empire. The Dark Ages. The Tudors. The English Civil War. She'd seen everything. Leah must have been through so many unimaginable, horrific things throughout history. It was amazing she was functioning at all.

And she'd listened to Rima babble on about *The X-Files* for decades.

It made sense that there were older ghosts here though. A few years after her death, Rima had gone exploring Mulcture Hall as a mouse, slipping into crevices under floorboards and down the sides of radiators. She'd found all sorts of lost things – tiny ceramic models, buttons, letters from old students stuck down the sides of their beds before they moved out, Polaroids, jewellery, even some money – but all of the things she found were relatively modern. The building hadn't been there for a few decades before she'd died. But dozens of generations of people must have lived and died here before that. There must be so much hidden under the ground.

Leah being Roman felt right, in some bizarre, inevitable way. She was dressed in a white linen dress, knotted around her waist. It *could* be an old, *old* shift of some kind.

"I don't understand why you didn't disintegrate centuries ago. How have you never run out of energy?"

Leah shrugged. "There never used to be any rules against taking energy from other ghosts. That's a modern phenomenon. For centuries, it was kill or be killed. So to speak. I had the advantage on any attacking ghosts – I used my power to see what attacks were coming."

This was so surreal. Leah was some kind of warrior ghost. Why had she been content to spend the last few decades just play-fighting with Rima? No wonder she seemed so utterly bored all the time.

"You must be the oldest ghost in the building. Older than the Tricksters, even."

At the words, Claudia let out a tiny wail. Her eyes bored into Rima like she was trying to convey a message.

Rima shivered, breaking eye contact with the baby.

What could Claudia be thinking? What had she seen over the last two thousand years? How could she *stand it*? Never ageing beyond a child, or expressing the thoughts that were clearly trapped inside her mind. She was begging to be understood, and – unlike with Cody and other animals – Rima had no way of hearing her.

Rima swallowed the lump in her throat. "It's not right, that you're both running out of energy after surviving *centuries*."

She wasn't ready to lose her. Not now. Not ever.

Leah squeezed her elbow. "It's time."

"It's *not*! There must be something we can do."

"If we did, we'd be no better than Harriet, Rima. You know that."

Rima bit her lip, looking away. "I can't imagine this place without you, Leah."

There were three ghosts watching from the far end of the corridor. She twisted, so that they couldn't see that she was crying. Everyone was always waiting now, hoping for more drama and gossip. They made her skin crawl. No wonder Felix had hidden himself away.

"*Hey,*" Leah said softly, and wiped away her tears. "I'm not going anywhere yet. And my only regret is that I didn't tell enough people to piss off while I had the chance."

Rima snorted, and wiped her face on her sleeve. "There's still time."

Leah grinned, and turned to yell "*Piss off!*" at the ghosts watching them. Rima's tears turned into helpless giggles.

"Feel better?"

"Much." Rima pulled Leah and Claudia into a hug. "I love you so much, Aeliana."

Leah held her tightly. "I love you, too. In fact…" She pulled a *Best Friends Forever* necklace out of her pocket – the one Rima had given her, years ago.

Rima touched the other half of the locket, which hung around her neck. "You kept it? All this time?"

"Don't make a big deal out of it."

"I'm totally chill, promise! I actually don't care whether you wear it or not!" Rima had to physically bite down on the corners of her lips to hide her grin as Leah put on the necklace.

Leah hummed in disbelief. "Now, let's go find the boys. If I'm disintegrating soon, then you better bet that I'm taking Harriet bloody Stoker with me."

I don't remember being alive. I died too young. But I've looked back at our lives. I've seen what it was like in the Roman fort where we lived. It was nice there – muddy and full of people, but a lot cleaner than some of the buildings that came later.

Leah grew up in a town full of Roman soldiers, caught in constant battle with the Celts near by. She had a speckled cat who ate out of her hands. She sang constantly. She was happy. By the time I was born, she'd lost all of those things. And by the time she died, I was all she had left at all.

Honestly, I prefer being dead to any life I could have had among the living. It's so much less messy, being a ghost. There are fewer expectations on a girl here.

I enjoy how much people underestimate me. They happily spill all their secrets in front of a baby, showing their true loyalties. I'm not saying that I'd choose to be like this if I had another option. But I've made the most out of a bad situation.

The most frustrating part about being so young is that I can't tell my mother any of the things I see happening in the future. That never used to be a problem, because Leah could see the future herself. But since she stopped using her power, I'm the only one who can see what's coming. I've got no way to warn her.

I've known about Harriet since the English Civil War. Leah and I saw out the war in style. This site was being used as an encampment for a troop of Roundheads. They all died like locusts. Honestly, you've never seen such poor hygiene.

For a season, we feasted on newborn ghosts all day and night, until we couldn't do anything but lie around and dream, swollen with energy. Too much energy sends ghosts wild and crazed, destroying them from the inside out. The white hair is an early warning sign, an indication to cut back on your indulgences. We all had it, back then.

It was around that time that I started testing how far into the future I could look. It was just a way to burn up the excess energy, at first.

A decade into the future, I saw a vision of my father learning to knit with the wool from a sheep spirit who'd died before a shearing. It was a hobby he continued for many years. It would have been endearing if he wasn't using two human fingers as knitting needles, taken from a ghost who'd upset him.

Fifty years away, the old barn had been burnt to the ground, and we were all huddled together under the charcoal remains of the wooden frame.

A hundred years, and we were pale and weak Shells,

floating around a few stray stones on the ground.

I should have stopped looking, then. It was already too dangerous, trying to see that far ahead. Time becomes unstable. Just looking could affect things – a little stray energy could cause chaos if it slipped through time.

I wanted to know how long it would take for us to disappear, like all the other ghosts around us. How could we keep surviving without people or animals or a building of any kind?

I skipped ahead in time again, and saw Harriet. It was just a flash – the vision was too small and fragile to last longer than a few seconds, stretched so far across time – but I saw a girl with a hole in the back of her head. Leah and I were there. Harriet was kneeling down beside us, a glowing chain of energy stretching from her hands to ours.

I wish I could have told Leah what I saw. But my mother doesn't realize I have a power at all.

I try my best to help her avoid danger – crying out in warning, or leaching energy from a threatening ghost until they leave us alone. I've kept my mother here for much longer than she'd have managed on her own. For a helpless child, that's about the best you can hope for.

Leah has no idea that Harriet is just the beginning. I'll fight alongside her, when the battle starts for real. I'll be their secret weapon – so secret, even they aren't aware of it.

FELIX

Felix sat on the fire escape outside Oscar's old student bedroom on the second floor. Rain trickled down his spine in an
ice-cold stream, making his teeth chatter.

Oscar's room had been emptied of his things years ago,
but Felix liked to pretend that Oscar had made some of
the pen marks on the desk. Just so he had *something* of his
brother.

His death was the worst kind of nightmare: so outrageously
awful that it couldn't be real.

He kept reliving the terrible moment when he'd understood
that he wasn't going to be strong enough to stop both Harriet
and Kasper from attacking Oscar. It had hit him like a punch
in the chest: the terrible dawning realization that his power
was going to fall short, and Oscar was going to die, and there
was nothing he could do about it.

If he'd practised using his power more, instead of being
stubbornly moral about hypnotizing anyone for all these
years, he might have been able to control them.

"Hi." Kasper was leaning out of the window, raindrops falling through him.

"Hi," Felix said back, automatically. They stared at each
other for a moment, then Kasper climbed out beside him.

In silence, they watched dark grey clouds rolling across the
landscape. He knew Kasper must be feeling guilty, in the worst
kind of way, but he didn't know how to tell him that this wasn't

his fault. Not without bursting into tears. He was teetering on the brink already.

"Felix..."

"I know we have a lot to discuss. But can we just ... sit?"

Kasper bobbed his head. When he held up his arm, Felix fell against his chest, tucking his face into Kasper's side. His familiar touch anchored something deep inside him, making his pain feel so much more bearable.

Kasper pressed his lips against Felix's head. "Tell me about him."

"He was always so much braver than me." He was trembling, letting out short, muffled sobs against Kasper's chest.

Kasper let Felix talk, holding and supporting him. They moved closer with every inhale, until Felix was half sitting in his lap.

When he finally pulled away, the rain had stopped. Kasper rubbed water away from Felix's cheek with one thumb. Felix pretended that it was rainwater instead of tears.

"You're going to survive this. I promise." Kasper swallowed. "This wouldn't have happened if I hadn't been there."

"He died because of Harriet, not you," Felix insisted.

"You had to stop me. Again."

"I'll always be here for you. What I said before – I was wrong. I'm not going anywhere. If you need me, I'm here." Just like Kasper was there for him.

Kasper's hand came up, pressing at the back of Felix's head until their foreheads touched. His pupils were blown wide open. "I'm not going anywhere, either."

When his gaze dropped to Felix's lips, Kasper sucked in a stuttering breath. Felix was shocked once again by how close they were. Kasper kept pushing at the boundaries he'd erected between them; creeping closer each time they touched, then darting away again. But maybe now, maybe finally, this was—

Someone yelled, "There they are!"

Felix's heart stopped. Kasper's head reared back.

Rima and Leah were barrelling across the room towards them.

HARRIET

Harriet was waiting for Oscar's power to manifest. She'd done this enough times now that she could tell from the way it was bubbling under her skin that it was almost ready. She hadn't given up the hope that it might be something useful. Even if it didn't let her get back to her gran, it could still help her to defend herself if the others came after her again. She'd barely managed to hold them off last time.

She had felt sick and dizzy ever since Oscar's death. Her lost eyelid and the incisions down her back from Rima's claws had been oozing constantly. Her whole body felt torn to pieces, like a scab that wouldn't heal. She itched and itched and itched until she wanted to scratch her skin off.

After the fight had ended, she'd turned invisible and slept

in the shadows, lost in the wracking torments of energy. Slowly, as light turned into darkness turned into light turned into darkness, Oscar's excess energy died away until she could think again.

Regret overwhelmed her. She hadn't meant to kill him. All she'd wanted to do was use Oscar's body to get home, but everything had somehow spiralled out of control. The energy and chaos and adrenaline had got mixed up in her head, and he'd just tasted so delicious, better than anything she'd tried before.

Killing humans was different to making a Shell disintegrate. Killing Oscar ... that was murder. She'd *murdered* him. Felix's twin brother.

Was she a monster, or was this how everyone felt on the inside? Were they all somehow wishing for blood and death and fear, too? Was everyone else just better than her at pushing those urges down?

Harriet focused on making Oscar's power manifest, because that felt like the only thing she could control any more. She had tried hunting rats to get a burst of energy, but she hadn't been able to catch one. There was no one around to trade with, either. The whole population of ghosts in the building seemed to have disappeared. They must be hiding away somewhere until the fighting was over for good.

Gradually, Harriet realized that heavy electronic music was playing near by. It vibrated through the floorboards and made her head pound. It was coming from a group of human students who were making their way through the hall.

They were clearly hours into their pre-drinks, and covered in glowing fluorescent paint. Shining phone lights into the shadowy corners, they kicked old beer cans across the concrete, making room to set down their own bottles of vodka in the corridor where Harriet was hiding.

"All right, Squash Club!" one of the boys said, clapping his hands together. "Where are the freshers at?"

Four pasty students stepped forward, looking nervous. The boy poured lemon juice into a bottle of Baileys, and shouted, "What team?"

"SQUASH!"

He eyed up each of the freshers, then handed the bottle to a blonde girl, who looked dismayed.

"We like to drink with Charlie, 'cause Charlie is our mate," he began, and the watching students joined in, shouting the rhyme as the fresher choked down the congealed liquid. *"AND WHEN WE DRINK WITH CHARLIE, SHE GETS IT DOWN IN EIGHT ..."*

The fresher was chugging the drink, looking green.

"... SEVEN ... SIX ... FIVE ... FOUR ... THREE ... TWO ... ONE!"

Only recently, Harriet had been like them. A naïve, innocent fresher, whose biggest problem was finding new and disgusting ways to get drunk. She'd changed so much since then.

Charlie held up the empty bottle, looking proud and

nauseous in equal measure. The boy clapped her on the back, then shouted, "Let's get this seance started!"

Seance? Harriet suddenly clicked to attention.

The students gathered in a circle, hooking their arms together, as Charlie wandered off down the corridor, presumably looking for a corner to throw up in.

"Spectres of Mulcture Hall, hear our call. We wish you no harm," a fresher intoned.

"Give us our girl back!" one of the boys yelled.

The students all burst into giggles, except one boy, who looked terrified.

"We call upon the spirit of Harriet Stoker…"

They were here for *her*? She'd only been dead a few days, but apparently she had become a university myth already.

"If Harriet is still present in the building, please can she make herself known to us."

A sign? They wanted a sign?

Harriet walked into the centre of the circle, spinning around to look at them all. Surely it wouldn't hurt to take a little from one of these humans? Just a smidgen of energy would be enough to make Oscar's power manifest. They had so much to spare, and they were practically offering it up to her. It could be the difference between life and death; between holding her ground against the others or being destroyed. Could she really…?

Should she?

"Harriet Stoker! Your life was taken too soon! In tribute, we offer up this … er – bottle of tequila!" One of the boys poured out a trail of liquid in the middle of the circle, right through Harriet's spirit. It was a cold dart to the heart.

The circle was moving, students swaying back and forth as they took swigs of their drinks. Before she could make a decision, one of the boys stumbled into her, passing through her body. Her instincts kicked into action involuntarily. She latched onto his energy, sucking it out of him in waves. She fought to stop it but it was like her hooks had caught onto him and she couldn't move away.

Oscar's power pulsed inside her, coming to life as the student convulsed and fell to his knees. Something popped inside her head, a deep pressure swelling and pushing against the inside of her skull. She shook out her ears, trying to dispel it.

A girl yelled, "Guys, I think there's something wrong with Eric!"

The students dragged him to his feet, carrying him away as they fled. Harriet was left alone, kneeling on the floor. She tipped her head back, energy burning up inside her. The power sprang into life. To her surprise, her whole body began to morph.

She had transformed somehow, like when Rima turned into an animal. Though she was still human, something had changed. Her hands were smaller than usual and covered in wrinkles. When she peered into the cracked glass of a window, it was her grandmother's face that stared back at her.

Harriet skittered away in fright. It was only when her gran's expression contorted in fear that she realized she had transformed into her. Harriet's new power let her change her body.

She focused her power again, thinking of Rima. Within seconds, her gran's face morphed into Rima's, looking first surprised then happy. This could come in handy. Incredibly handy.

LEAH

Leah was relieved to see that Felix was still here. She'd seen ghosts commit suicide when their loved ones disintegrated, in the hopes of following them into whatever afterlife came next. But this existence was all they had for certain, and it would be a waste for Felix to give it up in search of something more with his brother.

"It's *pouring* out there, you guys. Come back in," Rima said to Felix and Kasper on the fire escape. "Back at it again with the pathetic fallacy, eh?"

"It's only drizzle," Kasper said.

Rima snorted. "*Only drizzle.* It thundered a second ago!"

Felix watched them, looking a little stunned. Leah gently touched his shoulder. "My condolences on your loss, Felix Anekwe."

Taking her completely by surprise, he pulled Leah into a hug. She held still. Before Rima and the boys had appeared in her life, she hadn't touched anyone except Claudia in centuries. She'd tried her hardest not to, in fact.

"I'm sorry that I couldn't warn you in time."

Felix kissed her cheek. "Don't. Please. It wasn't your fault, not even a little bit."

She took a deep breath and nodded. "I know. But I'm sorry, anyway."

When Claudia tugged at his hair, Felix took her from Leah.

"Hey, munchkin," he said. "I bet you're glad your mum's finally woken up, aren't you?" Claudia *adored* Felix.

Leah stretched out her arms. More and more, her whole body was a mass of pins and needles. Holding Claudia didn't help.

It wouldn't be long before she disintegrated. She'd accepted that; now she was just impatient to get it over with. She'd had more than her fair share of time. Except … there was Claudia. There was always Claudia.

Leah had been alone for most of the time she'd been alive. Her family's goals were directly opposed to Leah's own desires. She had always just been a pawn in their plans, miserable and lonely except for Claudia. At least she'd had her, someone on her side who she could trust.

What would happen to her if Leah disintegrated? At least when they became Shells, they could stay together. She didn't want Claudia to disintegrate with her. If there was an after-life, it contained people who she didn't want Claudia to have to see again. The two of them were safer here in Mulcture Hall, hiding out in the place between now and whatever came next.

To Leah's surprise, Rima looked at Claudia and asked,

"Why couldn't *you* have done something about Harriet, huh?"

Claudia wriggled in outrage.

"Next time," Leah whispered in her ear.

She wished there was a way for Claudia to talk to her. She could see just how much she wanted to say. Her eyes would fill with frustration, as she searched desperately for a way to communicate with Leah.

"How are you doing, Felix?" Rima asked. "Seriously."

"I'm … coping. I think."

"Do you want to talk about it? Or would you rather we carried on pretending like nothing has happened?"

Felix smiled. "Can we stick with the forced humour for right now?"

Kasper was staring down at his hands. He had been touching Felix's cheek when Rima had found them, but now he had pulled away. Leah wished that he would love himself as much as he loved the rest of them. Kasper was his own worst enemy, sometimes.

It wasn't his fault, though. Society was different now, compared to how it had been since she was alive. Most of those changes were good, a sign of progress – women could be their own people, with careers and incomes and bank accounts. But some things were bad. Over the centuries, she'd watched sexuality become something malicious and evil and suppressed. It was a step back, even as everything else in society progressed. Poor Kasper had taken the brunt of that.

Rima said, "I think it's time we discussed Harriet. I have

a plan, but can you *please* get out of the rain before we start plotting? I know we can't catch hypothermia, but this *really* isn't a rom-com. Not every dramatic conversation needs to take place in the rain!"

"Please stop with the genre criticisms," Leah said. "I just woke up. It's too early."

"Oh, be quiet, Miss Angst-and-Misery," Rima said. "You've been awake for at least an hour."

"Have any of you seen Harriet recently? How do we know she's not listening in again?" Felix asked, voice quavering. He looked around the room nervously.

Kasper jogged a lap around the room, waving his arms madly. He didn't bump into any invisible figures.

"Satisfied?" he asked Felix.

Felix rolled his eyes but nodded. "Carry on, Rima."

"Well, I've been thinking a lot about what we can do about her." As Rima spoke, something in her posture changed minutely. The girl who had been teasing Felix only moments before was gone. In her place stood a commanding, determined figure. Leah had never been prouder.

"I think we can all admit that we aren't going to be able to stop her with force," Rima continued, striding up and down as she spoke. "None of us have ever dealt with anything like this before – and Leah's too weak right now to help, so it's just the three of us. We can't beat her with strength anyway. She must have four or five powers by now, between her own, the Shells', and O— your brother's. She might even have Greg's power, too, seeing as we don't even know what she did to him."

Leah shivered. Greg had used his power on her once. He'd waited around the corner to pounce on her. His touch had made her trust him unquestioningly. Against all her better judgement, he had convinced her to come down to the basement with him. He'd almost managed it, too – only Claudia's insistent screaming had made her pause and reconsider, just before she passed through the lightning barrier. If Harriet had Greg's power, they were all in trouble.

Rima continued, "At this point, we can't even predict what things she could do to us. We have to assume any power is within her grasp, if she's started picking off weaker ghosts. If we fight her, we're going to turn into Shells long before she even gets tired."

Kasper ran a hand over his scalp. "Can you get to the solution? This summary is stressing me out."

"Sorry. Basically, I think we need to use something other than brute force. There must be some way we can combine our powers to get her under control without fighting, right? That didn't work last time and she's only grown stronger. We need to use our brains instead of muscle."

Leah considered this. There was a chance that Rima was on to something. The idea of combining powers reminded her of some advice an old ghost had told her. They'd been living in the building when she was newly dead, and had disintegrated soon after. Leah had never tried it out, but she'd kept the idea in the back of her mind – just in case she needed to use it one day.

"You know, I've heard of something we could try. It might take some preparation, though."

Rima asked, "What is it?"

Leah frowned, trying to remember the details. "If you can get hold of a body part, then we can use it as a connection to her energy. We can draw out the excess energy until she's weak enough that we can subdue her. Something like a strand of her hair or a fingernail would work. Anything that used to be part of her body. It will still be running off her energy, and we can tap into that connection."

"Maybe we can distract her and steal some hair without her noticing?" Felix offered.

Rima winced. "She's on her guard now. I don't think she'd let *any* of us get that close. She knows we want to lock her in the basement."

Felix held up a hand. "Wait – the basement. Couldn't her ... eyelid be down there? It was torn off by the Tricksters, remember?"

Rima gasped.

"An eyelid could work!" Leah said.

"What if we made a trade with the Tricksters for it?" Rima suggested.

Kasper looked frightened. "Rima, you know what they did to Lisa. We can't risk it. They'd take everything from us."

She shook her head, expression taut. "I can't see how we have any other choice. I'd rather be in debt to the Tricksters than let Harriet keep killing people."

Leah said, "I agree. I can show you how to suck out Harriet's energy using the eyelid, once you have it. But I'm afraid I won't be able to come to the basement with you. The Tricksters and I have … unfinished business. My presence might make it harder to negotiate with them."

It had been decades since she'd seen Rufus and Vini, and she had no interest in repeating the experience. She *definitely* wasn't letting her daughter get anywhere near them.

Rima looked intensely curious, but to Leah's relief, she didn't ask any questions. "I've got loads of credit on the black market from all the squid ink they've ordered for tattoos. We can use that to trade for it."

Kasper sighed. "Do we really have to go and see *the Tricksters*? Would they even still have it? Everyone knows that Vini likes skin. He's probably eaten it by now."

"Rufus wouldn't let him," Leah said firmly. "He will know how valuable it is."

"Does he know that he can control people with part of their body?" Felix asked.

"I think so." Leah winced. She was lucky that he'd never managed to get hold of anything from her or Claudia. He'd have destroyed them both in an instant.

Felix said, "Sorry Rima, but I don't think your credit on its own is going to be enough for this. He'd be stupid to give up part of Harriet's spirit unless there was something even better on offer. She's the most powerful ghost in the building right now."

"What could we offer that he wouldn't be able to resist?"

Rima asked, frowning. "What can possibly be better than a way to control the most powerful ghost in the building?"

Kasper had gone pale. "Me."

It's been eighty years since we last saw Rufus and Vini. And that's nowhere near long enough for them to forgive me for what I did.

I don't think I'm ready to talk about it yet. I'm sorry.

Leah would do anything to protect me, but she can't avoid this confrontation for ever. Time is running out, and when we see Rufus and Vini again, I'm going to do what I was never brave enough to do before. I'm going to end this, once and for all.

Chapter 18

KASPER

"I really, really don't want to do this," Kasper groaned, standing outside the basement. He was so nervous that he could taste acid in his throat. The Tricksters had been trying for so long to get Kasper to use his power for them. Now he was actually going to give it to them.

They hadn't seen anyone on the way here. Everyone had gone into hiding while Harriet was on the loose. Only Rima and Felix were foolhardy – and brave – enough to try and stop her. If they hadn't been here with him, Kasper would be hiding away, too. He definitely wouldn't be preparing to go inside the basement.

He hated this dark, dingy floor, where everything was damp and the sun never shone. He hated even thinking about it, let alone coming down here. But this plan was their best shot at stopping Harriet. When Kasper thought about Harriet, his brain screamed *Stay away!* and *Not a good idea!* It offered up no suggestions about how to defeat her.

"Are you sure you want to do this?" Felix asked, worrying at his bottom lip with his teeth.

"I need to help. She *killed your brother*. I have to stop her."

Felix dropped his head. "It's too much. We'll try something else. We'll—"

"There's nothing else." There must have been something final in his voice because Felix stopped talking.

"Rock, paper, scissors to go in first?" Rima suggested. She was doing a very good job of hiding her terror. Or maybe he was the only one who was terrified.

Felix gritted his teeth. "No. I'll go in first. I can protect you both, then."

A shiver ran down the nape of Kasper's neck. He really, *really* didn't like the sound of that. Did Felix think he would have to hypnotize someone today?

He touched the back of his hand to Felix's, and he immediately interlinked their fingers. Kasper was carefully not thinking about Felix's confession earlier. Obviously, it hadn't come as a surprise to Kasper that Felix liked him. He wasn't that oblivious. But Kasper never, ever, ever let himself think about Felix's feelings. It was off limits; an existential crisis waiting to happen.

Kasper had been perfectly happy burying it at the back of his mind, never to be acknowledged or addressed. But now, he had to face it, even though his mind kept skittering away in absolute terror. Felix wanted things from him. Things that Kasper couldn't let himself give.

Whatever happened, all he knew was he absolutely couldn't lose him.

He focused on the warmth of Felix's skin, and tried not to think about what they were about to do. He gulped.

With Felix leading the way, they stepped inside the basement. Kasper's heart was thudding in his ears like he was underwater and he knew the Tricksters would sense his fear and try to feed off it.

Everyone in the basement turned to watch them enter.

"Hi," Felix said, into the roaring silence. "We've come to ask for a trade."

His voice sounded steady. Only someone who knew him well would be able to detect the tremble of fear laced through the words. Kasper squeezed his hand.

No one moved or spoke, until Rufus stepped out of the darkness. The Trickster glowed with energy, looking as mind-numbingly awful as Kasper remembered.

Terror swept up his spine, but he ignored it. If any of them panicked, this was all over. Once you entered the basement, you were fair game. Any sign of weakness or fear, and the Tricksters would pounce.

"Felix Anekwe. What a pleasure."

When Rufus sniffed the air, Kasper flinched. He could feel Rima trembling beside him. The Tricksters had been here long before him. They were *old*, and that hadn't made them weak, like it had Leah. It had made them strong.

"Would you be willing to trade with us?" Felix repeated.

Vini was inching towards them, eyes fixed on Kasper. He must be able to feel the fear pouring off him.

"What, no time for chit-chat?" Rufus rolled up his sleeve, looking down at the tattooed spreadsheet on his arm. He counted up the Roman numerals, then said, "I see you're in credit. I'm always happy to do business with someone reliable. This is the first time you've come to us personally with a request, though. Are things not working out to your liking upstairs?"

When Rufus took a step towards them, they all jumped back involuntarily. Felix held out one hand. "I know that you know what my power is. I will use it. Please stay where you are."

He straightened his glasses and added, clearly trying to be diplomatic, "Sir." A pang of affection hit Kasper's heart.

The Tricksters both stopped moving, though they looked ready to pounce whenever the time was right. Kasper bit the inside of his cheek.

"I've always admired your power, Felix," Rufus said. "Are you sure you don't want to join us down here? We have much to offer you."

Kasper thought he must mean a share of their black-market tradings. If Felix agreed to use his hypnotism on people who disobeyed Rufus, then they might give him first dibs on anything that turned up on the black market. The most valuable rewards were exotic animal spirits or the opportunity to use someone's unusual powers. You had to be willing to sacrifice your morals to get the best things.

Felix shook his head, twice, and then again. Kasper couldn't believe how calm he seemed. How controlled.

Rufus sighed. "It's an open offer. Please consider it. Time is running out, though."

Before Kasper could ask why, Felix said, "No, thank you. We're here because we know you've got Harriet's eyelid. We need it. Rima has a lot of credit built up from black-market trades that we'd like to cash in. On top of that, we've got something else you might be interested in."

Vini was still creeping towards Kasper. He swallowed again and again, trying to ignore his fear. When Felix pushed Kasper behind him, he let himself be moved. Unlike Felix and Rima, he had no way of protecting himself, if this became a fight. His power was useless against other ghosts. Physical strength didn't mean much when your opponent could summon monsters inside your head.

"What might you need this eyelid for, Mr Anekwe?"

"That's none of your business," Rima said, and then flinched when Rufus turned his attention on her.

"Rima Hamid, is that correct?"

"Yes, sir." She shrunk in on herself.

"Ms Hamid, you are also welcome to join us. We've always dreamed of a power like yours. The possibilities are endless," Rufus said dreamily. "Have you ever thought about producing hallucinogenic snake venom? We've become so bored with all the usual methods of having fun, after all these years. Venom would add a little edge to our days."

There was an uncomfortable pause. "No, thank you," she said, very politely.

"I suppose the same is true of the coward in the back? Mr Jedynak, it's amazing that you've survived this long. You reek of fear like a frightened little rabbit."

Kasper's heart raced. He couldn't think of a reply.

"Do you still have the eyelid?" Rima persisted.

"We still have the eyelid. But there's only one thing you can offer that we'd accept."

"What?" Felix asked, sharply.

"I want Kasper's power, of course," Rufus said. "And not just to borrow. I want to take it off him for good."

"Absolutely not," Rima spat out, while Kasper was still remembering how to breathe. "You can't take it off him. He could disintegrate!"

Kasper felt sick. He'd been planning to let them use it once, not give it up completely.

Vini laughed.

Rufus sighed. "How disappointing. No power, no eyelid. I look forward to seeing what Harriet does next."

"You can't do this!" Felix snapped. "You can't give her the knowledge to destroy people and then let her run wild."

"And why not?" Rufus said. "None of you have ever done anything for us. In fact, your alignment with Aeliana proves that our interests are in direct opposition."

Rima gasped.

"Aeliana?" Felix asked, looking confused.

"Leah," Rufus said. "I'd hoped you'd have brought our dear sister with you. Please pass on our regards to her – and our niece."

"Wait, *Leah*?" Rima asked in shock. "Leah is your *sister*?"

Kasper was surprised, to say the least. Why had Leah never mentioned this?

Rufus continued, "Well. Sister by marriage. We haven't seen her in far too long. She shouldn't feel like she can't pop in for a visit. I'm sure we can find a way past what Claudia did." His eyebrow twitched.

Leah was related to Rufus and Vini? *Really?*

"*What Claudia did*," Felix repeated. Kasper looked at him out of the corner of his eye, confused.

"Don't tell me she hasn't told you. Aren't you all a *family* now?" When none of them responded, he laughed. "Well. I suppose Leah has complicated ideas about what being a family means. You know how it is with brothers, Felix. Have a little sympathy."

Felix grimaced. Kasper didn't know what they were talking about, but he couldn't stand here and do nothing. They had to stop Harriet. He wanted to offer up his power, but since Oscar's death, he knew first-hand why the Tricksters should never be trusted with it.

Kasper was too afraid to think of any other ways to help. His fear got in the way of everything, eating away at him and hurting the people around him. He wanted to tear that feeling out of his chest, so he could be useful for once. Greg got on just fine without his worry, didn't he?

Kasper suddenly knew what he had to do. He spoke up, interrupting Felix's increasingly frantic attempts at negotiation. "I want to talk to Rufus alone."

Felix started. "What? Kasper, no!"

"I know what I'm doing. I promise."

He touched Felix's wrist, but he just looked hard at him, not moving an inch.

"Felix, let him talk." Rima tugged him outside, leaving Kasper alone.

Utterly defenceless now, Kasper looked straight at Rufus.

"So, Mr Jedynak. What do you want to say to us? Have you changed your mind about giving up your power? There is a chance you'd survive it, you know."

Vini crept closer to Kasper, slow and smooth. He pressed his back against the wood of the door, focusing on the thought of Felix waiting for him on the other side, centimetres away.

"I'm not giving you my power. That is non-negotiable. But I'll give you my fear. I know you took Greg's worry. I want you to do that to me too."

Rufus blinked. He took an eager, hungry step forwards. "Your fear? *All* of it?"

"I know you can feel it. I'm terrified, all the time. I hate it. I want to be able to fight without terror freezing me in place. Please. Take it."

"You understand that you'll be different, afterwards. It's not something that ever comes back. Being fearless will impair your judgement."

Kasper would survive. Felix could tell him when he was doing something stupid, just like he did now. "I understand. Do it."

Rufus cradled Kasper's jaw in his hand, breathing in deeply.

"Last chance, Mr Jedynak. Do you want this?"

Kasper closed his eyes, tilting his head back. He was absolutely, bone-deep terrified. And he wanted to be rid of it. "Take it. Take it all."

When the pins and needles started, Kasper had to hold back a scream. He'd made a mistake – Rufus wasn't going to stop at taking his fear; he was going to take all of Kasper's energy, he was going to destroy him, and Harriet would run wild for ever, and she would kill Felix and Rima and Leah and Claudia, and—

The fear dropped away, immediately and completely. He felt calm. Confident.

He reached up and pulled the hand off his neck, pushing him away.

"That's enough," he said. "You've got it all."

Rufus was glowing. "Oh," he cooed. "You were so *afraid*. How delicious."

Kasper raised an eyebrow. "Great. Glad to be of service."

Rufus had taken enough of his spirit from him that he was weaker than he'd ever been. And he had no back-up now, with Felix and Rima waiting in the corridor.

None of that stopped him from pushing Rufus so that he tripped backwards, falling into his brother.

"Now, get the eyelid, yeah?" Kasper said, hard.

Rufus licked his lips. "I suggest that you call your friends back in, before you embarrass yourself."

Chapter 19

FELIX

Felix was trying to listen through the basement door when Kasper stepped out, grinning. "Guys, the eyelid is so gross and gooey! You have to see it!"

Felix blinked at him. "What?"

Kasper rolled his eyes, bouncing up and down on his heels. "Come see!"

Throwing a bemused glance at Rima, Felix followed Kasper back into the basement. The lightning barrier glowed and then turned into darkness.

Rufus and Vini were leaning back against the pool table, smirking. Felix looked at Kasper, who was arranging his hair in the reflection of the door handle. What was *happening*?

"It's all yours," Rufus said, gesturing to an eyelid on the pool table. Behind it, some ghosts were having a wrestling match that seemed to involve tentacles of some kind. Or, rather, Felix hoped that it was a wrestling match. He grimaced and looked away.

"Thanks?" Felix said, looking searchingly at Kasper. Was this a trick? Were they going to get eaten if they went close enough to pick it up?

Rima was staring fixedly at the leering Tricksters.

"So why does Harriet have white hair like yours?" Kasper said, wandering over to Rufus. He hopped up onto the pool table to sit next to the Trickster.

Kasper had been so terrified he was almost frothing at the mouth earlier. Why was he engaging the Tricksters in casual conversation now?

Rufus looked at Kasper out of the corner of his eye. "Harriet's hair is white from energy overload."

"What, because she took energy from all those Shells?" Kasper leant forward and picked a stray thread off the shirt Rufus was wearing. It was like he was drunk.

Felix's heart rate tripled. What was Kasper playing at? He was going to get himself destroyed.

"It happens when there's too much energy for one spirit to contain," Rufus explained.

"That's horrifying!" Kasper said, sounding delighted. "Please continue."

"That's really the whole explanation," Rufus said.

Kasper nodded. "Well, it suits you guys, and I honestly can't imagine you without white hair, but Harriet looked better before. What colour was your hair before, by the way?"

"It was brown!" Vini said. "Mine was kind of light brown, like honey, and Rufus had chocolate-coloured hair, and Fabian had—"

"Vini," Rufus said, in a "that's enough" kind of way.

Felix should probably do something about this conversation,

but he could only gape at them. Rima wrinkled her nose at him in confusion. At least she agreed that none of this was normal.

"So you can taste fear, right?" Kasper asked next. "Can you tell what people are most afraid of?"

Rufus nodded. He seemed amused, in a patient sort of way. Felix didn't want his patience to run out. "I suppose. Fear has a different taste depending on what type it is – success, romance, obligation, spiders, you know. For most people, the thing they're most afraid of is themselves. Like you, for instance."

Kasper grinned. "Well, I knew *that* already. What is Harriet afraid of?"

Vini made a cut-off noise of delight.

Rufus tilted his head, then turned to meet Vini's gaze. "You can tell him."

Vini looked flattered. "Her grandmother."

Felix blinked, interested despite himself. Harriet loved her gran. Hadn't she been trying desperately to leave the building so that she could get back to her?

Kasper pushed on. "Boring. I was hoping it would be snakes. Hey, is Leah really your sister-in-law?"

Felix cast a desperate look at Rima, begging her to do something.

"Indeed," Rufus said. Strangely, he was humouring Kasper's endless questions. Felix hoped that his entertainment value lasted long enough for them to leave the basement.

"Man, that's wild. What was she like when she was alive?"

Felix frowned, but Kasper ignored him.

"Aeliana has always been completely herself."

"Legit! She's the best."

Rufus raised his eyebrows.

In desperation, Felix leant over the pool table and scraped the eyelid into his palm. It was slightly warm and sticky, leaking a clear, viscous substance. It might have been his imagination, but it wiggled slightly when he curled his fingers over it.

"Kasper, come on! Let's go, now, now, now!" He dragged Kasper off the pool table and away from Rufus, ushering him through the door.

"What the hell was that?!" Felix hissed at Kasper when they were safely outside.

"What? I was just chatting!" Kasper shrugged.

Felix rolled his eyes. "Rufus was probably seconds away from strangling you."

Kasper examined his cuticles. "It wouldn't have made any difference if he had."

Felix gave up. Whatever was going on with him, it could wait. "Let's get the eyelid up to Leah."

"What do we do if Harriet comes after us on the way?" Rima asked.

It was disconcerting to think that Harriet could be here, right now, maybe metres away, invisible and waiting in the shadows for them to leave. They couldn't fight her until they were ready. Who knew how many other ghosts she was preying on? She could be growing stronger by the day, gathering powers all the time.

There was a beat of silence.

"Cross that bridge when we get to it?" Felix suggested, voice tight with stress.

Kasper started, inexplicably, to chuckle. What had he done when he was alone in the basement? What if he'd given them his power after all? Felix brushed away the thought. Whatever he'd given the Tricksters, they would deal with it later, once Harriet was out of the way.

RIMA

"It's all going to be fine," Rima said, for the third time, sitting cross-legged on the floor while Leah examined the eyelid.

"Relax," Kasper told Felix, who was pacing back and forth across the room.

Rima was intensely curious about what kind of deal Kasper had struck with Rufus. She really, really hoped that Kasper hadn't done anything stupid just because he felt guilty about Oscar.

"I am relaxed," Felix said, then immediately started biting at his nails. Cody was hunting a mouse, and kept looking up at him in annoyance, his pacing disturbing her prey.

"Nearly got it," Leah said, staring at the eyelid. "It's like tuning into a radio frequency. I can feel her energy. She's … she's so strong."

Rima crossed her fingers, hoping this would work. Leah

said she could use the eyelid to leach Harriet's energy out of her spirit, wherever in the building she was hiding. But Leah had never tried it before. She was basing this on something she'd been told hundreds of years before. Was it even possible?

It was their best shot at making Harriet weak enough that they could get her into the basement. If they tried to take her down now, then she would probably destroy them.

"Leah, are you related to the Tricksters?" Rima asked.

Leah breathed out through her nose. She kept her focus on the eyelid, but she'd gone completely still. "Rufus and Vini are my brothers-in-law."

"You were married to their brother?"

She nodded. "Fabian. Claudia's father was their older brother."

Claudia whined.

There had been *three of them* when they were alive? Rima couldn't imagine anything worse.

"Why did you never—"

"I don't really want to talk about it. And especially not right now."

Leah looked utterly miserable, so Rima decided not to ask any more questions, even though she was burning with them.

"Can we just get on with this?" Kasper asked, lounging back against the wall.

"I think it's ready, actually," Leah said. "We need to make sure we've found Harriet before I use it, though. Once she's weak, we'll have to get Qi to help us move her into the basement as quickly as we can, before she fights back. She'll still be able to use her powers, even if she's not got much energy."

Rima nodded. It wasn't like they needed to do a vote with the whole building. Harriet had killed a living human. She had to go to the basement, there was no question.

"How about we make a big commotion, so she'll come and see what's going on?" Felix said. "As soon as we start talking to her, she won't be able to resist answering back. She's never turned down the chance at an argument yet."

"It's a plan," Rima said. "We can play the rest by ear, as long as we have the eyelid. If Leah waits out of sight with that, then the rest of us can handle Harriet."

Some of the other ghosts would have helped them fight Harriet, too, but most of them had hidden away inside the walls since Oscar's murder. They probably wouldn't come out until the danger had passed.

Leah rolled her eyes. "If you just want me to stay out of the fight, that's ridiculous. There's no way I'm going to let her hurt you if she starts—"

"I'm not risking you disintegrating, Leah. It's not worth it. If there's a fight, we're more than capable of dealing with it."

"*Yeah,* we are. She's going to regret ever coming near this building." Kasper was clenching and unclenching his fists, desperate for a fight.

Leah shrugged. "Fine. I guess I'll stay out of it seeing as Kasper has decided to fight her single-handedly. Are you *drunk*, Kasper?"

"I'm just – ready. I'm done with this. I want to get it over with."

"Well, let's get on with it, then," Rima said. "Let's huddle, guys. Come on, Leah – you too."

"Pass," she said.

"Liven up, squad!" Rima said. "This is our *moment*!"

Leah reluctantly let Rima pull her into the circle, intoning, "I will treasure this moment for ever."

"Same," Rima said, entirely serious.

Then Cody started yipping behind them. Someone was coming. Though it wasn't Harriet. It wasn't even another ghost. It was a human.

Fabian. The lost brother. The worst of the Tricksters.
I haven't mentioned my father much, have I? Rufus and
Vini might be unpleasant, but in comparison with my
father, they were practically doting aunts. At least they
knew my name.

I can show you the moment that Fabian disintegrated,
when Leah lost all the loyalty Rufus and Vini had given
her. It's the biggest mistake I ever made.

This is how I destroyed my father.

Here's what happened. Fabian was curious, power-
hungry and insatiable. He and his brothers ruled the
ghosts here with an iron fist. Everyone did what he asked,
and he set Vini on them if they refused.

He was convinced that he could do more with Leah's
power. It wasn't enough that she was pushing herself
to look into the future for him whenever he asked. He
wanted to know when he would disintegrate.

He couldn't believe that he'd disappear one day. All his
power, all his work – it wasn't enough. He had to make
sure he avoided the final death.

One day, some time back when war rationing was still
in operation, he told Leah she had to look five hundred years
into the future. He wanted to see if he ever found a way to
survive that long as a ghost, without becoming a Shell.

Leah knew that it would drain her completely. It's

a dangerous thing to do anyway – looking that far through time is unstable. It could have damaged both the future and the past.

When she refused him, Fabian cradled me in his arms and wrapped his hands around my neck. He threatened to tear off my head if she didn't do it. His own daughter. The threat was enough to make Leah try.

At first, it seemed like it might work, until she started to waver. She dimmed and went black and white, and her atoms started to separate.

I panicked. My father had proven once and for all that he didn't care about me, whereas my mother was willing to sacrifice herself to save me. The choice was simple. Cradled in his arms, with his hands around my neck, I took his energy and pushed it all into her.

He was gone before he even noticed. Leah glowed with his energy, and re-formed. Then Rufus and Vini realized what had happened, and we had to run and hide. They've been haunting us ever since.

The Tricksters have never forgiven me or my mother. If they weren't locked in the basement by Qi, they would destroy us both in vengeance for Fabian. One day we will have to face them again. All we can do is delay the inevitable. As you've probably guessed, time is running out for all of us.

RIMA

An old lady in tweed was climbing the stairs to the fourth floor, looking carefully around Mulcture Hall. Her hair was white like the Tricksters', tied back with a silk scarf.

"Who is she?" Rima was whispering, even though the human couldn't hear her.

She seemed to just be looking around, taking in the rotting mattresses, ivy-covered glass windows, and rust-stained puddles.

"Do you know her, Felix?" Kasper asked, frowning. "Could she be here because of Oscar?"

Felix shook his head. "I've never seen her in my life. And the police have already taken him away."

Rima froze. "Wait. Is she – could she be Harriet's grandmother?"

Now she was looking more closely, the woman did look like Harriet. There was something familiar in the shape of the nose and the way it wrinkled as she flicked dirt off her coat cuff.

Kasper frowned. "What would she be doing here?"

Rima's heart hurt. The lady must be mourning her granddaughter, on a pilgrimage to the place Harriet had died. Harriet had said she lived alone. She must be so sad and tired and lonely.

"Can we use this?" Leah asked. "We needed a distraction. This might be the perfect opportunity to lure Harriet here while we use the eyelid."

Felix's eyebrows rose. "That could work."

It might be a good way to make Harriet back down, too. Seeing her grandmother could snap her out of her chaos.

"I'll go and find her!" Rima was hopeful for the first time since Oscar's death.

"How are you going to do that?" Kasper asked. "She's probably hiding out somewhere, invisible."

"Can you – I don't know – get Cody to sniff her down?" Felix suggested.

"Ghosts don't have scents, Felix!" Rima replied.

He ran a hand over the back of his neck. "OK, OK, I was just spitballing!"

Leah said, "Try the fifth floor. She spent ages there hunting Shells, she might be hiding out. We'll make sure the grandmother doesn't leave."

Rima twisted into an owl and flew up to the fifth floor, turning back into her human form as she landed.

"Harriet?" she called.

She was the best person to come up here – if Harriet threatened to manipulate her emotions, Rima could just fly away. But that didn't stop her feeling nervous.

At the far end of the hallway, a shadow shifted.

"What's good, Rima?" Harriet said, her face completely blank.

Rima was shocked. There was barely a trace of Harriet left in the person before her. She was covered in cuts and wounds from the fight with Oscar, and skin was hanging loose across her eye. She looked like a zombie. She would never be mistaken for a living human again.

"Harriet." She swallowed. "I'm not here to fight you."

"I should hope not."

"I'm here to help. You've – you've lost your way. I think you need some … help."

"Have you come here to *preach* to me?" Harriet hissed, suddenly furious. "You've done nothing in all this time. It's too late now. You should have killed me when you had the chance!"

Only days earlier, Rima had said the same thing as a joke while play-fighting. She felt like she'd been punched in the heart.

"Harriet, don't – I didn't mean…" She stopped. She was going to antagonize her even more. "There's an old woman in the building with white hair and a silk scarf. We thought she might be your grandmother."

Harriet went completely still. "What?"

Rima blew out a breath. "Do you want me to take you to her? She's on the floor below."

Harriet's face crumpled in on itself. Without another word, she ran for the stairs. Rima turned back into an owl and followed her.

Chapter 20

HARRIET

Harriet raced down the stairs two at a time. She had been practising using her new transformation power when Rima arrived. Why was her gran here? Even though she wouldn't be able to see her, Harriet was still nervous.

Leah and Felix were standing in the corridor, while Kasper was watching from a distance, clearly trying to keep his power under control. Harriet strode past them, searching for her gran. Had this been a lie, to trick her into a trap? Her back prickled, as she prepared for a fight. Then she turned a corner, and saw her.

Her grandmother, in her tweed jacket and second-best blouse.

She looked smaller and older than Harriet remembered.

Harriet realized that she was trembling.

Rima landed on the banister in an undignified flapping of wings, morphing back into human form. "Stay calm. This is a good thing, isn't it?"

Her gran even smelt the same – part floral laundry powder and part cat hair. She must have called a taxi to get here. She couldn't drive with her broken ankle.

Rima was still talking. "She loves you so much, Harriet. Enough to visit here, because this is where you died. She would hate to see the way you've been behaving."

Her gran stopped walking to peel off her scarf. She folded it up, clasping her hands around it. Familiar paper-thin hands, with brown spots and lumps of bone from arthritis. They could move so quickly when she was knitting, jabbing the sharp needles back and forth. She used to prod Harriet with them when she wanted her attention, hard enough to make her wince.

"You should stop this terrible behaviour. For your grandmother's sake," Rima pleaded.

"Norma." Harriet's mouth was dry. "Her name is Norma."

For some reason, her feet were glued to the ground. She'd imagined this moment for so long. This was their reunion, at last. This was what she'd been working so hard for. Why, then, did she feel so numb?

Norma licked her lips. "Are you there, Harriet?"

They all froze.

"What?" Harriet asked.

Harriet and her grandmother first visited the university on an open day last spring. Let's take a look. They're standing in that crowd by the tour guide. Doesn't Harriet look young? With straightened hair and too much eyeliner?

Her gran has a too-large handbag tucked under her arm; a visitor badge sticker peeling off her tweed jacket. They're cutting through the car park on their way to view the library, so quickly that you'd almost miss them. But I sifted through the days, opening up moments until I found this. It's the first time Harriet saw Mulcture Hall.

She points it out to her grandmother, comments on the lack of car parking on campus, frowns into the sky as it starts to drizzle, and then she's gone. Her grandmother is slower, old and stiff, and lingers in the shadow of Mulcture Hall to catch her breath. She looks up at the building for the length of a heartbeat, and then she's gone, too, following her granddaughter to admire the library.

Did you see it? The starting point for another story? Or, rather, the start of the next chapter. Maybe next time I tell it, I'll begin here. With the grandmother.

Chapter 21

HARRIET

"I assume by now that someone has fetched my granddaughter," her gran said. "If not, can one of you please find her?"

"Does she believe in ghosts?" Rima asked, out of the corner of her mouth.

Harriet shrugged helplessly. She pinned her hand against her side to hide the way she was shaking. "I don't know! She must do! Why is she *here*?"

Nothing about this felt right. She couldn't understand the thick sludge of foreboding in her belly, spreading cold through her bones. "I'm going to go. Keep an eye on her until she leaves, will you?"

"Harriet?" Norma asked, tilting her head like she had heard her. She turned to look behind her, and then stumbled. Her bad ankle crumpled under her and she tripped forwards. Norma gasped, throwing her hands out to try to catch herself. The silk scarf drifted from her fingers.

"No!" Harriet shouted, as they all lunged towards her gran, but their hands passed through her as she fell. It happened in slow motion. Norma let out a surprised cry, and her knees gave way. Her head knocked into the wall, ricocheting off the concrete. She lay there, blinking dopily. There was a trickle of bright-red blood dripping down her temple.

Harriet sobbed. What could she do to help? There was nothing. If she still had her phone, she could call for help, but she was dead. All she could do was watch.

Norma raised a hand to her forehead, touching the blood. Eyes closed, she winced deeply, rolling over onto her back.

"Harriet," she said, and then paused, taking a deep breath. Blood pulsed from the wound, leaking down to pool in the dust. "Harriet. I'm coming to you. I'm coming for you."

Rima moved forward to help, and Harriet pushed her back. "Don't!" she said, shock making the words come out angry. "Don't touch her!"

She crouched at her gran's side, desperately ignoring her instinct to take the energy seeping out of her grandmother.

Norma let out a weak moan, eyes fluttering under her lids. She convulsed in pain. The blood might be clotting. Maybe she'd survive this. But she was old, and the wound was on her head. What if it had done some damage, deep in her brain?

"It's OK, Gran. I'm here. I'm here for you." Harriet couldn't watch. She closed her eyes, listening to the rough, weak noises of anguish coming from Norma until finally she went silent. A wave of golden energy flooded through Harriet, exploding out from Norma's body.

Harriet drew in a shaking, appalled gasp. Why did this keep happening? What had she done to deserve this – any of this?

Her parents, her grandfather, *herself* – and now her grand-mother? She'd never been as desperate to see her parents as she was at that moment.

Harriet waited for what felt like an eternity, wishing that none of this was happening. She was cursed. She had to be.

Finally, a cold hand pressed against the top of Harriet's head.

"Hello, Harriet," Norma said.

Harriet took a deep breath. She squeezed her eyes shut. "Hi, Gran."

Norma's ghost shone bright with fresh energy. There was a loose curl of scalp hanging down her forehead, where she'd hit the wall. She tied her scarf neatly around her head, hiding the wound away from view.

Patting her hair into place, Norma said, "Come away from the corpse. It's uncouth."

Harriet climbed to her feet obediently, eyes averted from her gran's body. "Are you – how are you?" she asked, forcing out the words between frozen lips.

The others were watching them, completely still and alert.

Norma twisted her mouth. "Making do. It's been hard without you, these last few days."

Harriet winced. It must have been impossible for her, all alone and hobbling around on her cane. Though her gran hadn't brought the cane with her to the hall. In fact, the plaster support around her broken ankle was gone, too.

"Your cast is off," Harriet said, surprised.

Norma looked down at her feet, which were both covered in white tights and patent leather shoes. "The doctor took it off early," she replied without missing a beat.

"I thought it was going to be another four weeks!"

"No, just one. You're misremembering."

Harriet frowned.

Norma waved her hand. "Never mind that. It's hardly important now, is it?"

Out of the corner of her eye, she saw Rima and Felix shake their heads at each other. Heat trickled through Harriet. She hated that there was an audience to see this. She wasn't ashamed of her gran. She loved her. But Norma was a little ... unusual.

"Gran, you know that you've died, don't you?" Harriet asked. She was taking this all very calmly.

"Of course I know that! Do give me some credit."

"Oh. And are you ... all right with that?" Harriet wasn't expecting her gran to cry, exactly, but some emotional reaction would have been appropriate – if only for their audience.

Norma tilted her head. "Well, it's a lot to process. I'm sure it will all hit me at some point. What I don't understand is how you could let this happen?"

"I was taking photographs of the building and tripped. It was an accident." That day was a lifetime ago now. Harriet could barely remember being that person, concerned with nothing more than getting a good grade on her Photography coursework.

Norma shook her head dismissively. "I don't mean your

death. I mean *this*."

She ran a finger over the torn skin of Harriet's eyelid, reaching down to adjust her collar. "You look … well, the white hair suits you. I'm not sure about the open wounds, though."

Harriet winced, turning to the side and cupping a hand over her eye. She'd forgotten about her battle scars.

"Sorry," she muttered.

"That was our fault, Ma'am," Rima said, stepping forwards. "I'm afraid that Harriet has had a bit of trouble settling in. But maybe now you're here, that will all stay in the past. Don't you think, Harriet?"

Norma turned to inspect Rima, looking her up and down. Her eyes skimmed over Felix and Kasper, landing on Leah and Claudia. She sniffed. "Oh, hello. And who might you be?"

Leah answered, since Norma was still looking at her. "I'm Leah, and this is Rima, Felix and Kasper," she said, pointing each of them out.

Norma took a step closer and pulled Claudia out of her arms. "And who is this little angel?" she asked sweetly.

"Claudia." Leah looked like she wanted to take the baby back off her. Claudia's face scrunched up. She went red, like she was about to cry.

"What a darling." Norma tucked Claudia against her hip, and turned back to Harriet. "Well, I'm sorry that you've been making a fool of yourself in front of all these nice people. Have you apologized yet?"

Harriet was abruptly mortified as she saw the last few days

through the lens of her grandmother's judgement. Harriet had come up short, failing to follow her gran's advice in every respect. Her torn eyelid was proof of that.

"Oh." Harriet forced herself to look at Rima. "Sorry. But, Gran – I've been trying to come home to you. I didn't mean to abandon you when you've done so much for me."

"I suppose it can't be helped. It's not like you meant to die. And we're both here now."

Harriet felt nothing but numbness.

Claudia twisted in Norma's arms, reaching back towards Leah.

"Be still now, that's a good girl." Norma's voice was firm.

A memory flashed through Harriet's mind, before she could stop it. Once, as a child, when her parents had still been alive, her gran had taken her for a long, silent walk in the park. She'd tripped and scraped her knee. Her gran had helped her to her feet, and then knelt, pressing a thumb to the bleeding wound, which was full of gravel.

"Does it hurt?" she had asked, watching her carefully.

Harriet had bitten her lip, nodding, trying to hold back tears.

"I've got to get the gravel out," she'd said, and scraped into the wound with her nail, tearing skin out alongside the grit. When Harriet had cried out, pulling away from her, she had calmly taken out a handkerchief and wiped the blood off her thumb. "Much better."

Harriet suddenly wanted to grab Claudia from Norma's arms. She swallowed. "Can I hold Claudia for a moment?"

Norma shook her head. "I'm not done with her quite yet."

Harriet looked at Rima, wishing that anyone here was on her side. If this had happened a few days earlier, they would have been defending her right now. Protecting her. But after everything she'd done, she was on her own.

She didn't even know what she wanted them to do. Take her away from Norma? Or did she want Rima to embrace Harriet, to show Norma that her granddaughter had finally collected some followers?

Norma cupped the back of Claudia's head, eyes fixed on Harriet. "What's your power, Harriet?"

Harriet closed her eyes. "Um." It was like her brain had been turned inside out. She was wading through slush, trying to process everything.

Norma's ankle was confusing her. The cast must have been taken off as soon as Harriet died. But then, Harriet had never even seen her go to the doctor's, after it was broken. It had been so convenient, how her accident had happened just in time to keep Harriet living at home instead of moving away for uni. Keeping her within her control for another year.

"You do have a power, don't you, Harriet?"

Her mind was blank. She couldn't remember anything right now. Casting her mind back for an answer, Harriet remembered transforming into Norma using Oscar's power, just before her gran had arrived in person.

"I can turn into other people."

Norma's eyebrows raised. "Well, well, well." She looked

down at Claudia, considering this.

"Mrs Stoker, I really would like it if you'd give my daughter back to me," Leah said quickly, her voice pulled tight.

Norma rocked the baby in her arms. "Anyone that you like?"

It took Harriet a moment to realize the question was directed at her. "I think I can turn into anyone, yes."

How did Norma know about powers? Harriet had needed Felix to explain it to her after she'd died.

Norma seemed to be lost in thought. Her hand was still cupped around the back of Claudia's scalp. After a long moment, she released her and passed the baby back to Leah, whose worried expression relaxed slightly.

"Come with me, Harriet. I'd like to talk to you in private. It was very nice to meet you all," she added to the others.

She strode away from her corpse without looking back. Harriet followed her, head dipped. She couldn't make eye contact with any of them.

Let's go back two thousand years. To another beginning, of the strictly chronological kind.

When the Romans first invaded Britannia, they would take in members of the local Celtic tribes as a method of keeping things civilized. It was a kind of peace treaty – We have your son/daughter/favourite dog, so please don't attack our fort. You won't like what will happen to them if you do.

Leah was the daughter of the leader of the Celtic tribe nearest to the Roman encampment, and when she was six or seven, she was "adopted" by an army general as one of these hostages.

She was mostly happy in the Roman encampment and liked her adopted family well enough. Her Roman father had actually been to the real, proper city of Rome when he was a young soldier. Everyone respected and admired him. The camp itself was clean, with good food and sanitation, and travelling theatre troops for entertainment. She was even taught to read, write, and speak new languages. But despite that, she always wanted to go home to her Celtic family.

When she was a teenager, a promising young centurion named Fabian decided that the general might make a good father-in-law. He was determined to make his way up the ranks, and he would gain a lot from having the eye and ear of someone of a higher rank.

Fabian asked the general for his daughter's hand in marriage over a fine dinner, bought with a month's salary. Leah was fifteen at the time, meek and quiet, staring down at her plate and barely sneaking a peek at Fabian. But the girl was practically irrelevant. It was the father that Fabian needed on his side.

With much flattery and wine, a marriage was agreed. The girl said "Hello", "Good morning" and then "I do" to the man who then became her husband. She could have objected. But nobody would have listened.

Fabian took his new wife to meet his younger brothers, Rufus and Vini. They congratulated him, teasing him for his keenness to settle down. They didn't think much of the silent girl, but said she'd probably liven up with a little time. She must have barbarian blood in her somewhere, they said, loud enough for her to overhear.

For a while, the four of them got along well. Rufus, who was the fort's priest, heard Aeliana singing one day while she brushed her hair. After that, the pair of them sang together after every evening meal, while Vini picked out his teeth and Fabian schemed.

Vini, never good with numbers, used to come to Aeliana for help with his coins. And Fabian – well,

Fabian had many uses for Leah. He taught her how to get information from other soldiers' wives – explaining what he wanted to know, and how to find it without suspicion. He made her steal papers and money, intercept letters and plant rumours, working his way up the ladder until he was ranked alongside his father-in-law.

There was always a new political goal, something he needed or wanted or wanted to avoid. Leah enjoyed the intrigue, even if nothing they achieved actually helped her. Fabian controlled everything from behind the scenes, planning out all of the three brothers' moves in minute detail. Rufus had a lot of leverage as a priest, and he did everything Fabian told him to. Vini was the muscle, of course.

Even after Fabian made it clear that he didn't love her the way that she wanted to be loved, all was not lost for Leah. She had a baby to give all her love to, anyway.

But good things don't last. When Leah was seventeen, there was a rebellion in the local Celtic tribe. They were upset with the amount of taxes being taken by their Roman overlords. They infiltrated the encampment and killed everyone inside by putting poison in the water supply. Or at least that's how the story goes. At any rate, it's true enough that the the five of us all died without warning on one cold evening.

That was just the beginning, of course.

Chapter 22

KASPER

"What do we do now?" Rima asked, once Norma had walked off down the corridor, with Harriet trailing after her like an obedient dog. Harriet's grandmother was clearly taking delight in embarrassing her granddaughter in front of other people.

Norma was just like Harriet, Kasper realized. He'd seen that look before, in Harriet's eyes: blank and condescending. There were *two* of them now.

"I don't like this," Felix said.

Kasper had no idea what they should do next. He wondered what would happen to their living arrangements if Mulcture Hall continued to acquire new ghosts at this rate. He would probably have to take in a roommate.

"Maybe she'll calm Harriet down," Kasper suggested, even though he suspected it was more likely to end in another battle. But Felix seemed like he was about to start hyperventilating.

Kasper was ready to fight now. He wasn't scared any more. He almost wanted to thank Rufus, for giving him this ability to protect them. Now, he wouldn't hesitate to do what was needed. He was willing to disintegrate to make sure his friends were safe.

"Is it just me, or was that thing with Claudia kind of weird?" Rima asked, baffled.

"It was." Leah had her lips pressed against Claudia's forehead, holding her tight. "We should be ready to use the eyelid to subdue Harriet if Norma can't calm her down. Or worse, if she riles her up even more. I know we're all hoping for the best here, but we need to prepare for the worst."

Kasper nodded. "I don't think this is over yet. Not by a long shot."

They walked to Rima's room in quiet shock, as they tried to process everything that had happened.

"How can one family be filled with so many creepy people?" Rima asked. "Her gran gives me the shivers."

"But they both have such *great* hair," Kasper added.

"How did Norma know what to do?" Leah asked, ignoring him. "She didn't miss a beat. She knew exactly how ghosts work."

"Maybe that's her power," Felix suggested, mainly joking. "Infinite knowledge of ghost mythology."

Rima let out a tired laugh, trying to be appreciative but mainly sounding exhausted. "I hope not. That sounds like the last thing we need right now."

Kasper couldn't stop looking at the shape of Felix's shoulders under his shirt. He used to avoid looking at Felix. Now, he couldn't remember what had been so frightening about that.

"Can you come with me?" Kasper asked Felix, stopping him before he could follow the girls inside Rima's bedroom. "I have something I need to say to you."

HARRIET

"Now, Harriet," Norma said, once they were out of hearing distance of the others. "We have some work to do. We need to move quickly. There's a ghost here called Qi, is that right?"

"How did you know that?" Harriet asked, hurrying after her.

Norma shook her head once. "Never mind that. She lives on this floor?"

"Yes…" Harriet said, a little late. She was too confused to pay attention to where they were going, until she realized that Norma had led them right to Qi's room.

In a lowered tone, Norma said, "Right. I have a job for you. I need you to turn into one of your friends. The plump girl, maybe. Knock on Qi's door and make up a lie to get her out of her room. Say there's been an accident or something – you make it up, you've been here longer than me. Then I want you to lead her down to the basement."

Harriet's mind raced. She was asking her to do the very thing that Harriet had been attempting only a few days ago. It was uncanny. How did Norma know all this? "Could you hear ghosts when you were alive?"

It was the only way to explain it. She must have heard some

328

of the ghosts talking about Qi and the basement.

Norma nodded shortly. "Yes, of course. I heard the ghosts talking before I died. They were saying that it's very important to get the ghosts in the basement on our side if we want to survive here."

Harriet considered this. Norma was right. She did need to get help from the Tricksters, and they wanted Qi more than anything in the world. By giving her to them, they'd be in debt to Harriet and Norma. Harriet had a power that might help her do it, unlike last time. But choosing to condemn Qi wasn't the easy decision it was before. Now it made her stomach twist into knots. The only reason she'd ever considered it was desperation, when her emotions had been burnt away by her energy highs.

"I don't think I can, Gran. I'm sorry, but you don't really understand. Once they get hold of Qi, the ghosts down there aren't going to have a friendly chat with her."

"Harriet," Norma said sharply.

Harriet took a step back, flushing hot in panic. Every muscle in her body knew what was coming.

Norma pinched her ear between two sharp fingers. "Harriet, I am a fragile, elderly woman who has just died, all alone. You are already going against my pleas for help. Out of everyone, I thought you'd support me here. Are we not a family any more?"

Harriet tried to shrink away, but Norma's grip on her ear kept her close.

She continued, "Have you no compassion for what I've been through? You've been defying me for your entire childhood, and you're going to continue doing so now that we're both dead? It's clear from the state of you that you're still not mature enough to make responsible decisions. It's a good job I'm here, for your sake."

"Sorry, Gran," Harriet mumbled.

Norma's touch gentled, releasing Harriet's ear and moving down to cradle her cheek. "It's time that you grew up, young lady. I'm only looking out for you. Doing what's best for us, as a family, like your parents would have wanted. Only, you're making it very difficult. Don't you want me to look after you, like I always have? I need you to do this. For us. Please, darling?"

"OK. Whatever you need, Gran." Something had shrivelled up and died inside her.

However wrong it might be to send Qi down to the Tricksters, she would do it. No amount of guilt was worse than disappointing her grandmother.

"I love you, Harriet." Norma kissed her forehead, hand cupping the back of her scalp, just like she'd done to Claudia. Her voice was satisfied, like a cream-filled cat. "Good girl."

KASPER

Kasper drew Felix away from the others. He couldn't stop staring at him. He knew Felix's face so well, yet it seemed completely new. There was no longer a lens of fear distorting everything between them.

Kasper touched Felix's cheek with the back of his fingers. Something had been building up inside him since they'd left the basement that he could no longer ignore. He wanted him. He couldn't hold back any longer.

Felix blinked at him, startled. Then his expression changed. The sudden awareness between them felt familiar. Felix had always watched Kasper through half-dipped eyelids, with a barely-there intensity that made Kasper shudder. The only difference was that now Kasper was looking back.

Kasper had told himself that everyone looked at men, as well as women. He'd thought that he could still be straight.

Now he was fearless, it was so easy to see the truth. He had been frightened that people would think he was greedy, or a cheater, or confused. It had been easier not to think about it at all. But he wasn't straight. He'd never been straight. Felix had always been more than just a friend.

He couldn't take his eyes off Felix's lips, plump and dark and parted just slightly. His breathing kept hitching. Kasper was overcome with the trembling feeling that he didn't deserve this. This delicate, new thing was going to be torn away from him before it had time to solidify.

"What is it?" Felix asked, the words barely a whisper, like he didn't want to interrupt the moment.

Their mouths were so close. Kasper bent his head, infinitely closer. He wanted Felix so badly that his teeth ached.

Land this plane, Kasper, he told himself. *Land. This. Plane.*

HARRIET

Harriet could barely focus enough to make a transformation stick. Every time her body changed to Rima, she caught sight of Norma watching her, and flickered back to herself again. Norma's frown was growing deeper and deeper.

She paused and took a large breath. She could do this. There was no way that she could let her gran down.

Harriet focused on Rima's smile, her constant laughter, her compassion. She let memories of her fill her mind and the transformation took hold. Harriet didn't pause to give it a chance to flicker away. She strode up to Qi's barricaded room. She could feel the electric of the lightning barrier run over her as she approached.

"Who's there?" Qi asked.

"It's me, Qi!" Harriet said, imitating Rima's sweet, chirpy tone.

"Rima, come in! I have some new research to discuss with you." The lightning barrier dropped away.

Norma nodded encouragement from further down the hall-way. She gestured for Harriet to go inside.

Qi was bent over a desk in the far corner of the room, inspecting something. "Hello, dear. Did you bring that sweet little fox of yours?"

Harriet cleared her throat, pitching her voice high again. "Actually, I didn't. I came to get you because we've finally got Harriet under control, and we need you to lock her behind the barrier, in the basement."

Qi wiped her hands on her trousers. She had been handling a thick misty liquid that was pooling into a puddle.

"Well done!" Qi said, impressed. "How did you catch her?"

Harriet rolled her eyes. "She got into a fight with some other ghosts and they took most of her powers."

Qi hummed, clearly amused. "Well, let's go, then."

It was working! She really believed that Harriet was Rima.

"Do you not need to –" Harriet gestured vaguely at the puddle of goo, lacking the words to describe it –"finish up?"

"The ectoplasm can wait," Qi said, as they left her bedroom. Harriet couldn't see Norma anywhere in the corridor. She must have hidden out of sight.

A beat too late, Harriet replied, "Is that what it is? What are you doing with it?" She should keep her talking, to stop Qi from thinking too much about where she was taking her. Harriet barely wanted to think about it herself.

"I'm researching disintegration. That ectoplasm used to be a mouse. I'm trying to find out what happens to ghosts after they disappear. I managed to break apart the spirit with a careful application of electrical shocks, until it lost its form. The next step is trying to track where it goes when it disintegrates fully. I've not managed to get that far yet."

Harriet remembered how her atoms had started separating when she'd tried to leave the building. It would be impossible to track where they all went. Qi had a long road ahead of her.

"Where do you think we go when we disintegrate, then? Do spirits just dissolve into the air?" Harriet could feel something tingling across her shoulders. Was her transformation fading?

Qi shrugged. "I've always been a fan of the reincarnation theory, myself. All our energy has to go somewhere, doesn't it? There must be a finite supply of spirit that gets recycled, somehow."

Harriet focused hard on Rima's face, trying to keep it from sliding away from her. It was like flexing a muscle that had never been used. She was already trembling with the effort.

Drawing in a quick gasp of breath, she said, "But surely if that was possible, people would remember their past lives?"

"That's true," Qi conceded. "The very oldest ghosts would see the same souls appear repeatedly. Though maybe they wouldn't notice if the souls were in different bodies. It's a weak theory, which is why I'm researching it. I'd happily switch to a more convincing hypothesis if I found one."

"How intriguing." Harriet could feel sweat trickling down her brow. One more flight of stairs and they'd be at the basement. She was so close.

"How is Harriet, then?" Qi asked. "She's a troubled one.

I think there's been a lot of disturbance in her life."

"She's fine, actually. Misunderstood, more than anything." Harriet tried not to sound too offended. The muscles of her upper back tensed as she hid her intense concentration.

They turned the corner to the stairs outside the basement. Harriet was so busy concentrating on keeping Rima's face that it was only when Qi said, "Hello, little one!" that Harriet noticed the fox sitting on the stairs.

Cody was stretched out, licking her paw. Harriet froze in her tracks.

"That's your fox, isn't it?" Qi crouched down to the spirit. Cody sniffed her hand politely, then stared at Harriet, perplexed.

"I'm not sure," Harriet said weakly. Her feet were changing back. She was losing Rima, bit by bit. "We'd better hurry, before Harriet manages to escape."

When she took a step past Cody, the fox growled, deep in her throat. She raised her hackles.

Surprised, Qi said, "Rima, I've never heard her make that noise before! Do you think she's ill?"

Harriet laughed. "Oh, it's just a game we play. Come on!" The transformation was creeping up her calves now. She was gaining height as her legs grew longer, pyjama bottoms rising up her calves. She straddled two steps to try and hide the height difference. As soon as the change reached her chest, she was done for. Harriet's body was a completely different shape to Rima's. There was no way that Qi wouldn't notice.

She tried to move past Cody, but the fox snapped at her,

fast and quick. Harriet jumped back, pressing herself against the wall.

"Oh!" Qi said. "That doesn't seem like a very fun game!"

She was going to work it out any second. Harriet grabbed her elbow, guiding her past the snarling fox and down the last few steps to the basement door.

Harriet hesitated, unsure if she could actually do this. Then she caught sight of Norma, watching from the shadows. She mimed a pushing motion at Harriet, a fierce look on her face. Harriet's hesitation disappeared.

Qi was still looking back over her shoulder at Cody. "Are you—?"

Harriet shoved her through the basement door. There was a flash of light as she passed through the barrier, and Qi made a small, frightened whimper. That was all it took for Harriet to realize that it was a step too far. How could she possibly have been considering sacrificing Qi too? She had to pull her out again.

Harriet reached through the door, but it was too late. The Tricksters were dragging Qi into the depths of the basement. She screamed, writhing to get free.

Harriet backed away, filled with horror, and bumped into Norma.

"Good girl! You've done so well for your granny!" Norma hugged Harriet to her chest, ignoring her stiff and unyielding reaction. "We'll be safe now. You've done the right thing!"

This was a mistake. This was all a huge mistake.

FELIX

Kasper was staring at him with some new and determined expression, fingers looped around his wrists. He wasn't speaking.

"Is everything OK?" Felix asked, wondering if he should go and fetch Rima.

"Felix." Kasper said Felix's name like it was a sacred word, savouring it on his tongue.

"What are you – what is—?" Felix said, but before he could make it to the end of a sentence, Kasper kissed him.

Felix let out a tiny, soft noise, and sunk into him, fingers clenching and unclenching against the muscle of his shoulders.

"Is this really happening?" Felix laughed.

"I think I'm finally ready. For this. For us." Kasper kissed him again. Everything had changed about Kasper. He moved and spoke differently now. He was more alert and confident.

"You're really ready?" Felix breathed out.

Kasper touched the side of his neck, rubbed his thumb over Felix's eyebrow. "I am."

Felix closed his eyes, and let Kasper kiss him. Something had made him brave enough to finally look back at Felix, to take the risk of trying this. He must be really convinced that Harriet was about to destroy them, if he was taking this leap now, of all times. After so many years of pining, he finally had Kasper all to himself. However much torment and pain Harriet had put them through, at least something was finally going right.

HARRIET

Harriet stared at Norma. "I don't understand any of this. Why are you making me do these horrible things? Even now, after we're both dead?"

Norma repeated, "I want what's best for you."

"No, you don't. You never have! You just made me condemn someone to *death*, Gran!"

Norma folded her arms, gaze fixed distractedly on the basement door behind Harriet. She looked completely unconcerned.

A hundred little things twisted in Harriet's memory, becoming knives instead of needles. Her whole life, her gran had been trying to control and hurt her.

Norma had never cared for her, not really. She didn't love her like her parents had. Everything Norma did had a purpose. This was what she'd always been like, ever since Harriet was a child.

The time she had forced eight-year-old Harriet to eat peas, which she hated – that hadn't been because she'd cared about Harriet eating her vegetables. It had been because she liked seeing her cry into her plate.

Refusing to take her to the doctor's when she was sick.

Feeding her foul, inedible food until her stomach hurt.

Pinching and prodding her until she got her own way.

How had she never noticed that those weren't things done out of love? Her parents' love had been simple and kind, not filled with booby traps and trick questions and poison disguised as nectar.

If they hadn't died, Harriet would only ever have seen Norma at Christmas. For the rest of the year, they would have been out of her reach in America. They'd been so close to getting away. It had been such terrible timing, that they'd died from food poisoning only weeks before leaving Norma behind for good.

It was an odd coincidence, actually. Her parents had usually been so careful with cooking properly. But by chance, on one night at Norma's house, they hadn't paid proper attention and had eaten slightly raw meat. By chance, that piece of meat had been product-recalled after a salmonella contamination. By chance, they'd died from it.

It was an awful lot of coincidences, to all happen in her grandmother's house. Almost like they weren't coincidences at all.

Harriet stared at Norma, who was still watching the basement door.

Had – could – what if Norma had been trying to make her mum and dad sick on purpose? She could have been desperate to stop them leaving, to keep them in England with her. One final act of control when nothing else had worked.

Had she *poisoned* them?

"You killed my parents, didn't you," Harriet said. It wasn't really a question.

KASPER

"We should probably go and find the others," Felix whispered eventually, resting his chin on Kasper's shoulder. "We've got a lot to discuss."

He spoke the same way he always had, but now it made a shiver run up Kasper's spine. "Do we have to? I'm not ready to go back to dealing with the Stoker Family Monsters just yet."

They were silent for a moment. Kasper noticed with satisfaction that they were breathing in sync.

"Are you gay, do you think?" Felix asked, his face still buried in Kasper's shoulder.

That was the question Kasper had been dreading for years, but for the first time, it didn't make him panic.

"I think I'm bi." Kasper had never said that out loud before.

Everything about being bi had been scary to him. He'd been afraid that girls might not like him as much if they knew he wanted to kiss boys as well. He'd been too intimidated by LGBT culture to even start learning about it. He'd been sure that he would do something wrong and offend people, or say stupid things and become a laughing stock. He'd had no idea how to even try to be with a man, after only ever being with women.

He could still see all those reasons to stay in the closet. They made sense to him. But somehow … they didn't matter as much any more. Who cared if he embarrassed himself, and every other gay ghost in the building disowned him? So what if no girl ever wanted to date him again? It wouldn't change anything. Inside, he would always feel like this. Being true to himself had to be more important than avoiding those worst-case-scenarios.

He wanted to tell Felix all of that, but he didn't have the words to explain. "It just felt like the right time to come out."

"I'm really happy for you. I'm glad that you feel comfortable being who you really are. But – Kasper, there's no pressure. There are other guys in the building, if you want to experiment. And you know you can come out without dating someone, right?" Felix's face was still hidden against his shoulder, like he was avoiding eye contact.

"Felix, I liked you even before I realized that I liked guys as a general concept. That part was a lot harder to accept, actually. If it had just been you, there would have been less pressure."

Felix finally pulled back, looking flattered. "Really?"

"Really. I'm bi, but I'm also very much into you. Do *you* want to be with *me*? Or is this just an adrenaline thing? There's a lot going on right now."

"I want to be with you," Felix said, the words tumbling over each other as they left his mouth.

"That's settled, then."

For one peaceful minute, Felix let Kasper kiss him, and then he pulled away to ask, "Can we tell the others?"

Kasper looked over his shoulder, where Rima was walking up behind them. "I think it would be hard not to."

She let out a squeal. "You guys! Are you – is this…?"

Kasper couldn't help the grin that broke out on his face. "It is."

Felix made a tiny, embarrassed noise.

Rima gasped again. "I can't believe this is finally happening. Felix! Oh my god! It only took you almost three decades of pining to get your man!"

"Three decades?" Kasper said, surprised, just as Felix said, "Shut UP, Rima!"

Rima's eyes sparkled. "He's been completely gone on you for the whole time I've known him. He used to stare at you in the dining hall while you ate your porridge."

"Since we were *alive*?" Kasper asked, stunned. He wasn't sure he'd even known what emotions were *for* back in freshers' week.

"Since, like, freshers' week." Rima wasn't about to let it go.

Felix, mortified, made claws of his fingers, dragging them down his face. "Rima," he moaned. "Rima, stop, no."

Kasper leant in and whispered in Felix's ear, "I'm glad you waited for me."

Felix melted against him.

"Are you two going to do this all day?" Leah called from Rima's bedroom. "Because we've got a serial killer to deal with. We need to find Qi, so she can take Harriet down to the basement when we use the eyelid to subdue her. Do you, like, *remember*?" she added in a Valley-girl drawl.

"If that was supposed to be an impression of me, it is not accurate. I will not respond to it!" Rima yelled back.

"No rest for the wicked," Felix said, ruefully.

"Don't let Harriet hear you say that," Kasper said. "Come on. Let's work out what terrible things we're going to have to do next."

"What's got into you lately, anyway? You've changed so much."

He kissed Felix's shoulder. "I'm just happy."

Kasper wasn't ever going to tell him about the fear thing, if he could help it.

HARRIET

"You killed my parents," Harriet repeated, unable to believe it. Norma looked away from the basement door. "You mean you didn't already know? I was sure that you'd guessed years ago. It seemed so obvious." She sounded genuinely astonished.

"You put something in their food. You've – I know you've tried to do it to me, too. All those times I passed out after eating your cooking. You used to say that my body just needed a long nap, that I must be coming down with something, that I had a sensitive stomach. You were trying to murder me."

"Don't be so dramatic, Harriet. It was nothing bad, just some natural herbal remedies. I was teaching you a lesson. You've never known how to behave yourself. What happened with your parents was an accident – it got out of hand, that's all. I'm not a *murderer*."

How had Harriet not seen this before? Had she really been so under her grandmother's thumb that she hadn't even recognized the abuse for what it was? Or did Harriet somehow, deep down, hate herself so much that she thought this was all she deserved?

Why had she ever wanted to go back to this woman's house?

"An accident," Harriet repeated. Her grandfather had died before she was even born. Hadn't the circumstances been mysterious then, too? Some kind of problem with medication after surgery? What had he done to deserve that – threatened to leave as well?

"It might have been an accident the first time," she continued. "But you've been doing it to everyone, for years and years. What about your husband?"

Norma shook her head. "You never listen. Just like your parents never listened. Like your grandfather. None of it would have needed to happen if you'd all just *done as I told you.*"

"Mum – Dad – they—"

"They knew," she confirmed. "They tried to keep you as far away from me as possible. But they couldn't keep their guard up all the time, I suppose. And then it was just me and you."

Harriet took one furious step towards her. "You *sadist.*"

Harriet knew first-hand how easily power could turn into something worse. She'd inherited her dark desires from her grandmother, after all. Harriet had never known anything else. She had reflected that back on Rima and the others, because that's what she had always been taught.

Norma grabbed her chin. Her voice was hard, unamused. "Where did you think you got it from? Did you really think that you were an original?"

Harriet could let this go. It would be easier to forget about it, to keep the peace and save her last remaining family bond. But she was going to spend eternity being tortured by this woman.

Harriet spat in her eye.

Norma froze, and then carefully wiped it away. She pinched Harriet's cheek with a sharp finger and thumb. "Don't pretend any of this comes as a surprise, young lady."

Harriet gasped. It wasn't just a pinch this time. Now, Norma was pulling the energy out of her. She was leaching it through her fingertips.

"No—" Harriet tried to tear away, but she couldn't make herself move. Even now that she knew the truth, Harriet was the same person who'd spent her whole life trying desperately, hopelessly, to please her granny. She still loved her.

How did her gran even know how to do this? She'd only died a few hours before, and now she was stealing energy? None of this could really be happening.

"I hate you," Harriet said through clenched teeth. "My parents hated you, and so did your husband. We were all willing to die to get away from you. Nothing you do will keep me here with you. I'd rather walk outside and disintegrate right now than spend eternity with you, I swear on it."

Norma's eyes blazed with rage. She went completely still,

and then lunged forward and bit into Harriet's neck.

The pain spurred Harriet into action. She wrestled her, breaking free and sprinting for the stairs. But Norma had the energy of a fresh young ghost, not an elderly woman. Before Harriet could make it across the foyer, Norma leapt on her back and pinned her to the ground.

She squirmed, pushing a dizzying kaleidoscope of emotions into Norma – pain, anger, sadness, lust, grief, one after the other. Norma just gritted her teeth, and bent Harriet's head backwards. A bone at the top of her spine snapped.

"Give it to me," she crooned. "That's a good girl. You've collected so much energy for me, haven't you? Now let it all go."

Norma started glowing as all of Harriet's hard-won energy left her. Her gran had clearly decided that she was useless, so she was taking everything she could from her weak, pathetic excuse for a granddaughter. Part of Harriet wanted to let her, so that this would all be over.

Something vital tore free then, leaving an aching hole behind. Norma had taken one of her powers. It hurt so much; raw and aching, deep in her soul. Was this what the Shells had felt, each time she had taken their powers? Once again, Harriet was freshly horrified by all the things she'd done under the energy's influence.

Norma sucked up Harriet's energy. It was too much for her body to hold, and the power shot straight out of Norma's hands, tearing her skin to shreds and cracking the delicate bones of her wrists and fingers.

Pain scraped at Harriet's bones until she felt weak and dizzy. There was no *way* Norma could be doing all of this on instinct. From the moment she had died, she had been calm and collected and ready for anything. There was something bigger going on here.

Norma let go of Harriet when she'd emptied her out. Harriet fell limp, too weak to move. Her neck must have broken, because her head hung to the side, and didn't respond when she tried to look at Norma.

Dry-heaving, she searched for any power inside her. But there was nothing. Her invisibility, emotional manipulation and shapeshifting were all gone. But she had stopped before Harriet disintegrated completely. Why hadn't she killed her?

"Thank you," Norma said, smoke pouring from her mouth.

Harriet tried to hold her head upright on her broken neck, watching as Norma inspected her fingers, which were charred black with burnt energy. She was incandescent with energy, burning up from the inside out.

She walked away from Harriet, staggering like she was drunk. Without looking back at her granddaughter, Norma turned herself invisible using the now twice-stolen power.

As she melted into the depths of Mulcture Hall, Harriet let her head fall slack and slipped into sleep.

Would you like to see what's happening down in the basement, while Harriet and Norma talk, and Kasper and Felix kiss away their pain?

Qi is suffering.

As soon as she entered the basement, Vini bit off her head. Rufus tore away her limbs, each one jerking with involuntary movements of pain. He wasn't even trying to eat her, just dismantling her so that she couldn't fight back. Qi managed to shoot off just a single burst of lightning, misfired and useless. Vini picked up an arm, sucking it down in one gulp.

They consumed every part of Qi in only a few minutes. When Vini swallowed her last little toe, the lightning barrier on the basement door glowed, then faded into nothing.

Rufus climbed to his feet, brushing off his hands. He walked through the door, passing to the other side without challenge. Triumph clear on his features, Vini followed him.

There was a pause, then every other ghost in the basement rushed for the exit in a huge wave, surging up the stairs into Mulcture Hall.

Chapter 23

FELIX

They were still discussing what to do about Harriet when Felix heard a scream from the floor below.

"What was that?" Rima sat up, disturbing Claudia, who had been sleeping against her shoulder.

There was a distant roar. The building shook, and three ghosts ran past. Felix's heart jumped. What was Harriet doing this time?

"Oi!" Kasper yelled at them, "What's going on?"

"They've broken out of the basement!" a girl shouted over her shoulder.

"What?" Kasper roared after her. "Who?"

"EVERYONE!"

Felix didn't process what this meant at first, and then he saw the horror on Leah's face. The Tricksters, and their loyal army of criminals and murderers, were roaming free. This was worse than anything he could have thought possible.

"I have to get out of here. Now." Leah grabbed Claudia and stepped right through the wall of the building.

"Where is she—" Rima began, but Felix said, "Go, follow her! Quickly!"

He grabbed Kasper's hand, tugging him into the empty space between the plasterboard of the hallway and the concrete breeze-blocks of the external wall. It was filled with pipes and cables, supported by metal girders. Leah was striding down the length of the space, walking purposefully through plaster and concrete.

Felix stepped inside, walking after her. It didn't hurt, but the sensation of things being pushed through his eyes made him shiver.

He could hear Rima huffing behind them. Cody darted ahead, excited that they were on the move. He had no idea where Leah was going, but they all had to stick together. That was the only way they'd survive this.

Leah said, shortly, "Down, now."

She sank through the floor at a steady pace, controlling her descent. Claudia giggled, blowing a raspberry when her head passed through a pipe.

Kasper started sinking, too.

"How are you doing that?" Felix asked, panicked. He couldn't even begin to focus enough to do the same.

Rima dropped in a sudden rush that was nothing like Leah's elegant, stately descent.

"Relax," Kasper said, and tugged Felix down after him. Felix's stomach flipped over itself as he fell. After a long fall, Leah brought him and Kasper to a stop. Rima was clinging to her other arm.

"Here," Leah whispered. She carefully bent forward,

pushing her forehead through the wall. Felix did the same. Rima had a hand hooked around Cody's chest, stopping her from leaping out of the wall.

They were inside the wall of the foyer, high up near the ceiling. Below them, hordes of ghosts were surging out from the basement stairwell into the main building. They were attacking anyone in their way, tearing apart ghost after ghost. A few even transformed into giant beasts, using their individual powers to make themselves as terrifying as possible.

Felix swallowed back a gasp of horror. There was nothing he could do to help them – not against such a huge mass. All he could do was watch while their building was taken over and everyone inside was destroyed.

The army rampaged through each floor, with Rufus and Vini striding ahead of their monsters. They weren't destroying ghosts – instead, they seemed to be searching for something.

"They're looking for Claudia and me. They want revenge." Leah tugged them back inside the wall. "Come on. We're not safe here."

She pivoted and stepped out through the wall into a narrow hallway that Felix didn't recognize. It was some sort of supply corridor, hidden behind the bedrooms on the ground floor. There were hatches in the walls, which were raw and unpainted. It must have been designed as an access route for caretakers to fix the heating systems, but now it was a breeding ground for spiders.

"Come on, keep up. There's a chance Rufus knows about

this place." Leah strode down the corridor.

Wincing, Felix stepped through the cobwebs as he followed her. He hoped that any spiders inside were very, very alive. He would rather not find a spider's spirit down the back of his shirt, sucking away at his energy. It had happened before, and it wasn't pleasant.

When they reached the external wall of the building, Leah stepped through a breeze-block wall and sank down again. They passed through the basement, then into the hard-packed soil beyond the building's foundations. Leah kept sinking.

Kasper was whooping for joy, clearly thrilled. Felix just tried to ignore his terror as they left the building far above them. Finally, they fell through the ceiling of a brick-lined tunnel.

"EPIC!" Kasper said, spinning on his heels to take it in. "I had no idea this was even here!"

"Keep it to yourselves." Leah brushed invisible dirt off her shoulders. "We don't want it getting around."

"Is this where you come? When you disappear sometimes?" Rima looked like she was having an epiphany. Felix had been witness to many rants about Leah's mystic hiding skills.

"Occasionally," Leah admitted. "This is where I used to live. It was here long before the university was founded. Judging by the state of the halls, I think it'll be here long afterwards, too."

Felix inspected the solid red brick arch of the tunnel's ceiling. "I don't doubt it."

"We'll be safe here for a while. Rufus and Vini won't come down here until they've exhausted all other options."

HARRIET

Harriet woke up to the sound of screaming. She stirred, forcing her eyes open even though she felt like she could sleep for a hundred years. A ghost jumped back. He had been hovering over her body, but he backed off slightly when he saw that she was awake.

It was one of the ghosts from the basement, she realized with a jolt of shock. She'd seen him playing pool down there. What was he doing in the foyer? Qi's lightning barrier was supposed to keep them all trapped inside. But Qi was gone now.

This was why the Tricksters had been so desperate to get hold of Qi – why they'd been willing to grant a favour to anyone who managed it. They'd been searching for freedom, and Harriet had foolishly given it to them.

The ghost licked his lips, looking her up and down as he prepared to eat her. Around them, dozens of imprisoned ghosts were fighting and killing and laughing viciously.

"Back off," Harriet croaked.

The sound was so pathetic that he laughed, right in her face. "What happened to you?" he asked, looking at her wounds and broken neck. "The fight has only just started!"

"Stay back unless you want to find out," she said, with entirely false bravado.

He smirked. "Uh-huh."

Harriet stared him down, knowing there was nothing she could do to defend herself. This was it. After all her efforts, this was how she would finally die.

Behind his shoulder, she caught sight of Rufus. He was strolling alongside Vini, his arms held behind his back in the picture of relaxation.

Harriet jolted. "Rufus!" she shouted at the top of her voice. The words twisted into something grotesque as jagged shards of bone ground together, where Norma had snapped them. "Wait!"

He beamed when he noticed Harriet sprawled on the floor at his feet. "Oh, hello! I've just been hearing about the exciting time you've had today. Your grandmother sounds absolutely fascinating, darling."

"Please," she begged, ignoring his teasing. Her eyes bulged in their sockets as her head dropped to the side. "Don't let him eat me. You owe me a favour!"

Rufus cast a look at the boy, who shrank back slightly. "I don't recall owing you any favours." He rolled up his sleeve to inspect the spreadsheet tattoo on his arm. "It doesn't say anything here about a debt."

"I was the one who brought Qi to you," she said. Why should Norma get the credit for that, when Harriet had done the dirty work?

Rufus raised his eyebrows. "I was wondering which secret admirer had left me that little gift. How did you manage it?"

"I … pretended to be Rima. She followed me straight downstairs."

Rufus laughed. "Brilliant! Congratulations on such a useful power. Well, I suppose I can help you out. Just this once. You're practically family now, aren't you?"

Harriet frowned at him. He gestured to his white hair, and hers, a secret smile lighting up his eyes. "Matching features! It's as if we're related."

Beside him, Vini snorted.

"Right," she agreed. She'd agree to anything, if it would help save her.

Rufus turned to the pool-playing ghost. "Sorry. This one's off the menu for now."

The boy nodded and turned to leave, but Rufus grabbed him by the back of the collar. He thrust him towards Harriet.

Her reaction was automatic. As soon as the boy's skin touched hers, she tugged at the edges of his soul and sucked up his energy. The boy screamed in rage, wriggling in their grip. But Rufus held firm as Harriet drank until the boy disintegrated into nothing.

Rufus drew his hand back, flexing his fingers. He nodded at Harriet in approval. Why had he done that for her? He must dislike being in someone's debt for any longer than necessary.

The boy had filled the empty place inside, quenching her thirst a little. She was safe from becoming a Shell now, and could probably defend herself if someone else attacked her. Every muscle in her body ached, though she couldn't even tell if that was real, or some pain-induced hallucination. Had her gran really attacked her? Surely that had been an impossible nightmare, not real life. Though, why had Norma left her with enough energy to stop her from disintegrating? Why hadn't she gone ahead and destroyed her completely, instead of leaving her on the verge of becoming a Shell? It was like Norma didn't actually want to get rid of her.

Harriet shivered. It was no use thinking about this. She was just going to stay as far away from her grandmother as she could. Forcing herself to sit upright, she pushed her head back up to centre. "Thank you, Rufus."

"Why don't you come with us?" he said. That strange glint reappeared in his eyes. "I think there's something you'll want to see."

FELIX

Leah led them down the red-brick tunnel, stepping lightly over stones worn from centuries of footsteps. Claudia was more active than Felix had seen her in ages, burbling and skimming the bricks with her fingers. Cody hopped along too, stopping to do invisible little wees up the wall every few paces.

They passed a ghost dressed in a long gown, with her hair covered in a cap. There was a purple bruise on her cheek. When she smiled, Felix caught sight of sharp fangs jutting out of the corners of her mouth. He skirted past her, though Leah said a friendly hello in something like medieval English.

"Her skeleton is still sealed up in that brick wall," Leah said to him, as they moved on. "Poor thing."

Felix shivered.

Finally, Leah stopped walking. "This is far enough. This wall here is right up against the property edge. They won't be able to get behind us."

They all sat down, with Leah keeping a close eye on the hallway.

"Qi must be gone," Rima said. "If the ghosts have escaped the basement."

"Oh, no," Felix said, devastated. He hadn't thought of that. "Do you think Harriet got to her?"

"Or Norma," Kasper said darkly. "I wouldn't put it past them to have teamed up."

Rima asked Leah, "Why are the Tricksters after you? You have to tell us this time, Leah. You can't keep it a secret for ever."

Leah sighed. "Fabian wasn't a good man. Worse than his brothers. The three of them used to work as a team, completely in sync. Rufus and Vini would take down other ghosts like prey, feeding on their fear. Then Fabian would extract their memories and use their weaknesses against them."

"His power let him see memories?" Rima asked.

"Fabian could visualize people's memories and create fake ones. He was very good at playing with people's brains. The three of them would implant fear into their servants' minds to make them compliant. Then they could use them without damaging their bodies through torture. He put fear in me, too. Even after he disintegrated, it took centuries for my brain to stop being afraid of all the things he wanted me to fear."

Leah swallowed. "Anyway. Fabian's power gave him utter control of the ghosts in this building, but that wasn't enough for my husband. He wanted more. He hated that he'd died young, before he'd achieved everything he wanted to do as a human. He had plans in the army, you see. He was always ambitious, even after his death. We spent the first few centuries as ghosts living alongside the human Roman soldiers. But eventually, the army started withdrawing from Britannia. The Roman Empire was falling apart.

"After our encampment was abandoned, Fabian became fixated on searching for a way to get more energy, more powers, more spirits. He couldn't stand the thought of ever disintegrating. He wanted to live longer, survive and outlast everything."

Felix was so focused on Leah's story that he forgot to even breathe.

"The reason I can't use my power any more is because he was always asking me to look into the future. He wanted to know everything that would happen, stretching over hundreds of years. When I started telling him things he didn't want to hear – about a time when he was gone, and the rest of us were here without him – he started looking for a way to stop it."

Leah closed her eyes. "He became convinced there was a way to come back. He was sure there must be more. That it couldn't just *end*. With all his knowledge, he thought that he must be able to trick the system. He used to ramble about it constantly – how he just had to look far enough, cast the net wide enough. How, eventually, he'd get it right and then he'd survive for ever."

Leah looked down at her daughter. "And one day, he was testing a theory. He was trying to see if he'd managed to bring himself back. He asked me to look hundreds of years into the future. I started to disintegrate."

She stopped talking. Claudia made a noise that almost sounded like "Mama".

Leah shook herself. "Claudia was in his arms. He was using her against me. Threatening to hurt her. When I started fading, she gave all his energy to me. To save me."

Felix tried to imagine being a ghost like Harriet or Norma or Fabian. They all seemed obsessed with amassing power and energy and it only ever seemed to make their lives more complicated. Usually shorter, too. If Fabian hadn't been messing around with experiments, he would have survived centuries more.

"That's why Rufus and Vini hate you?" Rima asked. "Surely they've forgiven you by now. If this was – when was this?"

"Sometime in the forties."

"They must have realized that it was an accident. They've had over eighty years to get over it."

Felix tried to imagine being here eighty years ago, when Fabian was still a ghost and Leah was under his contol. What sort of changes would Fabian have made to Felix's memory, to stop him rebelling? He shivered.

"They're never going to get over it. I know they aren't. He was their brother; their hero; their role model." Leah rubbed her eye. "This can only end one way. Either they die, or we do."

She touched Claudia's cheek. "And I'm not going to let it be her."

There was a silence, and then Kasper said, "Go on then! What do we do?"

"*Kasper,*" Felix hissed. "What has got *into* you?"

Kasper must be in shock. Did he have a ghost's version of PTSD?

Kasper shrugged at him. "We should plan something! The Tricksters could burst down here any second now. Listen, why don't we go up to the foyer and yell until they come and find us? Why are we hiding here? Let's get on with it."

"You'd be destroyed instantly," Leah said flatly.

"Right, that's it!" Felix said, holding up his hands. "Kasper, you have to tell us what the hell the Tricksters did to you. Because this isn't you. You've never been this impulsive. What did you give them, to get that eyelid?"

Rima added, "You heard Leah. They can mess with your fear and your memories. They're dangerous, and they had you alone in the basement. They could have done anything. Tell us what happened!"

Leah gasped. "Oh, Kasper. You didn't give them your *fear*, did you?"

Kasper's expression dropped. "How did you know that?"

Felix's stomach heaved up into his throat, as Leah said, "They've done it before. It's one of their favourite tricks."

"What do you mean, he gave them his fear?" Felix felt like he was going to faint.

"They took it," Leah said. "The whole thing. That's why he's been acting so strangely. We're all terrified, and meanwhile he can't feel a thing."

"At *all*?" Felix felt all the blood leave his head.

Kasper reluctantly nodded. "Nothing. Not even nervousness or anticipation. It's all gone."

Felix had known that the Tricksters fed on emotions, but he hadn't realized that they could take them away completely.

Leah winced. "Kasper, I wish you'd spoken to me before you did this. The Tricksters always ask for fear or worry, because that sounds like no big deal. People think they can live without these emotions, so they agree, in exchange for getting whatever it is they want. And then they regret it."

"Why?" Felix asked, terrified. "What happens to them?"

"Well, you know how strange Greg was. Humans *need* fear. All our instincts revolve around it. Once ghosts lose that, it's like they've lost the last of their humanity."

Felix imagined Kasper acting like Greg. He would lose everything that made him Kasper. Everything Felix loved about him.

"This can't be happening." Felix ran his hands through his hair. "We didn't even need the eyelid in the end. Kasper, that trade wasn't worth losing your *humanity* over!"

Leah rushed to add, "It won't happen immediately. That kind of thing takes a while. But it will build up, over time."

Kasper looked resigned. "You're right. It's changed everything. I can't trust my own judgement any more. I don't know if I'm making the right decisions. If—" He looked at Felix, and cut himself off suddenly.

Felix froze. "If what?"

No one spoke. Rima coughed, in the way she did when she was suddenly feeling very awkward.

"Oh God." Felix's voice was higher than it had been a moment ago. "This is why you kissed me, isn't it?"

Kasper rubbed the back of his neck, staring at the ground. Acid rose in Felix's throat. Kasper had been desperately avoiding confronting his feelings for Felix for twenty-five years. Of course he would only ever give in when he'd lost his fear. When he had nothing inside him, monitoring his behaviour.

"You only kissed me because you'd lost your fear," Felix said, the realization hitting him like a hammer to the head. "Do you – do you even want to be with me? Or was it just – a bad decision?"

Rima and Leah turned away, giving them a moment of privacy. When Kasper reached for him, he backed away. His entire chest was collapsing.

"*Tell me*," Felix said.

"I – I don't know," Kasper admitted, against his will. "I've been asking myself the same question. I'm sorry. It all happened so fast."

Felix shuddered. "How did I not *see*?"

"Felix…" Kasper said, looking guilty. "It's OK."

"I don't think you're qualified to decide what is and isn't OK right now!" Felix tipped forwards, burying his head in his hands. The implications of this kept rolling over him in waves, until he was drowning. "I've taken advantage of you. That's basically what this means. You aren't in a position to give consent right now. And I –" he stumbled to his feet – "I need a minute."

He walked blindly down the tunnel and sank to his knees, pressing his forehead against the brick. It was over, then. His biggest dream had come true for the grand total of an hour. And then it had been shattered.

Kasper was never going to be able to do this. Not in a way that Felix would allow. He'd never know if Kasper really wanted it, or if it was just the easiest path to take.

Kasper had said he didn't feel nerves or anticipation any more. Was it even possible for him to fall in love, without those things? What was love, if not the small moments of human-ity and vulnerability that came along with trusting someone to catch you, when you fell for them? If Kasper never felt any of that, then any relationship they built wouldn't mean a thing.

He couldn't have him. Ever. However much Kasper insisted that he was fine.

He let himself cry. Even now, he knew that Kasper wasn't worried about any of this. It was like his pain was doubled, with Felix feeling it for them both.

Eventually, his crying stopped feeling real and became self-indulgent and selfish. What was he doing, sobbing over a single kiss when ghosts were being destroyed above them?

He had to forget this had ever happened, shrug off this pity party and destroy the men who had done this to Kasper.

He stood up, realizing awkwardly that the medieval lady ghost had been watching him this whole time.

"Lovely day, isn't it?" he said inanely, then winced. *Lovely day?* She lived *alone. Underground.* Next to her *own skeleton.* And *didn't speak English.*

He hurried back to the others, who all stopped talking as he approached. Kasper was frowning, but it looked artificial, like he was forcing his forehead into a frown to make Felix feel less embarrassed about the whole crying thing.

"I'm ready." Felix looked away from Kasper. "So how are we going to end this?"

HARRIET

Harriet wrapped her scarf around her neck over and over again, until the stiff fabric propped up the weight of her head. As long as she stared straight ahead, and didn't make any sudden movements, it was only *mildly* excruciatingly painful.

She was still weak, even if she wasn't in danger of becoming a Shell any more. As her energy levels stabilized at a safe amount, her mind was starting to heal from the damage it had taken while holding all that stolen energy inside herself. She could think properly for the first time in days.

She'd turned into someone she didn't recognize. The memory of Oscar's dying moments haunted her. His eyes had just gone dark and empty, staring desperately at nothing as he tried to work out what was happening to him.

What had she been thinking? None of that had been her – it had been the powers inside her, burning out her mind.

She'd acted mindlessly, following her instincts without considering who she would hurt along the way. She had condemned people – the Shells, Qi, Oscar, Jonny, Greg, the squash student. So many lives, gone because of her.

That was never, ever happening again. Perhaps her gran had done her a favour by taking the extra energy away. She had been so close to turning into a monster, just like Norma.

In the meantime, she was going to stick close to the Tricksters. Harriet was too vulnerable to fight right now. Norma had multiple stolen powers, including whatever her own turned out to be. She was probably unconscious somewhere from her overdose, but there was a chance she was on the prowl already. Harriet needed allies to survive, and Rufus and Vini were the strongest people here.

Harriet followed in their wake, as the Tricksters' army rampaged through Mulcture Hall. At first, she'd been certain that this was just a celebration of their freedom, after years in the basement. Surely they'd rein everyone in, once the excitement had worn off? The Tricksters wouldn't let their army kill every ghost in the building, would they?

But it carried on, and on, and on. They were planning to destroy everyone in their path. Harriet could barely watch. What if they came across Rima? Felix? Kasper? She couldn't stand knowing that she'd been the death of any of them, even after all their fighting. There was a part of her, buried deep, that still wanted to be friends with them.

When they reached the roof of the building, Rufus breathed

in deeply, knocking his fist against his chest. "Ah, fresh air. It's been a while since we were last allowed outside."

Vini spat out a chunk of gristle. "Smells like petrol out here. That's new. The humans really are destroying the sky, then."

"There's no escape route up here," Harriet said, looking around for Norma. "We should go somewhere safer."

Rufus smiled. "Don't worry, we'll protect you. In the meantime, keep an eye out for those friends of yours. You should kill them on sight – except for Leah and the child. Only we're allowed to deal with them."

Harriet was surprised. What did they want with Leah and Claudia? The thought of killing any of them sent a pulse of revulsion through her.

Vini laughed, seeing the disgust on her face. "She's not going to do it, I can tell. Having regrets already, are you? I thought you had bloodlust in your bones."

"I'm not interested in torturing every ghost I pass, that's all," she spat. "But I can still stand up for myself."

How had she ended up here, rather than with good, kind people like Rima? Harriet hadn't realized what a precious gift she'd been given, when they'd offered her their friendship. It had been instinct to reject them, before they could reject her first. She'd been pushing people away her whole life. If she didn't have anyone, then she couldn't lose them. After her parents had died, it had been safer to think that she only needed her grandmother, that it was the two of them against the world. Look how well that had turned out.

She saw every conversation she'd had with Norma in a new light now. Norma had isolated Harriet, making her dependent on their home life, telling her to stay away from other people, who would use her for their own interests.

Her gran abused her. She'd been denying it for years. Harriet had been fixated on her gran, not because she loved her, but because she was afraid of her – and even more terrified of ending up like her.

If her life didn't revolve around constantly negotiating her gran's feelings, then who was she? She'd never even had the chance to find out.

Leah, Rima, Felix and Kasper were lucky to be together. That was what she wanted now, more than anything. Friends. People she could trust to guide her into doing what was right. To back her up when she couldn't manage on her own.

"Where are they, then?" Vini asked Rufus. "We've looked everywhere."

"Who are you looking for?" Harriet asked.

"Someone important. Someone we've been waiting to see for a long time."

Harriet guessed that they wanted to see Leah, if they'd told Harriet not to kill her. What could possibly be so urgent that they needed to see her as soon as they left the basement?

Rufus tilted his head and sniffed the air. "Do you know, Harriet – I think that someone might be here now."

He gestured behind her. A figure was striding across the

rooftop, glowing bright with energy, white hair blowing in the wind.

It was her grandmother.

"That's my gran!" Harriet hissed, skittering back behind Vini. "She's dangerous. You can't let her get near! Do something, please!" Her heart was going to beat out of her chest. But Rufus and Vini could take her on. They were both bright with energy, too. It would be easy, for the two of them.

Rufus surged forwards towards Norma, arms outstretched to seize her and tear her apart. Harriet gasped, bracing for the sight of her gran being torn limb from limb.

Instead, Rufus brought his arms around Norma and … hugged her.

Chapter 24

HARRIET

"Brother!" Norma said, and kissed Rufus on the cheeks, one after the other. He beamed so widely that he developed dimples.

Harriet was too stunned to even react. *Brother?*

Vini wrapped his arm around Norma's shoulders, laughing out loud in joy. "Oh, it's good to see you!" He giggled – actually, full-on giggled.

Norma rubbed his hair, clapping Rufus on the back. "You've both been keeping well without me, I see!"

She seemed to be completely ignoring Harriet, who was standing behind the Tricksters.

"It hasn't been the same," Rufus said. "But you're here again now. That's all behind us."

"It is. I want this place back under control as soon as possible, do you understand? After we've dealt with the child."

"We haven't seen them yet!" Vini said. "We thought you'd want us to wait for you, anyway."

Harriet gaped at them, her deep fear replaced by pure curiosity.

"You did well, brothers," Norma said. "Rufus, do you have anything to report?"

"A few things." Rufus fell into step beside Norma like an obedient servant. He updated her on the number of ghosts in the building, as well as the last place that Leah and Claudia had been seen.

Harriet had never imagined he would give up control. Why was he treating *her grandmother* like his long-lost leader, totally calm and submissive?

"Vini, what's going on?" she whispered.

Vini wrapped an arm around Harriet's shoulders. He was gazing at Norma in worship. "That's our brother, Fabian! We've been waiting for him. He promised he'd be back, and I didn't believe him. But here he is, after all this time!"

"No, that's my grandmother," Harriet hissed. "Not a man. How can she be your brother?"

"He brought himself back. He made sure he was reborn after he disintegrated. He's home, at last! After eighty years!"

Her grandmother had been here with the Tricksters before? She'd been *a ghost* before? It must be a trick. But it made sense, in a way that Harriet couldn't explain. Norma had known an impossible amount about ghost powers from the very moment she'd died. Was that because she had been doing this for a long time, as one of the Tricksters?

Harriet froze under Vini's touch, unable to process what this meant. Was this why her gran had attacked her, and taken all her powers? Had she been trying to grow strong enough to rejoin her old brothers?

"Does this mean we're…?"

"Related!" Vini said. "Didn't you wonder why we've been helping you so much? You're family!"

Harriet grimaced, feeling a twinge in the remains of her eyelid. Rufus had said the same thing to her earlier, but she'd thought he was joking. If this was how they treated family, she didn't want to see how they dealt with everyone else. Her eyes latched on to Vini's torn earlobe.

"I see you've met your great-uncles," Norma said, and held out her arms to Harriet. "Come here, dear. Let's make up, shall we? Family needs to stick together. And there's a lot we need to do to get this place shipshape again. It's become very disorganized in my absence."

"What?" Harriet spluttered.

"Join us," Norma said. "Together, the four of us can take control of this building. All the other ghosts will be our servants, if they want to survive. We'll have a huge supply of batteries to feed on whenever our energy runs low. We'd never become Shells or disintegrate. With the four of us ruling, we'll live for ever in total domination. Together."

Vini started clapping. Rufus was crying.

Norma smiled lovingly at them. "Harriet, you've been leading a very reckless afterlife so far, but you're going to behave yourself from now on. Aren't you?"

"I don't understand who you are. Are you Norma? Or are you…?"

"Fabian," Norma finished. "I'm both. I didn't remember any of my time as Fabian. Not until we came to the university for an open day last spring, do you remember? We walked past this building on a tour, before we went to see the library. I got this sense of déjà vu. I knew I'd been here before, and this used to be a hugely important place for me. My mind opened up and I remembered everything. It was like turning a key. It unlocked all the information I'd kept safe inside myself."

Rufus and Vini were listening carefully. They must not have heard any of this, either.

"Do you think your old power made it possible?" Rufus asked. "You've always been able to manipulate memories. Did that help you remember?"

Norma nodded. "I think so. When I first became a ghost, I started testing the limits of my power to control my own memories. I managed to train myself to remember who I was, just in case I could come back in a new body. It worked. As soon as I saw this building, my brain knew what to do. If I'd never come to Mulcture Hall, I might have died without knowing who I really am."

"No one else could do what you did, brother," Vini said, bursting with pride. "You've changed history. You're a genius!"

Norma smiled, her wrinkled cheeks creasing with pleasure. "Oh, you young fool. Stop it." She rubbed her knuckle against his cheek affectionately. Vini leaned into it, like a touch-starved kitten.

They loved her. Both of them really and truly loved Norma, in a way that Harriet never had. They adored her – *him?* – to the depths of their souls. Somehow, they saw Norma as someone good and admirable and worthy of love. They'd grieved her for eighty years, and patiently waited for her to come back. Just because she'd said she would. They'd trusted her implicitly.

How could it be possible?

"So when you killed my parents, you didn't know that you were Fabian?"

Norma's smile dropped. "Still caught up on that, are you? Do let it go, Harriet – we have a lot to be getting on with. You should feel lucky that it wasn't you, too."

Harriet flinched – Norma really didn't regret a thing.

"But I suppose it was all Norma," her gran continued. "I had no idea I had ever been anyone else when I killed your parents." She smirked at Rufus. "I guess it was natural talent."

"You've always been precocious!" Rufus said. "Barely seventy years old and you were already taking the initiative. So admirable!"

Harriet rubbed her eyes. How was any of this real? Could this be happening? "You just ... killed them, then? There was no special ghostly reason for that?"

Norma waved her hand airily. "It was a long time ago. If I'd known that ghosts existed, I would hardly have killed them in some little house in the suburbs of *Coventry*. What use is that? They're still stuck there on their own. I'd have put them somewhere they could have been useful. I killed them because it had reached the point where they were refusing to do what I said any more. They had to go. They were taking you away from me, Harriet. You're the only one of them who listened to me. My little protégée."

Harriet blanched, acid rising in her throat. So she was just easily influenced? She'd been indoctrinated since she was a child.

"Tell us what happened after your real memories came back," Rufus said.

Norma patted his hand, which rested on her arm. "Well, I remembered how strong and powerful I'd been here, ruling unchallenged for so many centuries. After that, I couldn't be happy any longer in this body." Norma gestured down at herself. "I was frail and weak, disrespected and ignored. I wanted – needed – to be my old self again, reunited with my dear brothers. Even if that meant becoming a ghost."

Harriet had been so upset when Norma died. It had seemed such a pointless accident, just tripping and hitting her head. Was she saying that it wasn't an accident at all? "You committed suicide?" Harriet gasped.

Norma sniffed. "I don't like that word."

"But you killed yourself? You hit your head like that on purpose?"

"Well, yes. I wanted to be back with you all! My loved ones!" When she held out her arms, Vini tucked himself under her armpit and squeezed her waist. "Now we can all be together for ever. A family again," Norma said, in satisfaction.

This wasn't right. Norma wasn't telling them the whole story. If Norma had planned to kill herself here, then it must have been a huge surprise to find out that *Harriet* had died here only days beforehand.

Unless…

Now she thought about it, Norma had been the one who suggested that Harriet come to Mulcture Hall to take photographs of the abandoned building in the first place. Otherwise, it would never have occurred to her.

She had been on the phone with Norma just before she'd tripped and fallen. What if it had never been an accident? What if her ankle had caught on something – some kind of tripwire, maybe – left by her grandmother? The hazard signs had been hidden out of sight, too. She'd only noticed them afterwards. Had they been deliberately moved?

Norma kept saying that she wanted to spend eternity with the three of them. Not just her brothers, but Harriet, too. She could have killed herself here on the day of the tour when her memories returned, over a year ago. But she'd waited until Harriet was here.

Norma had killed Harriet. Just like she'd killed her husband, her son and his wife.

"Did you set up my death?" Harriet asked politely, suddenly completely calm.

"Not at all," Norma said, sounding surprised. "I would never do that to you, Harriet."

Vini looked at Rufus, mouth tightening.

Harriet asked him, "Did she visit you in the basement? Before she set up the wire?"

Vini looked somewhere over Harriet's shoulder. "What?"

"She must have done, you were expecting her today! And – Greg told me that you were looking up a woman online using my phone. That was her, wasn't it? You were talking to her. She planned all of this with you two. When did she come here? Was it this summer, before uni started? Before she 'broke her ankle'?"

Norma snorted. "Oh, tell her whatever she wants to know. She's too clever for her own good."

Given permission, Vini said, "That all sounds right."

Rufus elaborated. "She came down to the basement a few months ago. We thought she was some old lady at first. We were about to take her energy and kill her when she started speaking out loud. She said that she was Fabian, and she hoped that her brothers were listening. She explained who she was, and what she was planning. She told us that her memories had only just returned, and she really missed us." He was getting teary-eyed as he recollected this.

"You knew all along that I was Fabian's granddaughter, then?" Harriet asked, feeling breathless. "From the first time I came to the basement and traded my phone for information, you knew I was your great-niece."

"We didn't expect to see you that soon," Rufus said. "You surprised us. You definitely have the family blood. Fabian told us that she'd leave a few days between the two deaths, to make sure they looked like accidents. Otherwise the building would have been overrun with police for weeks and weeks. So once you died, we started preparing for Fabian. But you turned up in the basement the very next day, asking us for a trade. We took the opportunity to get things ready for him."

"*Her*," Norma interjected. "If you please. It has become a bit of a habit. It's been a long time since I was a man, now."

"Sorry, sorry," Rufus said. "For *her*. We decided to use you to make a bit of a disturbance upstairs. You did very well, Harriet. Even without any training, you were more trouble than we could have ever imagined."

"We've been guiding you from the very beginning, so you were ready when the time came. We made sure you knew how to kill and take powers, how to fight back. You've made us so proud."

Harriet rubbed her temples. They'd been systematically stripping away her humanity ever since she'd arrived in the building, turning her into the monster that Norma had been crafting since Harriet was a child.

"You're just like Fabian, you know," Vini added. "You're definitely one of us!"

Harriet went cold.

"I am *not*," Harriet said severely. "Not in a thousand years."

Norma had been smiling at Rufus. At this, her smile turned thin as she looked at Harriet. "Oh, dear. Well, it seems that a decision needs to be made now, doesn't it?"

Chapter 25

RIMA

Hidden in the rafters of the roof, Rima couldn't believe what she was hearing. They had crept through the walls of the building, searching each floor until they found the Tricksters on the rooftop. To her surprise, Norma had appeared, hugging Rufus affectionately. Harriet was there too, standing by her grandmother with a fraught, terrified expression.

"Let's attack them," Kasper hissed, lunging forward like he was about to leap out onto the roof.

"Wait!" Rima said, grabbing his arm in exasperation. "Let's just listen first. I want to hear what they're saying."

"I want to fight," Kasper mumbled.

Felix snorted, ignoring him completely. Kasper and Felix weren't talking to each other. She couldn't believe that after all that build-up, their relationship had lasted only a few hours. They were already in the awkward exes phase.

Rima strained to hear what Norma was discussing with the Tricksters, keeping her hand on Cody's scruff. If the fox wandered off, she would be consumed by an energy-hungry ghost from the basement.

She heard "Fabian", and frowned. Why was Norma discussing Leah's husband? This conversation didn't make any sense. Then with a start, Rima understood: Norma was Fabian, somehow. He'd come back.

She turned to Leah who, judging by the colour she had turned, also understood. "Leah, it's OK. We're going to kill her. I promise. You never have to speak to him again. You can stay out of sight if you want to."

Leah shook her head, tight-lipped. "This isn't going to work. We might have had a chance when it was just the two of them. But I've tried before, Rima. I've never managed to defeat the Tricksters when they're all working together. They're too strong."

Above them, Rufus and Vini were hugging Norma. Harriet had drifted closer, still looking uncomfortable. She clearly hadn't known any of this either, which was at least some comfort.

Rima frantically wracked her brain for a plan. If this turned into a fight, their main advantage was Leah's ritual to leach away energy. But they only had Harriet's eyelid. Rather than fighting, they would need to focus on darting in to steal some hair or skin from the other three too.

Perhaps Rima could fly in as a small bird or insect, and bite the Tricksters and Norma? She might be able to take some hair while they were talking.

"Does this mean Leah is Harriet's step-grandma?" Kasper said, looking awestruck.

When Rima frowned at him, he leaned in to whisper to

Claudia, "The evil one is your new niece!"

Claudia reared her head up, trying to look over Leah's shoulder. Leah supported her head, so she could see. Rima wondered if Claudia remembered her father. What was she feeling about his return right now, if she was as intelligent as Rima had suspected she was?

Suddenly, the discussion on the roof ended, and Norma raised her voice. "Are you with us, or are you against us, Harriet? I'm sick of pandering to you. Decide, once and for all. If you want to be part of this family, then you will never mention your parents after today. Otherwise, I don't want to see your face again."

Harriet looked like she was thinking deeply, which sent dread through Rima. What would happen if she agreed? The four of them were like some strange boy band, all with matching snow-white hair.

"What's it going to be, Harriet?" Norma asked.

Rima couldn't even begin to guess what she was going to decide. Based on the conflicted look on Harriet's face, she didn't know herself.

Vini had started pacing, looking bored by the discussion. He circled his brothers in wide loops, patrolling the perimeter. When he turned in their direction, Rima realized she'd lifted her head too high. She tried to duck down out of sight, but she wasn't fast enough.

Vini's face lit up. "She's here!" he yelled, breaking into a run towards Rima.

They didn't have time to flee. All they could do was stand their ground and fight.

Burying her panic, Rima dived forward towards the Tricksters, transforming into a bear. As Felix tackled Vini, she jumped onto Norma's back, sinking her teeth into her hair. She felt the strands catch on her teeth, and pulled back, hoping that one would snag and come free.

Cody was biting at her calves, copying Rima. Norma let out a furious yell, grabbing at her as Kasper took Rufus down.

"Stop it! Go to sleep!" Felix shouted at Vini as he tried to hypnotize him.

For one small second, it seemed like they might have a chance. They had the three Tricksters on the ground, writhing and tugging at each other. Then Vini pressed his hand to Felix's chest, reflecting the command back at him. Felix's knees crumpled beneath him.

Rufus let out a deafening roar and then there was a sudden thunder of feet from the floor below. The Tricksters' army surged onto the roof. A ghost with worms writhing in the sockets of her eyeballs dragged Kasper away from Rufus by his feet. Another, whose teeth were coated in blood, kicked Felix in the flat of his back.

Kasper lashed out at his captor, who fell backwards off the roof, disintegrating into dust as she passed through the boundary of the building.

Rima tore at the ghosts who were trying to drag her off Norma. She fixed her bear jaws around limbs and pulled until she heard the bones snap and crack. However many she fought, the wave of attackers kept coming. There was so much energy bursting free from all of them that it filled the air and stung her eyes.

This was it. She knew that the battle was lost. They couldn't fight against hundreds. Rima kept tearing off chunks of Norma's skin anyway, pushing them into her cheeks to store them. She clamped her huge molars around Norma's skull until it creaked. At the very least, she could weaken her.

Norma gripped her paw to suck energy out of her. Rima twisted into a snake and plunged her fangs into Norma's shoulder, injecting venom. Norma tore her away, flesh clinging to the snake's fangs.

Rima prepared for the end. Then there was a roar from below – the stomp of feet and cries and smacks of flesh against flesh. Rima reared up, peering over Norma's shoulder. More ghosts were surging up onto the roof – the students who usually kept to themselves, or spent most of their time sleeping to conserve their low energy levels. They were fighting, too, attacking the Tricksters' army to defend their building.

Hope surged through Rima. It wasn't just the four of them! If the other ghosts could keep the army distracted while they dealt with the Tricksters, then they might still have a chance.

With renewed determination, Rima began to transform in rapid succession. First a poisonous frog, covering Norma's skin in toxic goo; then a skunk, spraying her face with musk; then a fox, like Cody. Cody and Rima tag-teamed Norma, hopping close to bite her, then away. Rima even got close enough to tear an eye out.

They could do this. The fight wasn't over yet.

FELIX

Felix hacked away at the clawed fingers gouging into his forearms, fighting off an injured ghost whose jaw hung loose and unhinged. Vini was struggling to get free, but Felix managed to slow him down with his hypnotism.

White lightning crackled around them; thunderclouds rolled around the rooftop, covering everyone in ice-cold water. As power crashed into power, a tidal wave of reactions spread across the roof.

Felix could barely see through the frost forming on his eyelashes. A ghost burst into flames in his arms, then disintegrated into dust, coils of smoke spiralling away in the wind.

Someone tried to bite off his nose. He headbutted her until she backed off, flared nostrils dripping blood. The air was full of dust now, as the wind scattered energy from disintegrating ghosts. There were enormous shapeshifting beasts everywhere, crashing through the fight and searching for easy prey.

Felix couldn't tell which side anyone was on, so he focused on Rufus, Vini and Norma. The rest could wait.

Rima was keeping Norma at bay as a fox, alongside Cody. Norma grabbed Cody's tail, sucking out her energy. She yipped, skittering back, but Norma had a grip on her soul.

Rima let out a guttural, horrified growl, twisting back into a human. *"No!"*

Rima tried to pull Cody away, but it was too late. The fox tumbled over onto her side, whining.

Norma didn't stop to finish the job. She raced for Leah.

"Cody, no!" Rima desperately pushed her own energy into the fox, trying to stop her disintegrating.

Watching this, Felix was so distracted that he lost control of Vini, who broke free of the hypnotism and ran after Norma. All three Tricksters converged on Leah and Claudia.

Felix tried to hypnotize them enough to give Leah a chance to escape. He visualized a huge chasm appearing in the roof, and threw the vision towards the Tricksters to make them see it too. They stopped at the edge, staring down into the canyon that had opened up.

Norma took a step back, then narrowed her gaze at Felix. "It's not real. Get him."

Rufus and Vini ran at Felix. Before he could turn and flee, his blood suddenly ran cold with fear. They were doing something to his emotions, amplifying his terror until it was bigger and stronger, incapacitating.

Felix's knees gave in, his eyes rolling back in his head. He could feel himself frothing at the mouth as waves of fear swelled through him. Rufus and Vini grabbed him by the elbows, dragging him to Norma.

She touched his temple, sending a searing burn through his brain. She shuffled through his memories, scrolling past snapshots of Oscar and Rima; computing lectures; battling Harriet.

This must be their team torture that Leah had talked about. She had said that *Fabian was very good at playing with people's brains*.

Norma came to a stop on a memory of Kasper from earlier that day – their kiss and immediate break-up. Felix rewatched the blank look on Kasper's face, as he explained his lack of fear. It still hurt Felix to see Kasper like that.

Norma replayed the memory, but this time it was slightly different. This time, it showed Kasper turning to grin at Leah and Rima after Felix stormed away down the tunnels. *"Well, that got rid of him!"* this version of Kasper said. *"Good story, guys."*

The three of them sniggered, and Rima rolled her eyes derisively. *"Can you believe he actually fell for that? As if you've lost your fear!"*

Kasper snorted. *"At least he won't follow me around like a sad puppy all the time now."*

"Do you think we can get him to leave the rest of us alone, too?" Leah asked, and the three of them laughed and laughed and laughed.

Felix couldn't look away. The new memory replaced the real thing, until he wasn't sure what had happened and what Norma had added.

Felix's fear was still cresting over him, getting stronger and stronger as Rufus and Vini pushed the emotion into him through their hold on his elbows. The altered memory sent him over the edge. He screamed and blacked out.

HARRIET

Harriet stood in the eye of the battle, frozen with indecision. She wanted to support Rima and the others, but her scared heart was telling her to flee while Norma was distracted. She could find somewhere small and safe to hide, and never come out again.

But she couldn't leave Rima and the others to be destroyed, not after everything else she'd done to them. They'd done nothing to deserve all this.

Felix went limp in the Tricksters' arms, red froth tumbling from his lips. He hit the ground with a thud, and the canyon disappeared into mist. The Tricksters turned to chase down Leah again.

Harriet knew that Norma was going to do to Leah what she'd done to Harriet and her parents. How could she let that happen again? She had to protect Leah and her daughter. They were the only family that Harriet had left.

Without even knowing what she was going to do, Harriet's body jolted into action. Energy started bubbling inside her chest, then surged out of her sternum, rolling towards Norma in a great wave.

It was like all the powers she'd stolen from other ghosts, but so much stronger that it made those little talents feel like card tricks. It must be her true power manifesting at last. Not a stolen one. Hers – the one she was meant to have all along.

Harriet's power flooded over Leah and Claudia, curling around the girls in a glowing white dome. It solidified, just as Norma reached them. When she ran at the energy bubble, she bounced away.

Growling, Norma tried to tear open the bubble, as Leah cowered against the far side. Rufus punched at it, but it was immovable.

Harriet had made a shield. Her power was a *shield*? This must be why it had never manifested before. Until now, she'd never cared enough about anyone to feel the urge to protect them.

She'd felt the same bubbling feeling in her chest before, when Kasper had nearly tripped on the stairs as he was talking about their Halloween date. Sunbathing on the fire escape, something had started to form inside her, too. She had pushed it away every time, not trusting the feeling, which had been formed from affection and love.

It must have been inside her all this time, just waiting for the moment Harriet decided to protect her new friends. Her power had woken up to defend them.

Harriet grinned. She had been right. She really was a good person, somewhere deep inside. She hadn't even believed it herself until this moment. Now she could start trying to prove it.

"Wait!" Norma said sharply. "Just stop for a moment."

Rufus and Vini stopped clawing at the shield. Norma

rearranged her hair and stepped forward, peering through the shield at Leah and Claudia.

Something inside Harriet told her that if she manipulated a little bit of the energy, she could...

The shield went see-through.

Leah stood inside, posture straight and calm, holding Claudia in her arms. She touched the shield in wonder.

Harriet gave her a reassuring nod, and Leah's expression cleared.

Leah focused all her attention on Norma. "Husband. How are you?"

Norma sighed. "I was hoping to surprise you with the good news."

Norma seemed to be ignoring her missing eye, which was weeping blood veins down her cheek. The socket flexed and moved as she spoke, revealing the white flesh and blue veins inside.

"I wouldn't describe it as good news. I would rather you were burning in the depths of hell than back here." Leah grinned a sharp-toothed smile.

"We're skipping the trivialities, are we? Very well. That barrier of yours isn't going to last for ever, and when it falls, I am going to kill you and our daughter. Your time is coming to an end."

Leah met Harriet's eye again. Harriet nodded once, trying to convey to her that the shield was strong, and that it wouldn't break. She thought that she could keep it running forever if she wanted to. It wasn't like those stolen powers, weak because they hadn't been designed for her. This was made to fit her. It took barely any of her energy to keep it going.

"You can't kill me," Leah said. "Not in any way that matters. You've proven that. I will come back again even if you destroy me now."

"I can make sure I never have to see your face ever again," Norma spat out. "Or that child's."

Norma looked at Claudia in pure hatred. Harriet remembered how her gran had taken the baby away from Leah. It was one of the first things that she'd done when she'd become a ghost. Harriet had thought that Norma had been using the baby as a distraction. But even then, Norma had been planning to kill Claudia. She'd just needed to get her brothers out of the basement first.

Harriet shivered, and the shield tightened, growing a little stronger and a little thicker. Norma wasn't going to do this. Not again. Not to anyone else. Harriet would make sure that she was Norma's last victim.

Norma said, "I should have wrung that baby's neck the moment she was born. She's been nothing but trouble, watching and judging me with those beady little eyes. For centuries, she's sneered at everything I do. She thinks she is so much better than the rest of us. It makes my skin crawl."

Leah said, very quietly, "She's just a baby. And you have no right to talk about her like that. Not after everything you've done to us."

Norma rolled her eyes.

"You know I was the one who killed you, don't you?" Leah said.

"It was the child, not you," Norma said dismissively. "Don't bother trying to protect her now. It won't make any difference."

"Not then." Leah smiled. "Not your disintegration. Your death, the first time. Two thousand years ago."

Norma actually took a step back, her shock throwing her off her stride. "What? No. What are you talking about? That was poison. An attack from the Celtic tribe."

Leah shook her head. "It was me. I overheard you discussing the rebellion in the Celtic tribe with Rufus and Vini. You were planning to kill my father, their leader. Or had you forgotten that I was taken from the Celtic tribe when I was young? That night, I took your poisons from under the floors. I used them to stop you hurting my real family. And I don't regret a thing."

"You poisoned yourself, too? Your *baby*?" Norma said, blinking. She didn't seem to believe her yet.

Leah shuffled Claudia onto her hip and untied her shift dress, revealing deep scars running down her chest. They were stab wounds, gouged through her stomach. "After you died, I tried to get away, but I was caught by the general. When he saw your corpses, he killed me and Claudia. He called me a barbarian."

Norma stared at the stab wounds. It was clearly undeniable evidence – Leah hadn't been poisoned like Fabian. The story she had thought she'd known was wrong.

Norma's lip curled over her teeth, but she still looked disconcerted. "Well. Thank you for telling me. That's going to make your death all the sweeter."

My father – Norma, Fabian, the Trickster, whatever you want to call him – is right to hate me. I really was judging him for all those years and if I could, I'd kill him too. I don't blame him for disliking me.

I can recognize so many of my father's tactics and methods in how Norma chooses to do things. The manipulation, the poison, the control, even the knitting needles – that's all Fabian.

I only found out the truth about Norma recently. A few weeks before Harriet's death, I saw a vision of Norma hugging Vini. It baffled me. I had no idea who this old woman was, or why Vini was treating her with such tenderness. It took me a long time to scan the past and future for enough information to work it out. Finally, it was the vision of Harriet and Norma on a campus tour that helped me connect the dots.

Since then, Harriet's behaviour has made a lot more sense. She was raised by a monster. Not the horrifying kind, but the human one. Whether man, woman or ghost, Fabian is always the same: swollen with self-interest, but without human decency.

I understand Harriet better than anyone. She was abused and made to feel like nothing, just like my mother *and me. I don't blame her for basing her behaviour on her grandmother's. Being a good person isn't an option when someone so strong-willed tells you that you're weak, makes you feel helpless and spends all their time chipping away at you. Just being functional is hard enough.*

Chapter 26

KASPER

Kasper ran over to Felix, who was slumped on the ground, totally limp. "Felix, are you all right?"

Kasper's finger had been torn away by a shapeshifting ghost and the wound was leaking blood down his wrist.

Felix groaned, squeezing his eyes tightly shut. "I can't do this. Please, go away."

"You have to get up, Felix. We need your help."

"You don't need me. I'm weak, I can't do any more."

Kasper grimaced. "Rima has lost her fox. She's no help. It's just us, buddy."

Felix groaned. "Please, don't make me."

Kasper hooked his arms under Felix's armpits and dragged him to his feet. "Tell me what we're going to do," he demanded, pointing at where Norma was interrogating Leah. "We can't leave them there."

Felix slumped. "I have no idea." A tear rolled down his cheek. He looked completely broken, like his spirit had been destroyed. He seemed ready to let himself disintegrate.

Kasper didn't know how to behave around him, after what

had happened in the tunnels. He was desperate to curl his fingers around Felix's, but now wasn't the time to try to fix what was broken between them.

As Felix staggered to his feet, the Tricksters seemed to be at an impasse now. None of them could get past the mysterious shield that had sprung up between Leah and the Tricksters. Kasper wasn't even sure who had made it.

"How have you been, sis?" Vini said to Leah.

"Not too bad, Vini," Leah said, eyes fixed on Norma. "How's the ear?"

"Still aches." Vini touched his earlobe, which was torn away.

"I'm sorry about that," Leah said. "I don't know if I ever said."

Kasper coughed. *Leah* had done that to him?

"Seeing as we haven't seen you in four score decades, I'd say you haven't apologized for anything," Rufus said.

Moving away from the Tricksters, Rima came up to Kasper and Felix, with Cody cradled in her arms. Tears were streaming down her face. "She went straight for Cody, like she knew I would stop fighting immediately to save her."

"Cody is going to survive," Kasper said. "Look at her, she's getting better already!"

The fox wasn't a Shell yet. She was taking in the energy dissolved in the air from all the destroyed ghosts. The Tricksters' army were still fighting the other students all over the roof, leaving a wide circle around Leah's bubble. Motionless, Harriet watched them, too.

Rima spat something bloody into her palm. It was a chunk of hair and skin. She held it out, looking proud. "I got this from Norma. We can use it to destroy her using Leah's ritual, like we were going to do with Harriet's eyelid. We need to get rid of the other Tricksters and their army first, though. We can't do anything if the three of them have Leah trapped like this."

"I can attack Vini first?" If Kasper could get Vini out of the way, that would make it easier for Felix and Rima to destroy Rufus. Leah had said they were strongest as a trio, and Vini was the weakest link.

Rima shook her head. "I have a plan for him. But you two need to be ready to finish him off. Then we'll go after Rufus. OK?"

Kasper nodded. It was something to do, at least. Better than standing here, watching. "Yeah, Felix? That sounds good, right?" He nudged his arm.

Felix was grinding the base of his palms into his eyes blearily, glasses askew. "Whatever," he mumbled. "It's not like we're going to win, anyway."

"That's the spirit!" Kasper said under his breath. "Go, team!"

If they didn't start this fight now, Felix would probably decide to have a nap instead. Whatever they'd done inside his head, the Tricksters had wiped him out.

Rima laid Cody on the ground, kissing the top of her head. She handed the disgusting lump of hair and skin to Kasper. "Hang on to that. Wait here."

Then she disintegrated into atoms. No – not atoms – but a cloud of tiny gnats.

One of the flies headed straight for Vini, a little speck that he wouldn't even notice. He was glowing with a golden light that kept getting brighter. He must be feeding off the fear of every ghost on the rooftop.

Kasper strained his eyes to watch as the gnat hovered by Vini's ear, then darted inside, quick as a flash. Vini rubbed his earlobe absently, but nothing happened for a long moment.

Then Vini brought his hand up to his ear again, rubbing it hard. He shuddered, and crumpled to the ground. Rima must have done something deep inside his ear.

Kasper lunged forward, grabbing Vini's head and twisting hard while Felix pinned him down. A ghost from the basement yelled out, turning away from her fight with a second-floor girl to run at Kasper. She engulfed Kasper in crackling flames.

Kasper gritted his teeth and kept pulling at Vini's head, until the skull came free of the spine with a crisp pop. Rufus ran at Felix, tearing him away from Vini as he disintegrated into atoms. Rima flew at Norma's face, covering her skin in gnats.

The flames were burning his skin, so Kasper threw himself at the floor, rolling until the searing pain disappeared. He climbed to his feet, smoke oozing from his skin. When he looked up, Felix was dragging Leah away. Kasper gaped at them, confused. How had Felix got all the way over to her while Kasper was on fire? The protective barrier around her and Claudia must have broken during the fight.

Norma swatted the flies away, her face swelling up from bites. She peered out through half-closed eyelids, and her eyes widened when she saw that Leah was free of the bubble shield.

Norma ran towards Felix, knocking him around the head and tearing Leah away. Felix crumpled to the ground and didn't move.

Norma held Leah by the back of her neck and shook her hard. Something like surprise crossed Leah's face, like she'd realized what a mistake she'd made. And then Norma took her energy, making Leah and the baby in her arms dissolve into dust.

Rima re-formed, crying out, "Leah, no!"

She jumped forwards, trying to stop them. Kasper grabbed her arms and held her back.

"Let me *go*." Rima turned into a bird and slipped free.

By the time she'd reached Norma, it was too late. There was nothing left of Leah except a shred of energy drifting on the floor. Norma tilted her head back in ecstasy as she absorbed it.

Rima cawed, circling the room in long flaps of her wings, screaming as loudly as her raven throat would let her. Felix rolled over, grimacing and climbing to his feet.

"Rima!" Felix said, holding out his hand. She flew to him, curling into his chest as a mouse. He cupped her in his hands as she whined desperately against him.

Kasper wanted to do something for her, but he couldn't. He stood and watched Felix comfort her in the middle of the battle.

"Rima!" a voice said. "I'm right here!"

Kasper spun around to see Leah was standing in the middle of the roof. She was still trapped with Claudia inside that glowing shield.

Rima stopped sobbing and morphed back into human form. Felix staggered, letting her go.

"What?" She wiped her face. *"What?"*

Kasper looked around. Rufus was missing.

FELIX

When they had finally defeated Vini, Felix had known that he needed to think fast. The three of them weren't going to be able to overpower Norma and Rufus together. The only way Felix could think of getting rid of them was to use trickery.

When Rufus had run at him, while Kasper was covered in flames, there had been a moment when Rima covered Norma's eyes in flies. While she couldn't see, Felix broadcast a subtle command to everyone on the roof, making them see Rufus as Leah. It looked like Felix was fighting her instead of Rufus. He'd hidden the real Leah and Claudia out of sight, hoping that Norma would assume Leah had escaped while Norma couldn't see.

He'd maintained the hypnotism as Norma swatted away the flies and saw Leah grabbing at Felix. Rufus had kept fighting him, with no idea what Felix was doing. He'd dragged Rufus away, trying to make it look like Leah was escaping.

Norma had attacked them, picking Rufus up by the collar. He'd stared at her in surprise – using Leah's face. Then Norma shook her brother and took all his energy, until there was nothing left but dust.

Exhausted, Felix let the hypnotism drop. Leah and Claudia flickered back into visibility, still safely hidden in their bubble. He'd never used such a huge command before, and he would have lost control if he'd needed to hold it for any longer. But it had worked.

Rima stared at Leah, joy transforming her features. There wasn't time for Felix to explain what had happened. Instead, he gestured at Norma, who was still enjoying her new rush of energy. "Rufus is gone. What are we going to do about her?"

"Whatever we do, we're going to need Harriet's help," Rima said. "I've got a plan."

HARRIET

Harriet had seen everything, and thought Felix was unbelievably clever. Norma was swaying on her feet, stoned out of her mind with all the new energy she'd taken from Rufus. In a few seconds, she'd open her eyes and the fight would continue. Harriet had to act now. She could use this.

If she could convince Norma that she was on her side, and would help her fight, then maybe Harriet could keep her distracted while the others came up with a plan.

She tightened the scarf holding her neck in place, and pushed away all her fear. She had to act like Rufus – as confident and relaxed as him. Norma would respect that. There was nothing she hated more than cowardice.

Harriet was just bracing herself to go over to her gran when a bird landed on her shoulder.

"Harriet, it's me!" Rima said. "Listen, we need your help. We have a plan. We're going to take away Norma's powers, so she'll disintegrate. But we need time. Can you distract her?"

Harriet didn't hesitate. "Yes. I promise."

Rima whispered, "Thank you, Harriet." She flew off back to the others, her tiny wings working hard as she darted between the fighting ghosts.

Harriet watched her go, and then turned to Norma, who was just coming out of her energy high.

In a drawl, Harriet said, "Congratulations! It must be thrilling to get rid of her at last."

Norma grunted. "Where are my brothers?"

Harriet winced. "We lost them. I'm sorry."

Norma's expression went blank and taut. She seemed taken aback for a moment, like the possibility of their disintegration had never even occurred to her. "I see. Well, there's a lot for us to do without them. Time to tidy up the rest of this mess."

Harriet's heart jumped. She had started to relax, but this wasn't over yet. Just because Rufus and Vini were gone didn't mean that Norma was harmless.

Harriet tried to steer her away from Leah, expanding the protective shield to include Rima, Felix and Kasper, too. She made it as solid as possible, so that there were only blurred shapes visible inside, with indistinct features. As long as Norma didn't look closely, they were hidden. Harriet was going to protect them until her dying breath.

LEAH

Leah cradled Claudia close to her chest, unable to believe they'd faced down Fabian and survived. For now, at least.

But there wasn't time to comfort each other. Rima flew back from where she'd been talking to Harriet, and immediately launched into business. "She agreed. Let's do the ritual!"

Harriet was talking to Norma, who kept playing with her empty eye socket, touching the edges with her fingers.

They would have to work fast. Harriet wouldn't be able to keep her distracted for long.

Leah had tested this with Harriet's eyelid, working out how to isolate the frequency her spirit vibrated at, then amplifying it. She would be able to use the small piece of Norma's spirit as a connection to draw the excess energy out of her. They could make her weak enough to destroy, hopefully. Leah would die trying in any case.

"Form a circle," she told them, taking Rima's hands.

Rima held Kasper's wounded hand as he winced. Felix finished the circle, looping his hand around Leah's arm where she held Claudia. Claudia gripped on to his thumb tightly.

Leah took some strength from Rima and Felix's warmth. Whatever happened with Norma, she couldn't lose her friends. Not if there was a chance they might survive this.

She tuned into the hair, searching out the specific wavelength of Norma's power. It tasted so similar to Fabian's that it almost repulsed her, but she swallowed down her bile and focused on making a connection.

There was a click, and she connected. She could feel every movement Norma made. If this worked, Leah would be able to drain away Norma's powers by pulling them out of her, through the hair and skin.

"Got it! Now, give me your energy. As much as you can spare. I need it all."

A pulse of energy came immediately from Rima and Felix, pushed from their hands into Leah's.

Norma must have felt something strange because she spun around, searching for the source. When she spotted Leah, her expression changed to absolute fury.

HARRIET

Harriet was still doing her best to distract Norma, watching over her shoulder as Leah and the others formed a circle. She didn't know how that would help them weaken Norma, but she trusted Rima.

"We should gather some more servants," Harriet said, gesturing to a ghost on the far side of the rooftop, who was shooting thunderclouds out of his arms.

"Good idea." Norma started walking through the mass of battling ghosts. They parted in her wake, wary and respectful, even mid-fight. Harriet followed her, relieved that her suggestion had worked.

Then Norma paused. "I would like to taste Aeliana's loved ones, though," she said, and cast a longing look over her shoulder.

Harriet couldn't move fast enough to block her view. Norma caught sight of the figures inside the cloudy bubble and realized that one of them was holding a baby. A look of tremendous anger passed over her face.

"They're back!"

Harriet frowned in false confusion. "Oh, no! What could have happened? She must be too powerful for us."

She could see the cogs ticking over in Norma's mind. If Leah was still alive, then Norma must have eaten someone else. She licked her lips, as if recollecting the taste.

"Rufus?" she asked, fury growing. "They made me eat *Rufus*?"

Harriet's expression clearly conveyed some kind of guilt, because Norma grabbed her by the neck, hoisting her up into the air. "That shield is yours, isn't it?"

"Gran – no—" she spluttered.

It was too late. Norma had worked it all out. "You're working with them? Harriet, how could you do this to me? To us?"

Harriet ignored the pain, and focused all her control on maintaining the shield between Norma and the others. The only thing she could give them was time.

"I'm – I'm sorry, Gran," Harriet choked out. "But I can't let you hurt them. They're my friends."

LEAH

Leah maintained the line of connection between Norma and the circle. The shield was still in place. If Harriet could keep that going, then they were safe.

"She's really helping us," Kasper gasped, looking over at Harriet in surprise. "I didn't think she would!"

Leah pulled energy from the circle, focusing it on Norma. Pulses of energy kept coming from Felix, Rima and Kasper. There was so little of it, compared to Norma's towering, glowing mass of strength.

Holding Harriet in the air by her throat, Norma shivered as if she was getting a slight chill. If it had been anyone else, they would have been on their knees by now.

"More energy," Leah gasped. "I need more."

There was another pulse of energy from the others, weaker this time. Rima was dimming as she gave Leah everything she had. It was too little, barely a drop in the ocean of what they'd need to overpower Norma.

"It's not enough," she managed to say, between breaths. "We need more!"

Claudia looped her tiny fingers around Felix's thumb. A huge wave of energy passed through the circle, more than anything the others had been able to give. Rima gasped, but Leah wasn't surprised. Claudia had always been the strongest of them all.

She focused the extra energy at Norma, who had sensed something was wrong now. She was frowning down at her arms like she had an itching sensation. Leah could see so much of her husband in Norma, though she'd changed, too. There was a whole other life there, lived without them. How furious must Fabian have been, if even eight decades weren't enough to dull his anger at Claudia? Norma's fury consumed her. Leah was more grateful than ever that they'd escaped Fabian when they did, before he could wear them down to nothing.

Harriet dropped a centimetre closer to the ground as Norma's grip faltered. She'd gone pale from the pain, but her shield was still holding.

The flow of energy from Claudia ended and the connection went weak again. Norma still hadn't collapsed, and they couldn't sustain this for much longer. They'd lose their chance, if they had to stop now. They were all weak and dim from the effort.

"More energy!" she gasped again. "It's not working!"

Rima looked around desperately. "We could get a ghost? Take their energy?"

"Don't break the circle!" Leah said, in one breath. She was relying on them to sustain her own energy now. She'd given too much of herself up to the ritual. If they broke apart, Leah would collapse into atoms.

"What do we do? This is hopeless!" Felix wailed.

"The only one of us with a free hand is Claudia!" Rima muttered, frustrated. The baby had one hand wrapped around Felix's thumb, the other waving in the air freely.

Leah could feel herself sinking into the blackness. She was about to pass out. She forced herself to hold on, hoping they'd think of something in time.

Just a little longer. She could do this, if it meant getting rid of Fabian.

I should take over for a moment here. As you can probably tell, I've always been good at quietly watching and waiting. Biding my time. I've had centuries to learn how.

I've been waiting for this specific moment for a long time. Whenever I looked at this moment, I was baffled. Something happens here – an odd little thing, so small that it took me many viewings to pin down exactly what it was. I helped them here – I will help them here – I am helping them here, right now. Right now.

I must bring them some more energy.

Enough to make them glow bright white with it. Enough for this to work. I can steal it from a moment in the past which has energy to spare, bringing it forward to the present day. Just like I did when I sent some energy back to Lisa, at the moment when she needed help the most. That never worked, but I can try again here.

Maybe this time it will make a difference.

But when? Where can I find enough energy? They need a whole life's worth – five lives, ten lives, maybe more. More than I can steal from any ghost in the past or the future.

I go back to 1994. To the night that Rima and the others died. Kasper is sleeping in his bedroom. It's clean and white, with blue curtains covering the window.

I'd almost forgotten what he looked like when he was a real, living human. He sings with life. His skin is so pink, blood pumping below the surface. He's snoring like he doesn't have a care in the world.

This is it. The moment that Rima, Felix, Kasper and all the other students in the building died. It wasn't a gas leak, or an explosion, or a fire that killed them. It was something mysterious and unknown. It was me.

I killed them. I'm going to kill them. I am killing them, right now, at this moment.

I can take their energy – their life forces – and use it to stop Norma. I can kill them in the past to protect their spirits in the present day. This is the only way to ensure Norma is gone for good. I have to do it. I need my father dead.

I reach to Kasper in 1994, asleep in his bed. I suck up his energy and bring it through into the present day, sharing it with the circle. It pours through me into Leah like a tsunami from the past.

The living Kasper's head falls back in agony. He's still asleep, until he isn't. Until he's dead. And then I keep going. Because, if this is going to work, I'll need the life force of every single student in this building.

It might be selfish, but I would sacrifice far more to destroy my father one final time.

FELIX

They were losing. Their circle was struggling, collapsing inwards as they ran out of energy. Felix pushed more into Leah as fast as he could, focused on nothing but summoning up every dreg. Leah was so dim and see-through that he could barely make out her outline. She was about to disintegrate. Felix's gaze flickered to Kasper's face, desperately memorizing his features one last time.

Then a tornado of energy exploded out of nowhere, flowing through them. Claudia was glowing golden, funnelling it all into Leah.

Norma dropped Harriet and collapsed to her knees, flickering from bright white to dim monotones. She wailed, clawing at her own face and keening.

"What's happening?" Norma shouted.

The new energy kept pouring in – more than any one ghost could provide, more than ten ghosts, more than a hundred. Claudia was sparking white, crackling like lightning or fireworks, like a nuclear explosion in slow motion.

Norma writhed. "Help me," she begged her granddaughter, as her arms split apart into dust.

"Rest in peace, Gran," Harriet said in a flat voice. Felix couldn't tell if it was a threat or a wish.

Harriet lunged forwards and sucked down the last of Norma's energy, tearing her apart and scattering her to the wind until there was nothing left but her scream, echoing around them.

The roof went silent. All the battling ghosts stopped to look.

Leah released the connection, and the energy flowing around the circle disappeared. The stump of Kasper's finger was sizzling and sparking from the energy transfer.

"We did it," Leah said, awed. "He's gone." Her face crumpled up. "I'm free. At last."

Yes, I killed them all. I'm not sorry. What else could I have done?

Without me, they would have all lived. They would have graduated university. They might have lived happy lives. Instead, they're all trapped here inside their eighteen-year-old bodies. Because I wanted to get rid of my father.

I needed them here, to defend us.

Does that make me worse than Harriet? Yes. So be it. I have always found modern ethics hard to grasp, I have to admit. What's a little murder, between friends? All that matters is that he's gone now. For good, I hope. Though there's always the chance he's being born again right at this moment, a new life beginning that's ready to be terrorized. I can't see far enough ahead to know for sure that we've escaped him. But I can hope. All any of us can do is hope.

Chapter 27

HARRIET

Norma was gone, and Harriet was free. The deaths and fear and violence were over, and she never had to think about her gran again. She could be her own person for ever, at peace at last.

Somewhere behind her, a long wail turned into sobs. Claudia was curled in Leah's arms, screaming. The ritual had been too much for Leah. She was fading fast, about to disintegrate.

Rima was pushing energy into her, but Rima was dim herself now. It wasn't going to be enough.

Harriet couldn't let them go. Not now.

She sprinted towards Leah, dropping the shield away.

Kasper was crouched down by Felix, who was sitting in an exhausted heap. He moved to block Harriet's path as she approached Leah.

"Let me help her," she panted.

Kasper looked wary, but let her through.

Harriet pushed her energy into Leah. Her atoms were unravelling fast, and it would take a lot to bring her back. But she was willing to sacrifice anything for these people who had welcomed her into Mulcture Hall, who had given her opportunity after opportunity to redeem herself, who had finally let her escape her grandmother.

Even if she'd ruined everything, she could still give them this. Friendship was about more than taking what she wanted from people.

Harriet closed her eyes, growing dizzy as Leah started to brighten. Even with Norma's energy, Leah was going to need more than she could give.

"Thanks, kid. But you need to stop," Leah whispered to Harriet, weak and barely audible. Claudia's crying faded into hiccups.

Harriet shook her head. This deserved to be Leah's energy. No one cared if Harriet lived or died, but Leah would leave mourners behind if she disintegrated now.

Harriet felt herself fading away as she gave Leah the last dregs of her energy. She closed her eyes and prepared to disintegrate. Then, hands gripped her shoulders and tugged her backwards.

"That's enough," Rima said. "Thank you. But that's enough."

Harriet nodded, closing her eyes. Then she crumpled to the ground.

RIMA

Harriet lay still on the rooftop, face pressed into the floor. This girl had done so many monstrous things. She deserved nothing more than death. But she'd helped them. She had been willing to sacrifice herself for Leah.

There was a tingle of hope in Rima's belly. Perhaps it wasn't too late for Harriet Stoker, after all.

Rima didn't understand what had happened while they were completing the ritual. Somehow, energy had appeared out of nowhere, right when they had needed it most. Claudia had started glowing brightly, so she must have brought it to them from somewhere.

Was that her power? Could she create energy out of nowhere?

There was a yip behind them, and Cody rubbed along her legs.

"I thought I'd lost you!" Rima said, and grinned so hard that her cheeks hurt. They'd got rid of the Tricksters, and they were all still here, weak but clinging on. This wasn't the end of everything, after all.

The last few members of the Tricksters' army were still fighting the students. Everything had slowed down, though, growing less intense without the Tricksters' influence.

"We made it," Rima said, beaming at the others. "We did it!"

KASPER

Kasper staggered over to where Felix had been sitting since the ritual ended, too exhausted to move. Kasper ached all over. It was possible that he had broken a rib at some point.

He knelt at Felix's side, terrified he was hurt.

"Felix?" he whispered. He hadn't turned into a Shell. That was good, at least. This couldn't be the end, not yet. Kasper's chest seized up in fear.

Felix opened his eyes, in degrees. "… Kasper?"

Something inside Kasper relaxed. His fear dropped away. Felix was OK. The ritual hadn't destroyed him.

With a shock, Kasper realized that he'd actually been scared. He should have felt numb, shouldn't he? Rufus had taken his fear. But now that Rufus was gone, maybe Kasper's fear had come back to him.

He was relieved for a moment, and then instantly crippled by the realization of how much danger they were all in, surrounded by ghosts intent on killing everyone in the building.

He managed to smile down at Felix, tears pooling in his eyes. "Are you OK?" he asked, in a thick voice.

Everything made sense to Kasper now. He'd been right. He did love Felix, really and truly, even with his fear. Yes, he was scared of the consequences. But it was worth it, to be the person he really was.

Felix's eyes locked with Kasper's. He was too close; not close enough. "I'm fine. Are you?"

Kasper considered the pain in his chest, the ache in his ribs. He nodded. "I thought you were gone. That I'd lost you."

Felix pressed a thumb to the corner of Kasper's mouth, pushing the frown into a smile. "I'm right here. I told you, I'm not going anywhere."

"I got my fear back when Rufus died," Kasper admitted.

Felix's expression changed slowly, until he was smiling radiantly at Kasper. He couldn't look away.

Rima and Leah walked over to them, both beaming.

"I got something back when Rufus died, too," Leah said. "I didn't realize I'd even lost it. He must have taken it from me centuries ago."

Kasper frowned. Leah could already feel fear. What else could he have taken?

Leah grinned. "My joy. I got my joy back!" She laughed giddily. "I'd forgotten! I'd forgotten how happy I used to be!" She kissed Claudia's nose, who giggled. "I know, darling!"

Rima gaped at her. "Oh, Leah, you're glowing!"

She hugged her, but Leah turned the hug into a dance, dipping Rima over her arm.

"I'm back, baby!" she sang, trilling in delight.

RIMA

"What are we going to do about Harriet?" Rima asked. Harriet looked so small, curled in on herself like a tiny child. Her neck was broken; she was covered in open wounds and she didn't look like she'd be able to hurt a fly.

"Did Harriet say that Norma *killed* her parents?" Kasper asked.

"Yeah," Rima said, tiredly.

"That's… It's no wonder she's the way she is. If that's who raised her." He frowned down at her. Harriet was stirring, wincing as she moved.

Rima knelt down beside her. "Hey. Are you OK?"

Harriet sat up, hand pressed against her lower back. "Are you going to send me down to the basement?"

Rima was surprised by the question. Though, helping them defeat Norma didn't really redeem all of the bad things Harriet had done, did it? She had still destroyed lives.

Rima looked at Leah, who shrugged. Neither of the boys seemed to know what to do, either.

Eventually, Rima said, "The lightning barrier is gone, isn't it? We'd have to find Qi to remake it."

Harriet hung her head. "Qi is gone. I'm sorry. It's my fault."

They all stared at her in silence. Rima had thought she'd reached the peak of her sadness, but knowing that Qi was gone too made the pit inside her stomach drop even further. Could this day get any worse?

Though, if Norma's arrival had done anything good, it had taught them one thing they hadn't known. Ghosts' souls were reincarnated when they disintegrated. Qi, Greg and the other lost ghosts were probably reforming as unborn babies right at this very moment. They were starting new lives. Maybe some of them might even remember their lives here, like Norma had done.

Harriet swallowed. "I'll stay in the basement anyway. I won't come out even without the barrier, I promise. It's what I deserve."

"It is," Rima said. Harriet looked so pathetic, but she was right to feel guilty. So much of what had happened was because of her.

"I'm sorry for everything I did," Harriet said. "It's no excuse, but my gran spent her whole life treating me like I treated you all. I thought it was normal. I don't expect you to forgive me, but…"

"We can see your point of view," Felix said. "That doesn't mean we have to forgive you."

"Harriet did save Leah's life," Rima pointed out. "She didn't have to do that."

Leah sighed. "I feel like the more urgent question is: what are we going to do about this lot?" she gestured at the ghosts fighting around them. "We have to end this, before they tear themselves apart."

HARRIET

There were only a few weak ghosts still fighting. The majority were lying on the roof, stoned on the rich energy they'd taken. Harriet recognized most of them from the basement. None of them would even be out here if it wasn't for her.

There had to be a way the ghosts could be locked in the basement again, even without Qi's lightning power. Harriet's power had shielded Leah and Claudia from Norma. That was a kind of barrier, wasn't it? If her power could shield people, then it might be able to keep them imprisoned, too. It was a trap as much as a shield.

She could restore the basement to how it had been before she'd broken it open. She saw now that there was a reason those ghosts had been inside. They were out of control, in a way that could only be isolated and contained. Even at her most furious, Harriet had never been like them.

She shouted at the top of her voice, "LISTEN TO ME, NOW!"

The nearest ghosts fell silent, and the quiet travelled like a wave through the rooftop until everyone was staring at her, waiting to hear what she had to say.

Harriet gulped, and then summoned Norma's confidence. She would use her gran's advice to get what she wanted, one last time. Then she was going to pretend that Norma had never existed. That was all she deserved.

"The Tricksters are gone," she said, voice raised. "I'm in charge now."

Several ghosts reacted in shock. They must not have noticed that Rufus and Vini had been destroyed. There was a pause, as they all took in what this meant. Some of them looked at Leah, and then back at Harriet.

Harriet paused, not daring to do anything that might endanger this grab for power. She tried to convey that she was tough and strong, like her grandmother. Finally, one of the ghosts dipped her head in Harriet's direction. One after another, they started bowing to her. A few even knelt.

They were going to accept her. This was going to work. "I want all of you to follow me now. The battle here is done. There is a lot we need to discuss."

Harriet summoned up all her strength, trying to convey an aura of strength and calm. With pain creaking in the deepest marrow of her bones, she strode across the roof and down the stairs, not letting herself turn her head to see if they were actually following her. She walked at a regal, steady pace – the kind of walk her grandmother had used.

The Tricksters' army split apart from the students of Mulcture Hall, following her down the stairs to the basement. She stood in the doorway and waited until the room was full of ghosts. They glowed so brightly that the room was almost white with light.

Rima and the others stood in the hallway, watching her in confusion. Harriet raised one hand. "You've done well, my friends," she told the ghosts.

Then she expanded her shield until it filled the perimeter of the basement, just like Qi's lightning had done. It made a new barrier of solid glowing energy between her and the ghosts, glowing in the doorway, opaque and thick and impassable. Several of the ghosts ran at it and were flung backwards, snarling at Harriet.

Satisfied, she turned to Rima. "There. They won't be able to get out. Not for a long, long time."

Rima said, "Thank you. You've saved a lot of lives."

Harriet shook her head. "I owe you a lot more than this. I'm sorry for what I've done and if you ever need my help, it's yours. I owe you all a life debt."

She held Rima's gaze, and then nodded once.

None of them spoke, but she didn't expect them to. They didn't have to forgive her. She didn't deserve that. But she had time – a whole eternity of it – to get back what they'd offered her when she first arrived in the hall. She'd gain their friendship one day. When she had earnt it.

FELIX

Harriet nodded at them, and then stepped through the shield into the basement. She moved through the crowd of furious ghosts, a new shield protecting herself from their wrath.

She had made the right choice. They couldn't let her go unpunished for what she'd done, even if she had helped them at the last moment. Her crimes were too terrible for that.

Harriet had to repent, at least for now. The basement was the best place for her.

When Felix turned away, Kasper was staring right at him. Suddenly, nothing in the universe existed except the two of them.

"I'm sorry," Kasper said. "Fear was the worst emotion I could have given Rufus. I ruined our chances before we'd even started."

"You're back now. That's all that matters."

When they kissed, Kasper made a soft noise of approval in the back of his throat.

Felix said, "You know, bonds made in times of high peril don't usually last once the shock has died away. People find each other too boring after everything calms down."

Kasper kissed his nose. "I already know you're boring, Felix. That's not going to happen with us."

"I'm going to hold you to that." Felix swallowed down the bubbles of perfect, complete happiness that were rising from his stomach.

"This is too pure for my sinful eyes," Rima said. When they finally pulled away from each other, Felix saw that there were literal hearts in her eyes. Cody was sprawled in her arms, splayed out on her back in complete bliss as Rima rubbed her belly.

"You needed your fear back, Kasper," Leah said. "Without the bittersweet, there's no sweet."

She smiled down at Claudia, a happiness on her face that Felix had never seen before. Felix still didn't understand how

Claudia had found so much energy for them, when they were forming the circle. Perhaps it was better if he didn't. They were safe, and that was all that mattered.

"Though, can I go and have a nap, now?" Leah asked. She was holding Claudia in exactly the same position as Rima was cradling Cody.

"No!" they all chorused together.

Leah rolled her eyes.

"Get over here, Aeliana," Rima said.

"Fight me," she mumbled, and then sighed in contentment when Rima pulled them all into a hug.

"We did it, guys," Kasper said, looking around like he was waiting for something to leap out at them. All was still and silent. Once again, Mulcture Hall was peaceful.

"Good work, squad," Felix said.

"And they all lived happily ever after," Rima said.

"We should be so lucky," Leah muttered.

Here it is. The end. The only one that matters. I don't have anything to wait for any more. It's all done now. All the tangles have been untangled and most of the visions make sense.

You've seen the end and the beginning, and hopefully you have more of an idea than me of which is which. But we have time for one more beginning, I think. Just a little one.

A few months from now, Rima will babysit me. She spends a lot of time talking to me these days. I think she's worked out that I'm listening to everything. She includes me in conversations even though I can't reply.

She talks about Oscar sometimes. About how much she wishes there was a way she could have saved him when he died. How, if she'd given him a bit of her energy, he might not have disintegrated. Felix could have had his brother back.

I don't think she's so disappointed for his sake alone.

I think there's something I can do to help. I look back into the past, to the moment that Oscar died. I pull his

ghost through into the future, just before Harriet can
consume him totally.

It won't change anything in the past – in the confusion
of the fight with Harriet, they'll all think that he
disappeared because he disintegrated. It was all so quick
and strange, that maybe this is what happened all along.
Harriet could never have consumed all his energy, not
when she was already filled to the brim with stolen powers.

When I tug Oscar's ghost through into the present day,
he re-forms into a dim and weak Shell. Rima is surprised
at first, but she quickly jumps into action. She has to give
him half her energy before he stops being a Shell.

Rima tries to calm him down, explaining that he's
dead, a ghost, and his brother is here waiting for him.

Once the shock leaves him, Oscar looks at Rima,
frowning. "Are you Rima? Rima from uni?"

She blushes bright red, and stutters out, "Yes."

Oscar grins and shakes her hand. "Good to see you,
after all these years. You look … great."

The years have made Oscar distinguished. Maybe even
handsome. Rima clearly thinks so. She says, "You too!" in
a too-high voice.

He tries to pull his hand away, but it takes her
a moment to let go. "Sorry!" she says. "It's just so nice to see
you, after all these years. Let me show you around?"

He grins. "Lead the way, Rima Hamid."

Rima sneaks glances at him all the way to Felix's bedroom, trying to hide a smile.

That's a small beginning. And another, bigger, one: a week after that, while Rima and Leah are trying to make Cody play with a badger spirit that Felix found on the ground floor, a car pulls up outside Mulcture Hall. None of them notice the caretaker who staples a poster to the fence, whistling to himself.

Not Felix, who is busy providing Rima and Leah with helpful comments – despite his insistence that he has no interest in the badger at all, and has never wanted a pet. Or Kasper, who is busy wrapping Felix as tightly in his arms as he can.

The caretaker drives off, leaving behind a sign. It says that the building is scheduled to be demolished in one week, due to a recent spate of fatal incidents on the site.

But, like I said – none of them notice any of this. Not even me. Not yet.

ACKNOWLEDGEMENTS

Thank you to my editors, Annalie Grainger and Frances Taffinder, and my agent, Claire Wilson, for guiding this messy book through the many, many rounds of edits it took to turn it into something readable. It was a long process, but worth it in the end!

The team behind the scenes – thank you to Miriam Tobin at Rogers, Coleridge & White Literary Agency, and Kirsten Cozens, Rosi Crawley, John Moore, Georgie Hookings, Jenny Bish, Anna Robinette and Chloé Tartinville at Walker Books.

And my writer pals! Thank you to the irreplaceable Alice Oseman, Lucy Powrie, Non Pratt, Emma Mills, Beth Reeks, Laura Wood, Sarah Barnard *and* Sara Barnard, Kat Harris and Beth Worrall and Clare Samson (who has always been a big support of #ghosthouse!). You all guided me through the aches and pains of creating such a long and complicated narrative.

Mum, Dad, Chris, Charlie – thanks for being so supportive, always. And Cody the dog, for donating her name to Rima's fox.

AUTHOR BIOGRAPHY

Lauren James was born in 1992, and has a Masters degree from the University of Nottingham, UK, where she studied Chemistry and Physics. Lauren is a passionate advocate of STEM further education, and many of her books feature female scientists in prominent roles.

She started writing during secondary school English classes, because she couldn't stop thinking about a couple who kept falling in love throughout history. She sold the rights to the novel when she was twenty-one, while she was still at university.

Lauren lives in the West Midlands and is an Arts Council grant recipient. She has written articles for *The Guardian*, Buzzfeed, Den of Geek, The Toast and the *Children's Writers' and Artists' Yearbook*. She teaches Creative Writing for Coventry University, Writing West Midlands and WriteMentor.

Her books have been twice-nominated for the Carnegie Medal, and include *The Loneliest Girl in the Universe*, *The Quiet at the End of the World* and *The Next Together* series, as well as the dyslexia-friendly novella *The Starlight Watchmaker* and serialized online novel *An Unauthorised Fan Treatise*.

You can find her on Twitter at @Lauren_E_James, Tumblr at @laurenjames or her website, laurenejames.co.uk, where you can subscribe to her newsletter to be kept up to date with her new releases and receive bonus content.

"A HUGELY REWARDING READ."

SFX MAGAZINE

How far would you go to save those you love?

Lowrie and Shen are the youngest people on the planet after a virus caused global infertility. Closeted in a pocket of London and doted upon by a small, ageing community, the pair spend their days mudlarking and looking for treasure – until a secret is uncovered that threatens their entire existence. Now Lowrie and Shen face an impossible choice: in the quiet at the end of the world, they must decide what to sacrifice to save the whole human race...